# JOSEPHINE

## THE
## SCOTTISH
## LIONS

# ANNE GREGOR

OLIVER HEBER BOOKS

Josephine Copyright 2024 © Anne Gregor

Cover art by Dar Albert at Wicked Smart Designs

Published by Oliver-Heber Books

0 9 8 7 6 5 4 3 2 1

# JOSEPHINE

F ind a nice man.
      Fall in love.
  Marry.
  Have children.
  Hand-in-hand and side-by-side. Forever.
  Such lovely sentiments. The problem... she tried that path, and it turns out that those societal norms aren't for everyone. Those opinions were shit.
  Unneeded. Unwanted. Unsolicited.
  Love was a lie.
  Promises are lies.
  Forever really meant never.

# 1

SIXTEEN YEARS AGO, ROYAL MARINES BASE; RM
CONDOR—ARBROATH, SCOTLAND

"Christ, Tommy, ye bastard," Coll, Thomas' best friend, needled, shaking his head and chuckling as they entered the facility's shower room. "You wrecked the new recruits."

Thomas grunted in response as he found his locker, more than ready for the pounding, hot water to ease his sore body. The five new commandos weren't the only ones who felt the grueling pace he'd set today.

Thomas made captain early and was determined that the men in his unit were the best. Showing mercy now wouldn't keep them alive in the field, and from chatter funneling down from the higher-ups, a mission was imminent.

He'd only been back to base in Arbroath for three weeks, and between the promotion and the new recruits, he'd yet to make his way home to visit his family. He wouldn't admit this to anyone, but he missed his mom, dad, and grandma. He desperately missed his little sister.

Catriona was a surprise baby for his folks and one he'd been embarrassed about... briefly. He *had* been a fifteen-year-old boy who knew how babies were made. However, he could have died happy with the belief that his parents didn't partake in baby-making activities.

All misgivings ended the moment he'd held her. Tiny and screaming with a shock of red hair sticking straight off her head — she was perfect. His little Cat, as he called her, was six years old now and the most precious, maddingly ornery little person in his life.

He and Coll joined the Royal Marines at eighteen. Now, at twenty-one, Thomas had made a name for himself. Coll had as well, except the bastard wouldn't take command over his own unit. They'd made a promise to stay together no matter what, and even when Thomas told him to accept the promotion, the stubborn jackass refused. He was selfishly relieved. He and Coll were closer than brothers, and it would feel strange to go it alone.

They grew up in the gentle countryside of Bunchrew outside Inverness, Scotland. Coll worked on his parents' cattle farm, and Thomas worked in his parents' greenhouses. MacGregor Farm shipped plants all over the UK. Tending the green beasts was exhausting, but it was satisfying work and one he missed.

Thomas grabbed his shower kit and beat up Motorola from the top shelf of the locker, looking at his messages while Coll flexed in the mirror. Coll was asking him something, but Thomas was too busy reading messages that had the potential to ruin his life.

Sitting heavily on one of the low metal benches that ran down the middle of the rows of lockers, Thomas heard a slight moan leave his lips.

No way. No way. No fucking way. *She* would *not* ask this of him.

Coll was in his face instantly. "What the hell, man? Show me," he demanded, holding his hand out for the phone.

This news would devastate Coll as much as it had him. "It's Aileen." Coll's face lost all color as he took the phone. Aileen was his younger sister and Thomas' ex-girlfriend. The three of them had grown up together. Aileen was only a year younger. She and Thomas had become more than friends when he'd been sixteen to her fifteen. Coll had been pissed, but Thomas promised his best friend that he would respect his sister always in all ways.

He loved her as only a teenager could. He walked her to classes, took her to school dances, and held her hand. They kissed every moment Coll wasn't around, which wasn't often. Thomas believed they would eventually marry. She was going to go to university to become a teacher. He and Coll had planned to join the Royal Marines since they were young boys. He promised to save as much money as he could to buy her an engagement ring and eventually their own home close to both their families.

He'd kept his promises. Aileen had not.

Thomas and Coll were on a short weekend leave some two years after they'd joined. He was going to surprise Aileen at uni. She attended the University of Edinburgh. They spoke on the phone when they could and wrote letters all the time. Thomas loved the Marines, and Aileen said she'd never been happier at school.

She also said she couldn't wait to be his wife.

That day, Thomas had found his girlfriend easily enough. She was standing outside her dorm building, locked in another man's arms, kissing him as though her life depended on his tongue never leaving her mouth. Her slight form was completely enveloped, and her light-brown hair blew in gentle waves around them. He stood on the brilliant-green grass that covered the campus and watched as a stranger gripped Aileen's ass and pulled her tight against his body.

He'd been shocked, frozen, and incredibly hurt. Betrayed. He wanted to leave without her seeing him, but he was a big man, much bigger after all the military training. She lifted her head and turned just enough to catch his movement as he'd pivoted on his heel to go. He watched as her body bent toward the man as if she'd been punched in the stomach, a look of horror marring her delicate features.

The man turned and stared at Thomas. When Aileen took a step toward him, Thomas said one word clearly and quite loudly. "No."

He walked back to the car park, only running once out of sight.

He'd saved her virtue and his own for marriage. He'd kept his promise to Coll and kept his desires tightly checked. She was it for him. She'd *been* it for him. Aileen was supposed to be his end-all. Now, she was just a memory that hurt to look at.

A year later, he'd forgiven her. Mostly. It had taken months and many letters, digging deep to find a level of maturity to move past it. Mostly, it was his grandma that forced him to relent. She'd swatted his hand with a ladle and told him that no man or woman was without sin— that he would want forgiveness for something someday, and hopefully, that person wouldn't be as stingy giving it as he was.

Also, Coll had begged him to remember they'd all been friends before anything else. That he and his sister could be friends, only friends, again. Coll had been furious with Aileen and had refused to speak to her for a long while, but they'd always been extremely close. Their parents were solemn and strict. They'd learned to laugh and hug and embrace life between the two of them. Thomas never wanted to come between their relationship.

Thomas and Aileen had only seen each other once since they'd broken up. It wasn't as painful as he'd feared. He'd laid in bed that night wondering why he hadn't felt... more. He was relieved to have her back as a friend, but truly, he hadn't felt gutted in the least. It made him wonder if maybe they hadn't been as in love with each other as they'd professed.

With two missed calls and three texts, Aileen had managed to knock him on his ass once again. Coll sat heavily next to him, a look of utter bewilderment smothering his usual smile.

7:12 am

> I need your help, Tommy. I've screwed up bad.
> Call or text me as soon as you can.

10:34 am

> Oh God, T. I'm pregnant. Mom and Dad will
> disown me. I'll have to leave school.

4:03 pm

> Please, please call me. I'm already five months
> gone. Can I tell my parents it's yours?

## 2

## PRESENT DAY

"Jesus Christ," Jo growled, fumbling for her phone, the one currently ringing at an ungodly shrill volume at... she finally managed to bring the damn thing to her face. "Three!" She'd only gotten to bed at one-thirty. "Damn it!"

Jo had been attempting to enjoy her last night at The Fitzwilliam Hotel in Dublin. She'd come to Ireland to celebrate Thanksgiving with the Byrnes and their families and attend her good friend's wedding. Saoirse Kennedy was Saoirse Daniels now. Tomorrow, today now apparently, she was flying to Rome to meet her folks and O'Connor Hospitality LLC's newest clients. Jo was relieved to have another big job to drown herself in.

She sucked in a harsh breath as her eyes finally focused on the bright screen. International number. This could be an inconsiderate client, but it could be Thomas, and if he was calling her at three in the morning, it had to be an emergency.

Clearing her throat, Jo swiped right to answer. "Hello?"

There were two heartbeats of silence before, "Josephine O'Connor?"

A woman. Scottish. Jo's pulse painfully thumped... neck, wrists, heart.

"It is." Jo wasn't in the habit of curt phone etiquette, but it was three o'clock in the damn morning, and anything related to Scotland was on her don't ask-don't tell list. She scooted further up her padded headboard, crossing her long legs at the ankle, fearful and impatient to find out the caller's identity and message.

Jo could hear several deep inhalations before, "Good. Good, then. This is Aileen, ahh... Aileen Barr... MacGregor."

All of Jo's facilities shut down. She couldn't speak, or hear, move, scream, or press... End Call.

She was speaking with Aileen MacGregor.

Thomas MacGregor's wife.

The woman he had failed to mention when he'd held Jo in his arms and told her he loved her.

So, how was Jo supposed to respond? *I'm so happy you called. I've been dying to get to know the woman whose husband I slept with.*

"Umm, okay. It's three in the morning. Perhaps we can schedule a time to talk later." Her voice barely shook. *Nicely done, Josephine.*

"I meant to wake you up."

*The hell?* This was getting more bizarre and uncomfortable by the second. However, if she'd had a husband who had cheated, waking up the mistress would be the least of her crimes.

"I see." Jo didn't see *anything*.

"Damn it," Aileen cursed softly. "This isn't how I wanted it to go. I wanted to wake you up in the hope that... that is... I hoped you were too disoriented from sleep that I could get out what I wanted to say to you before you hung up on me." Several awkward sighs and then, "Will you? Hear me out, that is."

Jo felt her eyes begin to burn. If the woman needed to tell Jo personally that she was a homewrecking whore, then... she'd take it. She hadn't meant to be a homewrecker, but that probably wouldn't matter to this woman. Understandably.

"Yes," Jo answered, resigned and silently screaming at MacGregor in her head.

Jo had broken things off with Thomas four months ago. She'd been devastated at his betrayal then. She still was now. She'd flat-out refused to tell her best friends, Raven, River, and Rowan Byrne, who she'd met in Oklahoma before the women moved to Ireland, anything about the matter. She cringed, thinking about admitting what had happened.

Jo would tell them when she could speak about it without crying, and that time had yet to arrive.

Her friends loved Thomas. To say they would be devastated at the betrayal... They loved her too, of course, but Thomas' security firm had provided men and women to protect Jo's families and theirs when a stalker had been after their families. Thomas had also been instrumental in helping find Rowan when she'd been abducted this past summer.

It had been hell, not knowing where her friend was or even if she was alive. The abduction happened right after Jo and Thomas had broken up. What was she supposed to do once Rowan was back home and recovering? *Hey, I know you were kidnapped and held for ransom by a monster, but I have a pretty big problem of my own to deal with.* Not likely.

The woman... Aileen... cleared her throat, obviously gearing up for the verbal beatdown.

"I'm sorry for what's happened between you and Tommy."

*What in the ever-loving hell?* Was this woman serious? Perhaps her husband's betrayal had pushed her too far, and she was... Jo didn't know, but *something* was amiss.

Jo forced words past her numb lips. "I'm truly very, very sorry, Mrs. MacGregor. Not knowing Thomas was married doesn't mean a whole lot at the end of the day. I hurt you. I didn't mean to, but I did." She leaned her head back on the headboard and used her free hand to cover her eyes. She didn't want to cry. This woman shouldn't be forced to listen to a cheater's tears.

"No, no, no, Miss O'Connor, you misunderstand me. Christ, have mercy, but I'm screwing this up!"

She sounded annoyed... at herself. *What?*

"I found out from one of your acquaintances that you are leaving Dublin tomorrow," she paused for a moment and cleared her throat apologetically. "Today, I guess. I would ask that you fly to Inverness first. I can meet you there. At the airport. I need to speak to you. Face to face."

Jo's first thought was 'who does this woman know that knows me... besides Thomas?' Her second thought was no way on God's green Earth was she doing a face-to-face with Mrs. Aileen Macgregor. No way.

Jo WAS ten minutes from landing at Inverness airport. *What in the actual...* Sighing and massaging her temples for the thousandth time, she wondered at her sanity. She also wondered why she was allowing her emotions to take a worse beating than they'd already endured.

Jo's brain was coming up with no solid explanation, but then, cognitive thought had taken a hiatus weeks ago. Jo had puked every refusal over the phone to Aileen except for screaming, *Hell No!* Thomas' wife was nothing if not persistent. Fine. The woman obviously wanted to face the person who had wronged her. A phone call was too impersonal— not enough. Fine... again.

Jo was a glutton for punishment. That was the only reason that made sense in this scenario. She wanted to be hurt even more than she already had been. Fine... for the third time.

She groaned aloud, receiving side-eye from the jet's steward. Perhaps Jo realized that nothing, and she meant *nothing*, could be worse than the day she found out that Thomas MacGregor was a big, fat liar.

The moment when the falseness of their relationship was unveiled... one moment, a monolith to last the ages... the next, a discovery of fractured lies... There was no poetic way to describe the crushing hurt. *Jo watched dreamily as Thomas walked away from her. He was off to shower and get ready for dinner with her mom and dad, who were stopping through Dublin with the express purpose of meeting her "boyfriend." Dad had met and spoken with Thomas on several occasions when he'd hired MacGregor's security firm during the stalker debacle.*

*This was the first time Dean O'Connor would meet Thomas MacGregor as his daughter's... something more. Jo was nervous as she fidgeted in their Dublin hotel suite, anxious for the evening. Thomas, of course, appeared cool as a fresh spring day. The bastard.*

*When she told him she was nervous, he'd kissed her to an almost mouth-to-mouth orgasm again before swaggering to their bedroom.*

*The bliss only lasted a minute after he walked around the corner. Jo began chewing her fingernails and cuticles, a disgusting habit but thankfully passed the time. A vibrating phone interrupted her escalating anxiety. Thomas had left his phone on the kitchen counter— where he'd left his girlfriend stewing over her parents.*

*Jo picked it up, considering it might be one of his employees.*

*The screen flashed Mirren. Jo didn't recognize the name, but MacGregor's security firm had a gazillion contractors. She swiped right to answer as she walked toward the bedroom and the steamy bathroom that held an equally steamy naked man.*

*"Hello," Jo answered.*

*"Omg, please don't tell me Dad can't talk," a young girl— a young Scottish girl began. "Mom!" The same girl hollered. "A woman answered Dad's phone. Now what? If he doesn't let me go to the movies with Aric, I swear to God... murder! You're his wife! Make him!"*

*Jo's steps faltered before completely halting. She was six feet from the bathroom door and a million miles from sanity.*

*"Umm... your dad?" Jo queried shakily, her body already feeling the damage her brain knew was about to hit.*

*"Oh, sorry," the girl stated, clearly unaware that this nuclear meltdown of a conversation was imploding Jo's mind. "Do you work for Dad? Whatever," she interrupted herself. "Tell him his daughter said if he doesn't let me go on a date this weekend, I'll never speak to him again," the girl growled. "I'm sixteen for flipping sake!"*

*"Sure thing." Jo huffed a shaky laugh. "Who is your dad, exactly?"*

*An elongated sigh— very teenager— escaped the girl's mouth before she answered. "Thomas MacGregor."*

*"I'll tell him you called," was all she managed before ending the call.*

And just like that, Jo's whole world had shattered. Blindly, she made it back to the kitchen, dropping Thomas' phone back on the counter, wishing desperately she'd never picked it up. That she'd stayed in happy ignorance. Swallowing the bile attempting to flood her mouth, she grabbed a pen and notepad and wrote a message.

*Your daughter and wife called while you were in the shower. I'll make this short. I realize you do not respect me, but if you have any decency, please never try to see or speak to me again. Not. Ever.*

She then took her phone out of her pocket and dropped it on the floor before stomping it into an early grave. The cheating bastard wouldn't be able to get a hold of her for a while, at least. She'd grabbed her purse and nothing else, fled to the lobby, and asked the sweet young lady working at the front desk to use her phone. She needed to charter a flight to Switzerland since her parents had the family jet, and then she needed to call her mom and dad to cancel dinner. Hopefully, they hadn't left Zurich yet.

She'd left everything behind and rented the suite for another week. However long it took to make sure MacGregor was gone before she retrieved her things. Toiletries and clothes could be replaced. Her heart couldn't be.

Jo had practically barreled through The Fitzwilliam's stately front, glass doors and hit the pavement running. She'd flagged down a taxi because she had no phone to order an Uber. Jo's rapid blink and swallow that had worked so far to keep her tears at bay stopped working five minutes before she slid into the back of a cab. It was a miracle the driver spoke sobbing woman language because he'd gotten her to the correct side of the airport for private jets.

She was running away with her tail tucked between her legs.

By the time the plane's front wheels had lifted off the tarmac, Jo had managed to stop her tears. Stop her thoughts. Stop her emotions. Stop... everything.

She'd learned her freshman year in college that she couldn't trust her judgment where men were concerned. She should have remembered what eighteen-year-old Josephine O'Connor had learned the hard way.

No more.

Never again.

# 3

Thomas walked through the front door of his small two-story home situated on his family property. He wanted to slam the heavy wooden door behind him, if only to give some of his pent-up rage a target. Instead, he closed it gently, breathing deep and steady as he dropped his duffle bag to the well-worn wooden floor.

He just got home from Dublin. He'd been invited to Saoirse Kennedy's wedding— well, he'd been invited when he and Jo were still together. He hadn't wanted to miss it even though he was bone tired. Thomas would take every chance to see Jo.

He'd been gone for three weeks prior to that, overseeing a tricky surveillance assignment in Bolivia. Drug trafficking had grown at an obscene rate there. Bolivia bordered Peru, the world's main producer of cocaine, and Paraguay, which kept the drug runners flush with marijuana.

Several members of Thomas' firm had been living in Bolivia and the surrounding areas for three years now. His best friend, Coll, had left the military when Thomas had. Even though MacGregor Security was Thomas' brainchild, Coll helped build it right along with him. Between their contacts in the Royal

Marines and the other military forces, they'd gathered an elite team that was hired by high profile families and businesses for cyber security and bodyguards. They also picked up occasional contracts with government agencies.

Coll had been the first to infiltrate the Bolivia scene, gathering names, pictures, and locations that would one day take down some of the most violent offenders.

A year and a half ago, Coll had been scouting some newly made paths through the dense Amazon rainforest that might have led to a new cocaine manufacturing facility. He stepped on a buried IED. Before losing consciousness, he'd been able to put out a distress beacon that showed his exact location. An extraction team got to him before he could bleed out, though he lost his right leg from below the knee for all that.

Thomas insisted that Coll go to Johns Hopkins Limb Rehabilitation Center in Baltimore, Maryland. Their program for amputees was world-renowned. Coll deserved the best.

He got fitted for several styles of prosthetics and did the work. He did his PT plus his usual Marines workout that he and Thomas had never stopped doing. He did everything he was supposed to do, with the exception of moving past his disability. Coll only took desk jobs now, claiming he would be a liability in the field— which was complete bullshit.

He was one of the team that worked tirelessly on Rowan Byrne's kidnapping case. His childhood friend now lived a hermit's life in the wilds of the Scottish Highlands and refused every invitation to visit home or have visitors, including Thomas and his sister Aileen.

Thomas' mood was sour for more reasons than his best friend's MIA routine.

He missed Josephine O'Connor.

He missed her. Jesus, God, how he missed that stubborn, golden-haired vixen. Thomas lost his best friend and the woman he loved in just over a year's time. Life felt unbearably suffocating.

The door he'd closed not one minute ago was thrown open with such force, that the handle slapped the whitewashed wall behind it. Thomas spun on his heel, ready to give the person responsible for the unwanted intrusion a tongue lashing they wouldn't soon forget when he caught sight of a sea of red hair swinging in the breeze from the battered door.

His wee sister was quite obviously in a mood. "What the hell, Cat?"

"Don't start with me, you giant shithead. I've just come from seeing Aileen and Mirren. They're hiding something. Neither of them is a good liar, thank Christ, but you'll have to discover what they thought to keep from me," his sister breathlessly demanded.

Cat was five foot nothing and slight enough to carry around in one palm. He wasn't scared of her physically, but his little sister was the very devil when she was on a rampage, which she was clearly in the throes of now.

"They both practically pushed me out the door, and I'd only been there ten minutes!"

She threw her hands up in the air as if she couldn't conceive of someone wanting to shove her out of their house. The irony was clearly lost on his sister.

"Mirren mentioned a Diana before Aileen shushed her. Are you acquainted with a Diana?"

His body stiffened at the name. He only knew one, but it couldn't be. Diana Gaines. Haughty, Oklahoma money, and friends with the O'Faolains and O'Connors. Surely, *that* woman would not have found out about Aileen. "Fuck."

# 4

Jo disembarked from her plane, Inverness' blustery wind cutting through her many layers, setting her teeth to chatter. She'd agreed to meet Mrs. MacGregor, Aileen rather, as the woman had insisted on a first-name basis, at a small café inside the airport. Hopefully, it served something stronger than coffee. Vodka? Gin? Whiskey? Wine?

Jo could feel her hands shake inside the pockets of her camel-colored Burberry wool trench coat. She asked herself for the thousandth time why she had agreed to this. Jo shouldn't feel guilty. Hurting this woman hadn't been intentional. What had Thomas said to his wife about Jo? Had she forgiven him? Was confronting Jo the last piece of this woman's reconciliation puzzle?

Jo walked through sliding doors into the blessed warmth of the airport's interior. *Deep, calming breaths, Jo.* She paused to unbutton her coat and slip her thin leather gloves off, shoving them into her pockets before smoothing her long, honey waves of hair behind her shoulders. She'd gone casual for the meetup. Camel-colored yoga pants and a cream-colored soft wool sweater, paired with her favorite Salomon tennis shoes— also in camel, cream, and muted black.

Check, check, and check. Another deep breath, and she was moving toward the rendezvous spot. Everyone used the word surreal in instances such as this. Jo now understood the overused cliché. Four months ago, she didn't know Thomas had a family hidden in Scotland, and now, here she was about to meet his wife over coffee. Surreal defined.

She'd almost broken down and called one or all of the Byrne sisters for advice, but since she'd never fessed up to what had divided her and Thomas, explaining that she was meeting the actual dividing wall felt exhausting.

Jo closed in on the little open front café, tables dotted here and there with passengers eating breakfast while scrolling social media and news apps until their flights were called. She cursed herself for refusing to try to find out what Aileen looked like, because if she was already here, Jo would have no clue. Nice time to remember that.

Jo needn't have worried. A small woman with a chic, light-brown long bob, wearing a dark shade of corduroy pants and a thickly ribbed, light-blue sweater stood suddenly. She looked at Jo while biting her lower lip and fidgeting nervously with the seam of her pants.

Aileen was tiny and lovely. The small smile gracing her lips was disorienting as Jo closed in on her table... *their* table. Jo felt lightheaded as another woman, no, girl, rose to stand beside her... mother. There was no mistaking who she was. The resemblance was undeniable. She'd brought Thomas' daughter. Here. For this conversation. *Run, Jo!* She didn't run. *Idiot, Jo!*

Stalling out awkwardly four feet from their table, Jo wasn't sure what comportment manual explained meeting the woman whose husband had intimate knowledge of the tiny mole gracing the inside of her thigh. There was an empty third chair, which Jo took advantage of. She shucked her coat and draped it over the back, finally forcing a second go-round of eye contact.

Holding her hand out in the hopes it wouldn't be rebuffed or, worse yet, slapped, Jo extended her diseased olive branch. "I'm Josephine O'Connor, you must be Aileen." As the woman eagerly took Jo's hand, pumping three times and even going so far as to use her other hand to pat the top of Jo's, she looked toward the teenager.

"You must be Thomas' daughter. Nice to meet you." It wasn't nice to meet her. Not at all. Nothing about this farce was *nice*. Jo's mother had raised her daughter on Emily Post, though. Too bad Mrs. Post didn't have a chapter on mistress etiquette.

"Mirren," the younger girl replied.

She was stiff and formal but not belligerent by any means. If Jo had been forced to meet a woman who had cheated with her father, the woman would be mopping a Diet Pepsi off her face by now.

"Might we sit?" Aileen asked, nervously encompassing the three empty chairs with a small wave.

"Of course," Jo replied, thankfully melting into one of the uncomfortable, plastic-covered seats.

Both women fidgeted with the napkin holder and straightened the menus three times. Were they going to force Jo to start things off? Apology or something mundane like the weather?

"I'm flying to Rome once I leave here. In Italy," she added unnecessarily. At their nods, she plowed on. "I hope you two didn't have a long drive to meet me." Jo barely bit back a curse at her stilted attempt at breaking the ice.

Mirren straightened in her chair, direct eye contact on point, and asked, "Do you love my dad?"

*Jesus Christ. Lord have mercy. Kill me now.*

Jo's panicked gaze flew to Aileen's. "I'm sorry. So very sorry. I didn't... he didn't tell... I never meant to hurt *either* of you." Jo felt tears begin to squeeze from the corners of her eyes. She swallowed the extreme emotion and tried to continue.

Looking at Aileen, she admitted, "I came here today so that you could say your piece, destroy me further, all in the hopes that you might find closure."

Both women looked shocked and distressed at her emotional outburst. Jo kept feeling like she was missing something, but for the life of her, the explanation escaped her.

"Mom," Mirren pleaded. "You've got to tell her everything. Dad has screwed everything up," she stated, clearly exasperated.

Aileen wrapped her tiny knuckles against the table's laminate top— a judge bringing order to chaos.

"Forgive me, Josephine. I'm making a complete wreck of this. Let's order something to eat and drink. I've got a story to tell you. It isn't a short one, and it isn't one I'm proud of."

Mirren leaned into her mother, bumping their shoulders. "You got this, Mom."

Mirren was correct. Over tea, juice, and one of every breakfast item on the menu, Mrs. Aileen MacGregor laid her soul bare in that little airport café. In between bites and sips, Thomas' wife asked Jo not to interrupt. She promised to tell her everything and answer Jo's questions when she finished.

"Tommy and my brother Coll were the same age and best friends. I was only one year younger, so the three of us did everything together." She snorted in amusement at that. "I'm sure there were many times the boys wished that wasn't so. We grew up together in the same small farming community outside Inverness. My family raised cattle. The MacGregor's grew plants and flowers.

"Coll and I spent as much time as we could at the MacGregor's. His parents are wonderful people. They've since moved to Wisley, England. Margaret, Tommy's mother, always dreamed of retiring where the temperatures aren't quite as severe as the

Highlands. Paul, her husband, surprised her with a semi-early retirement and a lovely cottage. It was a semi-retirement because they opened a flower shop in town to sell everything their daughter, Catriona, grows on the farm."

Aileen gave Jo a rueful look. "Sorry, I went off track."

"I don't mind," Jo said quietly. In truth, Jo had learned more about Thomas and his early life and family in five minutes than all the months she'd spent by his side. It was eye-opening to realize how tightlipped he'd been with her. She still was unsure why Aileen was telling her all this. Jo had agreed to hear her out, and she would, but this whole experience was... bizarre.

"Let me move things along and stop torturing us both," she grimaced. "Fast forward to our teenage years. I asked Tommy to take me to a school dance because I was embarrassed that all my friends had dates, and I didn't. He was sixteen, and I was fifteen. It was the first time he'd ever held my hand.

"We were flush with teenage hormones," she stopped there and side-eyed her daughter, who frowned. "Don't start," Mirren snarked. "Anyway, you'll understand teenagers," Aileen continued at Jo's nod. "Coll wasn't happy but Tommy being Tommy promised to keep our relationship *mostly* friendly. We kissed and nothing more until he and Coll left for Royal Marine training.

"We used to talk about doing more... fooling around, but we didn't want to piss my brother off. I believe now that neither of us wanted to do *more*. We enjoyed having someone to always go on dates with, but really, it wasn't a whole lot different than when we were kids. Tommy and I talked about getting married after I finished college.

"He promised to set money aside for a ring and a place of our own, and I was content with the arrangement. Until I went to college." Her cheeks pinkened at the admission. "I was away from my folks, who are good people in many ways, but loving was never one of those, and the freedom opened my eyes—specifically, how boyfriends and girlfriends interacted with each other.

"I was asked out a few times in the first few months, and I refused, of course. But then, Coll and Tommy were gone so much. I was lonely." She shook her head at that. "Good Lord, it sounds like an even weaker excuse than it did all those years ago. Without a lot of arm twisting, I let friends talk me into going to parties. Parties led to drinking and dancing. Kissing boys. I felt guilt, horrible guilt but," she hesitated, "I ended up falling in love. I was a first year, and Charles Morrow was an assistant lecturer working on his doctorate. He was years older than me, but I knew without a doubt he was the one.

"I planned on telling Tommy when he next came home on leave. He came to my uni instead. To surprise me. Instead, he found me in Charles' arms. I thought at that moment that I'd lost my best friend forever. That he'd surely never forgive me.

"He eventually did, in large part, I'm sure, because of my brother. We rarely saw each other over the next year, but it was beginning to be like old times. I was... relieved. Charles and I got serious. We were discussing moving in together, though my parents would have disowned me. Before any of that could happen, Charles was invited to teach at Harvard in America.

"He was writing a book about early Scottish settlers in the Massachusetts area. Charles had been speaking with several scholars there for months until they finally asked him to come finish his doctorate there and eventually teach. He would have full access to their records. A dream come true. For him. Ugh, sorry, I got off topic again."

Jo waved off the apology. Without meaning to, she'd become engrossed in the story. "Continue, please."

"Okay. Charles took the offer. It was too good to pass up. I completely understood. He wanted me to move with him. I told my parents that weekend— some of it anyway. They threatened to disown me. Told me I was shameful and threatened to take all of their financial help away, which would make finishing school almost impossible. Or so my naïve self believed at the time.

"I left their house defeated. I wasn't quite twenty at the time. Uni was the furthest from home I'd ever been. I was scared to move across the world and scared of my parents' threats. I couldn't imagine leaving my brother. I broke it off with Charles. He begged me to reconsider. I didn't. He was hurt and angry. He moved away two weeks later. It was the first of some of the worst decisions I ever made.

"The first, of course, was not following my heart. I found out I was pregnant a few months later. I was scared and alone and knew going to my parents would not end well. I plucked up the courage when I was four months gone to phone Charles. He told me he was so happy to hear from me but that he was seeing someone new. I didn't tell him I was pregnant.

"I waited one more month to make my second worst decision. I called Tommy. He was at a military base not too far away. I told him I was pregnant and asked him if I could tell my parents it was his."

Jo sucked in a shocked breath. Christ. What in the ever-loving hell? Jo looked between mother and daughter, amazed that Aileen would discuss such... personal bombshells in front of Mirren. Aileen must have correctly interpreted Jo's question because she explained immediately.

"Mirren knows everything. She has for many years. I refused to hide the good, the bad, and the ugly from her. My parents iced Coll and me out. I wanted different things for my daughter. Learning that someone can make grave mistakes and come back from them is the best life lesson I could give her."

Jo was burning to ask questions. So many, many questions.

"Long story abbreviated. Tommy was too honorable for his

own good. Even when I changed my mind, recognizing that panic had distorted my thinking, he wouldn't back out. He claimed to my folks that the child was his. His family does know the truth. It took them years to forgive me. Everyone else in town believes Mirren is ours together.

"We got married. I finished school. Tommy stayed in the military for several more years. He bought Mirren and me a house. I teach at the local primary school. Tommy and I have never been husband and wife on anything other than paper."

"Never?" Jo asked, struggling to comprehend it all.

"We discussed it once when Mirren was about six. He and Coll had left the Royal Marines by then and were working on building Tommy's security firm. He'd rarely been home before that, so dating for him was easy to keep from the nosy neighbors," she chuckled. "Once he was around more, our relationship became strained. I knew he was struggling with being a husband in name only. Being a father, however, was never a struggle. He's a brilliant dad.

"So, we discussed whether we should give it a go. That conversation was agonizing for the both of us. We'd truly ever and only been best friends. We would never be more. Ever. Once MacGregor Security took off, he and Coll were gone for long periods of time. We talked about getting a divorce. We just... never did, which I see now is my third worst decision. Tommy saved me and Mirren, and I paid him back by keeping him tied to me for the past sixteen years."

Jo felt tears begin to prick her eyes. Jo tried to speak, but to say what?

"You and Tommy broke up because of me—"

Mirren cut off her mom. "Technically it was because of me. I'm the one who called Dad," she declared with a small smile. "I'm sorry, too, though."

"Neither one of you should be apologizing for crying out

loud," Jo stated as her brain came back online. "Thomas MacGregor had months to tell me your story. I wouldn't have even needed the whole story, but he chose to tell me nothing. For the past four months, he left me to believe I was a cheater, that I'd wronged another woman in the worst way. I appreciate very much that you cared enough to tell me. It does help to know that, I suppose, he didn't consider being with me as cheating. Still... withholding the truth is lying."

Aileen reached across the table and took Jo's hands in hers. "He's a stubborn jackass, to be sure. His reasons are his own because, in the weeks of me chewing his ear off, he never told me anything. He admitted to loving you and then yelled at me to drop it. He's been a bear the few times I've seen him since."

"Worse than a bear," Mirren added.

"I filed for a divorce yesterday. He'll be served papers soon. It's years overdue, and no matter what you say, I hurt you by not doing it sooner."

Jo expelled a long breath, bonelessly leaning against the back of her chair. Still in wonder at the story and all its revelations.

"Tell her the rest, Mom," Mirren insisted.

*The rest...* Jesus.

"I think she's had enough for today," Aileen chided.

"No. She needs it all. For Dad's sake, at least."

Jo sat straight again. What did she need to be told that would help Thomas? There couldn't possibly be more. Surely.

Aileen glanced at her daughter and shook her head no. Mirren might not be Thomas' biological daughter, but she'd taken after his stubborn ways beautifully.

"Mom found out last month she has breast cancer," Mirren began, holding her hand up to stop her mother's protests. "It's not too far along that treatments are hopeless, but" and here Mirren blinked several times rapidly, "it might be close. We've been researching places to go. Good places our insurance will allow. Dad being upset about you not seeing or talking to him upsets Mom, and she doesn't need to be any more upset than she already has been about the cancer. You can fix that part. The Dad part," she explained.

"Mirren Mór MacGregor!" Aileen whisper-yelled in embarrassment. "That is not why I wanted her to know about the cancer and upcoming treatments, and you know that very well," she reprimanded her daughter, who had the grace to look a tiny bit guilty.

"It seems I will be burdening you further, Josephine," Aileen sighed in exasperation.

"Call me Jo, please, and nothing you've told me is a burden. I think you're very brave for opening up to me, a complete stranger." Jo meant every word. This woman, Thomas' wife, and mother of his child, was brave and seriously pretty wonderful. "I'm sorry you have cancer, Aileen, and though I appreciate you wanting to meet me, I hate that you're spending any time fretting over Thomas and I breaking up. You should be thinking about yourself, your health, and especially, your healing and recovery."

"That's the thing. Your story, yours and Tommy's, affects me whether I want it to or not. I'm getting ready to enter a battle for my life. The three most important people to me, Mirren, my brother, and Tommy, may have to learn how to live without me."

Aileen sniffed back her emotions and briefly hugged her daughter and kissed her cheek. "Mirren and I have discussed my options and the probability of me beating the disease... it isn't bleak, but it isn't rainbows either."

Aileen stopped speaking and stared hard at Jo. Measuring her... measuring what?

"If the worst happens, Tommy and Coll will love Mirren with their whole hearts. My daughter will miss me, but she'll never miss love. Coll will miss me. He and I have been each other's rock since we were children. He's struggling with his own life issues at the moment, but I know that eventually, he'll make his way back. He'll need Tommy, especially if I'm not here.

"It's Tommy that I worry the most for. You were it for him, Josep— Jo," she corrected herself. "He screwed up, and he doesn't know how to fix it. He wants to fix it, and I'm asking you, a complete stranger before today, to give him a second chance. It doesn't have to be today or tomorrow. Just... someday."

Silence filled the bubble surrounding their table. Jo glanced at her phone. They'd been sitting here for an hour and a half. A long first-meet. A short time to irrevocably change a person's direction.

Jo stared at the two women staring at her. There were choices to be made. Promises to make and keep or promises to deny. First things first, and more important than Jo's broken heart, was the scared woman sitting across from her. A woman with cancer. A married woman without a husband. A mother.

Jo tapped her phone screen, mentally creating a list of things she *could* do. She excelled at lists. "Are you still teaching?"

"I just started a long-term leave of absence. Only the head faculty know why, but it's only a matter of time before word gets out to family and friends. It's why I was desperate enough to corner you into meeting me."

"When you get treatments, is Mirren going to take a few weeks off school as well?"

"Yes. Mom didn't want me to, but me not being by Mom's side isn't negotiable."

Heart squeeze and mental sniffles. "I may not have known Thomas like I thought I did, but you can't tell me he wouldn't move heaven and earth to get you into the best oncology hospital available."

"He would," Aileen agreed. "Soon, he'll be my ex-husband, and he needs to learn now that I will be making all decisions for myself... myself."

Aileen's explanation made sense. What better way to jump headfirst into single life than making life-and-death decisions? "Did you two drive here?" At their affirming nods, Jo tapped her nails against her phone a few more times.

"Okay. I have a plan..."

## 5

## THE INSTITUT GUSTAVE ROUSSY, CANCER CENTER—VILLEJUIF, FRANCE

"I still can*not* believe you got me in here, Jo," Aileen whispered, clasping her daughter's hand tightly in her own as they were ushered into a posh "hospital" room.

Even Jo was wowed by the facility's state-of-the-art opulence. Her mom had come through and then some. "I told you already," Jo teased, bumping Aileen's side as they took in the suite. "My mother's sorority sister is an exceptional oncologist and board member of this hospital. Gustave Roussy is one of the best cancer treatment hospitals in Europe and is only a five-hour flight from Inverness. It's perfect."

"I feel like I'm checking into a fancy resort. This is too much," Aileen said with conviction, halting Jo from opening the refrigerator.

Jo knew Aileen would resist. She was prepared. "My people are working with your insurance. What they don't cover, I will." Jo held up her hand to stall the other woman's protests. "First, I can afford it. Second, it would make me feel as though I deserved your kindness in telling me your history after what happened between Thomas and me." Again, Jo had to stop the woman from interrupting. "I know you say it wasn't cheating, but... it felt that way to me. It still feels that way. You've been so kind, you and Mirren both. Let me do this for all of us."

"Come on, Mom. This place is the best of the best. Plus, you know it's only a matter of time before Dad finds out about the divorce *and* the cancer. We agreed to call him tomorrow and tell him everything. Wouldn't you rather be settled in your treatments first? That doctor believes they can fix you. I want you here," Mirren pleaded.

And that was all it took. When a child was fighting for their parent, there really wasn't an argument to be made. Jo smiled and grabbed both Aileen's and Mirren's hands. "Thank God that's settled. Your beauty team and masseuse are due any minute," she laughed at the look of horror on Aileen's face. "Joking," Jo teased.

"You're a shit and no mistake, Josephine O'Connor," she laughed, sitting on the edge of her bed. "Truly, though, Jo. I never dreamed meeting you would land me here. I feel like I'm getting a miracle and a friend all in hours."

Jo understood why Thomas married this woman. She was the type of person who inspired loyalty and, most definitely, sacrifice. "I'm not crying anymore over you today, Mrs. MacGregor. I may be a badass from Oklahoma, but I have limits." Jo got up and walked toward the door.

"You guys get unpacked. I have a few calls to make and some documents the hospital wants me to sign. I'm going to book a room at a hotel just a few blocks away. I'll be heading to Rome tomorrow. My parents and our new clients won't be put off for much longer. I want to make sure you're settled before I go."

Mirren grinned at her mom. "I promised Jo I'd send her daily updates since we both know if you were puking your guts up, you'd lie and say you were enjoying a bubble bath or some equally lame lie."

"Hey!" Aileen playfully slapped Mirren's leg. "Not true."

"You've told me for years you aren't lonely. Lies." Mirren raised her brows, looking like a carbon copy of her mother.

"You aren't half so clever as you think, young lady," Aileen chided. "Plus, once all my hair falls out, my lack of a social life will come in handy."

Aileen started to chuckle at her joke, but her breathy laugh quickly turned into quivering lips and watering eyes. Jo took a step toward the bed. Mirren looked stricken as she grabbed her mom's hand.

Aileen shook her head and waved them both off. "No. No, no, no. Hair is not more important than living. I refuse to feel sorry for myself."

Jo nodded in agreement. "I'm glad you feel that way, though you should know that Paris has some of the best wig makers in the world, and it's only a thirty-minute drive away."

"Christ, what *don't* you think of?" Aileen asked, smiling.

"Not much." Jo grinned. "I'll be back in a few."

He'd texted both Aileen and Mirren after his sister left and received happy, short texts in return. Too happy and too short. Perhaps not if it'd only been Aileen, but Mirren. No. Teenage girls in general weren't *that* happy, and his daughter tended to text novels. He'd asked to take them to dinner. He'd been out of town and normally Mirren would jump at the chance to hear about his work. *They had plans. Sorry.*

He'd let it go while he spent hours at the farm working through the chore list that his sister had slapped against his chest before she'd stormed out of his house. He refused to believe that Diana Gaines, a wealthy old widow from Oklahoma, an acquaintance of the O'Connors, and not to mention an all-around busybody, had contacted his... wife.

Christ, sixteen years, and he still inwardly cringed at the designation. He'd never regretted his decision. Not once. Until Jo. God, he missed her. He deserved every ounce of her anger.

He'd lied by omission. Had he only come clean in the beginning...

Shaking his head in irritation at thoughts that only led to frustration, he again turned over what Gaines might want. If it was even that woman. It was too far-fetched for him to consider further. But... was she fishing for information? Would she tell the Byrne sisters?

Josephine never told anyone why they broke up. If she had, the shitstorm her friends would have brought down on his head would have been intense and swift. He almost wished she had told everyone. At least then, she'd have people to support her while she was hurting.

She was alone with what he'd done to her.

He lost his breath each time he thought it.

Today was probably not the day Jo would let him back into her life. He needed to focus on something he could fix, which meant going to Aileen's after he showered and visited Grandma. He'd get to the bottom of whatever was going on and hopefully put the Diana namedrop to rest. After all, this Diana could just be some new friend.

Thirty seconds after walking into his grandma's, Thomas felt like he'd been gut-punched. Verbally.

"Molly told me that her sister, the one that works for a solicitor out of Beauly, told her that Aileen filed for divorce. About time you two went your separate ways. Good on you, lad." She patted him on the back as he dropped into a chair at her small kitchen table. She hadn't noticed his stunned silence or lack of response as she loaded the table with supper, continuing to tell him the latest neighborhood gossip.

An hour later, Thomas let himself into Aileen's house when no one answered his knock and doorbell buzzing. Everything was neat and tidy. Nothing out of place or suspicious. He checked Mirren's room, not willing to enter Aileen's private space. Mirren's usual disaster was nowhere to be seen. Bed made. Not an article of clothing on the floor.

A closer inspection made his skin prickle. Her laptop and backpack were missing. Her phone charger was no longer on her bedside table, which also happened to be neat as a pin. No empty soda cans or plates of food. He moved quickly toward the small, attached garage. Aileen's old Ford Fiesta sat there in all its ugly glory. She'd refused his attempts at buying her a better car, always stating that he'd done quite enough. She never forgave herself for his "sacrifice." The thing was, he never once regretted being Mirren's father.

The mistake probably lay in the fact that he and Aileen never considered having the baby together without getting married. They were young and Aileen's folks were judgmental pricks. Instead of telling them to take a hike, they'd bound themselves together. There were times when he'd wondered if Aileen was lonely, wishing for a true relationship. He assumed she secretly dated but then, she didn't travel like he did. Her opportunities would have been slim.

*Damn it.*

He locked things back up and sat in his truck, frustration simmering. He hated to invade his daughter's privacy, but something was off. Mirren's tidy room, their absence but the car's presence, and then there was the divorce. He pulled up the tracker he'd placed on Mirren's phone.

*Oh, God. No. No, no, no. Hell no.*

*Gustave Roussy. Cancer Center.*

Thomas' body burned from the inside out. How fucking dare Aileen keep something like this from him...

A flight to Paris was booked in minutes. Panic wasn't so easily managed. Did Aileen have cancer? His daughter? The thought of Mirren... his baby girl... Cancer. Taking another deep breath to calm his racing heart, Thomas tried to think of a more rational explanation.

They could be visiting a friend— but in France? Without telling him? It could be this mysterious Diana. Again, why the secrecy? Who drove them to the airport? He texted Mirren one more time, wanting to give her a second chance to tell him what was going on.

> Hey, Mir. I swung by the house to see you, but no one was home. Can you come see me at my house later? I've missed you.

After a minute, bubbles appeared.

> Sorry, Mom and I went to Inverness with Stacy and her mom for a day of shopping. We're about to walk into a movie. Be home late. Promise to call you in the morning. Love you.

She was lying. As he drove back to the farm, he texted Cat that he had to make an unexpected trip and would call her the next day. He then tried to call Coll. No answer, which had become their new normal since his injury. He texted him next.

> Something is up with Aileen. Mirren is lying about where they are. Do you know anything she is keeping from me? I have Mirren's location. Leaving soon.

Finally, an hour later, Coll responded.

> She's told me nothing. Want me to call her?

Thomas was surprised at the offer. Coll had been so reclusive and withdrawn since he'd finished rehab that he'd only been home once to see his family.

> No. I'm locked on their location. Should be there by eight or nine tomorrow morning.

Thomas didn't want Coll to know they were currently at a cancer center in France yet. He wanted to know the why of it first from Aileen.

> Understood. Keep me informed.

Thomas was packed, but there was no reason to hurry to the airport. His flight didn't leave until two in the morning— the result of booking last minute. He would normally try to sleep a few hours. Soldiers learned to sleep when they needed it, no matter the circumstance.

However, his military training deserted him months ago— the moment he'd found Jo's note. It didn't look like it would resurface during this latest calamity.

He almost, *almost*, called her when he'd discovered his daughter and... wife's subterfuge. Jo's voice was a comfort. Her touch would be a revival.

He stared at her name on his phone for several minutes before putting it on his kitchen counter with more force than the phone deserved. It wouldn't matter if he called or texted her. She'd blocked his number four months ago.

Josephine O'Connor had trust issues. Thomas could read people. Most had tells. From the first moment she'd slid into the backseat of his car, her body language screamed leery. Stay away. She laughed and smiled and tried to pretend she hadn't a care in the world. She did, though.

It would have been only a matter of time before she trusted him enough to share her secrets. What sometimes darkened her smile or why she jumped at the occasional shadow. Except he'd blown up that tenuous bridge. She wouldn't trust him with shit now.

He still wanted to hope. She didn't trust many people, but she'd trusted him the most. She had to again. *She had to.*

He'd figure out what in the hell his family was playing at, and then *maybe* he'd allow himself to reach out to Jo. Blocking him could never stop him from finding her. With his computer skills and that of his team, there was nowhere in the world that Ms. O'Connor could hide.

"Screw this," Thomas said aloud. He'd find a bar near the airport. Anywhere that served good Scottish whisky, which was every bar in Scotland, would be better than staring at his home's four white walls.

Several hours and shots later, Thomas had gotten caught up on all his work paperwork. He commandeered a small table near the bar, setting his laptop up and only looking up to order more whisky or food.

So far, he'd drunk enough Glenmorangie to take the edge off his worry and eaten Shepherd's pie, a small loaf of fresh bread and butter, fish and chips, extra vinegar on the chips, and a triple patty bacon burger with a side of sweet beans. He had an unapologetically healthy appetite.

It was nearing midnight, and it was about time to go to the airport and check in. He'd already dropped his truck off at the extended stay airport parking before taking a cab to Tate's Pub. He checked in with some of his teams, mostly online, and Bran and Patrick O'Faolain called around ten.

He had become very good friends with the brothers after

the months of he and his men guarding the family from a vengeful stalker trying to hurt them, the same one who'd been after Jo and her brother. There were times when he preferred speaking to their father, Hugh. He and Thomas would say about five words a piece, sit quietly, enjoying the other man's company— silently— before hanging up. Uncomplicated with mutual respect and little effort expected. What all friendships should strive for.

He had almost asked one of the O'Faolain men if they knew what Jo was doing. Where she was. Was she happy? Dating?

If she was dating someone, he'd make sure they regretted their life choices. He shook his head at his reaction and decided to leave questions like that for a time when he wasn't drinking or worried about Aileen and Mirren.

When he went after Jo, she would be his sole focus. He just had to give her enough time to cool off. Perhaps forgive him.

How much time was enough? Four months?

## 6

"I have two more forms to sign before I head out, and then you two are on your own." Jo had gotten back to Gustave Roussy by eight and was chatting comfortably with Aileen and Mirren. She'd slept fitfully. Dreams of Thomas made her sleep restless. Her inner worrier was concerned that Thomas might think Jo helped Aileen as a kind of FU to him. She sighed, admitting to herself that Thomas would never believe that. He may be a liar, but he knew her better than anyone else. No feeling person could use someone as sweet as his wife for revenge.

She was relieved to see that Aileen and Mirren had settled in. More important, the fear that had marked Aileen's eyes had dimmed. Positivity was more than half the battle, and it was obvious she was going to fight.

Aileen was hopeful and far from the woman Jo had met only yesterday. That woman had been focused on tying up loose strings, dotting her i's, and crossing her t's. It was gratifying to see the change in her and eased some of the tension from last night's restless dreams.

"Are you sure you don't want to stay and call Dad with us?

If he knew you were listening, he might forget to be mad at Mom and me," Mirren teased.

"Not a snowball's chance in hell, young lady. Your dad. Your problem." Turning to Aileen, Jo grinned. "You really are about to enter a shitstorm with no boots or umbrella."

Aileen grinned. "I am, and I won't even deny that I deserve some of his anger, but thanks to you, Jo, I feel more hopeful for my future than I have in years."

Aileen hugged Jo tight, and then Mirren hugged them both, closing the circle. Within days, their wonky connection had turned into... something.

"You made this possible, Jo." Aileen smiled through her tears. "You made me believe that not only will I beat this damn cancer, but I'm going to kick its ass. No more guilt, no more... celibacy," she grinned at her daughter's fake gag. "Sorry, Mir, but you were right. I did lie when I said I wasn't lonely. I have been. I am."

"Hallelujah, amen!" Mirren laughed. "When you get a boyfriend, you'll have less time to be a helicopter mom."

Jo loved that Mirren said "when" and not "if" her mom dated. She felt lighter than she had in months. Four months.

"I have never hovered!"

"You used to sit in a car outside my friend's houses when I had a sleepover." She tilted her head and smirked. "In case I changed my mind," she finished with air quotes.

"If it looks like a helicopter and sounds like a helicopter..." Jo said, laughing at Aileen's blush.

"You could always date my birth father. He's single and still pretty hot, according to online chatter and pics," Mirren said, shocking the room into silence.

Aileen was looking at her daughter like Mirren was suddenly speaking an encoded, extinct tongue.

"What... what..." That's all Aileen managed to stutter out.

Mirren smirked as only a teenager could pull off. "Dad isn't the only MacGregor with computer skills."

With this announcement, the sixteen-year-old brought her nails to her lips and blew, buffing the chipped, mossy-green polish on her blouse.

"You looked up Charles? Without telling me?"

"Duh. I had his name, age, and last known employer. Finding him was a breeze. Getting into his bank accounts was a bit trickier. He has quite a nest egg. Not a big spender, obvi. He still teaches at Harvard. Never married. No children. Well, he has one, but he doesn't know about me. Yet. I plan on reaching out in a few months once we know how your treatments are working. I have a feeling you're going to need the extra support since we agreed I would only stay with you for a few weeks before I go back to school."

Aileen's eyes were bulging. That was the only way to describe her nearly manic look. She whipped her crazy look Jo's way, begging for... help, support, life support?

"You admitted he was the love of your life. Mirren might be on to something."

"I am. He's written a ton of amazing journal articles. His works are highly regarded. I have links for all of them, including his books, for you to read while you're here."

Jo felt laughter bubble up her throat, and once her shoulders started to shake and a snort slipped out, both Aileen and Mirren were laughing along with her.

"This is all going to work out, isn't it?" Aileen asked once their laughter settled.

"Yes," Jo agreed.

"It's the only option. You're going to beat this, Mom. Your whole life has been for me. You deserve a happily-ever-after."

"Okay, guys, before you make me cry, I've got to head out.

My pilot is waiting for me, and you have a fun call to make." Jo grinned at the women's grimaces at the reminder.

"Are you sure you won't stay for that?"

Christ, even Aileen was trying to puppy-dog-eye Jo into staying. "No. Thomas Macgregor is a you problem. He has nothing to do with me."

"Nothing, lass?"

Jo gasped and spun on her heel so quickly she almost tripped.

The giant Scotsman of her tears.

The breaker of her heart.

The man she'd once trusted above all others.

Thomas MacGregor had arrived.

THOMAS STOOD outside what must be Aileen's room. Not Mirren's. Relief had his body trembling. Aileen must have cancer. She didn't tell him. He... didn't know how to process... any of what he was hearing and seeing.

Jo, his Josephine, was laughing and joking with his family like they'd been friends for years. Mirren discussing her birth father was difficult. On one hand, he was proud of her hacking skills. On the other, he never wanted that man near his daughter.

Mirren was his.

It was clear she was doing this for her mother's sake, but Thomas wasn't a fool. He'd heard the awe in her voice when she'd spoken of Charles' accomplishments.

He hated the man for that alone.

More crushing— how they spoke about calling Thomas. The dread. Was he really so immovable as all that? Did Aileen think he wouldn't care that she had cancer?

The worst was hearing Jo say he was nothing to her. It seemed he'd managed to alienate the three most important women in his life, but he wasn't about to let Jo blatantly lie. Not about that. Not when she knew he loved her beyond reason.

"Nothing, lass," Thomas growled, his patience at an end.

And there she was. Jo spun around at the sound of his voice. The shocked look and pink cheeks were satisfying. He affected her. Still.

The three women's animation of seconds ago had vanished. They were all deer in headlights. He walked through the door then. Entering the room and placing his big body before them. He crossed his arms and waited.

Mirren was the first to break eye contact, probably nervous about lying to him but also probably realizing he might have heard her speaking about Charles.

"Sorry I lied, Dad."

She sounded so dejected. He couldn't let her think he was angry with her. He was, but it appeared she had enough on her plate.

"I'm only sorry you and your mother didn't think I would want to know what's going on. Did you think I wouldn't care?" Aileen and Mirren's eyes whipped up to meet his.

"Of course not," Mirren said hotly.

That soothed some of his hurt, at least.

"But that wasn't the only secret? Was it?" He spoke evenly, so his frustration stayed banked.

"We were going to tell you today. Listen, Tommy," Aileen began, looking decidedly nervous. "You've heard about the divorce then?" At his nod, she continued, "This mess with Jo made me realize how unfair it was for us to have stayed married all these years."

When he attempted to interrupt, she held up a staying hand. "Unfair to both of us. You've been miserable. I've been lonely," she looked at Mirren for a beat, "and then I found out I had breast cancer."

Before Aileen could continue, Jo cleared her throat. Thomas hadn't realized he'd stepped so close to her side until he felt cool air hit his side as she took a step back. Christ, after months of misery, his body was done with the separation.

"You three have much to discuss, and I have a plane to catch."

She refused to look his way as she gave hugs to Mirren, whispering something in his daughter's ear that made her grin, and then Aileen.

"I'll let you know when I touch down. I can't wait to hear what the doctors think of your new scans, but don't call me at three in the morning, or cancer won't be the only thing you'll need to be worried about."

The two women smiled at one another, clearly an inside joke. They were both trying and failing not to cry.

"I can't thank—" Aileen began.

Jo cut her off. "I'll send you my work schedule once I meet with Mom and Dad. I'll be back when I can."

They stood silently for several more moments. Before Aileen nodded and Jo nodded back. Some unspoken promise?

Thomas' brain was finally registering that Jo was leaving. Leaving the room, the hospital, France. Him. Again.

He took a step toward her as she turned for the door. "Jo. Please." Please what? Was he asking for forgiveness? A second chance? For her to tell him that she still loved him?

Without turning, she spoke to the door. "Take good care of them, Thomas."

Her words punched him in the stomach. "Please," was all he managed to say a second time.

"You had months to explain your situation when we were

together. You've had months since. Your family needs you now. More than ever. I... I will take care of myself."

She walked out.

She left.

She was gone.

"Dad! Go after her."

Mirren even shoved his back to get her point across.

"Don't, Tommy. Leave her be."

Turning from the door to frown at his... at Aileen, she took a step back. Probably because his face televised the storm brewing in his body.

Aileen gripped his forearm. "It hurt her to see you. It was unexpected."

When he tried to pull his arm away, Aileen gripped him tighter.

"No, Tommy. You don't get to hide this from me anymore. I've tried more than once to speak of Jo. You shut me down each time. Not this time. I was selfish not to insist on a divorce years ago. You were an idiot for lying to a woman you love.

"We've both made decisions that landed us here." She paused to chuckle. "Not here, in a cancer hospital, but here as in us slowly coming to resent one another and you losing Jo. Once I found out about the cancer, I decided to make some changes. For both of us."

"Here, Dad. Come sit down. There's loads to talk about, and if a nurse walks in with you Hulking out in our room, you'll scare them," she smiled, tugging him by the hand to lead him to a small couch near the window.

Mirren sat next to him while Aileen took a chair facing them both.

"The doctor at Inverness didn't give me a lot of hope. Breast cancer doesn't run in the family. I didn't plan on getting mammograms until I was in my forties. I've had it for a while. I told Mirren right away because, regardless of whether I lived or died, she needed to be a part of the process."

"And I didn't? You and Coll have been my best friends since we were little." Thomas was pissed and hurt.

"We're still your best friends, and of course, you deserved to know. I really was going to call you today. I should have known you'd sniff out our lies." She sighed. "I didn't tell you initially because you were dealing with your own things. You were hurting, and Coll... has his own things too.

"Before I told you, I wanted to have a plan. You've taken care of me your whole life. I wasn't going to let you take care of this. Mirren and I have been doing a ton of research the past few weeks on the best facility for treatments."

"I'd say you found it." He'd been impressed with the hospital and with all the articles he'd downloaded and read on the plane.

"Oh, this place never made the list. This was all Jo, but I'll explain that in a minute. I debated talking to you first before I filed for a divorce, but I knew you would refuse once you learned about the cancer." She held her hand up to stop his rebuttal. "Don't deny it. You would have cared only about getting me well. Your devotion is one of the many things I've always loved about you.

"But... I've never been your wife. Not your real wife. You saved me when I needed you most. You became a husband, which made your dating life hell, but you also became the best father our daughter could have had. I needed to do this on my own for you, Tommy, and for me."

He let her words sink in. He didn't love that she'd kept her diagnosis from him. She must have been scared. He knew Mirren would have been. Letting go of the initial hurt, he could admit that he did understand where she was coming from. And she was right, he wasn't her husband in truth. She didn't owe him her every thought and fear.

"So, what now?"

"Now, I get my test results later today. I promised Mirren she could stay a few weeks and do school online. My doctor will go over treatment plans when she brings the results. Once I know my schedule, I plan on renting a small flat near the hospital. Whether the treatments work or they don't, I do plan on moving back home. However, until then, Mirren will need to live with you."

Thomas placed his hand on his daughter's knee and squeezed. "I would like that." Mirren smiled. "How did Jo, umm, figure into all of this?"

"Oh, that," Aileen chuckled. "Diana Gaines. You know her?"

"Unfortunately," Thomas grumbled. His day just kept getting better. "The woman's disapproval is deadly."

"Ha ha. She was lovely. Blunt but lovely. She called me a week ago and insisted I help you and Josephine— and here, I'll quote. 'Unless Mr. MacGregor is more brawn than brains, as it appears is the case, then surely he might formulate some mediocre plan to atone for his ineptitude and egregious mishandling of Ms. O'Connor.'"

Aileen and Mirren were both giggling. Diana Gaines was a menace. No wonder the O'Faolains referred to her as a dragon. "It isn't *that* funny." He frowned at them both.

"It really is, actually." Aileen dabbed her eyes, sniffing back the rest of her mirth.

"She didn't know we were married in name only. Does the woman have no shame to call about your husband's girlfriend? Jesus, the nerve of the woman."

"Oh no, nothing like that. She had a private investigator

look into 'the situation.' She wanted to know what you'd done to Jo and why she was hiding it."

Thomas surged to his feet, furious. "She did what? She had me investigated? Christ Almighty. That woman doesn't walk, she oversteps every foot."

"Calm down and sit, for heaven's sake. Her reasons were well-meaning."

He sat, taking deep breaths. "And those reasons?"

"I guess three of Jo's best friends are married to Diana's best friend's family."

"They are. The Byrne sisters. Raven, River, and Rowan."

"Hey," Mirren started, "Rowan was the name of the woman who was kidnapped. And weren't the Byrnes one of the families you were hired to protect from that stalker?"

"Yes, to both."

"I hated the stalker case. I hardly saw you and FaceTime got *real* old," Mirren complained.

"I missed you too." It had been hard to be apart from his daughter. He castigated himself for the hundredth time that he hid her from Jo. If he hadn't done that, the separation would have been easier for all of them.

"You see, then," Aileen continued, "that Diana meant well."

"She's a meddler," Thomas groused, not willing to let the 'brawn over brains' comment pass.

"Whatever. We've had a family meeting. It's over. Are you going to call Jo or not?" Mirren huffed, clearly considering the past few months of deceit done and dusted.

"She blocked my number," Thomas admitted, feeling his cheeks warm.

"Use mine," Aileen offered.

He was tempted but didn't want to come between the two women. "No. Thank you, though."

"Then what?" Mirren stood, placing her hands on her hips. Clearly exasperated.

"I might be able to get her plane stopped so that I can at least speak to her before she leaves." He didn't answer Aileen's questioning look.

He took out his phone but hesitated, waffling. He despised asking for favors. He really despised airing his private business.

There was no choice if he hoped to catch her. He dialed the one person who might feel beholden to Thomas. The phone rang twice before it was picked up.

"MacGregor."

Dean O'Connor didn't sound happy to hear from him. Thomas didn't blame him. Dean might not know why he and his daughter had gone their separate ways, but Jo's father wasn't an idiot. He would know Thomas was at fault.

"I need a favor."

"What is it?" Dean asked, with just enough venom to burn.

"I need you to call your pilot and tell him not to take off."

Silence settled before, "Why the fuck would I do that?"

"I need to speak to Jo."

"Why?"

"I have to speak to her." Thomas looked at Aileen and Mirren. They were wide-eyed. Dean didn't say anything for a solid minute. Thomas could feel his shoulders knotting with tension, waiting for the older man's decision.

"I texted Conrad. They haven't taken off yet. He'll watch for your arrival. But MacGregor, I'm warning you now. You hurt my daughter again, I will make it my life's mission to ruin you."

"Understood."

Dean ended the call.

Thomas looked at his family, running his hand down his face. Christ in Heaven, his life had really taken a wrong turn.

Several wrong terms. "I'll be back whether I speak to Jo or not. I want to be here when the doctor comes."

"That isn't nec—" Aileen began.

"It is. Also, you need to let Coll know what's going on." He could see the argument begin in her eyes and stopped that before it could start. "I let him know something was going on before I left home. He's waiting for an update. You will be the one to give it to him." Thomas may not be her husband in truth, but Aileen had known him long enough to know when he wasn't going to change his mind.

"Fine," she reluctantly agreed, rolling her eyes. An exact replica of Mirren's irreverence. As Thomas left their room, he heard his daughter say, "You're on your own calling Uncle Colly. Dad's the only one *I* was in trouble with."

# 7

"Hey, Susan," Jo addressed the stewardess who was currently busying herself folding blankets. "What's the delay?" They should have taken off forty-five minutes ago. Susan's wide-eyed guilty stare was the first fissure of unease Jo had felt since boarding her family's jet.

"Conrad had to hold our position longer until further notice. I... I... I believe. Might I top off your unsweet tea, Ms. O'Connor?"

Susan's stammering sped up Jo's already pumping heart. Seeing Thomas had thrown her emotions into a tornado of emotions as strong or stronger as the day she'd walked away from him.

"I see," Jo replied, standing and moving past the flight attendant. "I don't need anything at the moment. Excuse me while I go speak to Conrad myself about the delay." At Susan's relieved sigh, Jo's suspicion that something was off solidified.

Conrad opened the cabin door at her knock. He turned, giving her his full attention, seeming unsurprised at the interruption.

"Please explain why we aren't in the air." Jo tried to

moderate her tone, but something was up, and she was getting more agitated with each second that ticked off. To give Conrad his due, the pilot didn't so much as twitch a hair follicle.

"I apologize for the delay, Ms. O'Connor, but you'll need to speak to your father about the flight change."

Her father? What in the ever-loving hell? Jo opened the phone that was already in her palm and called Dean O'Connor. Straight to voicemail. She called her mother next. Voicemail. It was the same damn time in Italy. What the hell was going on? She couldn't call her brother, James, because he and his wife were currently back in Oklahoma, and it was the middle of the night there.

Jo was in the process of opening her emails to see if the information her mother sent on their Rome apartment lease mentioned a landline when Conrad announced, "The person Mr. O'Connor told me to expect is here. If you'll excuse me, I need to let the door down."

What did he mean, let them in? "Is there going to be another passenger?" Why wouldn't Dad have messaged her about the change of plans? Nothing made any sense. Jo stepped back, allowing Conrad to proceed her into the cabin.

The doors swooshed open, and the automatic stairs extended, ending at the feet of... Thomas MacGregor. Jo's heart rate spiked, her breathing stuttered and tried to stop, forcing Jo to wrap her hand tightly against her throat, a reminder to force oxygen down her airway.

Cold air spun around Thomas' big body, rippling the hem of his wool coat. The same wind that whipped the Highlander with its icy tentacles pushed into the plane, swirling her long golden waves about her shoulders and sending shivers down her back.

Thomas didn't say anything, so Jo did. "Go." She crossed her arms across her chest, a defensive posture that was no defense at all. He'd stood so close to her in the hospital room, close enough to feel his warmth and catch his unique spicy scent. She was too weak when he was that close. "Please go," she weakly whispered, not caring about the spectacle they were performing in front of the crew.

"I am boarding, lass. Your father's given me permission to speak to you."

Did he now? "He didn't get my fucking permission, MacGregor, and I say no."

"I'm not giving you a choice. The sooner you hear me out the sooner you can be on your way."

Jo knew from experience that the granite set to Thomas' jaw meant there would be no getting rid of him. "Fine." Jo's clipped response didn't change the man's stoic look. Sighing in frustration, she turned toward the back, considering all the ways to make her father pay for this level of interfering bullshit.

She sat at one of the side desk tables located under a bank of windows. Jo had already set her laptop up on the desk earlier, hoping to get a few hours of work accomplished before she celebrated not begging Thomas MacGregor to take her back.

A bottle of Monkey 47 gin sat on the desk waiting for the party-of-one celebration. Her dad had bought her a ridiculously expensive bottle of the German gin for her birthday last year, and she'd planned on using this flight to make that bottle her bitch.

For such a large man, Thomas was as stealthy as a panther. River Byrne would have irreverently called Thomas a fart—silent but deadly. When Jo was riding high on one of her spiteful moods, she would wholeheartedly agree. However, most of her moods directed at the drop-dead gorgeous Scotsman leaned less toward spite and more toward longing. So... a panther, not a fart.

Jo took a seat, leaving Thomas to either sit opposite her or stand awkwardly. True to his domineering personality, he stood.

She clasped her hands together to conceal their shaking. He always managed to get a rise out of her.

Good, bad, and orgasmic.

He didn't speak immediately. He watched her fidgeting with still concentration. Jo felt perspiration bead the back of her neck. Christ, this man could try a saint's patience.

With a sigh, Jo broke the silence. "Why did you have my father stop the plane? I have a lot of work to do as soon as I land and would like to get on with it."

Thomas' hands briefly flexed at his sides. Jo had known him long enough to have learned a few of his tells. He became utterly still, like he was now, when he was feeling extreme emotion— humor, anger, passion. Hurt.

He was wearing his typical uniform of boots, rugged work jeans, and a black tee that hugged his mouthwatering upper body. She had kissed, sucked, and licked every inch of him. She knew how smooth his rippling muscles felt under her palm and what noises he made when she touched his body intimately.

He knew her body too.

Jo pressed her lips together in frustration. She didn't want to remember. It had been four months since she'd felt his touch. Saying she missed it, missed him, was a parody of the truth. She craved him, felt withdrawal as a bone-deep ache and felt his absence every moment of every day.

But... he had lied. He had concealed the truth. Despite his and Aileen's situation, he was a married man. It had made her feel dirty, like the worst cheater. She still felt that way, though admittedly, not as strongly after meeting Aileen. She just couldn't get over the lies. Thomas hadn't even tried to reach out even after all these weeks later.

He had a daughter. Mirren. He kept her from Jo all that

time. Jo hadn't been significant enough to meet the most important person in his life. His marriage had crushed her. Learning he had hidden a child... that was a knife in the gut.

"Speak or leave," Jo spoke sharply, causing his jaw to clench. She couldn't sit here another moment with him towering over her. She stood. He didn't retreat even a step, causing their bodies to brush as she moved by him to the middle of the cabin.

"Josephine," he began, clearing his throat, adding, "Jo. I should have told you. From the beginning— before the beginning. Of us, I mean."

He was nervous. That was an emotion Jo wasn't familiar with seeing in him. She stayed silent.

"I never considered myself married. Not really. I believe Aileen explained all that." At her nod, he continued, "She was my high school girlfriend. We kissed when we were teenagers. We've never touched each other since. Neither of us wanted that type of relationship. I got used to having..."

At his pause, she finished for him. "Sex." She was satisfied to see his cheeks pinken.

"Yes. When I was out of town on assignments. The... women weren't serious. I never considered telling one that I was married. You are the only woman I've ever... loved," he quietly admitted.

Jo felt her heart pound and gracelessly dropped in one of the padded seats behind her. Thomas slowly lowered to the seat connected to hers, staying at the edge and turning his body toward her.

"The longer we were together, the more daunting coming clean became. I feared you would leave me. You *did* leave me."

"I would have been angry, but had you been honest, even belatedly, I would have forgiven you. Especially having met Aileen. But your marriage wasn't the worst of your lies."

"Mirren." He sighed.

"Your daughter."

"I've thought about this since the moment you left me in Dublin. The only explanation, which is not an excuse because there is no excuse for hiding my daughter from you, is that I had lived my whole adult life as a loyal son, a best friend, a leader in the Royal Marines, a business owner, a boss, a fake husband, and a father.

"I wanted to simply be... only me for once. I wanted to be Josephine O'Connor's boyfriend. I wanted to love a woman for the first time and know she loved me back. I was selfish and a coward. I can't... I want... I'm begging you to consider taking me back."

Tears were leaking from Jo's eyes by the time his speech had run its course. "Why didn't you try to explain before now?"

"I hurt you even though I'd promised never to do that. I felt like I didn't deserve to be forgiven, I guess. I knew you needed time. You blocked me, and I didn't want to go through your friends. I wanted the choice to be yours. Another error on my part."

Everything he'd just said were the right things. God knew, he wasn't the only one who'd made mistakes in the past. And yet... Christ... Having met his family, their relationship would still feel wrong if they were to pursue it again. Right now, anyway.

"I can't commit to anything with you, Thomas, until your life is in order, and with Aileen's cancer... She has a long road ahead of her. She and Mirren need you now more than ever. Aileen will say she doesn't, but she does."

He deflated at her words, leaning slightly over his knees and rubbing his face as if he were trying to wipe away the truth.

"I love you. My God, I've felt like a dead man walking since you left. Do you still love me? If you can at least give me that, I can keep enduring you not being next to me."

Jo would never lie. "I love you. Of course, I still love you." She yelped as he scooped her out of her chair and into his lap.

"Kiss me. Just once, baby, so that I can have your taste in my mouth when I have to walk away."

He spoke against her neck, a plea that melted her resistance. She placed her hands on either side of his head, the blonde buzzcut scratching her palms, and pulled his mouth to hers.

"Are you still my HB?" Jo's husky voice touched his lips. When Thomas had assigned himself as her personal guard last year when that serial stalker had been after her, Jo had once teased the gruff, silent Scotsman by calling him Honey Bunny, Honey for short. His golden, honey-colored hair reminded her of a pet bunny she'd fallen in love with as a child.

"Forever and a day," he vowed.

They sighed at the first brush of their lips, then moaned at the taste and touch of their tongues tangling. His hands clamped around her waist, twisting her body so that she was now straddling his lap.

She needed this kiss more than air. She felt the hard ridge of his erection between her thighs and began sliding her hips up and down, his hands moving her harder and faster, a perfect pump and grind. Their groans increased in volume until she feared the crew would hear and come to investigate.

Thomas broke the kiss, nipping her bottom lip before demanding, "I need more. Will you give me more?"

Jo knew this was a mistake, but damned if her body hadn't taken over rational thought. "Yes."

The moment he got the green light, she was plucked off his lap, so she stood before him. He snatched her exercise pants and thong down her body. She kicked her slides off so he could get the pants over her feet.

She leaned forward and slid her hand over his chest and down the ridges of his abdomen, going for the button on his jeans. He helped by reclining the chair, giving her access to open things up. The zipper down, he hooked his thumbs in his jeans and boxers, yanking both down at once. She helped tug his boots off before pulling his jeans free.

His sex stood proud between them, the pearling precum hypnotizing. She bent further forward, licking her lips, about to taste him for the first time in months.

"No, baby, Christ. I'd never last. I need to be inside you. Now."

Thomas redirected her before she could take a single taste, pulling her back onto his lap, aligning their bodies perfectly. The slick head brushed her core, causing them both to shudder and moan louder.

They both watched as his arousal stretched her body, disappearing inside her inch by inch.

"Fuck, baby, you're so wet— so tight."

She could only whimper as he finally seated himself fully. Nothing felt better than Thomas MacGregor. She set a slow pace, moving up until his flesh almost left her body before gliding back down with a sigh. The building friction... a sweet torture.

He began rubbing circles against her sensitive flesh where they were joined. Her hips jerked and spasmed. "Don't stop. Close," she panted.

Thomas secured her hips, increasing the pace, pulling her down hard over him, faster and faster, while simultaneously rubbing her sex. An orgasm ripped through her body— four months of pent-up, rippling shockwaves.

The grip and release of her muscles spurred his release. He pulled her down once more as he filled her, holding her close so they were eye to eye. Love was there, but so was wariness. They were as close as two lovers could be, yet she still felt the remnants of hurt and disappointment shadowing her heart.

Regret quickly replaced euphoria.

Thomas was still married.

She was still the other woman.

"Jo," Thomas began, feeling her pull from him.

She shook her head, standing on shaky legs as he slid from her body. She quickly grabbed her panties and pants, slipping them on without further eye contact.

"Damn it, Josephine! What we just did wasn't wrong. I love you, and you love me. Don't shut me out," he pleaded.

She shook her head, hurt from being pulled in a million directions. "What happened between us just now didn't change the fact that you have a family that needs you. I'm not a part of that family." She closed her eyes, breathing deeply. She heard Thomas redressing, regret thrummed through her veins. She didn't want to part this way, but this ending was inevitable.

Her back was to Thomas so she could ignore the disappointment surely etched on his face. She faced the exit, the door that would take Thomas away from her.

She felt him move to stand sentinel at her back. His heat, normally a comfort, caused pricks of ice to pelt her sensitive skin.

"I will fix this. Promise you will wait for me."

He tried to make it a question, but it was definitely a demand. When it was important— and Jo knew she was important to him— he wouldn't risk a miscommunication.

"Waiting is a lonely business," she said quietly.

"Promise me anyway."

She wanted to pledge her love and place forgiveness on his broad shoulders. His pain was hers too. In the end, she could only nod her acquiescence. He wrapped a hand around the back of her neck, pressing his thumb against the soft flesh.

His breath fanned her ear, "I will always be yours,

Josephine Margaret O'Connor." He gently squeezed her neck once more. "Always."

Her body shook as she watched Thomas MacGregor walk away and exit the plane, disappearing into the bright Paris morning.

She took one more shuddering breath, forcing herself to remember why she couldn't afford to hand over her complete trust.

Men didn't always keep their promises.

Men weren't always who they said they were.

Men could look like angels but be devils.

It was a lesson she'd learned long ago and one that had haunted her for years. No. She wanted to trust again, but she wouldn't survive history repeating itself a third time.

## 8

EIGHT YEARS AGO, MONTAUK YACHT—
NEW YORK

"Oh, Ivy. You're stunning." Jo wasn't lying. Her childhood friend was getting married today, and a more lovely bride couldn't exist. She and Ivy had grown up playing at each other's houses in the Hamptons during the summers, and even though Jo's family visited less and less over the past couple of years, she and Ivy had remained close. "Hunter is going to pass out when he sees you walking down the aisle."

There were a dozen women hovering around her friend, making last-minute adjustments to the dress and veil. Ivy had chosen a fitted, sheer sheath, champagne with a slightly darker, body-hugging slip underneath. It was simple, yet stunning.

"That color makes your skin glow."

Ivy was born in Massachusetts, but both her parents had immigrated from Haiti years before. Her father worked for his uncle's real estate company before eventually taking it over. Real estate in the Hamptons area was a goldmine, which was why Ivy's family could easily afford this extravagant wedding at the Montauk.

"Ha," Ivy snorted. "Mamma says babies do that to a woman.

I call it the teen-mom sparkle," she said, shooting her mother a grin.

"Tone down your sass, young lady," her mother admonished.

Ivy admitted her mother had been furious when she'd broken the baby news. Apparently, as soon as her mom realized the upside, which was a grandbaby to dote on, the news had been much easier to swallow. She'd gotten her game face on after that.

It was easy to forget Ivy was pregnant. She'd only turned nineteen last month and was the youngest real estate agent at her father's firm. She'd grown up in real estate and had been killing it.

Jo was about to start her junior year at Cornell. She'd had two years of college completed by the time she graduated high school a few months ago— all it had taken was hours holed up in libraries studying and two summers of classes. She'd rarely had time to join in the Oklahoma social circle... *Worth it.*

Ithaca was only a five-hour drive from the Hamptons, so she and Ivy would be able to meet up more often.

Ivy had told Jo about meeting Hunter. He was a fourth-year law student at Yale. His family put the 'well' in 'to do.' Very posh and very much in the political scene. When they found out their only son had impregnated a teenager, they were not pleased.

The Cordon family assumed Ivy was after Hunter's money, but after they met her, they recognized that she was the real deal. However, to save the family from even a whiff of scandal, they insisted she and Hunter marry. Immediately. Hunter loved Ivy and was thrilled with the shotgun wedding.

Ivy's moan brought Jo's attention back to her friend. "I hate my hair. It looks horrible, and the veil only makes it look dumpier." She turned suddenly frantic eyes her way. "Jo?"

Wedding jitters had finally made an appearance. Her mother and Jo had been waiting. Iris gave Jo a pursed-lip pout with raised brows, almost causing Jo to snicker. "I know what the problem is, Ivy. You have the most gorgeous hair. It's curly and crazy, kind of like your personality."

Ivy's "Hey!" made the ladies in the room chuckle.

"Your updo is lovely, but it isn't you. You went simple with the dress, make a statement with your hair. Plus, you know it was your hair that first caught Hunter's attention."

"My ass too. Never forget the power of firm butt cheeks. You're right, though. Would you take my hair back down, Mamma?"

Once her thousands of spirals were released, Ivy sighed in relief. Her hair reached just past her shoulders, draping perfectly below her collarbones. Iris fussed a few more minutes before tucking the veil's clip in place.

"Perfect," Ivy sighed.

"Perfect," Jo agreed.

THE WEDDING WAS BEAUTIFUL. The breeze coming off the lake was a perfect nature-inspired touch. Ivy looked like a fairy princess. Her champagne dress dazzled as the sun began to set. It took an hour after the ceremony to finish taking pictures with the families and the wedding party. Jo was the only bridesmaid, and Percy Donovan, Hunter's best friend and fellow law student, was the groomsman. The dining hall had its glass doors open so the guests could enjoy indoor-outdoor seating for dinner.

Several bars were set up near the outdoor dance floor. Tonight promised to be one hell of a party. Jo smiled as she looked around the hundreds of well-dressed guests, not an O'Connor in sight.

A shiver went down her spine as she recalled Percy walking her down the aisle. He'd whispered in her ear that she was the sexiest woman there. Lies, of course, but Jo's body had heated at the compliment.

Jo was wearing a caramel-brown slip dress. It slithered over her body as she walked, not too clingy but fitted enough to show her curves. The low-heeled strappy sandals accentuated Jo's long legs.

At five-eight, she was slightly above the average height for women, and had legs for days. She'd left her long, golden hair waving down her back, a simple gold and diamond clip holding one side back. A light brush of smokey brown shadow framed her long lashes, making her gray eyes shine.

She felt very much like a woman.

Percy grinned at her as he and several other men leaned against one of the bars. He saluted her with a crystal glass of what looked like bourbon or whiskey. She was about to awkwardly turn and make her way inside when Ivy swept up beside her, wrapping her arm around Jo's.

The two friends grinned at one another.

"I did it."

"You certainly did."

"I'm married."

"And pregnant," Jo added with a grin.

Ivy sighed. "No alcohol at my own wedding." She pretended to pout.

Jo glanced Percy's way once more. The man exuded tall, dark, and handsome. Jo guessed his height was around an even six feet, the custom suit fit his body perfectly. His black hair was short and expertly groomed, not a hair out of place. His eyes were dark. Their intensity made her shiver, wondering what thoughts were going on behind them.

"Hunter's friend is gorgeous," Jo whispered so no one passing by would hear. Ivy stiffened, causing Jo to look at her friend in question. "What?"

She shrugged, shaking her head a little. "It's nothing, really. Only, he's nothing like Hunter. Percy can sometimes make me feel... uncomfortable."

"He does have a powerful presence. Surely, Hunter would know if his friend was, I don't know, a bad guy."

"You're right, Jo. I'm overthinking." Switching gears, Ivy grinned, grabbed Jo's hands, and swung her around. "Let's party! I just got married." She laughed. "I can't drink, but I can dance!"

The night was fun. The food was exceptional, the cake was even better, vanilla with fresh strawberry buttercream, and the G&Ts were manna from heaven— especially since her mom wasn't there to take the drinks out of her hand.

Jo had danced for hours. Her partners ranged from toddlers giggling as she twirled them to senior citizens cutting a rug with their walkers. It was nearing midnight, and the crowd had thinned considerably. She walked inside, not seeing Ivy anywhere in the outdoor area.

Jo was pleasantly buzzed and ready for bed. She could reach her room easily from one of the many beach paths around the Club. Her room had a gorgeous view of the marina, and she couldn't wait to enjoy the private beach after the races tomorrow.

Most of the guests had found their beds already so that they would be well rested enough to enjoy the regatta racing tomorrow morning. Brunch, mimosas, and cheering on a favorite racing team sounded like a perfect day to Jo. She spotted Ivy hugging her aunt and uncle goodnight. She was about to join them so she could hug her friend goodnight when a man suddenly appeared beside her, wrapping his large hand around her wrist.

"You weren't about to leave without giving me a goodnight kiss, were you, Josie?"

Jo blew off the unasked-for nickname and smiled at Percy. The man was smoking hot, but he had never approached her once all night. She would catch him watching her but nothing more. "Jo or Josephine works for me." She chuckled to take the sting out. "And yes, I'm exhausted. It's been a long day," she admitted.

Percy slid his hand around her silk-covered waist and left his warm palm resting on her lower back. Jo couldn't decide if she was entranced or discomfited. He touched her with possession— perhaps too much. He looked at her like he could easily make her follow him anywhere. *The Pied Piper of Montauk*. She had to hide her smile at the thought.

Jo was about to tell him, firmly, that she was going to bed. By herself. But then, he used his free hand to feather his fingers down her cheek and neck, gently brushing her hair to her back.

"I wanted to touch you all night, Josie. I watched you and wanted you, but you're so young. I tried to stay away. Have a drink with me. Let me tell you who I am, and you can tell me who you are. Then we won't be strangers anymore."

At her continued hesitation, he pushed, "Just one drink. Please. I promise to drop you off at your room and leave you alone... to dream about me," he whispered against her mouth.

His dark eyes were intoxicating. She didn't need another drink, but she'd be lying if she said she wasn't flattered by this man's attention. Jo had dated in high school, but nothing serious. She was a virgin by choice, not because her parents were hoverers.

She had goals. The first was to get her master's in hospitality management by twenty-two, and the second was to become a full-fledged partner in O'Connor Hospitality like her brother had this year.

That didn't mean she wasn't open to exploring her sexuality. She was becoming increasingly interested as Percy's body caged her much smaller one in a darkened alcove— interested but not sold. He did promise not to ask for more than a drink.

"One drink, and then I'll say goodnight."

"One drink's all I'm asking for, Josie."

Jo SHIFTED, groaning at how sore her body was. Dancing. Drinking. Oh, God, too much drinking. Her head was splitting, and the sunlight currently beaming through her room's glass doors was burning the skin off her squinted eyelids.

She managed to throw an arm over her eyes to block the worst of the rays. She took a moment to take stock of how hungover she was and if it would be possible to recover before the regatta began. Mouth, dry as the desert. Head, splitting. Stomach, nauseous.

"Shit!" she slid blindly off the bed to hobble as quickly as her shaky legs could manage to the bathroom, barely fisting her long hair before puking her guts out in the, God no, closed toilet. A projectile of putrid-smelling, watery spray covered her legs and half the floor.

"Damn it, Jo. You idiot." Swallowing the bile that kept trying to slip past her clamped lips, she forced herself to clean up the disgusting mess. There was no way in hell she was calling housekeeping.

She was leaning her palms on either side of the sink, sweating and groaning thirty minutes later. She'd had to stop twice more to throw up— this time with the lid up. Never trust an eighteen-year-old to make good life decisions. She groaned at her stupidity, shaking her head before wincing at the movement.

Forcing her head to lift, she looked at herself in the mirror. Not good. Her hair was a matted rat's nest, her lips were swollen, and as her hands traced her naked torso, she took in the multitude of red marks and purple bruises.

She recalled a slight buzz last night, but she certainly hadn't been that inebriated. Going to bed naked was also new.

Her hands gripped the counter's smooth, cold edge tighter. Fear started to trickle into her consciousness.

She attempted a few calming breaths before going over the last thing she remembered from the night before.

Wedding. Pictures. Food. Drinks. Dancing. Yawning.

Dark eyes followed her every step. Whispers. Hands.

One last drink... one last drink... one last drink.

Not enough to make her blackout drunk.

Percy Donovan.

She recognized the marks covering her body then. Oh God, bite marks. Her breaths were coming in heaving gasps, and she knew she was about to hyperventilate.

She shoved away from the bathroom counter and turned to the full-length mirror covering the back of the closed door.

And there it was. The tenderness between her thighs that she'd successfully ignored until this moment.

A smear of dried blood.

Hot tears began a scorching trail down her cheeks.

A moment that should have meant something, been special, been with a man she loved. Instead, she'd gotten drunk and allowed a man to... She felt bile rise once more. She stumbled into the bedroom, frantically looking for any clue... any fucking clue.

There was a note on the bedside table tucked under her phone.

*Last night was amazing, Josie. I love that you let me video our first time. You looked beautiful in every position.*

*Our night will be our secret... unless you want to be internet famous.*

*I know you'll be with other men over the years, but I want you to always remember— I was your first. PD*

# 9

## PRESENT DAY, THE INSTITUT GUSTAVE ROUSSY —VILLEJUIF, FRANCE

"Please tell me Diana Gaines' opinion was unwarranted, Dad. Tell me you won Jo back," Mirren demanded the moment Thomas stepped one foot back into Aileen's room. Unwarranted? Was his daughter dipping her toes into historical romances again?

Last year she'd told him a boy had been "forward" with her during a science lab, which was why she "accidentally" caught his two weeks of notes on fire. She had gone to the movies a week later with that same boy.

Save him from teenage girls.

*Nonsensical, thy name is Hormones.*

How did he answer her question when his body still felt the blistering heat of Jo's? Nothing was resolved, but everything felt... better. He would take care of his family, and she would take care of hers by working.

Jo was his, and he was hers. She did indicate she would wait. That simple nod of the head was the only thing that let him walk away.

Their meeting had been the end of one story and the beginning of a new one. He could say none of that to his daughter, however.

"Fine."

"Fine?" she screeched, throwing her hands in the air, a trait she'd obviously learned from his sister.

"Seriously, Tommy. Fine is all you have to say?" Aileen asked, managing to portray annoyance and flabbergasted in one question.

"Fine," Mirren repeated. "Good Lord, Mom. I'm beginning to believe your fake marriage to Dad saved some poor woman from committing murder."

Aileen stopped speaking for a moment and just stared at him, her head slightly cocked in thought. She must have picked up on one of Thomas' tells. Damn his fair cheeks, and damn her for knowing him so well. She tried to hide her grin but failed... irritatingly so.

"Leave your dad alone, Mir," she chided, swallowing most of her humor. "He's probably worn out after such a soul-bearing *conversation*."

Mirren stopped berating him and looked from her mother to him and back again. "Ohhh, I see. You guys had sex. Well, she must have forgiven you. That's encouraging. Though, with driving time included, you weren't with her that long." She sighed with a contemplative look.

Was she actually calculating how long he had lasted?

Thomas had been shot before and shot at several times between military campaigns and running security. That word... sex, coming out of his baby girl's mouth, produced more repercussions.

He looked to Aileen, waiting for the *child's* mother to scold Mirren— the woman looked amused. *Amused, for fuck's sake.*

Thomas opened his mouth to reprimand his daughter, who surely shouldn't understand anything about sex, let alone so blithely speak of the act, when a doctor walked in, effectively shutting down Thomas learning the extent of his child's birds-and-bees knowledge.

Thank God and all his Saints.

"I'm Dr. Delaloge," the petite woman introduced herself.

He liked that she spoke with authority. Her French accent was strong, perhaps as heavy as his own Scottish brogue, but she was precise enough in her enunciation that her words were not difficult to decipher. Aileen introduced Thomas as her husband, which felt wrong, considering he still had Jo's scent on his skin.

"Let's sit," the doctor suggested. She took one of the chairs, Thomas the other, and Aileen and Mirren sat facing them on the small couch. Dr. Delaloge pulled a packet of documents from her bag and a tablet, setting them both down on the coffee table set in the middle of the seating area.

Aileen's hands were fisted in her lap. She was clearly nervous about her results. The doctor looked at Aileen with just enough softness, he felt his lungs begin to restrict in panic. Thomas read people's body language for a living. She was about to speak words that they didn't want to hear.

"I'm sorry to give you this news, Mrs. Macgregor, but your cancer has progressed much further than your original doctor believed. You are Stage 3."

Aileen gasped. A keening whine escaped her throat before she could clamp her teeth together. He stood, moving to her side. The damn, tiny couch wasn't large enough to handle his bulk as well as theirs. He plucked Mirren up like he used to when she was a bairn, sitting beside Aileen and setting his daughter on his lap. He grasped one of his best friend's hands in his own and looked toward the doctor to continue.

"There are four stages of breast cancer," she continued, probably very used to a human's varying reactions to bad news. "Stage four would require aggressive treatments to prolong your life. That's it. Prolong, not cure. Stage 3 requires aggressive treatments as well, but the chances of survival exponentially increase. There are three stages of severity in Stage 3. 3A, 3B, and the most severe, 3C. You are 3B.

"Had this not been caught, 3C was breathing down your neck. This all sounds bad. I know it sounds like the end of the world to you right now, but Mrs. MacGregor—"

"Aileen," Aileen corrected as she continued to squeeze his hand, holding on tight.

"Aileen," the doctor acknowledged. "This is treatable. This is survivable. You need to be one hundred percent committed to the process. If you are, I believe your chances of a complete recovery are high."

Thomas squeezed Aileen's hand back while simultaneously squeezing his daughter's knee. "We're committed." He waited for his girls to nod in agreement before continuing. "Give us the treatment plan, Dr. Delaloge."

Forty-five minutes later, after reviewing x-rays, documents, pictures, and side-effects, he was satisfied Aileen was in the best hands. He was so thankful that Jo was the type of woman to care enough to find the best hospital and the best doctor for a woman she barely knew.

"Only your right breast tissue is compromised, but because of the aggression of your cancer, I believe you should choose a double mastectomy. Once you're healed from that surgery, we'll begin chemotherapy— shrink the remaining tumor.

"It's preferred to wait several weeks before beginning chemotherapy after the mastectomy. However, because you have a fairly advanced case, I'll want to begin within two weeks. Chemotherapy will run in two-week cycles lasting anywhere from three to six months. It all depends on how your body responds.

"I don't make promises lightly, Mrs. Mac— Aileen," she

corrected herself, "but if I say I'll do everything within my power to get you cancer free, I mean it. I believe in it."

"I trust you, Doctor," Aileen whispered, back to wringing Thomas' hand.

She was overwhelmed. *He* was overwhelmed, and nothing was happening to his body. For the hundredth time, he wished desperately for Coll's presence. Coll would be able to reassure his sister much better than the shitty job he was managing.

"I have a question, Dr. Delaloge," Mirren hesitantly lifted her right hand as if she were in primary school waiting for a teacher to call on her. "Is mom a candidate for reconstruction? I mean, can she get it at the same time as the mastectomy? Mom and I have been reading about that."

The doctor dipped her head in chagrin. "Oh, of course. I should have gone over that first thing. The answer is yes. I'll ask Dr. Leland to stop by to discuss your options; size, shape, and all of that. Your husband will probably want to be a part of that discussion." She smiled at Thomas.

Clearing his throat, he looked at Aileen. "I want Aileen to pick exactly the way she wants her... wants to look. She'll be beautiful to me no matter what." Aileen smiled at his words, not only because she knew neither of them would want Thomas anywhere near her breasts but also because she knew he meant what he'd said.

She would be beautiful to him no matter what.

"You'll need to fast after midnight. You'll be my first surgery tomorrow morning."

"Oh, so soon." Aileen spoke softly, dropping his hand to grab Mirren's.

"I'm afraid so. I don't want to take any chances of giving that cancer more time to spread. I should also note that my good friend, Mary O'Connor, the one who called me about you, requested I do everything in my power to save her daughter's friend. I would have anyway, but the sooner we get started, the sooner Mary will stop asking for updates." She chuckled.

That made Aileen laugh, releasing some tension, which was probably the doctor's intent.

"It sounds like Jo is a lot like her mom," Mirren said, elbowing her dad in the stomach with a laugh.

"Okay," the doctor said, grabbing her tablet as she stood. "I'll leave the information packet for you to review, and as I mentioned before, expect Dr. Leland for your breast augmentation consult within the hour. You'll stay here two to three days after surgery for recovery. Probably three since you'll be starting breast reconstruction and getting the expander implants placed to stretch your skin. Dr. Leland will be dealing with your breast reconstruction while I deal with killing the cancer. Then, I assume you'll be moving into the apartment Mary and her daughter found."

"What? I was going to look for a place today," Aileen said, clearly bewildered.

"Oh, well, I'll leave you now to figure things out. I believe Mary mentioned her daughter would be sending the information to one of you this morning," she said as she walked out of the room.

Between finding out about Aileen's cancer, her filing for divorce, flying to Paris... seeing Jo... he was in dire need of a shot or three of whisky.

Mirren stood as well, stretching her legs and swiping through her phone. "Here it is, Mom. Jo must have sent me an email after she saw us this morning."

"What does it say?" he asked.

Mirren smiled, grinning at her mother. *"I signed a short lease on a condo. It's only two blocks away, so on nice days, and depending on how your mom feels, you might be able to walk to the hospital once in a while. However, the building comes with a driving service—"*

Aileen gasped. "Really? A driving service. Christ, that woman. You two deserve each other, Tommy. Both as heavy-handed as they come."

Mirren ignored the interruption and continued, *"Tell your mom not to be dramatic about it. It's not just for her. There are three bedrooms. One for her, one for you, and one for me when I come visit. You two will want to go shopping in Paris, surely, and if your mom loses her hair, we'll need to visit that wig shop I told her about.*

*"I'm working in Rome for two to three months, so I'll be available to come a few times to see you guys, and I'm tired of sleeping in hotels. See? It's really for my benefit. Also, I don't believe you have any intention of returning to Scotland without your mother. You'll need the extra space the condo allows for studying."*

"What is she talking about, Mir? You most certainly are returning to school. My cancer is not going to make you miss cheerleading and dances and your friends."

"Your mom's right, lass," he said gently. "I'll be staying with Mom. You can stay for a bit, but that's it."

Mirren looked between her parents. "I will not leave. I refuse to leave you. What if something happened? Would you really want the guilt of me not being here with you? Do you really want Dad to hold your hair if you're sick?"

Aileen turned a frustrated glare at him and Mirren. "I never planned on you staying, Tommy. And before you try to mansplain the situation, I'm telling you, I need to do this without you. I love you, but our lives will be much different going forward."

"I'm not leaving."

Aileen threw her hands up in exasperation. "And you

wonder where she gets it," she sighed, shaking her head. "You can stay two weeks at what I'm quite sure is a ridiculously posh condo. Then you'll leave and take Mirren back to school."

"Dad can leave. I already let my cheerleading coach know that I needed to step down and to give my spot to Janet. She's been working hard and deserves it. I also sent a forged letter with your signature asking the school to set me up on their online program. I already received my work, and *you've* been inputting the parent part of logging my hours.

"Are you really going to out me with the school admins? They'll think you're a delinquent parent who's let her daughter run wild."

"You... you... you." Aileen turned to him for help. "Do something," she demanded.

Mirren wasn't the least bit remorseful. If anything, she looked smug with her arms crossed and casual lean. He was having a hard time not showing how proud he was of her subterfuge.

He knew Aileen wouldn't change her mind about him leaving in two weeks. She could be as stubborn as her brother when she chose to be. He also understood that she needed to have some power over something while she went through this nightmare.

Rubbing his hand over his face, he chose not to go with logic, trying love instead. "Aileen, listen to me. If Mirren were the one with cancer, would you leave her here alone to go back to work?"

Aileen's face went from pale to fire red. "What an idiotic question. I don't know what you're playing at, but you're being a complete prick."

"Jesus, Dad. Work on your delivery." Mirren walked over to her mom and placed her hands on her shoulders. "Mom. What Captain Opposite of Obvious meant was that you would never leave me when I needed you, so you can't expect me to leave you.

"We're done discussing this. As soon as Dr. Leland comes and we get your new boobs squared away, how about Dad and I take you to a fancy, early last dinner before surgery. Then, we can swing by the condo and check it out. We can have our new driver bring us back here." She laughed as her mother hugged her tight.

"You're a pain in the ass. You know that, right?"

"If showing my parents how killer my special op skills are... then guilty." She fluffed her hair and smirked. "Plus, I know you'll need my help keeping Uncle Coll off our doorstep. We only need one grumpy, old man breathing down our necks. No offense, Dad," she quipped.

"If you expect me to say none taken, think again," he grumbled back.

"Speaking of Dad and pains in the ass, you never finished Jo's email."

"Oh yeah." Mirren pulled the message back up. *"Listen, Mirren. I hate that I may have caused you or your mom any discomfort over my affair with your father. Regardless of your age and understanding of your parent's situation, it still couldn't have been fun meeting the woman your dad didn't ever plan on you... meeting. Awkward.* 😬

*"Remember, your mom is brave (the b!t@h called me at three in the morning). She'll beat cancer and have a new set of tits to show for the effort.*

*Hug your mom for me every day until I see you both again.*

*My love, Jo."*

Damn that woman, Thomas thought. Jo had sent Mir that email before they'd seen each other, but fucking hell, it killed him that she'd believed, or might still believe, that he'd never wanted her to meet his daughter. How had he been so blind? Mirren and Jo were everything. Everything.

Mirren was grinning like the Cheshire Cat. His daughter probably loved Jo's potty mouth and cheek. Aileen was dabbing her eyes. His family loved Jo after hours of knowing her. He understood completely.

From the moment that mouthy, intelligent, gorgeous, long-legged blonde slid into the back seat of his SUV, he'd been under her thrall. He'd not originally been assigned as her guard. He owned the damn company and hadn't personally taken security detail in years, preferring to do his work behind a computer, destroying his targets financially, but the moment he'd seen her... the combination of cheeky comments and flashing gray eyes had not been something he'd been willing to give up.

He still wouldn't give her up.

He had to win her back.

Jo would trust him again.

Thomas had always known there was something in Jo's past that had caused her skittishness. She hadn't been dating someone when they'd met. She didn't talk or text men. He knew because he'd looked through her phone more than once. She worked and then worked some more.

It wasn't that she was cold, she was warm to her family and close friends. She had fierce loyalty. When she befriended someone, it was for life. She was real, and yet there was a part of her that always seemed to be waiting for the other shoe to drop. A black cloud hovering over her joy only a moment from enveloping her smile.

She had trusted him. Truly and without reservation. He had seen it. Felt it. Until he'd crushed it.

He may have retired from the military, but he would always be a Royal Marine. He would create a plan, execute the plan, and win her back. He would slay every demon or dragon haunting her until shadows could no longer live in her bright light.

The first step in Operation O'Connor: Don't let her forget who she belonged to.

He would text or call her every day. She would try to put distance between them again. That wasn't going to happen. If he couldn't have her physical presence, he would at least have her words— her voice could sooth or inflame. He wanted all of it.

Aileen and Mirren needed him now, but as the day wore on, he was seeing more clearly that his little, tiny baby girl wasn't so tiny anymore, and his soon-to-be ex-wife was creating a life where his presence wasn't required or needed.

"Aileen. Text Jo, please. Tell her I said my number better be unblocked today."


LATER THAT NIGHT, Thomas was lying in bed at the condo Jo had leased. Mirren said he could use Jo's room when she wasn't here. Nice of her to dictate the terms of his stay.

Dinner had been one of the nicest the three of them had shared in... months, years? They'd been more honest with each other than they ever had been. He and Aileen were truly comfortable in the roles they played in each other's lives for the first time since they were kids.

When people are willing to admit that they wouldn't change a single thing about the past, their true north will sort of right itself.

Mirren stayed with her mom at the hospital. She said it was so she would have someone there to keep her from getting nervous about surgery. He and Aileen knew it was Mirren that needed reassurance.

He'd just gotten off the phone with Coll. Aileen wouldn't

be happy, but her brother would be there tomorrow. She'd downplayed her diagnosis to her brother, as he knew she would, but Thomas filled him in. Coll might be in hiding, nursing his own wounds, but he would never put himself before his sister.

Thomas told him that Mirren had researched her birth father, Charles Morrow, and that he was considering making contact. He'd contemplated waiting to see what Aileen wanted to do, if anything, but wasn't sure that was the right course. It was clear from what little of the conversation he'd overheard that she was still in love with the man.

Surely, it was better to find out if he held similar feelings. He didn't want her to get hurt. Again.

Coll's instant response was to let the bastard rot in ignorance, understandable since the man had impregnated his little sister, but when Thomas pushed, he said he'd do his own deep dive into the man's situation. Thomas agreed to wait.

Still palming his phone, he flipped it over and over in agitation. His other arm was braced between his head and the headboard. He knew exactly why his phone had yet to leave his grasp, but knowing what he wanted to do with it and whether it was an intelligent idea were two different things.

He wanted to call Jo. It was ten. She would definitely be up. Had she unblocked him?

"Fuck it," he said out loud. His heart started beating its way out of his chest when he pressed her contact. One ring. Two. Three. Four. Christ. Five—

"Hello."

She probably heard his sigh of relief. "Jo." He heard movement on her end. Shifting at her desk? Her bed?

"Thomas."

She wasn't giving anything away, and he was shit at verbalizing. "Are you staying with your parents?"

"I am. They rented a flat in the Piazza Navona neighborhood. It's lovely."

Thomas was sweating. This wasn't how he wanted the conversation to go. "When do you meet your clients?"

"Lunch tomorrow. We'll tour the building. It's a gorgeous four-story in the Campo de' Fiori district. A five-minute walk from our flat."

"That's convenient."

"It is. I spoke to Aileen and Mirren. Surgery in the morning, huh?"

"Yes." Shit. Shit. Shit. It was like he couldn't think of anything to say. He spent hours talking to Jo in his head. They talked about everything then. Effortlessly. They laughed and flirted.

Real-life discourse had become an over-reduced sauce of tepid and stale. His dick had been buried deep in her body mere hours ago. She'd been moaning his name over and over as she'd orgasmed. And now?

"She'll be in the hospital for three days."

"She told me."

*Jesus, kill me now.* "Thank you for the condo. Please let me pay you back."

"No."

Painful. "I appreciate everything you've done for Aileen and Mirren."

"Of course. They're your family."

"You're my family."

"You're married."

Thomas banged his head against the headboard. How could he fix this? Could he? "I'm getting a divorce, Jo. Please." Silence. Nothing but exhalations. *Please, Jo.*

"You aren't divorced yet. This morning... damn it, Thomas. I felt guilty once you left. I understand your situation is unique.

I listened to Aileen's story. You might not wear a wedding ring, but you have a family. A family you hid from me. Maybe you'll get a divorce. Maybe you won't."

"I am," he swore.

"I have the facts. Your wife gave them to me. You didn't trust me with your truth. I'm not sure I can trust you with mine. Goodbye, Thomas."

She ended the call.

## 10

Jo slid down the mound of pillows at her back. Tears of frustration dampened her eyes. She groaned at how out of step she'd felt since her breakup with Thomas. This melancholy wasn't her. She didn't allow her boyfriends to influence her emotions. Now friends, she wholeheartedly accepted her feelings for them.

Thomas had been the first man she'd let her guard down with since... eight years ago. Percy Donovan, damn him, broke something in her that night. She'd been walking around, not broken, but incomplete, always feeling that missing... thing.

She didn't like remembering. She tried never to recall the morning she'd woken feeling broken and abused. She'd been high on life and the hubris of a young woman feeling childhood restraints released for the first time.

And how did she handle her first dip into adulthood? Getting so drunk, she'd allowed a man she'd just met to use her body and take her virginity.

The worst— she'd consented to having something that should have been private videoed. All these years later, that thought alone took away her breath in anxiety.

There was one other thing that was worse than that. She remembered nothing. Her mind was a void from ordering that last drink with Percy until she woke up. She'd wondered if he was as drunk as her. He hadn't seemed drunk at all, but then, she'd thought she was no more than buzzed.

He had to have been drunk to have left that disturbing note. The words 'internet famous' still made her throat close in panic.

She had saved the note, hated herself for keeping the sick keepsake, but unwilling to let herself forget what could happen if she let her guard down.

She'd lived in fear of running into Percy again. She'd followed his career over the years with a single-minded determination. The sole purpose was to know where he lived, who he socialized with, where vacationed and where he worked so that she could make sure to never cross his path again.

He was a well-known attorney, working at first one prestigious firm and then another. No wife or children. Three years ago, he switched career gears. He became a corporate attorney for his father's publicist company, Donovan Public Relations, situated in New York City. It had probably been the senior Donovan's plan all along to use Percy's law expertise to help in the family business.

She'd managed to go eight years with no contact, praying daily that he'd destroyed the video. Jo lost touch with Ivy on purpose, unwilling to chance running into Percy because of his friendship with Ivy's husband, Hunter. If only she'd listened to her childhood friend that night... *Percy can sometimes make me feel... uncomfortable.*

That long ago morning, she'd had to shut off the part of her that wanted to break down, just break and break until nothing was left but bloody pieces.

Breaking would mean admitting to what had happened. To what she'd done. To Ivy. To her parents. So, she showered, packed, and left the hotel before anyone from the wedding party could see her walk of shame.

She texted Ivy and profusely apologized, saying she'd caught a bug or something and was sick with a fever and didn't want to chance getting her sick and ruin the rest of the weekend.

She drove straight to a pharmacy for a morning after pill and then made an appointment with the weekend clinic at Cornell's campus clinic. She didn't know if Percy had used a condom and needed to be screened for STDs.

She made it through that day and the next and the next. She gave herself tasks and goals, placing high expectations on herself. The grind her life helped create a barrier between that morning and the rest of her life— like a frosted window. Some days, she could kind of see through it, but mostly, it remained opaque.

She'd had a few boyfriends over the years. Nothing too serious. There was one boyfriend four years ago that she'd felt a connection with, enough so to try having sex again. It hadn't gone well. A feeling of claustrophobia would crush her until she was forced to close her eyes and endure until the end.

She wasn't a quitter, and Ben had been a really sweet guy. She'd tried different positions, locations, times of day... nothing changed. She became a good actress so he wouldn't think the problem lay with him, but after only a few months, she called it quits, and they went their separate ways.

She threw herself even more into work and put her hopes for more aside.

Until Thomas MacGregor. He changed everything. She had pined for him like a lovesick teenager for months and enjoyed giving him a hard time, teasing him mercilessly. He took everything she threw his way with grim-faced determination.

She had thought for the longest time that Thomas considered her only a job. The day he'd disabused her of that notion was the best day of her life, and when they'd had sex that first time, her mind had been blown.

She remembered thinking, *this is what it's supposed to feel like*. There had been no anxiety, no mental reminders to unclench her jaw, no praying for the end to come quickly or self-recrimination. Instead, she had been as voracious for Thomas' hands on her body as he had been to touch hers.

It had been a desperate coming together. She could still feel the glide of his skin against her own. When his giant body had covered her own, there had been nothing but fierce want and need.

She'd felt wonder at their joining for days. She'd begged for his touch. Craved his weight atop her own. There had been no dark thoughts— nothing but unfaked orgasms, moans, and groans.

Why had her mind and body finally righted itself? Trust. She hadn't trusted herself to make good decisions for eight years. She'd trusted herself with Thomas, trusted he wouldn't let her screw up. He was it for her— or he had been.

That was exactly why his deceit had hurt her so badly and kept hurting her. She'd finally trusted herself. When she'd left him that night at The Fitzwilliam, she was too furious to realize how easily she'd taken Thomas at face value. All that time together, and she hadn't asked him any of the tough questions. Childhood, family, school, work. *Are you married? Do you have children?*

Sighing for the hundredth time at her shitshow of a personal life, she threw some of her pillows from the bed to lay flatter and turned off her table lamp, hoping sleep would claim her sooner than later. She would get back to doing what she did best. Work.

She'd be flying to Paris to see Aileen in a month, give or

take, for a short weekend. Thomas was leaving Aileen and Mirren two weeks before that. Another sigh... she hated how their conversation ended.

Her phone dinged thirty seconds after placing it on the charging dock. She glanced to the right at her nightstand and made out the text notification. It was from Thomas.

Her conviction to shut down their communication evaporated as she grabbed up the phone so fast the docking station crashed to the floor. "Jesus, Jo. Get a grip," she chided herself.

I'm not giving you up.

Her heart thudded with need but also fear.

You aren't what I need right now.

The fuck I'm not.

Thomas.

Josephine.

You made me feel... like I'm less. I deserve more.

You do.

She didn't respond. This conversation was as pointless as the verbal one. Bubbles waved and waved and were still waving five minutes later.

Until...

Please let me prove myself.

Her thumb lightly swiped over the text. She might be able to forgive him eventually, but would she ever experience the level of trust she'd had before? Could she ever trust her own judgment on the matter?

She kept reading the first text. *I'm not giving you up.* Should she at least trust in that?

Would a small bit of grace and hope be so bad? Aileen had asked it of her.

> Eventually. Maybe.

Christ, I can't breathe without you.

I see your family in a month. I won't live in the same space with them as your mistress— and I won't have you rush a divorce while Aileen has many more important things to think about besides my feelings.

She is committed to her treatments and to divorcing me. She paid extra for an uncontested, expedited divorce.

Jo pulled the pillow from behind her head to cover her face, groaning at being trapped in purgatory.

Promise you'll wait for me. I don't have the right to ask, but I am. Wait for me, damn it!

Her chest ached as she read. There was no choice, really. She'd known from the outset that, despite the egregiously poor choices of her past and Thomas' secrets, she was powerless to deny him.

> I'll wait.

## 11

Her parents were taking a much-needed day off. Her mom booked a day of pampering at a luxury Roman bathhouse. Jo didn't mind them taking some time for themselves. The last couple of years, her folks had been sharing more and more responsibility with her and her brother.

She also had plenty of help on this job. Her two assistants were with her. Caren and Carla were twin sisters adopted by an Oklahoma couple from Russia almost sixty years ago. The women never married or had children. They were too invested in CC Sourcing. CCS was a genius little business the ladies had created that Jo had run across almost five years ago. Caren and Carla were experts at sourcing anything. *Anything.*

They excelled at locating service providers wherever Jo happened to be working. Plumbers, electricians, kitchen equipment suppliers, painters, chefs, or masseuses— the more difficult the ask, the happier they were. CCS was a hospitality manager's dream come true.

The best part was that they hated marketing, which was how one would normally find clients, and they loved to travel. That combination meant they worked almost solely for her and her brother. Her brother, James, and his wife, Jane, were about to begin working on a high-end retirement village golf course restaurant/bar in Oklahoma City. Caren and Carla were slated to help him until Jo flashed Rome in front of their faces— they were all hers after that.

The bonus was bagging CCS. The bigger bonus was sticking it to her big brother.

While the women continued their guru sourcing from the comfort of their hotel, Jo met with Aldo Russo, the owner of the new club the O'Connors were hired to launch, Veleno. Venom in English. She knew that each floor would have its own name. Veleno was the name of the building and would have a large, illuminated pylon on the rooftop.

Mr. Russo had pretty much given them carte blanche monetarily and artistically. It was one of the first jobs she had worked where the possibilities were limitless. The bar. The dance floor. The menu. Everything was trusted to O'Connor Hospitality.

It was just a shame that Aldo gave Jo low-key creep vibes. It was unfortunate, but Mom and Dad didn't seem to mind him, so she stayed focused on the tasks, not the man.

Today, Aldo was meeting her onsite to go over progress and timelines and to meet his PR people. Supposedly, he'd hired a company from the States. Jo would be responsible for feeding them enticing photos and teasers to put out on social media sites and entertainment magazines. This club promised to be the next on-trend phenomenon.

Veleno would draw all types— dance crazy clubbers, Zen cigar loungers, old-world polished bar goers that appreciated the classics, and fine diners— pub grub on one floor and white-glove service on another.

She walked up to the street-level entrance. Veleno's glass front was chic and modern, but somehow, the dark charcoal metal and full glass sliding doors matched seamlessly with the old brick of the building. On nice evenings, the lower-level, classic-style bar and eatery could open its doors to patrons, allowing men and women the choice to enjoy outdoor seating while listening to live music.

A huge glass elevator was built into the façade of the building and to the right of the bar's grand front. Floors three and four were membership only. Keycards were the only way to use the elevator and access the top floors. Cigar lounge on the third and a Michelin Star chef restaurant on the top. The spectacular views of the city while dining would be worth the exorbitant membership fee.

A deep staircase was situated around the side of the building to accommodate the dance club entrance. Queued lines of those wanting to party on the second floor wouldn't bother the flow of the front entrance.

Russo had thought of everything. Licensing had to have been a bitch for this monster of a project. Staffing this place and hiring general managers for each floor was going to be a huge task, but she was excited about the challenge.

Carla and Caren were setting up nonstop interviews. General managers had to be found first to help vet the staff they'd be working with. This behemoth would require hundreds of employees for the four floors' varying shifts, and they would all need training. Working with the interior design team was a separate level of intensity.

More than once, she had to tamp down her irritation that Aldo Russo had insisted on using a firm he'd previously done business with. They were good, to be sure, but they weren't Triskelion Territory Designs. Raven, River, and Rowan were exceptional designers. They had the benefit of being her besties and were a hell of a lot of fun to work with.

Russo might have given O'Connor Hospitality the American Express Centurion card treatment, but he was not budging on the tight deadline— which was why her parents already needed a spa day. Well, her mother, really. Her dad was just a supporting character in her mother's hospitality play. He spent his days agreeing to whatever his wife said and checking the stock market, where he'd made his original fortune.

She went with business attire today. Her normal yoga pants, sweaters, and tennis shoes wouldn't cut it. Mr. Russo seemed to be a stickler about maintaining a certain level of professionalism. She chose a sheer creamy-white button-up with a black camisole, black stretchy skinny jeans with her favorite black Louis Vuitton high boots, and finished with a black blazer and ankle-length, off-white wool coat. Her hair was in a soft, low bun with a few tendrils that had escaped during her brisk walk over.

She spied Aldo through one of the shiny glass doors, his austere face in profile, reading a newspaper and sipping what was most likely an espresso. He was just under six feet if she had to guess, slim, suited, in his mid-forties, and with the beginnings of salt in his dark hair. Nothing on the man was ever out of place.

He was never anything but courteous and professional. He was also... cold. His eyes, more brown than hazel, were lifeless. A shiver ran up her spine as she reached for the door's handle. Dreading the next hour or more. It was unfounded, but there were times... times when he seemed to look at her... It was silly. He didn't look at her in a sexual way. It was more... calculating. Strange.

*Suck it up, Jo. He's a client like any other. You are a professional.* As pep talks went, it wasn't bad. *Deep breath.*

"Good morning, Mr. Russo," she greeted her client cheerfully while pulling out the chair facing him to sit.

"Ms. O'Connor. *Buongiorno,*" he said as he stood to shake her hand.

Thank God, no cheek kisses today. She pulled her tablet out along with print versions. He tended to like bouncing between digital and print of the same documents— knowing this, she covered her bases.

Pulling up her spreadsheets while handing Aldo his packet, she explained, "I know you're a busy man, Mr. Russo, so I've tried to give you a fairly detailed look at what's been done so far and a timeline highlighting the next several weeks. Subject to change, of course." She smiled, though she was sure it didn't touch her eyes— as fake as his genial expression.

"Now that we've found the chef for the fourth floor, menu, staffing, and décor will move along quickly. We believe that the third-floor lounge and fourth-floor dining would benefit from a single general manager Most of your clientele that pay dues will want access to both of those levels. However, if you think a manager per floor is necessary, my team will absolutely do that."

"No, no, no. I like this plan. Very good. I see the benefit of one manager for the top floors. I am bringing on a senior manager of the entire building. A business associate of mine. They will need to meet all the managers once they're hired and trained. I want someone who I can speak with who knows all the floors activities."

"I understand. Once the GMs are brought in, I will get the information to you to pass on to your person. No problem. Have you named the floors yet? It will make a huge impact in design as well as PR."

"I have. The enterprise as a whole will be Veleno, as you know. I went over the final polling consensuses for the floors. The ground level bar will be called Adder, the second-floor dance club is Garden of G&E, we hope people will eventually reduce its name to G&E, which should do well with branding, the smoking lounge is Serpent, and the fourth-floor restaurant will be called Medusa."

*Shocker, a snake theme.* "The polls have spoken. I love it, and so will Rome," she schmoozed. "Now that names are locked down, PR can really start dropping some hints about what Veleno is all about."

"It is my hope."

She forced herself not to check the time, sure that less than five minutes had passed. The military should torture terrorists by putting Aldo Russo in a room with them.

"Will design be meeting us this morning with PR? I brought tentative menus for, uhm," trying to remember the slithery names, "Adder and Medusa."

"Yes, in fact, Angelica should be joining us. Oh, here she is," Aldo announced as he stood to greet a woman about Jo's age walking through the door.

Angelica had soft brunette curls that skimmed the shoulders of her navy wool coat. After the requisite air kisses, the woman removed her outer coat revealing a sharp suit. Jo stood to shake the newcomer's hand, barely repressing a frown. She could tell this woman was not going to be a pleasure to work with at first glance.

Angelica was perfectly put together, pristine and cold. Thankfully, the woman didn't try to smile. That would have been eerie on her otherwise expressionless countenance.

"Josephine O'Connor. Hospitality," she introduced herself, attempting to shake off the feeling of wrongness Aldo and Angelica exuded.

"Angelica Bluche. Bluche Design. Aldo tells me you've found Medusa's head chef. I would like to meet with you both as soon as possible. The menu will drive the design," she explained as they all took their seats.

"Of course. Adder's chef has also been hired. If you're available, they might be able to meet us when we're done here. I will message both chefs now."

"That suits." She slipped her tablet back into its sleeve before saying, "O'Connor Hospitality has made quite a name for itself in many countries."

Compliment? Question? It was very hard to tell with this woman. She settled on, "We have."

Aldo decided to add his voice to the stilted conversation. "Ms. O'Connor's father was already an extremely wealthy man before her mother started the hospitality business, Angelica. Mr. O'Connor was a well-known name on Wallstreet."

Jo was taken aback by Aldo's knowledge of the founding of her family's business. Before she could wonder further how he even knew or cared to know about her family, he continued his ill-mannered history lesson.

"My good friend was familiar with the family, and that's why I hired the O'Connors for this job. He assured me their reputation for excellence was well deserved. His family is the one doing the PR for Veleno."

Though this entire conversation about wealth was gauche, the cold sweat trickling between her shoulder blades had nothing to do with that. Aldo was looking at her with some sort of... she wasn't sure... a knowing smirk?

"Ah, speaking of the devil, here he is now. He's quite an admirer of yours, Ms. O'Connor."

She felt a cool breeze touch her hair as the door to Adder opened. *Oh my God, no.* Flight or fight? Prey or predator?

Flight if there was anywhere to run and most definitely prey.

"Hello, Josie. It's been years."

Four hours later, Jo felt the click of the apartment door close behind her like a gunshot. Percy fucking Donovan. He was the PR. He was the friend from the States. He was the one who had recommended her family for the job.

Why? Why? "Why?" she moaned to the empty kitchen as she kicked her boots off and made for the fridge. Her legs barely held during the short walk from Veleno to her family's apartment. Thank God her parents were still enjoying their day off, and the place was empty.

She wanted alcohol but grabbed a bottle of water instead.

Clear head. Clear mind. She certainly didn't need a mixed drink to open paths to things better left buried.

Next, she grabbed a notepad and pen, as well as her phone and tablet. Multiple devices to make lists.

This was happening. Percy was here. In Rome. She could get through this. She *would* get through this. One to-do list at a time.

Check. Check. Check.

By March or April at the latest, she'd walk away from this project and wash her hands of Percy Donovan. He never alluded to their night together. She was thankful and disappointed all at once. Thankful because she would have died of embarrassment all over again. Disappointed because she would have liked even the slightest glimpse into what they'd done.

During the tour of the floors, she'd caught Percy staring at her more than once. She avoided direct eye contact and did her best to remain friendly but focused on business.

Aldo had given her an all-floor passkey so she would no longer have to meet him each time she needed access. Small mercies.

Finally, Aldo and Percy left to meet friends for lunch so she and Angelica could meet with the chefs and senior manager. It was productive but Jo was so mentally tapped that in the last hour a horrific headache had been building behind her eyes and temples.

Sitting in the apartment's kitchen now, endeavoring to calm her mind so that she could make her lists and not fall completely apart, felt impossible.

She wanted Thomas' arms wrapped around her. She needed them. He was stalwart and fierce in her defense. She wanted to call him or text, but she couldn't take the chance of him figuring out something was wrong. She never wanted him to know about that night, Percy, or the sex video.

Lists would get her through. One task at a time until there was no room left for dwelling on things she couldn't change.

# 12

"I'm telling you, Dad, she's different. Something is wrong with Jo!" Mirren insisted over the phone.

Thomas wasn't going to jump to any conclusions based solely on Mirren's concerns, but he'd also felt Jo had been off for the past few weeks.

They rarely spoke, and by spoke, he meant text, and when they did, she seemed distracted. He assumed it to do with their rocky relationship and had written it off as skittishness, but if she acted strangely when she'd visited Aileen and Mirren, there might be something else going on.

"What does your mom think?" Aileen had started her treatments, and the nausea had been kicking her ass. He was relieved she had their daughter to look after her. Aileen needed someone with whom she was comfortable during such a difficult time.

She'd kicked both him and her brother out early, claiming she didn't need the two of them helicoptering. Coll had been quiet, but he'd held his sister tight when they'd reunited. They'd both needed to remember their bond.

Mirren answered his question. "She didn't think so at first, but the longer Jo was here, Mom had to admit she was different.

She looked close to tears a few times when she was reading something on her phone. When Mom asked her, she'd say it was nothing, that her current job was a difficult one."

"You didn't believe her?"

"No way. Neither of us. She barely ate during the three days she was here. Hang on, Mom's talking. Oh yeah, right," she agreed. "Mom reminded me that Jo's lost a lot of weight and looked pale. So?" she demanded.

He was getting alarmed. *Damn it!* He shouldn't have assumed it had to do with the two of them. Jo's life didn't revolve around him.

"I trust what you and Mom saw. I promise to look into it."

"How?"

"How what?"

"Dad..."

She sounded just like her mom when she took that exasperated tone with him. "I'd planned on surprising her in Rome in a couple of weeks." Since Aileen had filed for an expedited divorce and there had been nothing to divide up or contest, it should be finalized in the next two to three weeks.

"Good. You wouldn't want to go to Jo when you're still a married man," Mirren teased. Obviously, she was aware of the divorce timetable.

Thomas rubbed his eyes at Mirren's sass. "Correct," he gritted.

"I suggest putting a ring on it ASAP."

"Noted, Mirren."

"Mom said to let us know the moment you figure out what's going on."

"As if you'd leave me alone if I didn't."

"Correct," she mimicked.

LATER THAT NIGHT, Thomas was leaning against his kitchen counter, moodily staring at his phone. Since when had he become an indecisive prick? Christ, his sister had even yelled at him earlier to get the hell out of her greenhouse after he'd knocked over a second clay pot, making a mess and forcing her to replant.

He'd already checked in with all of his security teams, whether they were in the field or working from home. Helping Cat with the farm chores seemed like a good way to take his mind off Jo, but here he was, chastened like a child and sent home.

Catriona had been devastated to find out about Aileen and her patience had been thinner of late. He understood Aileen had been like a big sister to Cat. At almost twenty-two, she looked like a small child and had the temper and sharp tongue of an octogenarian.

Not even thoughts of his little firecracker of a sister could distract him from Jo. God, how he wished the divorce was final. He would call and put pressure on the damn solicitor tomorrow. Again.

He wanted to fly to Rome now, but he refused to disrespect Jo ever again. He would not stand in front of her as anything other than a man free to pursue her.

Picking his phone up, he texted.

What are you doing?

Three minutes later.

Working. Preparing for tomorrow.

Mirren called and said you'd left for Rome this afternoon.

It was good to see them. Aileen is being brave,
but she's really not feeling great.

I know. I'm glad you went to see her.

And then, because he couldn't help himself.

I dream of you every night.

Thomas.

Do you think of the plane?

He knew he was pushing it.

Stop.

Tell me. Do you think of it?

Finally.

Yes.

Last night, I dreamed you were riding me just
like you did on the plane. I woke with your
taste in my mouth and painfully hard.

Bubbles appeared. Disappeared. Appeared. Sweat broke
out on his brow. He had to adjust himself. Not exactly where he
planned on taking this conversation.

Did you do anything about it?

Oh. My. God. Why did she just text Thomas that? But in her defense— what in the hell was he thinking texting her suggestive... stuff?

Jo had been hunched over the desk for hours in her bedroom, knowing she needed to go to bed but not willing to chance letting her guard down unless she was tired enough to fall right into sleep. An active mind at night opened her mental pathways to the past.

Percy Donovan used to only take up memory space for one bad decision. Now that she'd been forced to work with the arrogant asshole for the past few weeks, she had to endure several new additions to her memory.

Recently, he'd made some suggestive remarks. Not overt enough to put her on high alert, but given their past, she would have preferred he just brought up the elephant in the room, so to speak, and then never talk about it again.

During a lunch the day before she'd flown to Paris, Percy asked Aldo if he'd seen the leaked sex tape of some famous Italian actress. Percy had glanced her way with a sly look on his face. She'd barely had time to excuse herself to the restroom to vomit. She rinsed her mouth, tidied her hair, and forced a smile on her face before rejoining the table.

God, she hated the smug bastard. Thankfully, her mom and dad were seated at the table. Mom was going over the cigar lounge seating configurations. She'd taken over the Serpent lounge, and the Senior Manager had been quite helpful with the restaurant, Medusa, leaving Jo more time to focus on the dance club and the street bar.

When her mother created O'Connor Hospitality, her father jumped into the contractual part of the company. He was the one that drew up the contracts for the clients. The only reason he traveled with Mom when she had a job was so that they could be close. She adored that her parents had such a loving relationship.

The meeting had ended well. Hiring and training wait staff was in full swing and took up hours each day, thank God, as it mostly kept her away from Percy. He'd texted her a few times while she'd been visiting Aileen and Mirren, work related— mostly— but he had a slimy way of adding an odd, unprofessional comment each time.

For example, *I hope you aren't already undressed and in bed,* or *I loved that silky brown dress you wore.*

She'd only worn a dress that fit that description once. Eight years ago.

Her phone dinged with a notification, thankfully pulling her out of her dark thoughts and back into her sexy text faux pas to Thomas.

**Yes.**

*Oh God. Don't do it, Jo. Nothing good will come of it except sexual frustration.*

**Tell me.**

**I'd rather show you. Turn your video on.**

Her thighs clenched at the thought. Sirens and danger warnings were clanging in her head, but in reality, she rationalized Thomas *would* be divorced soon, and the moment he was a free man, they'd be together. Probably. Maybe. Definitely.

Percy coming into her life again had confirmed a suspicion she'd long held— her past decision was still altering her present.

There was a possibility that not allowing Thomas to explain himself the day she'd left him had just been an excuse. She might never be able to give him what he wanted. If she couldn't trust herself, she couldn't trust him.

Those were worries for another day. Right now, Thomas had her body's full attention. Standing, she locked her door before slipping her shoes off. Grabbing her laptop off the desk, she tossed it on the bed and plumped several pillows that lined the headboard.

She was wearing a green silk blouse with tiny pearl buttons. She decided to leave that on but shucked her green, wool slacks. She settled on the bed and used a decorative pillow to prop her laptop, turning it on Messenger video and making sure the angle was on her face, no lower than her clad chest.

After adjusting the pillows at her back again, she had run out of reasons not to call. She texted him to call her from his laptop. She hoped she didn't have to explain that the computer screen would give her a better view of his body. It had been months since she'd seen all his densely muscled flesh.

The plane had been fast and furious and clothed. If he was willing to give her a show, she wanted to see all those rippling muscles.

Her Messenger app started ringing with an incoming video call. "Oh, God. Oh, God," she repeated through a suddenly dry throat.

Quickly dimming the bedside lamp, she tapped to accept the call.

And there he was. The most ruggedly handsome man she'd ever known. From his honey-blonde hair cut close to his scalp on the sides with the longer top combed and gelled messily forward, to his intense, brooding, brown-eyed stare, chiseled jaw, and firm lips... he was a feast.

The golden expanse of his bare chest lightly covered in pale curls and thickly ridged abs were on display.

Right now, she wanted to forget about her past, her work,

and Percy Donovan. She wanted to look at Thomas and pretend the giant Scotsman currently on her computer screen was in her bed, straddling her hips.

"Hey," she spoke evenly, trying to cover the slight wobble in her voice.

"You look beautiful, Josephine."

She felt the pulse in her throat flutter. The pulse between her thighs wasn't far behind. The deep timber of his thick Scottish accent had always made her feel... Christ, everything. "You look... naked." *Smooth.* One corner of his mouth barely lifted. A look of amusement on Thomas, a face tic for most others.

"How else would I be able to show you what the thought of you riding me does?"

She bit back a moan. He wasn't playing fair. He bent toward his computer, adjusting the angle lower. When he leaned back again, more of his body was exposed. The white sheet covering his stomach down did nothing to disguise the impressive erection lying thick and long against his lower body.

He seemed to be waiting for something. Approval? Directions? Reciprocation? He wouldn't get the last, but the first two were definitely doable.

"I wish I could touch you," she admitted. "Why don't you do it for me," she suggested, pleased when she saw his fists clench at his side.

One of her best friends, River Byrne, told her she ought to try video sex. She scoffed at the suggestion. She wasn't scoffing anymore. Thomas' cheeks pinkened, but otherwise, he didn't make a move to touch himself.

He cleared his throat, his face turning even rosier. "I've never done this. I... I... Damn it," he stopped, taking a deep breath. "I've done this to myself, of course, just not while someone watched me. On their computer," he finished through gritted teeth.

His honesty and nervousness made her love him even more. So, she took mercy. "I've never done anything like this either." *Only once when she was black-out drunk.* She would not let those thoughts intrude. That memory would not touch this moment.

"Get naked for me, baby, please. I want to see your little pink nipples begging me to suck them."

"No." She stiffened instantly and hated Thomas' resulting frown of confusion. To recover, she added, "I'm not comfortable being naked on camera. Not this time, at least," she amended.

"I understand, lass. You're beautiful with or without clothes."

She would give him something, though, and reached for the tiny pearl buttons of her blouse and began to flick a few open. His gaze was trained on every centimeter of skin revealed. Her top wasn't sensual by any stretch, but the way his eyes were glued to her chest, she felt as sensual as a burlesque performer holding her one-man audience captive.

Her blouse fell open, the wispy silk revealing the nude lacy camisole beneath. One deep breath and the silk would move enough to reveal her nipples pressing against the lace. Thomas was hypnotized, and probably unbeknownst to himself, his right hand had drifted over the swollen flesh between his legs.

"Let me see you, Honey," she said, using the old nickname for her former security guard. He was just as precious as the honey-colored bunny at the petting zoo when she was a child. She had wanted to take that bunny home with her. She definitely wanted to take this honey-colored god home too.

"I love when you call me that, baby." He hissed as his palm pressed tighter against his sex.

Jo used her fingernail to slowly slide a bit of green silk to the side to show him one lace-covered nipple.

"Christ," he growled.

Tonight was unexpected. If a woman could think negative thoughts while looking at this man, then they deserved their problems. "Move the sheet. Show me how you take care of yourself when I'm not with you."

Thomas' chest was pumping like a bellows. Without another word, he threw the sheet off, revealing his engorged sex that was leaking pre-cum all over his ribbed stomach. She would have swallowed her tongue if it hadn't been busy licking her lips.

"God, Thomas."

Still silent, his gaze unwavering from her own, he took himself in hand and squeezed himself firmly. A groan passed his lips in a pleasure-pain-filled gasp.

"Show me," she asked again.

He started out slow, never taking his eyes off her, using his own body's fluid to slick his skin. She was mesmerized as his pumping became faster and sweat began to bead his skin. The bunching and flexing of his muscles made her groan in frustration because she wasn't there to brush them with her fingertips.

Out of the camera's sight, her thighs were pressed tight together, and her shifting legs created just enough friction to leave her wanting. Probably because she knew her hand would be out of view, she boldly slid it down her stomach and ran her fingers over the dampened silk before sliding the material to the side.

The first slide of her fingers across her slit had her back bowing. Her eyes must have briefly closed because at Thomas' growled, "Fuck, baby, yes," they popped open. Thomas MacGregor looked like Celtic warrior— half-crazed and fierce. His strokes were frenzied, his hips jerking.

"Make yourself come. I want to see your face when you fall apart," he demanded.

She pushed two fingers deep, using her thumb to brush the

sensitive bundle of nerves. She kept her rhythm in time with his furious one. "I'm... close," she moaned.

"Keep your eyes on me. Come now," he barked the command.

He was propped against his headboard, similarly to hers, so as his body started to jerk and she saw jets of white hitting his stomach, her core practically exploded in clenching spasms.

She and Thomas were no strangers to each other's bodies, but what they'd just done had to be one of the most erotic.

"Jesus Christ," he muttered. "You are so damn sexy," he added while reaching for a t-shirt that sat next to him on the bed.

She pulled her fingers from her body, still feeling the occasional pulse in her core. Thomas was watching her closely as he wiped the cum off his stomach.

"Show me what fingers you used."

His request startled her. He was not normally this verbally... dirty. It was a total turn-on. She lifted the hand in question from the bed, holding her right hand like she was about to wave. She peeled back all but her middle and pointer fingers.

Thomas made an appreciative noise in his throat at her compliance. "If I was there, I'd lick your fingers clean."

"If you were here, you'd be licking your own fingers," she said, giving him a small smile.

He groaned, his flaccid sex filling again. It was fascinating to watch his body react to her. She frowned when he dropped his dirty shirt over his groin.

"I can barely work from thinking of all the things I want to do to you."

"What are the top three things you want to do to me?" she teasingly asked. Feeling lighter than she had in weeks.

"Top three things, hmm? Easy— driving first my fingers,

then my tongue, and then my cock in your wet heat, make you come with all three."

Her settling heartrate of a moment ago started to thump faster again at the mental picture his words conjured.

"Let me come to Rome."

She almost got whiplash from the sudden change of subject. There were two reasons why she didn't want Thomas to come to her. First, he was still married, though she could even see how silly that excuse was after what they'd just done. Second, Percy Donovan. There was no way in hell she wanted him anywhere near that slithering snake of a man.

Percy had become very unsubtle about his interest in her, or rather his interest in bringing up their past. She didn't want to take the chance of Thomas finding out about Percy— she would die a thousand deaths if he ever found out about how foolish she'd once been.

Of course, she couldn't give him any of those reasons.

She tried to hide her grimace before saying, "You're still married."

"I was married five minutes ago, and you still came while watching me do the same. We were intimate with one another even if it was by video," he countered.

"I know, damn it. I know," she pleaded, pulling her bare legs to her chest and resting her chin on her knees.

"Then why? I know I was wrong to keep Mirren and my situation from you. I deserved your anger, and I deserved you leaving me, but lass, you did agree that Aileen and I are in a very unique relationship."

"I know—"

"But do you?" Thomas interrupted. "Do you really? Aileen and I were sweethearts as teenagers. She and her brother are my best friends. They always have been. The two of us have never had sex. Hell, we've never even had our clothes off in front of each other except for when we were really young and swimming in one of the ponds on our property.

"I love you, Josephine O'Connor. It kills me that we're apart."

She deflated with every truth he gave her. She owed him her truth as well. At least some of it. "I love you, too, Thomas MacGregor, and you're right, we belong together. I know that too. I was hurt, devastated by your lies... but I *have* forgiven you. If you want to label us, then good. I'm yours, and you're mine."

His relief was obvious. "Thank fuck," he mumbled as he scrubbed his hands over his face before focusing on her again. "Then let me come to Rome. These past months have been hell. I need to hold you in my arms and know you're mine again."

*Damn it.* Deceit didn't come naturally to her, but she'd spent so many years hiding her mistake that she couldn't bring herself to speak about it. "It's a tough job. Now just isn't a good time. I'll come see you in a few weeks."

## 13

*It's a tough job.* Jo had never met a job that cowed her. Her strange behavior with Aileen and Mirren, coupled with not wanting him to come to Rome, had his gut cramping with alarm.

It couldn't be another man. She wasn't the type of woman to love a man and have another on the side. Plus, they'd just had sex— video sex but sex, nonetheless. She'd been alone and working when he called, not partaking of Rome's nightlife. Her parents probably had more of a social life than Jo did.

Something else was going on. Something or someone was bothering her. He could question her father, but Dean had an explosive protective streak where his daughter was concerned, which he appreciated. Jo wouldn't thank him for getting her father involved.

He could use the security software he still had loaded on her phone and laptop from when he was guarding her to find out if he could see anything, but again, Jo would take his head, and he refused to go that route without probable cause. If there was evidence that put her safety in jeopardy, his moral high ground could hang.

He decided to ask her a direct question and watch her reaction. "Tell me why you don't want me to come to Rome." And there it was... she flinched. "Jo?"

"Good grief. It's not that I don't want to see you. I'm swamped and won't be able to spend any time with you. Wait for me to get to a spot where my mom can take over for a few days, and I'll come see you."

One more try. "Even if I get to stand by you for one hour out of twenty-four, it would be worth it to me." If she denied him again, he would know...

"Give me one week," she tried to compromise. "One week, and I'll fly to Scotland. I promise."

As soon as he said goodbye to Jo and closed his laptop, he picked up his phone. Coll answered immediately. "I want to know everything about O'Connor Hospitality's job in Rome. Restaurant? Club? Spa? Who hired them and their history. Who else is on the job. Anything, Coll. Damn it, everything, I guess. Something's wrong with Jo, and she isn't talking."

"THE REPORT SHOULD BE LANDING in your inbox any second, but I can give you short of it," Coll told him the following morning.

"Give me the highlights, then."

"Aldo Russo is a playboy, or play-middle-aged-man, as he's pushing fifty, and the oldest son of Leondro Russo. Leondro's father, Elio, created the billion-dollar Russo clothing empire off the sweat of child laborers in Asia, most notably in Vietnam. They've been turned in for factory hazards in the past, including deaths of minors, but their money has managed to keep them out of trouble. A fine here and there.

"It's worth noting that I could find a lot of information on

Aldo's father and grandfather, but there is very little to be found on the man himself. Only what he pays social media marketers to share. It will take more time to dig deeper into his personal life.

"Aldo has spent millions renovating a four-story brick monstrosity in the heart of Rome's downtown social district. From what I could find, each floor is themed. He hired a long-time acquaintance for Interior Design, Angelica Bluche of Bluche Design. Wealthy Italian family— generational wealth. A few scandals in her twenties— sleeping with married politicians, sex tape scandal, that type of thing.

"Aldo hired an east coast PR firm, Donovan Public Relations, out of New York. The owner's son, Percy, a Yale law school graduate who, after working for other law firms a few years, took a senior position in the family business. He oversees the company's legal contracts and schmoozes their wealthy PR clients. Aldo and Percy have been photographed partying all over the world. A typical uber-wealthy dick club.

"Here's where it gets interesting. I put Aldo, Percy, Angelica, and Josephine's names in a search. Eight years ago, your Jo and Percy Donovan attended the same wedding— Montauk. There were hundreds of pictures to comb through. Josephine and Percy were in the wedding party. They definitely know each other.

"It was a full weekend party, boat races, the works, but Ms. O'Connor isn't in a single picture after the wedding day. I couldn't find any mention of her absence. She was eighteen at the time but enrolled as a junior at Cornell starting that fall. Overachiever.

"There is not one mention of her and Donovan again. If you want me to dive deeper, I will. It will take a lot to get into their private systems, but I can."

"I know you can. You're the best hacker the company has,

brother," Thomas praised his best friend. "Hold for now. I'm going to Rome to see things for myself. Something is off."

"Fine. How is my sister?"

"Ask her yourself," Thomas said before hanging up. He caught Coll's "Fuck y—" before the line went dead. He could be mad all he wanted. He would have to stop living a hermit's life if he wanted to be kept in the loop.

Thomas had to listen to his gut on this one, and something was telling him that Percy Donovan was at the heart of it.

He would do his own deep dive on Russo, Donovan, and Bluche. Then he was going to Rome.

Jo's body language had been all wrong when she'd been on screen. When he'd asked to visit, her eyes kept flicking to her right, avoiding eye contact. Even after she'd broken up with him and he saw her at the wedding and again at Aileen's hospital, she'd not acted like she had tonight. Whatever was causing her unease resided in Rome.

# 14

Jo was determined to work as many hours a day as needed to squeeze a long weekend in with Thomas. She'd promised him she would go to Scotland, and she would. Unsurprisingly, he'd gotten suspicious of her putting him off as his livelihood was dealing with exposing deception. She didn't want to make him worry, so she was working twelve-hour days to see him face to face and prove she was okay.

However, Thomas had to go back to Paris to be with Aileen because she had become so ill with the aggressive chemotherapy that she'd had to be checked back into the hospital to get her vomiting and dehydration under control. She was having a tough time of it. Mirren probably needed the support of her dad more than Aileen wanted Thomas standing over her. Regardless, Jo was sure that Aileen would appreciate the gesture as it was meant. One of Thomas' best traits was being solid in a crisis and a comfort in any storm.

Aileen wouldn't hear of Jo coming to the hospital. She believed she'd be out in no time and back to the condo. Jo wasn't as positive. The woman sounded terrible. She wanted Jo to wait until she felt better so they could go wig shopping. Her hair had begun to fall out.

Jo swallowed her tears, not wanting Aileen to hear. "I can't wait. Tell Mirren we'll look for some new shoes first. We don't want to go to some high-end wig shop if she's wearing those crusty turds with laces. They'll think we let a vagrant tag along," Jo joked, pleased when Aileen chuckled, and Mirren could be heard telling Jo to kiss her butt.

Regardless of the fact that her weekend with Thomas was out the window, she kept working long days, because eventually, she planned to see him or Aileen, and she really wanted to finish the job sooner rather than later. Espresso had become her breakfast, lunch, and dinner, and she didn't even like espresso. By six that morning, she was already on her computer, answering emails, scheduling, and reading reports from her mother, Caren, and Carla. She looked over the latest round of menus for the bar and grill, Adder, and the fine dining Medusa.

The smoking lounge needed less of her hospitality expertise. The senior and general managers and Angelica were handling that floor for the most part, but she would be checking each level as soon as she left the apartment.

She'd suggested to Aldo that the staff train on each floor. Even though the floors would be independent of one another, having employees that could seamlessly float when necessary, tended to minimize the imposition of servers calling in sick.

She stood up from her computer, stretched her lower back, and grabbed her phone, tossing it in her lightweight tote. She'd learned her lesson years ago about carrying a heavy bag around for hours. She had no desire to resemble Quasimodo by thirty.

Determined to head to Veleno early and get her work done before either Aldo or Percy showed their faces was priority number one. Percy had touched her on more than one occasion over the past couple of weeks, sending rivers of revulsion coursing through her every time.

A touch on her hand or his palm on her lower back. He even had the nerve to pick up a strand of her hair and place it behind her ear. He mentioned that her hair looked as lovely as it had when they'd met.

He was clearly toying with her. Yesterday, he'd told Angelica that he and I had a long history of firsts. He chuckled like he was discussing working on jobs together, though this was the one and only.

She had thought to ignore the innuendos, but he was making it harder and harder to turn the other cheek.

They'd had sex, not committed murder and covered it up. She was a grown woman now. He shouldn't have this much power over her emotions. There was just something about him... he was like a beautiful, shiny apple— full of rot.

She hated him and didn't fully understand why.

Men who thought too highly of themselves aside, it turned out to be a highly productive morning. The street-level pub's chef was a dream. Funny, sharp, and like most talented chefs, worked hundred-hour weeks. She had joined Angelica yesterday while she'd overseen the bar's dark Italian wood benches and barstools being installed. The counter and bar tops were coming today after lunch.

Caren and Carla had sourced the spirits and food vendors for the chefs and bar managers to meet and approve. The twins would be heading back to Oklahoma tomorrow. Their job in Rome was done. She would miss their quirky emails.

Mom and Dad told her last night that this would be Mom's final job. She was retiring. The business would officially become her and her brothers. She wasn't surprised, they'd been wanting to travel more. "Traveling without your mom working will be a nice change," Dean O'Connor had said as he'd reached for his wife's hand.

Jo was happy for them, of course she was, but there was a part of her that felt abandoned. Mom had finished what she needed to for Veleno, and she and Dad decided to fly home to Tulsa and take Caren and Carla with them.

"This apartment is paid through the end of the month. It doesn't look like you'll need more time than that." Jo must have let some of her feelings show— overwhelmed at being left and surrounded by people she didn't like or trust for starters. Because her mother leaned forward to pat Jo's knee. "The new POS system will take a few weeks to implement, and then you'll be free to come home," she added.

Jo wished doubly now that Thomas could come.

She wouldn't ask him to, even if she didn't have to worry about Percy. Aileen needed him, and Jo would continue to handle things in Rome.

"James has been acting cagey. So has Jane. I think she's pregnant!" Turning to her husband, Jo's mother gushed, "Oh, Dean, how wonderful would that be?"

Dad couldn't keep his grumpy face in light of his wife's excitement and simply said, "Very."

She managed not to tell her mother that James and Jane were probably acting weird because her brother could be an enormous ass. He'd most likely done something to piss his wife off and had nothing whatsoever to do with a positive pregnancy test.

Her parents had gone to bed early to pack and make arrangements with the pilot. She'd stayed sitting in the dark for another hour before brushing off the negative thoughts plaguing her and focusing on the day's remaining tasks.

The point-of-sale system for Veleno incorporated the latest in technology. She would be setting up several classes for the staff and management over the next couple of weeks to learn the program. It had the potential to make the wait staff's job more manageable. When an order was entered into the small handheld tablets, the employee's name, table, and customer order could be sent to any of the floor's bartenders or kitchen.

Though the initial cost had been high for this POS system, even Aldo could see the benefits, especially when she'd told him that the program kept track of all food and liquor consumed, creating lists that needed little tweaking for the managers when buying for their floor.

She finished her rounds, and the last of her morning meetings were with Medusa's GM. Jo decided she would find a lovely café to have a late lunch and finalize the training schedules. She would need to go over the list of employees and try to find a schedule that worked for most.

As she stepped into Medusa's elevator, she gave a sigh of relief that she'd managed to avoid Tweedle Dick and Tweedle Dickier. She was about to hold her pass key to the control panel and pick the bottom floor when her eyes caught on a fifth button. It was located near the bottom left of the panel. She would have sworn the button was a new addition.

There was no number, just an etched design, but the elevator was too dark to make it out properly. Digging her phone out from her tote, she pressed the flashlight and shone the beam directly on the mysterious button. Shocker, it was an etching of a Cobra.

Even mystery buttons were on theme. She hesitated for a moment until, finally, the pad of her finger pressed the serpent. What could she say? Curiosity hopefully wouldn't kill the cat.

The elevator began its descent. Not a secret sky lounge then. Basement storage? The space had never been discussed, and if it was only storage, why would it have a special elevator button. Clearly, the fact that she had an all-access pass key was the only reason she could reach it.

As the lift came to a soft halt, she had a sudden wave of foreboding. Curiosity might be a path best avoided. She'd just made up her mind to go back up to the ground floor when the doors opened.

Her pointer finger hovered again over the pad, but as her eyes glimpsed what stood beyond the gold metal doors, her hand fell back to her side. She took one step forward to stop the doors from closing, not ready to commit further. Her eyes scanned left and then right, trying to make sense of what she was seeing.

Every surface was done up in red and gold décor. Jo had seen the color combination create a stunning symphony in many a room. Here, it was overdone and tacky. There was no other way to describe the space beyond the doors but to call it a miniature Colosseum. Curved stadium seats surrounded a stage. She finally left the safety of the elevator to venture toward the raised platform. Sweat started to prickle her forehead as unease slithered through her abdomen. There were gold rings imbedded in the floor.

"What the ever-loving hell?" she whispered to herself. She continued to walk through the basement area, finding a beautiful, well-appointed bar and an alcove with drapes clearly meant for a small orchestra. There were dozens of seating areas with chairs, couches, chaise lounges, and beds on raised platforms.

It was shocking to realize she was standing in the middle of a sex club. She didn't know exactly what they should look like, except from movie and book descriptions, but this was ticking a lot of those boxes.

Moving through the enormous room, Jo made her way to one of the wide hallways that meandered through dozens of rooms. Some were private, and many had glass fronts. The ones with glass had outside seating to comfortably view... whatever was going on inside.

All the rooms she passed and peeked into had a disturbing amount of hardware. Rings were on the walls and embedded in the floors, and each was equipped with beds with more gold metal rings attached. It was definitely not her scene.

There were only two rooms left at the end of the corridor. It was darker the further she walked. The last room was double the size of the others. Two giant glass pocket doors were on either end, but it was still too dark to see what was inside. She assumed it was the same as the others but slid one door open and flicked the lights on. *In for a penny, in for a pound.*

Her breath left her in a whoosh. She stood in the doorway and took in... what was this place? Neat rows of gold handcuffs, whips, chains, masks with snake motifs, gags, paddles, switches, canes, and many other items that she didn't have a clue what they were lined the walls— a BDSM tool store.

The longer she looked around, the more disturbing items she saw. Several pieces had metal spikes, and there was one whole row of spiked paddles. Tears pricked her eyes. Surely, no one would consent to that.

That wasn't the worst— not close to the worst. One wall carried... Christ... miniature cuffs and masks... leashes attached to tiny collars. Child-sized. All were stamped with the same snake design.

She felt her stomach roil and her coffee begin an ascent up her throat. Before she fled the room and shut off the light, she took several pictures. Her breaths were sawing painfully in and out of her throat.

She didn't want to open the final door, but if this place was what it appeared, she needed to get as much information as possible. Mind made up, she opened the last. The door at the very end of the hall was wider, and she found it was much heavier as she pulled it open. Not wasting time, she walked in. The lights came on automatically.

If she'd been scared by the last room, this room was the true horror. Rows of cages stacked to the ceiling. One corner was a large, open shower with drains in the floor, open toilets, and what appeared to be hair and makeup tables. She took pictures with shaking hands and backed out quickly.

"Oh, God. Oh, God. Oh, God," she chanted, practically running down the corridor, changing her camera from picture to video as she went. She knew she was probably going too fast and shaking too hard, but her panic wouldn't allow a slower pace.

She'd just finished videoing the... stadium closest to the elevator when she heard it ding. "Oh, shit." She managed to shove her phone in her tote before the doors slid open.

It was Aldo. *Get your shit together, Jo. He can't know that you know.* "Mr. Russo," she began with a sly grin, "you've been holding out on me." She had to swallow back bile as the slimy pile of shit held the elevator door open, looking at her with suspicion.

"What are you doing down here, Ms. O'Connor?"

"Oh, I noticed a new elevator button had been added, so when I left Medusa, I was curious to see if the building had a basement. You never mentioned it. I assumed it was storage for Veleno." She stuck to the truth, knowing he could easily check her story. She only prayed this floor had no cameras to video the illicit behavior.

"Aren't you a curious cat," Aldo said, smirking but not as on guard. "What do you think?"

She would play whatever part necessary to get the hell out of here. She gave Aldo her back, making it like she was scanning the room again. "It's lovely. I've only been to a club like this once before," she lied before spinning once more to face him. "I'm not really a performer. I don't mind watching, though," she admitted coyly. If it was Thomas, and it was only the two of them. She added mentally.

"Come now, Josie. You're too modest."

Ice speared her like a knife. *Josie. The innuendo.* This sick bastard had seen the video of her and Percy.

These men were perverted monsters— and she'd had sex with one, and the other had watched it.

She couldn't lose her head now. She couldn't give away that she thought this space housed anything but a sex club. "You can't hold experimenting against a girl, surely, Aldo. Voyeurism suits me."

"It doesn't bother you that Percy showed me your video?"

She couldn't let him suspect... anything. Shrugging nonchalantly, she prayed her next lie was convincing enough for a reprieve. "I may seem fairly buttoned up compared to many women, but I'm not unaware that my body is desirable to most. Would I prefer Percy kept the video for his pleasure only? Yes.

"I'm a realist, however, and men do so like to brag about their conquests," she said with a light laugh.

"You were a virgin. The blood was beautiful between your legs."

It was then she noticed the bulge at the front of Aldo's slacks. Her mouth flooded with saliva. The need to vomit was overwhelming. She needed to end this.

"Too bad I was too drunk that night to remember." Thank God, really. "Now, enough about me. I assume some patrons will pay extra fees for membership. Very clever. Did Angelica decorate? It truly is lovely."

"She did, and I agree, she outdid herself."

She stepped past Aldo to enter the elevator, all no-nonsense business again. "I'm going to spend the afternoon setting up the POS training. Hopefully, I can email all the managers by tomorrow."

Aldo accepted the change of subject. He stepped off the elevator, trading places with her.

"I have a few things to check on while I'm down here. Have a nice day, Ms. O'Connor." Before the door closed, he asked, "Perhaps you might want to join us some evening once we're open. To watch only, of course."

Jo managed one more smile and said, "Perhaps," as the door finally slid shut.

As she stepped off the elevator at street level, she could have cried. Her body shook with relief. There were decisions that had to be made, and even though her mind and heart were racing a mile a minute, she wasn't going to let those... those rapists get away with what they were doing.

It was clear to her now that Veleno was a cover for traffickers. Disgusting, perverted, should be killed traffickers. And she and her parents had been working for them.

Jo took a seat at the lovely Caffe Novecento located only a block over from the Veleno building. They served the most delicious cheeses and cold cuts, and their tea was some of her favorite in the city. She ordered by rote but knew she would taste nothing.

She wanted to keep to a routine in case Aldo was watching her or having her followed. She prayed he bought her story of not seeing anything other than a sex club. If he thought she might have discovered the true nature of the business, she truly believed her life might be in danger.

Suddenly, what had been weeks of the tortuous rehashing of her past became so much more. She was not so naïve to believe that there weren't many men and women who partook in dark sexual practices. Had she not seen evidence pointing toward something much darker and depraved, she would have walked away.

The room of cages did not scream consensual— the

restraints sized for children? She took a sip. Her shaking hand caused some tea to slosh over the rim.

She cursed herself. She had to keep it together. Opening her laptop, she went to the POS website and began to settle into scheduling. She would do nothing— contact no one— until she was sure no one was following her.

She called her contact to see what dates their reps were available, how many people they could send, and how large the classes could be. She was still on the phone when Angelica walked in. She walked to the counter and placed her order before scanning the interior, acting surprised when she spotted Jo.

They did suspect her, then. She just had to keep playing the game a while longer. Thank God she was on an actual business call. Jo smiled and waved her over. "Excuse me, Evelyn, but I need to put you on speaker for a moment. A colleague just walked up." She asked Angelica to sit for a moment.

"Angelica, I'm speaking with Evelyn. She's Veleno's head contact for the POS software company. I met Evelyn when I attended one of their seminars in the States. I'm working on scheduling the staff's training, and when I saw you, I wondered if you might want to sit in on one of the classes."

At her surprised expression, she explained, "I know it isn't in your design description," Jo chuckled, "but this program is a game-changer for businesses, new and old. I think having knowledge of such a system would impress many of your future clients who would appreciate the recommendation."

Angelica seemed to contemplate the offer. So far, so good.

"Knowledge is power. I wouldn't mind knowing how the inner workings of the businesses I design for run," Angelica consented.

A waitress called Angelica's name, thank God. "Evelyn and I are going to knock the scheduling out. I'll cc you in the email with Aldo and the managers of class times and dates. Pick what time works best for you and let me know."

Angelica stood to go retrieve her order, saying, "Thank you, Josephine. See you soon."

Hopefully, never, Jo thought. For all the interior designer's newfound cordiality, the woman was as filthy as her employer, and she didn't have any doubt that Percy was as disgusting as his friend.

Two HOURS LATER, Jo finished setting things up with Evelyn and even got the training schedules sent out.

She believed she'd succeeded in throwing Aldo's distrust off. She'd never know how she managed to pull off normalcy after what she saw in that basement level of horror. As the apartment door closed and locked behind her, her legs literally gave out.

Sliding down the wall, she sat on the cold marble of the entry and curled around her knees, fat tears scalded her cheeks. Flashes of the last few hours burning permanent pictures behind her eyes.

*You were a virgin.*

*The blood was beautiful between your legs.*

Great gulping moans ripped from her throat, racking, heaving cries followed. Her every fear had come to fruition in a single moment. What if they released her sex video if she threatened to turn in their sick club? Her parents, her brother... her friends would see.

Thomas would see.

It didn't matter. She would go to the police. The shame of the video didn't matter in this scenario, not when so many depended on her shutting that horrible place down. How would she do it, though? She should tell her dad everything now.

She wanted to tell Thomas instead.

She wasn't sure how long she cried when her phone started ringing. She was still wearing her coat and rubbed the sleeve across her wet face. Her phone was still in her tote, and after a moment of digging, she pulled it out. Thomas.

"Hello."

"What's wrong?"

## 15

Thomas had just left Aileen and Mirren at their condo. Aileen had been released from the hospital yesterday and seemed to be doing much better. Of course, her next round of chemo started next week. The cancer was shrinking, and Dr. Delaloge was pleased.

They all were pleased. The hospital had a list of men and women who were licensed caregivers. Thomas hired a kind older woman to visit Aileen once a day and help her with baths for those times when she felt too weak. She didn't want to impose on Mirren for such things, so she hadn't balked at the help.

He felt comfortable leaving France now that things were squared away with his family. He'd planned on heading home to Scotland and dig deeper into Percy Donovan.

It was six in the evening, so he took a chance and called Jo on his way to the airport. He knew something was very wrong the moment she answered.

He immediately asked what was wrong. She didn't answer. His heart was hammering now. "Tell me now, Jo," he demanded.

"Long day. How's Aileen?"

He didn't bother to reply as he got out of the taxi and walked into the airport. She knew the answer anyway because Jo had called her that morning. He walked to the nearest ticket kiosk and was able to cancel his flight to Inverness and rebook for Rome. His flight didn't leave for an hour.

"Are you still there?" Jo asked.

She sounded so sad. What in the hell was going on? "Where are your mom and dad?"

"Tulsa."

"Caren? Carla?"

"Tulsa, as well."

He exploded, not outwardly as he didn't want security on his ass, but inwardly... he was raging. "Why are you there alone?"

"I work alone all over the world, Thomas," she answered, her tone flat.

"Damn it, Jo. Please tell me, baby. You're clearly upset, and it's killing me. I should be knocking on your door by nine-thirty. Let me in."

She didn't answer, but it sounded like she was crying. Damn him, he should have sent Coll to his sister and gone straight to Jo. He'd known something was off. "Josephine," he said her name gently, hoping to coax a response.

"You're coming here?"

There was a tinny quality to her voice. Panic? "I am, and I won't be talked out of it, so don't bother trying."

"I won't try. I need you."

THREE HOURS and forty minutes later, Jo heard a knock on the front door. Thomas had texted her that it was him at the door.

Ever cautious. She'd never appreciated him more than in that moment.

She showered to give herself something to do while she waited and now wore a long, silk robe belted at her waist and her thick blonde hair in a low, messy bun. Unlocking the dead-bolt, she opened the door.

Thomas went through the door so fast that she didn't even have time to blink. He locked the door behind him and threw his leather duffel on the floor. Then he wrapped his big arms around her back and lifted her up to press against his body.

Time apart always made her forget how huge he was. How safe he made her feel. She wrapped her arms around his neck and held on tight, letting her face drop to the vee of his neck. He seemed to understand her need to just be held before anything else.

He rubbed her back, over and over, as he whispered words above her head. "I'm here now, baby. I'm not leaving you. I love you. I love you. I love you."

He walked them into the living room and sat on the dark-navy, velvet couch. She felt the crush of the plush fabric against her bare legs where her robe had pulled high. He kept her in his lap, still rubbing her back, in no hurry to question her.

She sighed, letting the heat from his skin soak into her body. Her shaking was subsiding, and her tears were no longer a salt burn on her cheeks. She fiddled with his jacket zipper, not wanting to move but also not wanting to prolong the inevitable conversation.

There was so much to tell him. Her part in the story, though horribly embarrassing, didn't rate compared to what she saw under Veleno. He would want to know why she'd stayed working for people who made her uncomfortable. Why she hadn't told her parents she wanted off the job. Those questions could only be answered if she started from the beginning.

She forced herself to lift herself away from Thomas' chest. His arms loosened but did not completely let go.

She untangled herself from his lap and leaned her back against the arm rest opposite of his side, placing her feet on the couch and adjusting her robe modestly around her. She realized what a mess she must look like, having cried for hours and touched her cheeks and her haphazard bun.

Thomas placed one of his broad, capable hands over her feet, effectively stilling her actions. "You're beautiful."

*You're beautiful.* In that voice and in that tone, she believed *he* believed that and let her hands drop to her lap. She took a deep breath and began.

"The second part of this story is the most important part, and I'll need your help with it, but I think it would be best to start from the beginning." His complete attention was on her face— his brilliant mind probably dissecting each nuance and tremor. Watching him, too, she noted he was still in his boots and heavy coat.

"First though, please take your coat and boots off. I'm comfortable, and you're not." She knew discomfort wouldn't bother him at all, but she asked anyway. If only to delay the inevitable.

He stood, a great golden oak amidst the dark Parisian décor. He unzipped his jacket and tossed it on the nearest chair before bending to unlace his boots, placing them on the floor by the chair. He was now only wearing a plain white t-shirt and dark-washed jeans. Before he could resume his seat, she asked, "Did you pack any sweatpants?" *You're delaying, O'Connor.*

He only raised a brow but walked back to the front door and retrieved his duffel, placing it on the kitchen table to riffle through it. He found what he was looking for and pulled out a pair of navy sweats. Without looking her way, he shucked off his jeans and pulled the sweats on.

Without comment, he sat on the couch again. He placed his hand over her feet again.

"So, from the beginning." She sighed and then winced at the Once Upon a Time opening, knowing this story was anything but fairytale-like. "I moved to New York after high school when I was eighteen. I was accepted into the hospitality program at Cornell. My grades were excellent, and I'd already completed two years of college.

"I went in as a junior. Mom and Dad got me a small, single resident apartment on campus. The summer before the fall semester began, I drove to the Hamptons to attend a wedding. I was a bridesmaid. Ivy was a friend I'd made—" She interrupted herself, "Sorry, none of that is really important."

"Everything you're thinking is important. I don't care how long it takes," he assured.

It would be easier to explain her actions and keep them straight if she gave details, so following his advice, she explained her relationship with Ivy, that she was a year older and in real estate with her dad. Who Hunter was and that his family was political. She explained that Hunter had been attending Yale Law at the time and that his best friend was also a fellow law student and a groomsman.

"Percy Donovan was in his final year at Yale and several years older." She had to look away from Thomas' face briefly, giving herself a moment to get out the next bit. Jo brushed her finger over the velvet, allowing herself to focus on the patterns she was drawing.

"Jo," Thomas said gruffly, "Nothing you've done, nothing you tell me will make me think less of you. Tell me you believe me."

Looking into his eyes once again, she tried to explain. "I think less of me. For eight years, I've thought less."

"Have you ever spoken about this to anyone?"

"No."

"Tell me, then, and share the burden."

"The wedding was lovely. I was partnered with Percy, who, as I said, was older. He was handsome, and I was flattered by his attention. I was a naïve eighteen-year-old who thought she was a savvy, sophisticated woman.

"The wedding venue, Montauk Yacht Club, was lovely... magical. I danced for hours. I had a few G&Ts, not too many, but enough that I was ready to go to bed. Percy never asked me to dance, but I noticed him watching me all evening.

"I thought I might have made too much of his compliments earlier in the evening. He was simply being kind to Ivy's friend. I was about to tell Ivy goodnight when Percy found me. It was in a secluded corner of the clubhouse, and he... convinced me to have one drink with him at the indoor bar. I agreed to one drink. I remember ordering from the bartender. I remember taking a few sips, Percy flattering me, never touching me, just... talking about my... appearance.

"I didn't think I was drunk. When I was sixteen, a friend and I stole a bottle of tequila from James' not-so-hidden, hiding spot and got so shitfaced, I puked for two days. I know what being drunk feels like, but again, I was young and obviously dumb.

"I woke up the next morning and," she had to pause to swallow down her nausea. She hated thinking of that morning, let alone speaking of it to the man she loved. "And... I was in my room alone. Naked. I was sick— barely made it to the toilet before vomiting. It felt like I dry-heaved for hours.

"When I managed to look at myself in the mirror. I had bite marks all over my body. I ached everywhere. I had blood between my legs." She looked at Thomas helplessly then. She only just noticed his body was practically vibrating with anger.

He leaned forward, took her wringing hands, and placed them against his chest. His heart was pounding.

"God, Jo. My God, he raped you."

She pulled back in shock. "No, he didn't! I was dumb and drank too much."

"Okay, sweetheart," he sighed deeply... softly. "Tell me what happened next."

THOMAS WANTED to walk out of that apartment, find Percy Donovan, and kill him. That sick bastard had clearly drugged and raped an innocent girl. Jesus, he could barely stand to hear the words coming out of Jo's mouth. They would have to speak about what he believed happened, but not just yet.

"I was too sick to stay for the wedding festivities and too embarrassed to face Percy. I finally managed to shower and pack. I told Ivy I'd caught a bug and had to leave. I drove to the nearest pharmacy and bought a morning after pill because... because I didn't know if he'd used protection.

"I had a doctor check me out on the Cornell campus. And then I worked hard every day to not think about it. I tracked Percy and his family for years to make sure we never ran into each other. I allowed distance to grow between Ivy and me since her husband was friends with him."

He watched as she clenched her jaw, clearly not wanting to tell him something. "Tell me," he asked gently.

"I guess I let him video us... having sex. He left me a note."

Christ, have mercy. He had to clear his throat of the rage clogging his vocal cords to ask, "What did it say?"

She stood instead of answering. "Hang on. I still have it. Give me a sec," she said as she left the living room. When she came back, she handed the note to him. "I know it's weird that I kept it, but I never wanted to forget. I keep it in my makeup bag, so it goes wherever I go. I only have to catch a glimpse of the scrap of paper to remember to make good choices." She shrugged.

She still had the note from the man who'd raped her. He had to get a hold of himself before she came back. His anger was not what she needed. His sadness wasn't either. She just needed his love and support. He had to remember that. It was hard to remember that.

She returned and handed him a folded note. He opened it to find the Montauk Club's logo on the top and a sadistic message below written in neat, sharp lines.

> *Last night was amazing, Josie. I love that you let me video our first time. You looked beautiful in every position.*
> *Our night will be our secret... unless you want to be internet famous.*
> *I know you'll be with other men over the years, but I want you to always remember— I was your first. PD*

The note was clearly meant to demean and threaten. Had she said anything, he might have leaked the video. He hadn't realized he had tears slowly falling down his cheeks until her hands cupped his face.

"Don't cry for me, Thomas. I admit that the threat of the video, of my family seeing it, has hung like a noose over my head for years, but that isn't as important as what else I have to tell you."

She finished wiping his tears— she was comforting him... "I want to hear it all, baby, I do, but first, I have something to say before you move on."

At her nod of agreement, he told her, "You may have been naïve, but I don't believe you've ever been ignorant a day in your life. You said yourself that you knew what being very drunk felt like. You weren't drunk that night. The way you described his behavior throughout the evening was classic for a person stalking a victim. He drugged your last drink, Jo. He took the video for his own sick pleasure and to hold over your head in case you pressed charges.

"You did nothing wrong that night. The only bad decision you made was trusting that sadistic piece of shit, and that's on him, not you." When Thomas heard himself say the word trust, he flinched. No wonder she'd run far from him when she'd found out he'd lied to her. Trust was important to people, imperative.

It was survival to her.

"Christ, baby, I knew my lies had hurt you. I had no idea, until this moment, why it cut you deeper than most. Please tell me you've truly forgiven me. Jesus," he swiped his hand between them, waving away his words, "it doesn't matter right now. This isn't about me. Tell me the rest," he requested, chagrined.

"You matter. *We* matter. I have forgiven you. I promise."

She leaned forward and pressed her lips to his. He deepened it for just a moment, but it released a bit of tension for them both.

"That night with Percy," she began, touching her forehead to his, "is it possible... do you really believe he could have drugged me? I never understood—" She cut off with a whimper.

"Yes, and he'll pay for it one way or another."

"No! I don't want to ever bring that up to him. I just want to forget... more than what I have," she pleaded.

"Josephine," he grumbled low, bracing her face between his huge hands so that she was forced to meet his eyes, "do you think you are the only person to suffer at his hands?" He hated saying that. She'd gone eight years believing what happened was somehow due to her carelessness. She deserved to be free of that guilt.

Fresh tears leaked from the corners of her eyes as she stared into his. "No. If he truly drugged me, then no. I don't think I was his only victim." She swallowed several times, her nerves drying her throat.

He stood and walked to the refrigerator to grab a bottle of Evian. Coming back, he unscrewed the cap and cupped her hands around the cool bottle.

"Thank you. I need to tell you the rest, though. It is much worse than what happened to me."

He doubted that, only nodding for her to continue. Then his phone started buzzing. He looked at the screen, which Jo could see. It was Mirren.

"Answer it."

Obeying, he answered, putting the call on speaker. "Mir, what is it?"

"Jesus, Dad. Dickhead much?"

"Mirren Mòr MacGregor, you'll watch your mouth, or I'll watch it for you, young lady," he said, pretending offense.

"Fine. Whatever. A senior asked me to prom. Can I go? Mom said I had to ask you, which I don't understand why you'd have an opinion either way. Mom and Jo already promised to take me dress shopping if I got asked."

Thomas could practically hear the eye roll from his daughter. He glanced at Jo, her face was much rosier than it had been moments ago, presumably because she and Aileen had made promises to Mirren without consulting him. He didn't care. The fact that she didn't resemble a ghost was a relief.

However, he still had to play his part. "Why in the bloody hell is a senior so much as looking in your bloody direction?"

"Dad! You're so ancient. Of course, he'd look at me. I'm

smoking hot, and I'm a cheerleader," she paused, "or I was, but still. Hot."

He must have made some sound indicating he'd like to kill said senior because Jo was patting his knee and making tsking noises.

"Send me the date of the prom and the boy's name. I'll make sure Uncle Coll looks into the family."

"You wouldn't dare," Mirren growled, a decent imitation of her father.

"I would." He could hear Mirren whining to her mother and her mother taking none of it.

"Fine. I'm calling Jo, though, so she can plan on meeting Mom and me because I know Uncle Colly won't find a single bad thing about Stefen."

He had to bite his tongue so that he didn't say something unflattering about the— what did Josephine call people— douche canoe named Stefen. Christ, what a pansy-ass name.

"Jo heard you. She's right here."

"OMG, Dad! Why didn't you say? I would have talked to her instead of you. Put me on your shopping calendar, Jo. We only have four months to find the perfect dress," she trilled. Clearly ignoring every word her father had spoken.

"Jo, can you hear me?"

"I'm here, Mir," Jo answered with a smile.

"I wouldn't normally impose... but I'm imposing. Do whatever it takes, no matter how X-rated, to get Dad to stop being such a... Dad."

Despite his daughter's antics, he couldn't help but be amused, especially when Jo replied in American truck driver. "10-4, little lady." Message received.

"Thanks, Jo. You're the best. I hope Dad helps you figure out what's been making you sad," Mirren said, suddenly much more serious.

Jo glanced at him. "He is. See you soon, Mir. We'll go shopping if your Colly isn't a bigger dick than your dad," she teased, though there was a shine of tears in her eyes.

He said his own goodbyes, reminding Mirren to send the boy's credentials before hanging up. "Teenage girls," he lamented.

"Sixteen and already running circles around the great Thomas MacGregor."

Only two years younger than Jo when a predator had taken her innocence. Scorching heat thrummed through his veins once again. The reprieve from his daughter's call was negated in a moment.

"Finish your story, Jo, so I can take you to bed. You're exhausted." She raised her brows but didn't deny the charge.

"Okay," she said, seeming to center herself for the rest, "Aldo Russo hired O'Connor Hospitality to help open Veleno, a four-story brick-and-mortar. There is a ground-level bar, second-floor dance club, third-floor smoking lounge, and fourth-floor luxury dining. It's a premier luxe address in downtown Rome.

"I found out that this was Mom's last job a few days ago. They will be ceding the company to James and me within the month. I knew it was coming, but the date was unexpected. I didn't tell Mom or Dad that Aldo made me uncomfortable. I should have. Dad would have pulled no matter what it cost our company."

Dean O'Connor should have been paying closer attention to his daughter instead of his wife's early retirement. They would be discussing the oversight. He said none of this to Jo.

## 16

"I felt a weird vibe from the first moment I was introduced to Aldo. Like I said, he made me uncomfortable. There would be times he would look at me strangely like he knew a secret. Like he was almost playing with me. I ignored it, only wanting to do my job as quickly as possible so I could leave.

"Then I met Angelica. Her company had been hired to do interior design. Again, I felt something was off with her. Finally, I met the head of Aldo's PR, who, unbeknownst to me, was the person who recommended my family for the Veleno job."

"Percy Donovan," Thomas guessed.

"Yes. After eight years, the man I'd done my level best to stay far away from, was the person who recommended me. He knew we'd have to spend time together. At first, I ignored the oddness of the trio. Percy started slow, a touch on my hand or back, casual but uncomfortable. Then he began to text me. Not often and usually work-related. A few asked if I was in bed, but nothing too terrible. Once, he mentioned loving the silky brown dress I'd worn.

"That was the dress I wore for Ivy's wedding. Then I knew — he was definitely toying with me. I should have gone to my parents, even if I had to tell them about the possibility of a sex tape. It was foolish."

"Not foolish. What matters is you're telling me now."

Jo nodded. She was telling him now. "Again, I thought to just power through. I've been working long hours, and everything on my end should have been wrapped up in a matter of weeks. Today changed everything."

She described the new button in the elevator and that Aldo had originally given her an all-access pass key. She pulled up her photos and walked Thomas through the rooms, describing everything she'd seen. The rooms, the chains, the handcuffs, the cages... the child-sized things.

"Jesus Christ, Jo. Tell me no one caught you down there!"

She winced at his panic. "I did warn you this was bad. Aldo. Aldo caught me," she admitted. "I heard the elevator ding and quickly put my phone away. He was suspicious, and I knew I could be in serious trouble.

"He called me Josie. Only Percy called me that. I knew then that he'd seen the video. I kept my cool and played it off like I'd been to a sex club before. I said I wasn't into performing for an audience. That's when he finally told me Percy had shared the video." The vile things that man said would haunt her forever.

"Oh, baby," he said, placing a gentle kiss to the top of her head, "I wish I would have been there to protect you from that."

"Do you want to know what he said that I had to pretend didn't affect me?" At his nod, she told him, only because she prayed that in saying it out loud to Thomas, it might take some of the horror away.

"He said, 'You were a virgin. The blood was beautiful between your legs.'"

Thomas moaned as if he was in pain. "I wouldn't have rested until Aldo Russo and anyone involved in his trafficking ring were caught and prosecuted— but for what he said to you, Jo, I will make sure he's destroyed. My people will destroy them all financially and socially before the authorities arrest them. They won't have two p to rub together for defense."

"Do you think Percy is involved in... that part of the business?"

"Absolutely."

She felt ill. To think that perverted floor was being designed while she was working the floors above. "Oh, I asked Aldo if Angelica had designed the basement club. I pretended to think it was stunning. He admitted that she had. She knows too."

"Veleno is a cover. They've created an over-the-top experience to draw an extraordinary amount of attention. High-rolling predators could be seen coming and going from the venue, and no one would bat an eye."

"I can't believe my family worked for them— is still working for them."

"Aldo made a fatal error in taking Percy's advice to hire you. They thought they were too powerful and too clever to get caught. You were a toy to them, or at least to Percy. Aldo is wealthy, sick, and twisted and probably thought to use you as entertainment. But they underestimated you."

"After all these years of no contact, I don't understand why Percy would want to see me now. He's never tried to contact me."

"That is what we're going to find out." He picked her up and began carrying her to the back. "Thank you for trusting me. I'm honored, baby."

Resting her head on his shoulder, she pointed to which door led to her bedroom. "I've felt so alone, and not just in Rome, but for years. I've always had this sense of wrongness. Like something was wrong all the time, but I could never put my finger on it. I gave up dating because intimacy felt... I don't know, it just felt wrong." He placed her gently against the pillows and sat beside her, holding her hand.

"Do you think, if what you think happened the night of the wedding... I mean, if it was assault, do you think that my trouble with men... could it have stemmed from that even though I don't remember anything?"

"Yes, I do," he answered grim-faced. "Your subconscious mind remembered or knew something bad had happened. I'm not a therapist, but I believe you would benefit from speaking to someone. I think it would help you work through all of these new revelations. I think you would find closure. You need it, Jo."

She took a deep breath, letting it out slowly as she nodded in agreement. "What now? I mean with Veleno." She quickly told him about the café and speaking to Angelica, who had obviously been following her. "I think I convinced her I'm no trouble, and she surely relayed that to Aldo."

"I think you should continue to go to work like usual until we speak to the authorities. I'll be tracking your every move. Your phone and tablet already have my software on them—"

"What?" she choked over his casual reference to already having her bugged. It was comical. Before today, it might have pissed her off.

"You've been mine since the first day we met. Since the first time you told your friends you named me Honey Bunny after a zoo rabbit with golden hair like mine," he explained, giving her a small frown at the nickname. "I take care of what is mine. I won't lie. I considered putting a tracking device in your skin after Rowan was kidnapped."

"Jesus, Thomas," she shook her head in mock annoyance, but really, his level of protectiveness was exactly what she needed.

"I would like to come with you, but I looked up Aldo and his family before I had to go to France. It would take someone with his connections less than an hour to find out I run a security company. I don't want any more suspicion on you. They have to keep believing you haven't a care in the world and that BDSM clubs fascinate you. They can never suspect you believe it's a trafficking ring. Even when we take them down, I don't want anyone to suspect you had anything to do with it.

"I will call in a team to start working on this case. We'll need to notify Interpol National Central Bureau. One of our men has a high-up contact in ICPO who can help me navigate working with Rome's authorities. I am used to dealing with the FBI's international offices, but I've heard good things about ICPO. Their job is to work with people and organizations around the world. It will be very interesting to see what Roman authorities think of traffickers trying to set up shop in such a prestigious district."

"What all will you have to tell your people?" she asked softly. Already knowing the answer and dreading it.

"To shut these people down, they'll need all the information. They need to be able to piece together when Aldo and Percy first got involved. It would be almost impossible to develop a theory as to why he's bringing you in without some backstory. I'm sorry for it." He hesitated before adding, "How about we do this. I speak to Coll separately and ask him to research your connection.

"I trust Coll with my life. He's struggled with his own personal demons for a while now, but if I asked, he would treat this as if you were his own sister."

She didn't like it, but it was better than a bunch of the members knowing her past. She was also very aware that this was a dire situation. Her discomfort could not supersede the lives and well-being of the men, women, and children that the snake pit below Veleno would destroy.

"I would appreciate that. Can your team get into Percy or Aldo's phones or computers?"

"I plan on using the software installed on your devices to attempt to slide into their security. If your tablet or phone is placed near any of theirs, my team or I should be able to hack their programs. You just need to be in the same room with one of them. If we can get in that way, I'll have my team focus on their businesses, finances, and networking." He grasped her hand tight. "Coll can focus on finding the video and deleting it from their accounts."

"Oh, wow. Deleting it for good?" she asked hopefully.

"Saved only on our end if you decide to press your own charges, lass. But it will be locked away. I hope that once MacGregor Security is done with him, further charges won't be necessary to put him away. In that case, you can permanently destroy it."

"I see." And she did. Truly. Percy was a horrible man who probably did awful things to countless women. She was still shell-shocked that he might have drugged her. Eight years of thinking she was an irresponsible idiot was hard to let go.

"Do everything you can to avoid both men. Sit in on as many POS training sessions as you can. That will mean less time for one-on-one chance encounters. You said Angelica will be joining one of the training sessions. I'd prefer you not be around that woman either, but she's by far the safest option. Her phone or laptop is all we'd need to get into Russo's system and then from him, into Donovan's.

"Are you sure you can handle going back there?"

She didn't answer right away. She'd been around them for weeks. She'd hated every moment, but she'd done it. Now that she knew what they were capable of, she was angry. Angry that Percy had done something to her that had affected her for years, and angry that they had committed their lives to being disgusting human beings.

They did not value life. She did, and she would fight. She would suppress the eighteen-year-old girl who wanted to curl into a ball and hide. She was a badass, twenty-six-year-old woman now. She would fight.

"I can handle it. I will handle it," she confirmed.

"The strongest woman I know," he murmured against her lips while he slid some of the pillows from behind her back. "Try to sleep. I'll be working on a plan with the team most of the night, but I won't leave this apartment. Rest and know you're safe."

"Lay next to me when you can. Please," she asked quietly. Her eyes already felt so heavy she knew she'd be asleep before he left her room. "Thank you, Thomas. I love you."

"My heart has only ever been yours, Jo."

Thomas MacGregor's poetic words were the last thing she remembered before sleep pulled her deep into its depths.

## 17

Jo was asleep before Thomas closed the door softly behind him. He planned on setting up a temporary office in the kitchen. There was one man he needed to speak to before he called his people.

It was early evening in Tulsa, Oklahoma, and he wasn't surprised his call was answered on the first ring.

"MacGregor."

Jo's dad was as friendly as ever. He imagined Dean O'Connor would be even less welcoming by the end of this conversation.

"Have you noticed your daughter acting different lately? Before you left Rome." No reason to beat around the bush.

Dean paused for several seconds before clearing his throat and answering with, "Why do you ask?"

It was taking all of his control not to curse at Jo's father, but if he didn't answer his questions, this conversation was going to deteriorate fast. "Did you notice anything?" Thomas wasn't going to play the older man's games.

"She seemed more strained than usual. I assumed it had to do with you."

"So, you didn't ask her if something was bothering her before you and your wife left her alone in Rome?"

"What in the fuck is going on? I'm hanging up and calling my daughter."

Before he could make good on his threat, Thomas said, "Don't. She's sleeping. I'm at the apartment now."

A beat of silence, and then, "Tell me what is happening. Please."

Dean O'Connor said please. It was good to know he loved his daughter enough to humble himself. "I can't tell you everything. It isn't my place. I will tell you that one of the men she's been forced to work with on this project hurt her years ago. When she was eighteen." Thomas heard something shatter. Jo's father did not like hearing that. He could hear Jo's mother, Mary, scream and Dean shushing her and telling her he'd explain.

"Apologies. A crystal tumbler fell off my desk. Continue."

"Like I said, it's her story. She can tell you or not. The owner of Veleno has been making her uncomfortable for weeks. Aldo Russo is the worst type of trash, and unfortunately, Jo has been left to deal with it on her—"

"Don't you dare insinuate I'd leave my daughter in an untenable situation knowingly, MacGregor," Dean warned.

"Not knowingly, but was she a priority? Did celebrating your wife's retirement take precedence? Are you so used to Jo working fifteen hours a day and being unhappy that leaving her to the status quo seemed the best decision?"

"I've already texted our pilot. I'll be there tomorrow. Tell me what is happening, damn it. What is happening to my baby girl?"

Some of Thomas' anger dissipated at the older man's obvious distress. He was a good father, he knew that, but seeing

Jo left alone and so vulnerable triggered an impulse to make her father suffer as he suffered hearing her story.

"We've both failed her. I won't fail her again, and I trust you won't either, Mr. O'Connor."

"I will not," he replied stiffly, but Thomas could hear the man's emotions roughening his speech.

"Remember, I can't tell you everything, but I can tell you the owner, Aldo Russo, his interior decorator, Angelica Bluche, and his head of PR, Percy Donovan, are into some very bad shit, and O'Connor Hospitality has been working above the criminal activity for weeks."

Thomas described what Jo had discovered in the basement, the danger that she was now in, and his plans to take them all down.

The first question from her father was, "Will you stay with her?"

"I can't go to work with her because my presence would throw up an immediate red flag to Russo, but I will be taking every precaution to keep her safe. She knows what the protocols will be and is prepared to walk back in there. I will not leave her or Rome until the situation is resolved. I won't leave her ever," he added.

He heard a great exhalation come from the other man. Clearly, he was relieved. There was some mumbling, followed by Dean's muffled voice and a one-sided conversation between him and Mary. "I'll explain everything the moment I'm off the phone, my love. Please don't cry. MacGregor is with our Josephine. No, she's sleeping. We'll call tomorrow. I'm going back to Rome in two hours. You are not coming. Mary, please. Please, Mary. Stay home. Fine. Go pack for us both, then."

"Christ," Dean swore, "Mary and I will both be coming. What is she... why didn't she tell me... anything?"

"She had reasons, sir," Thomas said gently, more gently than he'd ever spoken to the man in the past. "She only just confided in me because of what she discovered today. I'm asking you not to mention her past. It might take her awhile to tell you. There's a chance she never will. She'll only know I told you about the underground trafficking club."

"I understand. Fucking hell, I've dropped the ball," Dean admitted, a sound of perhaps a fist thumping a desk in the background. "You were right to call me out. I've let my daughter down, but I can assure you, it won't happen again."

"I've let her down too. I won't let it happen again either," he promised. The call ended.

Now, the work began. He had hours of calls and planning to facilitate.

Coll answered before the first ring finished. "Is it Aileen?"

Thomas winced. He should have realized that calling him this late would make him think something had happened with his sister. "She's doing much better. Sorry to worry you. I only left her earlier this evening."

"Work then," Coll guessed.

"Yes... and personal." He took a moment, disliking telling anyone of Jo's trauma, even if that anyone was his best friend. She'd given him permission to tell Coll, but he hated it.

"MacGregor?"

"Damn. Okay," he sighed. "I've sent messages to four of our team. I'll patch them in next, but I needed to speak to you privately first." He forced emotion down. He could not allow his feelings to interfere with his work.

"Eight years ago, when Josephine was eighteen, she was drugged and assaulted. The man videoed the rape. She'd been a virgin."

"Fucking hell, Tommy."

Coll hadn't called him Tommy in years. Clearly, he was upset by the news. Their relationship may have been strained since his injury, but he was aware of how Thomas felt about Jo.

Coll was silent for a beat before saying, "I assume he's the target."

"One of them, and not solely because of Jo."

He spent the rest of their time giving Coll the pertinent facts, starting with the wedding eight years ago, family connections, etc., to Veleno and the trafficking. He sent all of Jo's pictures and video as well. He could hear Coll furiously typing from his end.

"I'm going to use our software on Jo's phone and her computer. If Russo, Donovan, or Bluche are anywhere near Jo with one of their electronic devices, we should be able to jump in. The team will need access to everything, but only you and I will have access in the beginning. The video needs located and removed.

"Jo is trusting you because I trust you."

"Understood. If we find it, does she want it destroyed or kept for the police?"

"She wants it destroyed, but she's agreed to wait until this is all over before doing it. I never want her to see it. She's believed for eight years that she must have been drunk, and that's why she didn't remember."

"No question. She was drugged. I already found her friend's wedding photographer and was able to pull up couple's entire album in the history."

"That was fast."

"I'm motivated," Coll said gruffly. "I'm sending you the file now. Jo is in several, dancing and laughing. Donovan is in a few as well, but he's always in the background. He's clearly watching her."

"I just sent you a picture of the note Donovan left by her bed," Thomas said, staring at the offending scrap of paper now lying on the coffee table.

Two heartbeats later. "She kept this all these years."

Grimly, Thomas replied, "She did. Russo has seen the video... he made a few comments, specific comments about Jo being a... about..." he trailed off. Too sickened to speak of the specifics. "It might be on his phone or computer as well. We won't know anything until we can get access. Coll... damn... you have to help me take down these people. You have to neutralize that video. I would owe you. Anything."

"For fuck's sake, brother. If I've become the type of man who needs owed for helping my family, then I shouldn't be allowed to keep breathing. You love Josephine, and she was hurt. I only needed one of those reasons to help."

"Fine, then," he exhaled some of his worry.

"You're close to this job, Tom. Bring the others in, but I will take lead. Your focus needs to be on Josephine's safety and nothing else. You'll be a member, and you can help, but I will call the shots. Agreed?"

Thomas' kneejerk reaction was pure fury at the suggestion, but he was seasoned in the business enough to know he was compromised, and he didn't want his attention divided. He needed to be focused on one thing only, and that was Jo.

"Agreed." He wasn't thrilled, but he agreed.

"When we're through with them, brother, they'll wish they'd never heard the name O'Connor. Now let's bring the others up to speed and bring these sick fucks to their knees."

Jo woke to heat— gallons of it. It was like she was simultaneously lying in a tanning bed, that was set in the desert, while sipping on Everclear. That was how combustible her skin felt.

The bright light piercing the curtain's edges meant she'd slept much later than her normal five am She felt rested and energized... before yesterday's events flooded her memory.

Veleno. Trafficking. The video. Thomas.

Jo slowly rolled to her side, and sure enough, the source of that lovely heat was the Scotsman lying beside her. She had no idea how late he'd worked but imagined he only got a few hours of sleep.

He was naked from the waist up. A sheet covered his lower body, but if memory served, and it most certainly did, Thomas preferred to sleep naked.

One hand rested flat against the deep grooves of his abdominals, partially blocking her view of the trail of golden hair leading to his groin. His other arm was thrown across his eyes, probably trying to block the flickering sunlight beams bouncing around the room.

Despite all the unknown variables of her life, having Thomas back infused her somewhat tattered soul with courage. Last night, she'd taken the first deep breath in what felt like forever. Sharing her story had released... well, it had released something.

One would think finding out she'd been assaulted versus having made a drunken mistake would send her spiraling. It hadn't. It had been a terrible shock, and she knew she desperately needed to speak to a therapist to work through it all, but it had given her some of her old confidence back.

Her real confidence. Not the show she put on for her family and friends. She hadn't realized how much she'd not trusted herself, mostly where men were concerned. The weight of that video— fear that her mistake had the potential to embarrass her family and affect her family's business— had been immense. To be able to sluff off the guilt was a renewal of her spirit.

Not wanting to wake him but not wanting to leave the bed without at least touching him, she sat up and slowly bent to place an ultra-light kiss on his mouth. Intending to slide off the opposite side of the bed and get ready for work, she squealed in surprise when Thomas had her flat on her back, looming over her, his normally serious face... still serious. Some things never needed to change.

"Hey!" She huffed out a laugh. "I thought you were sleeping."

"And I thought you'd only stare at my body and never touch it, lass," he growled close to her mouth.

"I need to get ready for work," she hedged, even though her hips couldn't help but roll into his.

He groaned and captured her mouth. "You'll have to get undressed to get dressed again. I can help you with that."

Tingles instantly touched her body, burning brighter as he pulled the silk of her nightgown up and over her head, leaving them skin to skin. She couldn't help but moan as their skin touched.

"Christ, Jo, I haven't felt you under me in months. I dreamed of it every day, but my dreams didn't let me feel you."

He kissed her neck, shoulders, and chest. She clasped his head and directed his mouth to her breasts. He kissed, laved, sucked, and nipped both breasts until her nipples were hard, sensitive points. "Thomas, please," she begged as he pulled away, but when he sat up to straddle her hips, his erection drug against her body, causing her "please" to hiss slowly between her lips.

"Now, Thomas. I need you in me now." To emphasize her wants, she wrapped her hands around his sex, which was now bobbing above her belly. He let her have only a few strokes before he took her hands from his body, holding them in one of his own.

"No, baby," he growled, "I'm not done tasting you yet."

And, oh God, he wasn't. He had her near orgasm before he'd made the first swipe of his tongue against her core. She was panting and grinding against his mouth by the second one. When two fingers joined— game over.

She screamed when her orgasm peaked. "Get inside me now. Now!" She didn't have to ask twice. He was back to his knees in a blink, lifting her ass with one large hand while the other gripped his sex. Another blink, and he was gliding through her pulsing channel.

Thomas was the one shouting as he fully seated himself. "Tight. God, Jo, feels so damn good."

He slid in and out in a controlled, punishingly slow measure. She wrapped her long legs around his lower back and tried to force her hips up to increase the pace.

He placed his palm over the top of her sex, effectively holding her still, his thumb slowly flicking back and forth, back and forth. Slow flicks that were quickly driving her mad.

"Faster," she pleaded.

"Slow," he countered.

"You're killing me," she whined, her second orgasm so close. If he would... "Just move faster!"

"Like I said, baby, you haven't been under me for way too long, and I'm going to remember every single stroke of me filling you up. I want my cum buried so deep in your body that you feel me every moment we're apart today."

His deep voice, those words... her body exploded. The moment she started to squeeze around him again, he moaned. He wouldn't be able to stay slow and steady now.

"Fuck me, Jo... no chance—"

He didn't finish the thought as he lost his will for slow

torture and began pistoning at an almost impossible pace. He reared back, grabbed her hips in both hands, and pumped three more times before stilling as deep as a man could get inside a woman. She moaned again as she felt his release.

He opened his eyes to stare down into her own. "I love you, Josephine O'Connor."

## 18

Before she called Coll, Jo hopped in the shower. Thomas joined her.

"Sorry, lass. I couldn't think of you naked and wet without seeing it for myself."

"You just saw me naked and wet exactly three minutes ago. How can you be ready? Already?" she laughed, making his lips twitch in a small smile.

He shouldered his way into the large walk-in shower, immediately crowding her against the back wall. There were no preliminaries or warmups— not that any were needed. He lifted her by the waist, and before her legs were even fully wrapped around his middle, his hard flesh was pushing in deep.

"God, Jo," he growled before taking her mouth.

He was in the mood for hard and fast, and she was in a mood to take whatever he gave her. His rhythmic pumping set a pounding cadence. It took less than three minutes for them both to orgasm.

Consequently, the meeting started late with Coll. She wasn't mad about it.

She'd never spoken to Coll before that morning. She knew

he was Thomas' best friend and Aileen's brother, but she'd never met him before. Thomas explained Coll's injury in South America and his subsequent withdrawal, so it was a surprise to find he was the lead on the case.

One of the team members contacted their man inside Interpol early this morning, and Coll had a video conference with the agency soon after. Coll had already learned that Russo's family had been suspected of involvement in numerous crimes over the past forty years. There was never enough evidence to convict, or if there was, it disappeared, including the accusers. The world's largest police cooperation would enjoy taking that family out.

She shivered again, thinking how closely she and her parents had been working with criminals of that caliber.

Jo was thankful for Coll's professionally gruff personality because as soon as Thomas connected the call, Coll started right in on the video— no need to anxiously await for the dreaded subject to come up.

"Once I find the video, I will use the file's unique code to find it on all the devices linked to the original device and whether it was sent to any others. With that information, I can delete or corrupt those sent files, as well. Do you understand?"

She had to press a tissue to her eyes to stop the tears from escaping.

"Coll," Thomas growled, clearly not happy the video was being discussed with her.

Before an argument could erupt, she said, "I understand." If her voice wobbled, Coll didn't react to it. Thomas looked about ready to Hulk out and destroy the apartment.

"No one, including me, will see it. I will know from the time stamp if it's the right one. If you choose to use the video as evidence against Donovan in the future, I'll keep it secure. It might be able to be used to help with character assassination in this case, though I doubt it will be necessary. If you bring charges against him yourself, a professional in law enforcement trained in sexual assault cases would have to watch it.

"Thomas and I will make sure no one involved will walk away clean. Questions?"

"None. Thank you."

And that had been that. The rest of the call dealt with the other members. One was arriving in Rome within the hour to begin surveilling the predators of Veleno. The ICPO contact would meet with Thomas and Coll via video before lunch.

Thomas was stiff with Coll. His answers were short and bordered on rude. Probably because Coll had spoken to her so openly about the video. She touched his hand where it fisted on the table and mouthed, "I love you." He unbent enough to loosen his hand and clasp theirs together, palm to palm.

After the call ended, it took another fifteen minutes to leave for work. Thomas practically bearhugged her, clearly not wanting to let her out the door.

"I can do this, Honey. Let me do this. You'll know where I am." She huffed a laugh. "You have more trackers on me than NASA does their rockets."

He sighed but finally let her slide down his body so her feet could touch the floor again. "Text me often."

"I will." She pecked him once more on the cheek and was about to step outside when he casually mentioned, "Your parents are on their way back."

"Why?" She pushed the door open a bit wider so she could see his face. Guilt? "What did you do?" She might have thought his pinkening cheeks were precious if it didn't mean he'd done something she wasn't going to appreciate.

Clearing his throat, he admitted, "I called your father last night. We had words."

"Words?" She prayed he hadn't brought up the video, swallowing the lump of shame that immediately followed.

"I told him he'd been thoughtless to leave you. I also mentioned that he should have recognized you were unhappy and working too hard," he said the last in a rush, hoping perhaps she wouldn't catch it all.

"Why would you do that, Thomas?"

"Because it's true, and he needed to know it."

Despite the blush, his crossed arms and granite face meant he wouldn't budge from the high horse he was currently sitting on. Sighing, she finally asked what she feared most. "Did you tell him everything?"

"You know better, Josephine," he chided. "He asked me why you didn't tell him about not liking to work with Russo or Donovan. I told him you had your own reasons, and you would either tell him what those are or you wouldn't."

In some ways, it would be a relief for her parents to know. In other ways, she worried they would be disappointed in her, or worse, look at her differently. She might not have been at fault for the assault, but she was at fault for bad judgment. She should have known Percy was a grade-A creep.

A worry for later. She needed to focus on work and helping Thomas' team gain access to the criminals. "Okay. I'll see you later," she said as she shut the door. Thomas caught it before it could close.

He pulled her against him once more, giving her a firm, close-mouthed kiss. "Text me."

She shook her head but managed to smile, her heart lit by his antics. "Yes, Mr. MacGregor," she shot over her shoulder, finally on her way.

Jo hoped she exuded confidence this morning on the outside, because she was a quivering mess on the inside. She purposefully wore a sleek camel-colored suit with black trim, a black silk shirt, black heeled half boots, understated diamond studs, and a gold James Avery fleur-de-lis ring.

Classy. Confident.

Scared shitless.

Thomas went over everything with her this morning. She wasn't supposed to seek out anyone other than the ground-floor bar chef, with whom she had a meeting scheduled first thing. Training didn't begin today, so Jo wouldn't have a chance to join Angelica's class yet. She would ensure her presence was noted by the staff and then leave as soon as possible.

The chef decided he had a problem with the menu. He believed that two of the items had ingredients that wouldn't be sustainable to get year-round.

Before she even sat down with the chef, Jo knew she'd take the items off the menu and reprint them. She would then suggest special printed mini menus when the chef wished to make the dishes. When the ingredients *were* available.

This was the stage of hospitality that consisted of putting out fires. So, she would meet the chef this morning and then speak to the managers to make sure they had contacted the employees who would be doing the first round of the point-of-sale training.

She hadn't admitted this to Thomas, but Jo hoped she didn't have to wait for the training classes to allow the team to hack into one of Aldo, Percy, or Angelica's systems. She wanted to run into one of them and get that part over with so Coll's team and Interpol could have access now.

The opportunity came swifter than she imagined. The meeting with the chef lasted less than an hour. He'd been more than pleased with the suggestions Jo made. An hour and a half after that she'd confirmed most of the employees had committed to their class times.

It was frustrating and disappointing to realize that so many hardworking people who had diligently trained for their positions would soon be jobless. Many had quit their previous jobs to have the opportunity to work for Veleno. She prayed that Russo's dark plan for the business was revealed quickly. It might not be much solace, but at least the employees would know why.

She was about to step onto the elevator, swiftly sending off what felt like the two hundredth text to Thomas when she glanced up and saw Aldo, Percy, and Angelica walking toward her. They'd obviously come to the lounge floor when she'd been in the back speaking to the GM.

She smiled. "Good morning." She held up a 'just a minute' hand gesture. "Let me finish this email, and we can chat if you wish." Willing her hands to stop shaking, she quickly texted Thomas again.

> Trio here. Third floor lounge. Have your system ready.

> I'm with you.

"There," she said brightly, indicating to her audience that she'd sent off her email. "Percy, I have what I believe are the final menu changes for Adder. I think your PR team will want to focus on Adder's sustainability concept. The bar will be one of few casual establishments in Rome to concern itself with the environment. Plus, the chef is committed to buying locally."

She explained all of this as they took a seat on the rounded, plush couches in the main lounge, praying she didn't sound nervous. She'd already opened her tablet, allowing Thomas to record and hear her conversation.

Percy grinned. To most people, he was a strikingly handsome man. Intelligent, put together. A catch. But when he smiled like he was now, Jo only saw a crudely painted, psychotic Joker.

"You're right, Josie. PR will be all over that."

Instead of shying away or flinching, she looked directly at the man who assaulted her and said, "Josephine, please. Or Ms. O'Connor if you prefer, but I do not like the nickname Josie."

"I remember you used to not mind me whispering Josie in your ear," he taunted.

Aldo and Angelica smirked. Each one of these people was disgusting. Knowing Thomas was listening gave her confidence. "Good Lord, Percy. That was like a hundred years ago and apparently very forgettable."

That wiped the sneering grin off his face. Angelica snorted in mirth, turning Percy's countenance darker.

Ignoring the growing tension and Aldo's strange watchfulness, she continued, "Anyway," she waved her hand in front of herself as if she were carelessly brushing away Percy's randomness, "I should have a complete list of each floor's unique features for your team by this evening, tomorrow at the latest. There will be plenty to choose from. It will make the public go crazy to get inside Veleno.

"This lounge, for instance, will boast one of the most prestigious cigar menus in the country. Mayan Sicars run close to half a mil per box. That will attract a lot of big fish. I tried to get Aldo to spring for a Gurkha Royal Courtesan Cigar." She laughed as if she hadn't a care in the world. "Serpent Lounge could house one of those bad boys for a cool million euros."

Her jest did its job, loosening Aldo's reserve. She wanted him to think she was a team player. A Veleno team player. When he finally spoke, she wished she'd never tried to relax his guard around her. The last thing she wanted to hear about was the torture chamber below, though it helped to know the information was being recorded by Thomas.

"I've decided to call the basement club Viper. What do you think?"

He was staring intently at her face. They all were, not wanting to miss her reaction, she was sure. *I'm with you.* She could hear Thomas' voice in her head.

"It's certainly on theme, though," and here she leaned forward as if she were slightly uncomfortable, "I did tell you, Aldo, I've only been to a sex club like that once, so I'm not the best person to judge anything except the name, which I think was a smart choice.

"The club I went to wasn't quite like yours. I'm not sure how many viewing rooms there were, but in the main salon, there were several raised platforms. Some were open, and some had cages with... equipment," she said in a hushed, hesitant voice, indicating to her audience that she didn't wish to be overheard.

It would have done her story wonders if she'd truly stepped foot in such a place. Hell, even a gambling den where rich men took women they'd hired to hang all over them. Alas, her lack of masculine interest before she met Thomas, of course, and working eighty-hour weeks wasn't conducive to experimenting with the baser elements of life.

"It was beautifully appointed, though not nearly as opulent as... as Viper. You did lovely work, Angelica." The other woman preened, glancing at Aldo who momentarily broke eye contact to look at his designer. They smiled at one another— a knowing smile.

She suddenly realized that Aldo and Angelica were something else to each other. Definitely more than colleagues. Aldo brushed his thumb over Angelica's lips, making Jo shiver in revulsion.

Did they get each other off while they watched children being victimized? Incarceration would be too good for them.

"Aldo tells me that you like to watch. Tell me, Josie," Percy said, continuing to use the pet name, "did you ever sit in one of the theater rooms to watch a scene?"

"Once."

"Who was on the stage?" Angelica asked, her eyes had a glassy look, almost like she was getting turned on.

Jo's stomach was beginning to churn. It wasn't that people enjoyed sex or sex clubs. That lifestyle simply wasn't for her. It was that these people weren't just engaging in sex in public or BDSM. They were selling people. Hurting people. Hurting children.

She felt filthy just sitting next to them.

"A woman and three men," she finally answered.

Percy's eyes lit up. He liked her answer. "Have dinner with us tonight, Josie," Percy said, a disgusting hint of arousal clouding his voice.

She sighed in relief. This would be an invitation easy to avoid. "I'm sorry, I can't. I already have plans with my parents."

Aldo looked up from his phone sharply. "I thought you said your parents went back to the States."

"They changed their minds and went to visit some friends in Ireland instead. They decided to stay with me until our job at Veleno is complete, and then we'll all return home together."

"Ah, yes," Percy said thoughtfully.

The tone of his voice put her on edge. Wishing this meeting was over, she began to gather her tablet and folders, putting them back in her tote.

"Were they visiting your college roommate? What was her name," he pretended to ponder, "Kennedy, right? Or were they visiting your interior decorator friends? Sisters, I believe. The Byrnes."

Jo's whole body turned cold. The warmth of the room created a condensation-like effect. Her clothes were suddenly clinging to her damp skin, and she could feel the beginnings of panic trying to inhibit her breathing.

Through stiff lips, she replied, "My parents love my friends." She hoped that had come out as relaxed as she'd intended. "But, Percy, I'm confused. How do you know so much about me? I haven't thought about you in years. Eight? Wow, that's right," she answered herself. "It's been eight years."

A brief look of rage crossed his face. The demon living inside him watched her through his eyes. Jo barely controlled her shiver of unease.

"Of course, I kept tabs on you, Josie. You made a lasting impression on me. You still do whenever I look at my saved history."

All pretense of congeniality faded after that. He grabbed her wrist, but no amount of twisting or turning could break his grip.

"You haven't guessed yet, but I think you and I have a bright future ahead of us."

"Let me go, Percy. I think I've had quite enough of your humor for one day." She stood as soon as he let her go. "I'll work the rest of the day from home and get your PR team everything they'll need to launch Veleno's campaign.

"Aldo," she addressed the other man, "my family's job here is all but complete. I will do my best to arrange things to stay through the grand opening, but I wanted you to know that if it doesn't work for my schedule, I'll be available by phone any time."

She may have to go in, but barring emergencies, she hoped not. Plus, no one knew how long Interpol would take to build a solid enough case to raid Viper and arrest the criminals. Veleno might not open at all. There were so many unknowns.

Aldo frowned at Percy before smiling at Jo. "Of course. It's been a pleasure working with you and your family. I would love it if you could make the opening, if for no other reason than to enjoy your success."

"Thank you, Aldo. I hope you remember us if you ever do another big project. We'd love to work with you again," she lied.

Jo felt nothing but heart-pounding relief as she walked away.

She stepped onto the sidewalk. The crisp air and sunshine filled her lungs and washed her face in warmth. She took her phone out to text Thomas and let him know that she was on her way home when a motion up ahead caught her attention.

"Oh, Jesus," she spoke out loud, awed by the site of the giant avenging angel pelting down the sidewalk toward her, scattering men and women in his wake. She would have been scared to see such a behemoth running helter-skelter through the streets of Rome too.

# 19

The whole team was listening to Jo's meeting. The software he'd placed on her phone and tablet did their work. It dug its sticky, hacking claws into any device in its proximity. It wouldn't feel like a victory until Jo was walking out of that building.

Thomas had been cursing since the moment he'd received her text. He alerted the team and sat down to listen. The need to pull her out, to get Jo away from those sharks, was visceral. The things she was having to listen to and the shit she was having to lie about... they were trying to see if she was willing to be drawn into their world. He slammed his fist down on the wooden kitchen tabletop.

"Steady, brother." Coll's rough voice attempted to soothe his friend. He was the only one Thomas had open air with.

Coll couldn't possibly understand what he was asking. Josephine was surrounded by evil, and Thomas had let her walk in there— had even encouraged her to keep up appearances.

Never again.

Never fucking again.

The things they were saying to her. The shit she was having

to say back. Christ, no... Coll would have to love a woman first, the way he loved Josephine, to understand how tenuous his grip on rational behavior was.

And then... *Let me go, Percy.*

Thomas was out the door and running toward Veleno in less than a second. Coll was yelling in his ear to stay the course. "Fuck you, Coll," he said before digging the buds from his ears and shoving them in his pocket.

As he ran, he considered how he would get to Jo. She was on the third floor, and he didn't have a passkey. Was there an outdoor fire escape? Maybe he could threaten the bar's chef to get him to the third floor if he was still there after his meeting with Jo.

He fumbled to pull his phone out as he ran, wanting to track Jo to see if she was still on the third floor.

And then he noted a flash of golden hair. Jo had stepped from the very building he'd been about to storm. She had her phone out typing and hadn't noticed him yet. He knew the moment he caught her eye. She came to a stop, her eyes widening and a look of bemusement touching her lips. He increased his speed, ignoring the pedestrians' annoyed curses.

He knew he was acting like a lunatic, a madman on a mission.

Jo raised a hand in front of her waist, making a stop gesture. He started to slow, realizing she didn't want him to give her away to anyone who might be watching from Veleno.

"Christ," he swore as he abruptly turned and started walking back to the apartment. Once he was out of sight of Veleno, he stopped to lean against one of the many brick buildings lining the street, waiting for Jo to walk by.

As he waited, he castigated himself over his loss of composure. He just needed to touch her, make sure that bastard hadn't hurt her, and then he'd be able to calm down. He was used to dangerous situations. He didn't want Jo in them.

"Josephine," he softly called as she was about to pass where he was leaning in the shadows. She barely startled, expecting him.

She didn't say a word, walking straight into his chest, where he could wrap his arms around her back and pull her in tight. Thomas wasn't fooled. He might pretend to be comforting Jo, but in truth, Jo was comforting him.

"I'm fine, Thomas. Remember, we had code words for me to use if something went wrong," she reminded him, still trying to smooth his ruffled feathers.

"It did go wrong," he countered. "He was holding on to you. Where?"

She stiffened briefly before pulling out of his arms to hold up her wrist. It had a bracelet of red welts. He took her hand gently, turning it carefully to take in the damage, and forced himself not to turn back around and storm Veleno after all.

"It wouldn't have been so bad, but I tried to pull out of his grip. I *would* have alerted you if I'd truly felt like I was in danger. Did you get into their... IP addresses?"

"We got into all three. It's only a matter of time before my people jump from one to another to another. Russo is a big target for Interpol, but he is connected to bigger criminals than himself. What you did today will give law enforcement the in they need to make arrests now and more later," he explained as they began to walk home.

"How long until those three are arrested?"

"Perhaps as little as a week. Maybe longer. The authorities won't be able to wait past the sex club's opening or risk innocent people being hurt. Though, in significant cases like this, authorities are willing to allow some injury if it means taking out more corrupt players.

"It takes time to build a case against a powerful family like the Russos. Donovan and his family will be much simpler to take down as their family will be easier to track stateside. My team will need several days to sift through Russo, Donovan, and Bluche's files.

"Mentions of the underground club would be gold— any reference to illegal dealings will dig their legal graves deeper. There's no way they aren't all three involved in something they shouldn't be, besides the club. The skin trade is as bad as it gets, so the team will also look for child pornography.

"There's a chance none of them are actually into assaulting children themselves, but if they have the club set up to handle such things, more than likely they are."

"Watching assault is no better than committing the assault yourself. These people—" Jo started, shaking her head, a look of sadness flitted across her features.

"Don't, baby. Don't try to understand them. Whether it takes one day or one year to take down Veleno, your part in this is done. I hope that Coll and his team will get ICPO everything they need to act quickly. I'll know more once we return to the apartment and ring Coll.

"As for you, we'll play it smart. You'll stay in Rome and check in on the POS training, and then we'll leave an appropriate amount of time after that. Together. I'm taking you home to meet my sister, parents, and Grandma." Thomas had her pulled tight against his side as they approached the apartment.

Jo's eyes widened at that announcement. "Your family?"

"Yes, and I want you to move in with me. I want you to make your permanent home in Scotland. Travel wherever work takes you, Jo, but come home to me." He hadn't meant to spring all this on her after the hell she'd just endured, but he desperately needed her absolute commitment.

"That's... that is... sudden."

"After today, I realized there's no halfway with us. There never has been. It's all or… that's it. There's only all. There will never be nothing with us. Say you agree. Say you'll move in."

They'd stopped outside the apartment, passersby moving around their still forms. Jo turned to face him, leaning her head back to look him in the eyes. He knew she loved him. It had to be enough.

"I'll move in with conditions that we'll negotiate at a later date. Preferably when you're naked, sweaty, and sated."

He allowed his lips to turn up in a small grin, loving the twinkle in her eyes. "Deal. Have your arguments ready before we get this door unlocked. I plan on having us both naked, sweaty, and sated very soon."

She laughed at his playfulness as they stepped through the door. "When are my parents expected?"

"They had a late start. I believe it won't be until eight or nine tonight. As soon as I touch base with Coll, I need to call the O'Faolains about Donovan's interest in your friends. Hugh will want to make sure the girls are protected. Saoirse Kennedy will also need to be made aware. Until things are settled here, I want your friends to be extra vigilant."

"I need to call the sisters too. I promised to be better at checking in. They'll kill me if they find out we're seeing each other again, and I didn't tell them."

"We're doing more than seeing each other, lass." He turned to glare at her, making sure she knew how displeased he was with her description of their relationship.

"I'm yours," she placated. "I'm also a day overdue in calling Aileen and Mirren. I can't wait to tell Raven, River, Rowan, and your girls that I'm going to be moving close to them. I imagine your daughter's reaction will be the most entertaining. She'll probably ask if we're having a lot of sex," she teased.

Thomas hated that he felt his ears and cheeks burning. He

kissed the grin off her lips, giving her just enough passion to make her forget about teasing him. *Where in the hell had his five-year-old Mirren gone?*

When Jo softened against his chest, he pulled back. "Make your calls, lassie, and I'll make mine. Then I'm taking you to bed until your parents arrive," he announced as he swung her around, giving her ass a light slap. He hid his grin at her yelp

Jo was safe again. Safe behind walls that he protected. His muscles began to ease one by one. This was it. She'd agreed to move in with him. He dared to hope the worst was behind them.

## 20

---

"I t's about damn time you called us, Jo," River Byrne's acerbic jibe made Jo smile.

"River's not lying," Raven agreed with her sister. "After months of secrecy, you finally drop the Honey Bunny of all bombs in our laps and then ghost us for another week."

Jo had finally felt comfortable enough to share the story of why she and Thomas had broken up. To say the sisters had been furious was an understatement. They wanted to hunt down Thomas and "medieval torture him," River's words, and they wanted to "give me a hug and then paddle my ass for not telling them," Rowan's words. Raven, the sweetest of the trio, said only, "Oh, Jo."

She should have confided in them long before she had for the sake of their friendship, but she'd finally got the guts to spill the truth because of Aileen and Mirren. She wanted the Byrne sisters to love Thomas' family like she did. The sisters were still irritated with Thomas, but true to their nature, they were also empathetic to his situation. They agreed to hold off plotting his "disappearance" until Jo decided if she would take him back.

"Don't mind me, Ms. O'Connor, I'm just miserably huge

and pregnant. I certainly don't expect you to check in every day," Rowan, the youngest sister, groused.

The sisters were all married to O'Faolain men. Rowan's husband, Hugh, was the father of Raven and River's husbands, Bran and Patrick.

Convoluted but incredibly wonderful.

"You're not huge, Row," Raven soothed.

"I'm the same size you and River were at five months, and you were both huge!" she countered.

"You're right, Row, you're huge," River agreed. "But remember the positives, you and I are taller than Raven. Raven seriously looked the biggest."

"Barely shorter, you dicks. Jo, my sisters are assholes," Raven grumbled, but laughter was bubbling through.

Jo couldn't help but chuckle. She was sprawled across her bed, enjoying the hell out of the Zoom video call. She'd been missing seeing their faces, which made her next news so exciting.

"Well, I've got news. Not as amazing as Rowan having a baby or Raven and River becoming aunts and sisters-in-law to Baby O Girl," Jo giggled at their combined groans— their family tree really was going to look wonky, "but still pretty exciting."

"Tell us."

"Tell us."

"Tell us."

"Thomas and I are officially back together," before the gasps could turn into questions, she added, "and I'm moving to Scotland. We're going to live together."

"Oh my God! I'm so excited for you guys, and I'm really excited you'll be closer to Nan since you two are throwing me the best baby shower in the whole wide world. Don't forget to look at my sex toy registry. Hugh really likes to use them on me."

In the background, somewhere out of view of Rowan's camera range, Jo heard Hugh growl, "Christ, Row."

"Sorry, babe. Baby O Girl has been making me extra inappropriate."

She didn't sound sorry at all.

The back of Hugh's head came into view to give his wife a kiss. "Girls, tell Bran and Pat to meet me at the bar. I just spoke with MacGregor. We have things to discuss." And then, "Hello, Josephine."

"Hello, Hugh. Congratulations on having a girl. They're so much better than boys. Just ask my dad," she teased. He only grunted, but she saw a small smile grace his profile as he pulled out of view again.

The multiple video screens on her laptop showed Bran and Patrick, Raven and River's towheaded husbands, giving their wives similar kisses before leaving to meet their dad. The best thing about having Thomas back in her life was not feeling jealous of her friends' relationships. She had that with Thomas.

Once the chat cleared of men, Jo admitted, "I know why Thomas called Hugh. Before you ask a million questions, you guys, let me give you the short version of what's been going on."

She went over working for Aldo Russo at Veleno and how she'd never been comfortable around him or his friends. How they'd been poking at her for weeks, and how just yesterday, she'd discovered the sex trafficking den below Veleno.

"Percy Donovan's family owns a PR company in New York. Percy practiced law for years before joining the family business. He and Aldo are friends. Percy recommended me for the job. Angelica Bluche owns an interior design company in Rome. She's dating Aldo, I believe, and she also knows about the 'club,'" she finished the last with air quotes.

"Damn," River swore. "It looks like you're still a shit magnet.

My sisters and I haven't brought any scary boys to our yard in a while."

"Six months, at least," Rowan said, shrugging.

"So why did Thomas need the guys to know, except for the obvious, your safety?" Raven asked.

She'd been dreading the question even though it was an obvious thing to ask. "Percy let me know that he'd been following my career... and he knew about my friends. He mentioned Saoirse because we were friends in college, and... he mentioned you three. Thomas wanted to make sure your husbands know to be more vigilant with your protection until they're arrested."

The sisters never looked more identical than in that moment. Their mouths were perfect circles of 'O.'

"So... what are you saying, Jo?" Rowan was the first to speak. "Have you known this Percy Donovan for a long time?"

"Were you friends?" Raven asked.

"No, guys," River started. "She already told us she didn't like any of those people. The question is, why was this man keeping track of her."

Bingo, Jo thought. She had already stripped out of her suit jacket and was left wearing her wool slacks and black silk button-up. She fiddled with unbuttoning a few buttons to give herself a moment to decide how much to say. If she wanted to say anything at all. The assault happened eight years ago, but she'd only just found out that it was assault. It felt too raw yet to speak about.

Her hesitation was noted by all three women. Three sets of hazel eyes were trained on her. "I met him when I was eighteen. The summer I moved to New York for college."

"Oh."

"But..."

"We don't need anything more," Rowan said quietly. "Someday, if you need us to lend an ear or six, we'll be there."

That was why these women were her best friends. She could only nod... and change the subject. "If you guys have a few more minutes to spare, I wanted to ask Aileen and Mirren to join us. I want you to meet them. I already texted Aileen to make sure she would feel up to it, and she said she did. I also wanted to make sure she had a stocking cap or scarf on. She's self-conscious about losing her hair."

Mirren said she'd finally talked her mom into letting her shave her head. She said looking like Natalie Portman when she shaved her head for the movie *V for Vendetta* versus Golem in *The Lord of the Rings* was a no-brainer.

"I'm not going to pretend this isn't weird AF, but I'm down to meet them." River grinned.

"What River said," Rowan agreed.

"If you love them, we'll love them," Raven said.

"Jesus, you guys, I sometimes forget how exhausting it can be to talk to all three of you at once." She laughed as she hit the add button for Aileen and Mirren to join their video chat.

"So Hugh tells me every day," Rowan said, laughing.

"You mean he has time to speak in between screwing your brains out like an apocalypse is right around the corner," River teased just as Mirren and Aileen came on screen.

"They're talking about sex already, Mom. This meet and greet's gonna be killer." Mirren grinned at everyone. Aileen just shook her head in exasperation.

"Whoops." River blushed for perhaps the second time in her entire life. "Sorry about that."

Aileen made a swishing motion with her hand, wiping away River's apology. "No worries. My daughter has decided to be her 'authentic self,'" she air-quoted, "which apparently means being inappropriate eighty percent of the day."

"I guess there's no need to break the ice with this group," Jo said. "I'll do introductions, at least. Aileen and Mirren, I'd like you to meet my good friends, Raven, River, and Rowan O'Faolain." Each woman raised their hand in greeting.

"You're all married to brothers, right?" Mirren asked.

Jo, Raven, and River stifled snorts of amusement when Rowan's cheeks turned rosy.

"Actually, I'm married to their husbands' father," Rowan clarified.

"Older man fetish. Nice!" Mirren fist-pumped the air. "I like to read a good age gap romance on occasion. I might have some questions for you, Rowan. At your convenience, of course."

"Jesus, Mary, and Joseph," Aileen muttered.

"What, Mom? A lot of women like them older. Are you forgetting you and Charles? Dad and Jo?" She put her hands in the air, all innocence.

For another thirty minutes, the six women enjoyed getting to know one another, and thanks to the inappropriateness of the initial conversation, which Mirren, the smart girl, probably did on purpose to put her mother at ease, Aileen stopped adjusting her head scarf within moments and allowed the Byrne sisters to do what they did best, entertain.

Thomas walked in as their conversation was winding down, and of course, Mirren had to announce, "Well, guys, it was nice to meet you, but it looks like it's time to say goodnight. Dad just walked into Jo's bedroom, and we all know what that means," she deadpanned.

Thomas flushed bright red, freezing in mortification. *Ahh... teenagers could be wonderful.*

"Nice to see you, Honey Bunny," Raven teased Thomas by using Jo's old nickname for him.

"You two going to try to make a kitten?" River asked, her small grin making her eyes sparkle mischievously.

"A kitten? What in the hell does that have to do with rabbits?" Rowan demanded.

"Baby rabbits are called kittens," River answered like everyone could pull out animal husbandry facts from their back pocket.

"Oh right, I forgot," Rowan said, rolling her eyes. "Jo, HB better *hop* on a plane soon and bring you to Ireland to see us."

"Dad, do you have a furry fetish or something?"

"I do not," he growled.

"Never worry, Mirren," River started, "once you and your mom are home and we come to see you, we'll tell you the whole Peter Rabbit tale."

"It's precious," Raven seconded.

"Everyone hang up. Now," Thomas commanded.

Jo grinned at the women who were all doing their best not to laugh. Good nights, love yous, and see you soons were spread around before the last face blinked off the screen.

Thomas stood next to the bed, scowling down at her, but she knew him well enough to recognize that he wasn't truly mad.

"Did you get all your calls done?" she asked as she slowly slid one button free at a time from her blouse. He stood as still as a sentinel, but his eyes were trained on her fingers.

"Yes. Hugh will take care of his family and Saoirse. An Interpol agent is flying to Scotland tomorrow to meet with Coll."

Her eyes must have shown her surprise. According to Thomas, Coll avoided speaking or meeting with almost everyone since his accident, preferring to live in the wilds of the Scottish Highlands.

Her hands had stilled while Thomas had spoken. "Don't stop." He spoke softly, but the demand in those two words had her sitting up straighter against the headboard so she could finish unbuttoning.

In answer to her unspoken question, Thomas said, "Where I focus on security, Coll focuses on taking down criminals like Russo. He must believe meeting the agent will help the case if he's willing."

She slid the silk from her shoulders, her nipples clearly pebbled against the sheer material of her black bra.

"Christ, if you knew how my mouth waters for your tits," he admitted, his voice rough with need. "Take your pants off."

He hadn't made a move to join her on the bed, clearly intending to stay staring down at her from his great height, arms flexing where they crossed his massive chest. Thomas' serious mien had always done it for Jo. She could feel her panties getting damp, the promise of... well... the promise of whatever his eyes held assured her compliance.

Reaching for the pants placket, she unhooked the metal fastener and slid the zipper south, using her thumbs to hook the waistband and slide them from her body.

The only thing covering her important bits was provocatively see-through. Thomas' swallowed moan made Jo's inner pinup girl pose, arching her back and letting one long leg casually fall to the side.

He started to rip his clothes off, cursing when he forgot to take his boots off before trying to rip his jeans from his feet. She was amused at the rush until he told her why.

"I want hours, no days, with you naked, but your parents will be here in fifteen minutes. That's what I came in here to tell you," he explained, voice slightly muffled as his t-shirt was pulled over his head.

"Fifteen minutes," she screeched. "Put your clothes back on! If Dad told you fifteen minutes, trust me, he'll try to beat the time." Thomas just looked amused while distracting the hell out of her now that his body was on full display.

"Seriously, babe, Americans live to beat their own travel times. It's... it's like a game!" He pulled her panties off before practically ruining the hook and eyes on her bra, wrestling it off her as well. "Thomas! Listen to me, damn it!" The thought of Dean O'Connor walking into the apartment to the sound of his only daughter moaning in ecstasy was not happening.

Thomas was busy pushing her back against the mattress and climbing over her body, using his fingers to swipe through her wet core. "God, Jo, you're ready for me, baby. I only need five minutes, and" he started, bringing his wet fingers to his mouth, "you'll need less than that."

He wasn't wrong. She silently admitted defeat by letting both her knees fall to the bed, spreading herself wide. A rare grin touched his square jaw, giving him an almost boyish appearance. However, the hand he was using to stroke his length was all man. She couldn't help the moan that slipped from her lips then.

When he used his fingers to swipe the moisture from the thick head of his erection and paint her thighs with it, she lost her mind. "Now, damn it. I need you inside me now," she demanded.

"I know, lass. I need it too," he admitted as he positioned himself between her legs.

With one hand, he lifted her lower back from the bed, making it easier to align his body with her own much smaller one. He rubbed the head of his sex between her legs, causing them both to shudder at the heightened sensation.

Time was ticking. Her parents would be here any minute, and he still had yet to enter her. To ask him to hurry would likely give her the opposite result. *Stubborn man.* Whispering his name to get his attention, he was instantly mesmerized by her hands cupping her breasts. She pinched and tugged her nipples, arching her back and moving her hips against his length.

"You aren't playing fair," he rumbled while finally, *finally* pushing through her folds.

She was so wet that all of him was able to breach her in one stroke. He filled her so fully that it was hard to do anything but hang on. He must have recalled that their time was finite and started to piston faster and faster, hitting her G-spot with toe-curling vibrations.

The moment his fingers touched her swollen bundle of nerves, an orgasm grabbed her insides and squeezed, setting off his own climax. A short shout burst from his throat as his body jerked repeatedly inside her.

His body curved over hers, and he gently placed his head next to her own. His breathing was ragged as he kissed her ear softly and whispered, "I'll love you forever, Josephine."

Those were the sweetest words, healing and devastatingly effective. They clogged her throat and eyes with emotion. Sniffing, she told him, "I love you too, Thomas. Forever... but if you don't get your ass out of this bed and dressed in thirty seconds, I won't be responsible for my actions."

She felt his chest rumble in amusement. The fine covering of blond chest hairs tickled her breasts. Unable to help herself, she stretched them higher until her nipples could more fully enjoy the friction.

"Not the best way to get me to leave our bed, lass," he chided.

"Whoops." She gave him a quick kiss on the cheek and then shoved, not that she could move the mountain from her body if he didn't want to go. With only a few grumbles, he sat up, allowing his body to slide from inside her own.

"I'm not done with you," he promised darkly.

"Later. My parents have to sleep sometime."

## 21

"That shortcut cut off two minutes," Dean announced proudly.

Jo, who'd only taken two steps from the bedroom when her father walked through the front door, looked at Thomas with a smirk and an 'I told you so' eyebrow raise. *Americans...*

"That wasn't a shortcut, Dean, you maniac. It was a narrow back alley loaded with debris and, most likely, criminals. We're lucky we made it here at all," Mary, Jo's mother, fumed. It would have been more effective if she hadn't been patting his arm like the old man was a hero.

To Dean's credit, he walked directly to Thomas and offered his hand, his shake firm. "I appreciate you being here."

He accepted the man's hand and nodded his head in acknowledgment, but his attention was focused on Jo. He knew she was dreading speaking to her parents. He'd told her she never needed to tell them the whole of it. She was committed to therapy, to making herself happier, to finally making peace with the truth that she was not to blame— had never been to blame.

When Thomas had gone to the bedroom earlier, he had every intention of telling Jo that Coll had already found Donovan's assault video. He was going to tell her that Coll had planned on erasing the video from his devices and destroy all evidence of it from those Donovan had shared it, but when he'd seen her smiling and laughing with the Byrne sisters and Aileen and Mirren, he couldn't bring himself to ruin her moment of happiness.

Interpol forbade all members of MacGregor Security to delete files from any person of interest in the case because it might make them wary, especially since the video was of Jo and Donovan and she'd seen Viper, which meant Coll could only copy the video and save it for if and when Jo decided to use it to press charges.

Coll had sent the team the video's URL and let them know that the material was sensitive and not to be viewed by anyone. He let them know it pertained to a potential assault case. Without question, the team agreed to be careful.

He would let Jo know, but the knowledge would only make her feel exposed. Interpol had effectively tied the team's hands, and though he understood, he wasn't ready to see Jo's hope of the video being taken from her attacker's hands crushed.

He watched as Dean and Mary turned to their daughter. Jo's shoulders tensed, but she managed to keep a warm smile on her face. Her parents didn't look convinced. Once Dean's eyes had been opened to his failures, the man wouldn't let Jo hide her true self behind a smile any longer. He could see the resolve settled on each parent's shoulders.

"I'm sorry you guys had to come back to Italy," Jo announced. "You both must be exhausted." She began to head toward the kitchen, asking over her shoulder, "Let me make some coffee."

"We never should have left. Forgive us, sweetheart," Mary implored.

The older woman was wringing her hands as Jo turned back

around. She looked toward him in alarm. He couldn't tell her what to share, but he could stand by her side and support whatever she decided to do. He could also help get at least some of the conversation rolling.

"Let's move to the living room. I'll update you both on my team's findings so far." As the group made themselves comfortable, he was pleased that Jo sat close to his side. Dean gave him a quick, sharp look. The man hadn't forgiven him for the breakup and was probably concerned that his daughter had taken him back because of the circumstances at Veleno.

"We have access to Russo's computer and phone. We've also infiltrated the devices of Donovan, the son of the owner of the PR firm Russo hired from the States, and Bluche, the decorator.

"Interpol is aware that you three have been handling Veleno's hospitality needs and are willing to keep up at least a modicum of normalcy here in Rome until more of a case can be made against all of them, including any of Russo's investors.

"After speaking to Coll, my associate and the lead on this investigation, I believe, as he does, that they will allow Veleno to open."

"Truly," Jo asked, surprised.

"They'll want to know who joins the sex club, Viper, but more importantly, they want to raid Viper once it's open— catch members and prove that it isn't just a typical fetish club."

"You mean they want to wait until some of those goddamn cages are filled so they'll have irrefutable proof." Dean swore.

"Yes." Thomas exhaled. He was disgusted with the entire process. Coll normally dealt with drugs and trafficking. Thomas' focus had always been on guarding individuals, cyberattacks, or hacking, not human monsters. "I dislike it, too, but from what little we were told, allowing the victims to be brought to Viper gives them a better chance of being rescued."

"I'm sick that my family worked for these people, but I don't understand why they chose our company to hire," Dean began, clearly trying to work out how his family got involved. "Russo mentioned to Mary that Donovan's PR firm recommended us. I looked back over our accounts. We've never worked with them prior to this job."

Thomas felt Jo stiffen beside him. Here it was. Deflect or confess. He slid his palm over her thigh and squeezed, deciding to help her avoid the question if she chose. "It's been a long day for Jo, Dean. Let's go to bed and reconvene in the morning," he suggested.

Mary stood quickly. "Of course. Oh my," she floundered. "Dean?"

Thomas felt bad for the woman. Clearly, her husband had enlightened her that their daughter had not been happy for years, and they desperately wanted to know why but weren't willing to push, which he appreciated.

He was about to stand himself and take Jo to bed when she spoke.

"Wait."

## 22

Jo took a deep breath and then another five. Her pulse was pounding. She didn't want to tell her parents about Percy, but she was exhausted, worn down from years of worrying about the video being leaked. For years there had been a space in the back of her mind that shuddered in horror at her secret being revealed. She'd continually shored up the space to keep that fear on lockdown, but she was tired.

Percy Donovan should have never been allowed that level of control. Hearing Thomas' explanation of what probably happened to her— she wanted him to pay for hurting her. She wanted to let go of the pain more.

And that meant telling her parents. "Wait."

Thomas settled next to her once more, taking one of her hands and placing it on his leg. She could feel his muscles tense as her parents sat back down in the chairs facing the couch.

"I want to tell you something. For two reasons. The first is that I should have told you eight years ago. The second is that it is the reason, though I don't understand why, that our family has found ourselves working for these sick bastards."

Mom and Dad were both quiet, bracing themselves.

"Do you remember my friend Ivy, who I used to play with when we went to the Hamptons?"

"Of course," her mom immediately answered. "I remember you going to her wedding, which was quite shocking considering she was only about a year older than you. You haven't spoken about her in years."

"Eight. Almost eight years," Jo confirmed. Thomas pressed her hand more firmly into his thigh but remained a silent supporter.

"I had moved to college that summer and drove to Montauk for the wedding. Guests were put up for the whole weekend with lots of fun things planned. It's where I met Percy Donovan."

She watched as the color drained from her folks' faces. "I was the only bridesmaid. Percy was the only groomsman," she began.

It took less than thirty minutes to explain the events of that night, waking up, the discovery of her abused body. The blood. The note.

"I've tracked him and his family through social media and news outlets for years. I didn't want to risk running into him. Thomas was the first person I told this story to, and only because of what I discovered in Veleno's basement. Trafficking is bigger than my secret."

She glanced at Thomas, needing a second from witnessing the devastation her story had wrought on her parents.

He lifted her hand to his mouth and kissed its back before holding it briefly against his cheek. Placing her hand back on his leg, he finished for her.

"What was obvious to me and would have been to Jo if she'd been older, perhaps, is that she was drugged and assaulted. Knowing this, Jo is understandably relieved that she can let go of the guilt she's been carrying around these years. Still, on the flip side, she's now struggling with what truly happened that night.

"We know the video wasn't just a threat. Donovan and Russo have made comments about it to Jo at Veleno. When Russo discovered Jo looking around Viper, he mentioned specific things that had been done to her in the video. It was meant to show their power over her life. To keep her in line and keep their secrets."

Her parents were so still Jo couldn't even detect breathing. "We aren't sure why Percy chose now, after all these years, to reconnect. Thomas believes that once his team finishes their deep dive into his life and his phone and computer's hard drives, we might discover what brought me here– us here," she corrected.

One minute, it was deafening silence. The next, her father hunched his shoulders and covered his face with his hands, great gasping breaths and choked sobs whistled through his fingers. Her mother continued to stare at her daughter, silent tears running rivers down her cheeks.

"When Dean told me that we'd missed something, that you might not be as happy as we thought, that," she hiccupped and pressed her fingers to her eyes in an attempt to stave off the worst of her emotion, "... that you... that you might have worked too hard all these years because—"

"Mom. Dad. None of this is your fault. Please," she begged. She slipped off the couch and kneeled before her parents' chairs. She grasped one of her mom's hands and pried one of her fathers from his face, forcing them both to pay attention.

"Listen to me. Physically, I'm completely healed. I have been for eight years. Mentally... well, I've promised Thomas that I'll begin therapy. I wish I had told you back then, but there's nothing to change that now. We just move forward.

"I'm done blaming myself for it, and I don't want the guilt of you two blaming yourselves either."

Her dad grasped her chin, briefly closing his eyes before meeting hers again. "I knew before coming back here again that I had failed you. No," he stopped Jo from speaking, "it's true. You are my daughter. My child. You needed me, and I wasn't there, but you're right, Josephine. Guilt won't heal a damn thing. I can only do better. I hope you know that there is nothing in the world that I wouldn't do for you, for your happiness and safety."

Jo could only nod, her own tears blurring her vision. "I do know. You and Mom both." Everyone hugged and kissed and spoke of their love and commitment to being more open with one another.

Through it all, Thomas sat as a sentinel behind her back. To help wipe away some of the room's melancholy, she said, "I have some exciting news to share."

Her mom perked up at that. "Oh?"

"Thomas asked me to move to Scotland and live with him," she said brightly, throwing a smile over her shoulder.

"Oh my, Jo. How exciting! When? We'll have so many things to get you." Her mother loved a love story. She really loved decorating the love story.

"Was there a proposal?" Dean O'Connor asked while glaring at the man over his daughter's shoulder.

At least things were getting back to normal. "Dad! Mind your own business," she admonished.

"You are my fucking business," he countered.

"Dean O'Connor," her mom chided. "This is happy news for Jo."

"So, you plan on moving in with a man who isn't even your fiancé?"

*Dog meet bone.*

"We haven't discussed—"

Thomas cut her off. "We've discussed everything, lass. We both agreed this was forever," he said roughly. He was clearly offended that his honor was being called into question.

"Forever insinuates a commitment," her dad rebutted.

Jo climbed to her feet and threw her hands up in the air. "Things will be easier once his divorce is final."

*Bomb meet detonator.*

Dad couldn't even speak, his mouth opening and closing over and over.

"His daughter Mirren loves me, so," she trailed off when her mother clutched her imaginary pearls and went into a half-faint against the chair's back.

"Jesus Christ," she heard Thomas mumble behind her.

## 23

I t had been past midnight before he and Jo had gone to bed.
Two hours... two hours was what it had taken to convince
Dean and Mary O'Connor that Thomas wasn't some cheating
profligate looking to use and discard their precious daughter.

After Jo's revelations about eight years ago, he couldn't say
he blamed them, but damn if Dean wasn't the most overprotective, infuriating father alive. Jo reminded him that he was just as
ridiculous where Mirren was concerned. So, he let the older
man have his say and then some.

Mary, for her part, had spent the majority of the disagree-
ment making lists of what she thought his house would need
to make Jo comfortable. In between dodging Dean's ninja
stars, he had to simultaneously answer questions about his
home's 'color story,' kitchen appliance brands, and thread
count.

Mary had been surprised to learn that the friend Jo had
been helping with cancer was Thomas' wife, but true to her
unflappable and kind nature, she assured Thomas that she
would call Jules, Dr. Delaloge, and get an update first thing in
the morning. Even Dean softened when Jo mentioned that

Mirren had chosen to do school online so that she could stay by her mother's side.

Jo had looked bemused by it all. Her dad's blustering and her mother's intrusiveness never dimmed her soft smile. Speaking of her past to her parents had loosened something in her. She'd always been loving and fun, but he'd always felt she hid part of herself. Josephine was a better version of herself, a more authentic version.

This was the third morning he'd woken up wrapped around Jo, which meant he could feel his lips hinting at a smile and the hardness between his legs nestled against the curve of her ass. One hand was pressed flat against her stomach, pushing her firmly against his body. The other was full of one breast.

Jo had been sleeping past six, which wasn't typical for the early riser he'd come to know. She was beginning to stir and would soon slip from bed to prepare to monitor the live streams of Veleno's employee training, mindful until the end. All of which meant he had only about one minute to change her mind about leaving their bed.

In anticipation, he moved his hand slowly down from her stomach, grasping her leg to tenderly pull over his thigh. She began to stir more, arching into his groin, causing him to groan. The pressure of the contact felt so good.

It was her turn to groan when he brushed between her legs. He slipped one of his thick fingers between her silky lips and pumped in a deliberately slow measure.

"Thomas," came her breathy response to his ministrations.

He squeezed the breast he was still holding, dragging his blunt nails over her sensitive nipple before tugging the distended tip. She was no longer a passive player this morning but actively seeking his touch.

He kissed the back of her neck and let his deep voice vibrate her ear. "Tell me what you want me to do to you, Josephine." He pushed a second finger deep into her sheath, causing her to moan deep into her pillow. "Shh, love, you don't want your parents to know what I'm doing to your body."

He moved his fingers faster, curling them slightly to hit her sensitive spot just right. "Are you going to come for me?" he asked gruffly against her ear, enjoying that she couldn't react vocally.

"Don't stop, Thomas. Right there, oh God, right there!"

Her entire body shuddered before he felt her spasm around his fingers, her panting moans muffled against the down feather pillow. He was done waiting, and even though her body was beginning to relax, she was still in the grip of her orgasm as he pulled his fingers out and quickly rolled her onto her stomach. Before she could so much as gasp, he was pulling her hips up, bringing her to her knees and plunging his heat into hers.

It was his turn to suppress noise. She felt so good. He wanted to roar with satisfaction. Grasping her hips, trying to control the firmness of his grip so he didn't bruise her creamy flesh, he watched his body disappear over and over, every intimate dip and hollow of her body spread wide for him.

Visions of all the dirty, sweaty things he wanted to do to those dips and hollows had his balls tightening and his control weakening. Knowing he was close to bursting, he demanded, "Touch yourself, baby. Come again for me. I'm almost there."

She disengaged one of her hands that she'd had fisted in the comforter. As it disappeared beneath her body, he had to pinch his eyes shut to gain a few more seconds of control. When her ass cheeks quivered from more than his thrusting, and her half-smothered mewling whines increased in volume and frequency, he couldn't keep from coming deep inside her body.

Her body must have liked the jerking of his release and responded in kind. Her body clenched and spasmed in time with his, drawing his seed even deeper.

He could have happily stayed buried deep in Jo for hours, but just as he was considering how he could lay his huge body over her without smothering her completely, his phone began to ring.

She managed to turn her head to the side as he reached to grab his phone. "Don't you dare answer that," she growled.

His dick had been softening, but her possessive words had the animal coming back to life. "Shit! It's Mir, and she's video calling." He cursed under his breath at the intrusion, but because it was Mirren and she was taking care of her mother, he couldn't not answer.

As soon as Jo heard who was calling, she screeched and started shoving him off her body. She was dressed in one of his t-shirts and throwing another at his head before he registered she'd left the bed.

"Jesus, Thomas, hurry up!" She was finger combing her hair like a mad woman, before jumping back in the bed to prop herself on the headboard. She grabbed her laptop and hissed at him to "Do what I'm doing," she demanded.

He answered the call as he got beneath the covers beside her. The glare she shot at him meant he hadn't followed her instructions correctly.

"Mirren," he answered.

"Hey, Dad. Oh, hi, Jo." She smiled but her whispered voice meant either Aileen was still asleep, or she didn't want her mom to know she was calling.

"Hey, Mir," Jo said, shutting her laptop as if she'd been working. It wasn't even on.

"Sorry for calling you guys so early. I didn't think you'd already be... working," she said with an obvious smirk.

He prayed the heat crawling up his neck wasn't visible. When had his daughter turned into such a sassy... person.

"Oh, don't worry about it," Jo kindly offered, "I was almost finished anyway."

"From your wild hair and Dad's hickey, I'm guessing 'work' is code for something that doesn't require clothes or spreadsheets."

And... there went his attempt at his blush going unnoticed. He *knew* he didn't have any hickeys, but the need to slap his hand to his neck was almost overwhelming.

Jo was thrown by his daughter's teasing, surreptitiously attempting to smooth her wavy gold hair behind her ears.

"You've had your fun, lassie. Is everything okay? With you, your mother?" He watched the smile disappear, and he was on instant alert.

"Do you need me to come to France, sweet girl?"

"No! No, no, no," she quickly sputtered. "I only—" she cut off, shaking her head, only to begin again. "I didn't want Mom to know I called you," she admitted softly.

"What's happening, Mir?" Jo asked. "Has there been a setback? Bad news?"

"No, nothing like that. In fact, Dr. Delaloge said Mom was better than ninety percent of her patients at this stage. She's expecting us to be able to come home within another month and only monthly visits for the next year."

If it wasn't Aileen's health that was the issue, then it had to be something with his daughter. "Are you having trouble, then?"

Jo laid her hand on his forearm, forestalling anymore questions. "If you need to talk to your dad about something personal, let me leave you two for a bit."

Jo's thoughtfulness was always a wonder to him. Mirren immediately reacted, fluttering her hand in front of the screen. "It's nothing about me, Jo, don't go. I wouldn't mind your opinion as well."

He relaxed a bit. If his daughter was good, he was good. "Tell me then, lassie," he urged.

"Yeah, lassie," Jo attempted to mimic his accent... poorly, "tell us. I have more *work* to do this morning," she deadpanned. Mirren giggle-coughed behind her hand. Women were the devil.

Clearing the last of the mirth from her face, she told them. Apparently, Aileen was doing very well, the doctor had confirmed all of that, but Mirren could tell her mom was sad.

"She gets sadder every day. I've caught her looking at herself in the mirror and crying."

"Your mother is beautiful, for heaven's sake!" Jo sounded incensed that her friend would think differently. "Is it about her hair? I can empathize. Only another woman can understand how important our hair is to us, but still, your mom is young, and she will get past this. Her hair will come back. Do you think the Byrnes and I should come for a visit?"

"No, everyone's coming to Scotland when Mom and I get home. That's soon enough. It isn't her hair, well, not all of it," she corrected. "She admitted the other night that she couldn't believe she was so old and still alone."

"The hell is she talking about?" he interrupted. "She's always had you and me."

Jo and Mirren simultaneously said, "Dad!" and "Thomas!"

"You're my father," Mirren started.

"But you aren't her husband, babe, not in the way it matters most," Jo finished.

"I think me bringing up Charles has thrown her. She's been... I don't know. She's been reevaluating things. Her life. I feel terrible," she admitted.

When he heard the sniffle in his daughter's voice and saw the shine of tears in her eyes, he wanted to curse. He wanted to fix the problem. Dean O'Connor's devastated, tear-streaked face flashed in his mind. Father to father, Thomas understood how a child could bring joy into a parent's life but that they could also bring frustration, worry, and aggressive overprotectiveness.

"Tell me what I can do." It would always be that simple for his family.

"She thinks it's too late to rekindle things with my birth father. I don't. I want your permission to reach out to him. I don't want Mom to know in case he's a total douche— but if he isn't... I want to invite him to our home to meet us once Mom is finished with her treatments."

He felt his chest tighten. It was a reasonable request. Very reasonable. She was being respectful of his feelings.

It didn't matter. He hated it.

When he felt Jo's hand slide under the comforter and clasp his upper thigh in support, he found the will to bite his tongue on every cutting thing he wished to say about Charles. The man didn't deserve his ire. He hadn't known. It was Aileen's choice, and he'd abided by her wishes, but coloring the man a villain wasn't fair.

He forced himself to say, "Do you think it would be less of a shock for... the man if I were to contact him instead of his... daughter?" Jo leaned over and kissed his cheek. She must have believed he deserved more than a simple leg pat for his thoughtful choice of words.

"Oh, Dad," Mirren gaped, her whispered astonishment clear. She hadn't expected the offer. "I never thought you might... that is, I know this doesn't make you happy, but I would appreciate your help. If I'm being honest, I was dreading the initial contact," she admitted.

"You have the best Dad in the world, Mir. Surely, you knew that already," Jo chided tenderly.

His chest thumped fiercely at the compliment. "I'll admit I'm not thrilled, but you never have to do hard stuff alone," he finished, barely. When his normally unflappable daughter began to blink rapidly to stave off tears, his own throat started to tickle. "I'm in the middle of a case, but I will make the time soon to reach out. I'll let you know as soon as I do."

"Good Lord, you two," Jo interrupted, "it's way too early for all this emotional baggage. Obviously, your father will handle the heavy lifting on the Charles Project." She air quoted the last. "You need to focus on school and sending me prom dress inspiration pics."

Mirren's face instantly brightened, and laughing, she admitted, "I've got a slideshow with mood music almost finished. You'll die at how many dresses are gorgeous this season."

Jo elbowed him in the side before patting his chest like he was some precious child. "A slideshow, Thomas. Your daughter is efficient and creative." He rolled his eyes at the antics, but he was thankful for the subject change.

"Perfect timing," Jo continued. "My mom is here and will love to look at them too."

"I bet having a parent roomie is really slowing down the baby-making, huh?"

"I will not confirm or deny," Jo answered, covering her mouth while snorting out a laugh when she looked at Thomas' face.

He was so done with the women in his family making him blush. "I'm hanging up now, Mir."

"I'll email you my file on Charles. Love you. You, too, Jo. Bye."

"She is so much like her mother, but I swear, Thomas, she could try a nun's patience— and that... is all you," Jo teased. When he only sat there quietly, she told him, "No one will ever replace you, babe. Surely, *you* know your daughter well enough to know that."

He sighed, long and loud. "I do."

She sat forward and maneuvered herself into his lap, dragging his arms apart where they were crossed over his chest. He automatically grasped her hips to position her more firmly against his groin, groaning at how good that felt.

"Remember," she whispered, "parent roomies."

He took her sassy mouth, deepening the kiss until she was the one groaning. "Shh, love. We'll have to try to make a baby the quiet way," he teased.

"Remove my NuvaRing, and I might be able to give Mirren a brother or sister in about three hours," she teased back.

All of a sudden, he didn't want talk of babies to be a joke. He wanted to have a child with Jo even though he was technically still married to another woman, and her family would most likely hire a hitman to take him out if he disrespected her like that— still... he realized he yearned for a wee Josephine.

"Tell me how to remove it," he said with a seriousness that gave Jo pause. She cocked her head to the side, watching him carefully.

"I'll tell you, the moment you're a free man, Mr. MacGregor."

## 24

Jo was still riding the euphoric high of being well satisfied this morning by her Scottish... Lover? Partner? Best friend? All of the above. Boyfriend.

Her body was warm and languid, her heart a solid thump under her breast, both from the sex and the conversation in the shower.

They'd been surrounded by steam and the echoes of their passion, still insatiable from their breakup and lengthy separation, when he gripped her hair just tight enough to tip her head back.

"Tell me you'll have me forever." Her bare back was pressed against the warmth of the shower tile, her front surrounded by... Thomas. At that moment, she would have promised him anything.

However, she didn't need the coercion of his heat, or her need, or want— she only needed to see him looking at her like he was then. The breakup had been equally hard on them both. Since they'd gotten back together, he needed verbal reassurance about her commitment. Often.

"Forever," she'd promised.

A shiver zipped from her toes to her scalp, remembering the poignant moment.

"Are you even listening to me, young lady?" her mother scolded as they were seated at a lovely café downtown.

In an attempt to hide her wide smile, she fidgeted with her purse before facing her mother's sharp gaze. "Of course I am," she lied.

"Then?" her mother prompted.

*Damn.* "Okay, I might have missed the last bit."

Her mom smiled and took her daughter's hand in her own. "You love him very much, don't you?"

"I do. Very much."

"Your father and I have that kind of love. You deserve it too... and more." She hesitated, swallowing thickly before continuing. "I don't wish to rehash your past, as we should only be celebrating your happiness, but I want to say something, and then I promise to give it space."

At Jo's nod of agreement, she continued, "I love you. Your father loves you. There are no two people more important to us than you and your brother. I wasn't there for you when it mattered most— when I knew something was wrong. I never want that to ever happen again. I don't want to smother you, but I want to know if you ever need me. Promise you'll tell me in the future. Do that... for me. Promise." She hiccupped the last, pressing the linen napkin to her eyes to blot away the tears that threatened to fall.

Jo squeezed her mom's hand back before replying, "I promise." Her mom took one more trembling breath before settling back into her chair.

They each picked up the tiny menu of today's specials. "Mmm, how about we share the bruschetta with tomato, basil, and balsamic. I definitely want the minestrone too. What sounds good to you?" Jo asked.

"Minestrone for me too," her mom answered.

The waiter took their order, and the bruschetta arrived within minutes. They remained silent for a beat, enjoying the layers of rich toppings on the perfectly grilled Pagnotta.

Eventually, their attention turned to the tablet her mom had set up between them. She wanted to go over the list she'd made of all the things Jo would need to pack from home to feel comfortable once she moved, with a second list of items that she might need to purchase for Thomas' house in Scotland.

"His bed is only a queen." She tsked. "I hope that isn't a representation of the size of the primary, sweetheart."

Her mother's wide-eyed look of pain made Jo snort in amusement. "I think I'll wait to buy anything until I see the house. Thomas told me that we would meet with an architect as soon as I saw the space and decided what I'd like to change or add to. He's only ever lived there alone, so it isn't large. Mirren has a room, of course, but she mainly stays at her mother's, which is nearby.

"I'm determined to keep the place homey. I quite like the idea of slightly closer quarters than I grew up with." She laughed at her mom's raised brows. "It's just... I think having my home base be something quaint and lovely will be the perfect place to rest and recuperate between jobs— and to raise a child."

Mom sucked in a breath so fast she choked. Thankfully she hadn't taken a bite beforehand. "Oh my. Oh my, oh my," she repeated. "I can't wait to be a grandmother." She took a sip of lemon water before adding, "Quaint and homey... but elegant?"

"Semi-elegant," Jo compromised. "Think garden chic. I want a flower garden like the Byrne sisters' nan has surrounding her home in Boyle, Ireland. I've shown you pictures," she reminded.

"Oh, yes." She tapped her lips with an index finger in thought. "The floral theme could be carried inside. I might need to be at the meeting with the architect. Your father too. He is the best at designing offices. Hiring Triskelion is a must, as well. Raven, River, and Rowan excel with florals."

"The first step is getting Aileen well and home."

"Of course," her mom agreed. "The divorce is up there on the priority list as well."

Jo couldn't help the chuckle that escaped. She'd been dying to tell her mother all morning. "Thomas received an email from Aileen's attorney before we left. The divorce is final." Jo almost bounced in her seat she was so excited.

"Jo! And you're just now telling me? You realize the wedding to-do list can be fast-tracked now," she added excitedly, flipping to another bulleted list, completely oblivious that she was stepping over a gazillion boundaries.

"Enough, Mom." She laughed. "We aren't even engaged yet. Technically, at least. Put that list to bed for a while longer, please."

"Technically?" her mom asked with a hopeful expression.

*Shit.* "I mean... he... we have an understanding," Jo finally got out.

Mary O'Connor, socialite extraordinaire, snorted in a very unladylike fashion. "I imagine there *is* an understanding. That man of yours isn't going to let you get away again. I won't bring out the list— yet," she half-heartedly conceded.

Lunch was lovely, especially when she called Aileen, and her mom got on the phone. She said it was just so that she could introduce herself, but it quickly turned into, "Surprise! I hired Mrs. Grady for you and Mirren! She is a widow who was looking for work."

Silence met the announcement. "Awesome," Mirren shouted from the background. "She's helped in the lunchroom at school a few times."

"But—"

Mom cut her off. "Mrs. Grady will help with cleaning and errands as needed. She's purportedly an excellent cook. She said she would work six hours a day, except Sunday and Wednesday. She lives only ten minutes from your place. I Googled it," she added proudly.

"I'm retired from hospitality now, dear. Surely, you wouldn't begrudge a woman in her twilight years the opportunity to lend a hand."

Jo snorted at the description. At fifty-six, her elegant mother was further from seeing twilight than anyone she knew.

"Plus, Mrs. Grady could sure use the income after losing her husband of thirty-two years."

The big guns closet opened, and the old manipulation trick was pulled out.

Mirren was wholeheartedly on board, leaving Aileen to finally, reluctantly, agree.

"You've already done enough, Mrs. O'Connor—"

"Mary," her mother interrupted.

"Mary, then," Aileen corrected. "You introduced me to Dr. Delaloge. You don't need to do anything else. Anything," she emphasized.

"That's for me to decide," her mom countered. "You and Mirren are Thomas' family, and he and my daughter are... a couple... of sorts. That makes you two part of my family."

After that, Aileen relented and agreed to just about every suggestion Mom presented until finally, with a look of satisfaction, the call ended.

"She's lovely," Mom said with a soft smile.

"She is," Jo admitted, wondering if her mother planned on working harder in her retirement.

JOSEPHINE SEEMED in high spirits later that afternoon when she and Mary joined Thomas and Dean at the apartment. He hated that he might ruin her good mood with the latest Veleno intel.

But first, he stood from his chair as Jo was about to walk by him to grab a drink from the small kitchen refrigerator. Her surprised look, as he was suddenly towering over her, quickly turned into a blush as he wrapped his arms around her and pulled her into his body.

"Was your lunch good?"

"It was," she answered with a bemused smile.

He noticed Dean trying to hide a smile as Mary dabbed tears from her eyes. He didn't care about the audience. "You look lovely, lass." He loved to see her cheeks darken— loved that he wasn't the only one who blushed in this relationship even more.

"Mom called Aileen."

Thomas couldn't help the slight stiffening of his shoulders. It wasn't because he believed Mary would ever be cruel. It had everything to do with his lingering guilt over lying to Jo.

"She was wonderful, Thomas," Mary said. "I can't wait to meet her and Mirren once they're home. Oh," she continued as if she'd just had a thought, "speaking of Scotland, do you happen to know what architect you'll be hir—"

"Mom," Jo interrupted, warning in her voice.

Thomas looked at Dean and both men swallowed their amusement.

"Mom hired a woman to help Aileen until she's back to her regular self," she explained, changing the subject.

Thomas felt his eyebrows lift in surprise. "And she... agreed?"

"Of course, she did, for heaven's sake. She's obviously an intelligent woman. I only meant it as a homecoming present.

Someone to cook and clean and do the shopping," she explained, flourishing her hand to and fro. "It's not like I bought her a new car," she defended.

"I... thank you, Mary." Jo must have seen his discomfiture because she patted his side before moving to grab water bottles for the table. "My crew sent the latest reports while you were out. If you sit with me, I'll catch you up."

Jo stood in front of the open fridge longer than necessary. Her parents watched her silently. He hated that he had to tell her anything, but to keep her in the dark wouldn't be fair or honest.

In motion again, she grabbed the waters and walked back to the table. "Sure."

He knew she wanted to take down the alleged traffickers as much or more than everyone else did. Russo and Donovan had been making her life the past few months hell, and she knew how sick and twisted they were. She was tense because she was probably concerned that he would mention the video. Her parents knew, but that didn't mean she was comfortable discussing it again so soon.

To put her mind at ease, he began with, "Coll's report included notes from our team and Interpol on what they've found on Viper so far." He touched her leg beneath the table in reassurance. She flashed a brief smile his way as her body visibly loosened.

"We have a list of members for Serpent and Medusa. There isn't a membership list just for Viper. It's only for the lounge and the restaurant. There were no distinguishing marks between regular members and those attached to the sex club. So, two of my team members started looking at Veleno's bank statements and those of all Veleno members.

"Veleno showed no additional funds coming in besides the normal fees. However, they found that close to thirty new members had recently withdrawn anywhere from a million to almost double that. The member's IP addresses show that the money was sent to six different accounts."

"Do they know who the accounts belong to?" Dean asked.

"Charles Donovan, Percy's father," Thomas answered, hating to even speak the name of Jo's attacker where she would hear it. "They weren't under his personal name but several subsidiaries. They are all legitimate businesses under the umbrella of Donovan's PR company. He's obviously using multiple businesses to launder the funds from Veleno.

"Interpol believes they are a front for more than just Veleno. They're working night and day to track the money trails, knowing it will lead them to other, hopefully even larger trafficking rings."

"I looked up the family last night. I remember them from a few summers in the Hamptons. Charles was a belligerent prick when he was drunk. I avoided him," Dean said.

"After I saw the pictures, I remembered his wife, Nadine, from the Club. She... well, I hate to say she was an alcoholic because she could have had a medical condition, but we... didn't run in the same circles," Mary added, sighing.

"Right now, everyone is focusing on trafficking links, but Coll said," he paused, squeezing Jo's thigh in apology, "Percy Donovan has a lot of dark web activity, which they hope to do a deeper dive into soon."

"I still can't believe we worked for them," Jo said, looking at her parents and shaking her head.

"Jo received emails and texts from Russo and one of the GMs early this morning about Veleno opening its doors this coming Saturday. The messages we've intercepted corroborate this. The training will be complete, but barely. Authorities believe they are fast-tracking the opening because they have human 'cargo' coming in," Thomas finished grimly.

"The GM, George, asked me to come in for the opening. He's worried about the kitchens running smoothly, but he's especially nervous about the point-of-sale system. A lot could go wrong, and that ultimately falls on the floor's managers."

"But you aren't going." Dean didn't so much ask as demand.

"I..." She hesitated. "I told George my boyfriend was in town, and we were celebrating a family event, but that excuse won't fly with Aldo. I know the program inside and out, and he won't accept my absence without an argument."

"Celebrating moving in with a married man," Dean mumbled under his breath.

As soon as the words left his mouth, the older man yelped. Mary clearly kicked him under the table. "The divorce is final, you ass," she huffed.

"Not being married to another woman is a step in the right direction, I suppose," Dean deadpanned.

Thomas sighed, refusing to rise to the man's baiting. It was Jo's turn to squeeze his leg in commiseration.

Thomas attempted to get the conversation back on topic. "The local authorities set up cameras around the entire block surrounding Veleno. They want to make sure they catch any hint of goods being moved through the basement stairway in the back alley, and by goods, they mean people. They believe a delivery will be made Friday night."

"Oh God," Jo started at the news. "Those poor people will be held for so long— in cages. Why can't they raid the place then?"

"The money trail from the members won't be enough. They want as many Viper 'special members,'" he air-quoted, "in house when they raid."

"I understand. I hate it, but I do understand. The more of them that can be put behind bars, the more innocent men, women, and children will be saved in the future."

"Yes."

"Jo's been done at Veleno for a while. Do you think we can leave Rome? She's already made her excuses about the opening," Mary added.

"Unfortunately, not until after the raid." He glanced at Jo, hating what he had to say. "Coll's Interpol contact let him know that because they found evidence that Percy Donovan has numerous searches and pictures of Jo on his laptop, they don't want her to officially finish her job at Veleno until it's over."

"Explain, MacGregor," Dean gritted out. Both of his hands were gripping his side of the table. He looked a half a second from breaking the heavy wood top in two.

"They've gone back far enough in Donovan's files that they know he's been keeping track of Jo for years. We don't know how invasive or for how long. Yet," he added grimly. Without permission, he plucked Jo from her chair and put her on his lap, wrapping his arms snuggly around her waist.

"You are safe with me, baby," he whispered in her ear because he'd heard her gasp at the news.

"I know."

Ignoring her parents, he turned her head to face him. "Should I have waited to tell you until we were alone?" He should have asked her permission before blurting out any information about her attacker in front of anyone. He cursed himself silently.

"No, Thomas. Truly. I think we all learned that keeping secrets from those who love you, especially if they pertain to psychopaths, only leads to more grief." She nudged his stomach lightly with her elbow.

She was referring to Percy Donovan and the stalker rapist, Samuel Delton. Thomas was glad every day that Delton was dead and could never threaten Jo or any other woman again. He secretly wished for the same outcome for Donovan, though he would gladly settle for the man going to prison for the rest of his life.

"I let Percy have power over me by staying quiet. I won't make that mistake again. I admit, I'm a little freaked out that he's... I don't know... kept tabs on me."

"I still don't understand why they want her to stay," Dean persisted.

"They believe that because Donovan has followed her, he'd know that she almost never leaves a job until after the opening in case problems arise."

"They're right. Plus, I know this place is going to be shut down, but hopefully someone will buy it and perhaps save all the staff and chefs their jobs. The point-of-sale software is new and has taken a lot of training. Everyone is excited, but nervous as well."

"I had always planned on being there on opening night. Aldo still expects it," she explained, drumming her nails on the tabletop. "I don't think my family excuse will work. I'm concerned it will tip them off that something is wrong if I'm not there. They know I know about Viper. I don't think they believe I know it isn't just a sex club, but surely my absence will raise red flags."

"I don't care, Josephine. That is for the authorities to worry about," Dean insisted.

Thomas was of the same mind. However, Jo was correct in her assumptions. Donovan might think he had Jo right where he wanted her, under his thumb and his to take as he pleased, but Russo didn't seem like the type of man who would take Jo's innocent act at face value. One wrong move could halt the mission.

It didn't matter. "I agree with your dad. Those in charge of the raid will have to contend with any fallout should any arise."

He watched as Jo rose slowly from his lap and moved to face

the table's three occupants. "These are bad people I'd rather avoid, but you three need to understand this, if I'm asked to come in Saturday, I will go. I let what Percy did to me..." She paused to swallow deeply. "It changed me.

"I don't want to let Veleno's staff down when they've been working so hard, but more importantly, I want those monsters caught. If my actions can make even a small difference for the authorities, if one more person or child can be saved by a few more hours of my time, I'm doing it.

"I'm texting George now that my plans were canceled, and that I'll be available. I'll only go in if it's absolutely necessary."

# 25

"Jo!"

Jo smiled as three dark-haired beauties ran at her as soon as she stepped through the heavy wooden door of Triskelion Territory Designs, the Byrne sisters decorating business in the heart of Dublin.

"I missed you guys," Jo said, laughing as three sets of arms caged her in, squeezing her ribs and hopping up and down. "Stop you guys, you're going to make me pee my pants! Thomas and I came straight here from the airport."

She looked behind her at Thomas' stoic face. She couldn't help but laugh harder than she already was. He looked so much like the first time he'd met the sisters— a shrine to resolution.

The other women turned their attention to the hulking man blocking the front door, military bearing engaged.

"Honey Bunny." Raven detached her limbs from Jo's waist and walked toward him for a hug, which he begrudgingly gave. No one could be mean to Raven, the oldest and by a mile, the sweetest Byrne sister.

River was next to embrace him. "It's good to see your cotton-tail back in Ireland." When she lightly patted his jean-clad behind where his 'tail' would have been if he'd had one, he turned three shades of crimson. He didn't react otherwise, which was an impressive feat with that crew.

Rowan was last, giving him a side hug to accommodate her growing baby belly. She looked up at him mischievously. "I've made a list of baby names for you and Jo if you finally decide to get with the baby-making program. Our kids will need a wee MacGregor to round out playdates."

"Tell him the top two boy names on the list, Row," Raven urged.

"Peter" Rowan started, "and Benjamin," River finished, clearly delighted.

At yet another rabbit reference, his eye was starting to twitch, and he had to unclench his jaw enough to growl, "Girls," with a slight nod of his head. He would cut out his own tongue before he acknowledged the jibes.

"The guys are waiting for you, Thomas." Rowan relented and called him by his real name.

"Yes, Thomas," River whined, "please keep them busy for a while so we can have some time with Jo. We thought Bran and Pat were bad about stopping by to interrupt work, but Hugh is the worst."

"Our sister doesn't seem to mind. She's always dragging him off to show him the breakroom for the hundredth time," Raven said as she skipped out of Rowan's hitting range.

"It's the damn hormones," Rowan groused. "I'm always hor—"

Thomas interrupted quickly. "I'm leaving now," he said with a pleading look in Jo's direction.

Taking pity, she moved to his front and gave him a quick peck on the mouth. Quietly, she told him, "Thank you for bringing me to see them." After she announced her intentions to go to Veleno's opening if they needed her, he didn't try to change her mind. Her father received a look from his wife that encouraged his acquiescence.

After that, in front of her wide-eyed parents, Thomas had wrapped his arms around her waist and told her to go pack. They were leaving directly for Dublin to spend a couple of days with friends. He said, "You deserve a bit of relaxation. Some time away from... here."

He'd kindly invited her parents, but they declined. Her dad even offered to call their pilot while the two of them packed.

His response to her thank you peck was to kiss her, and a lot more romantically than she had if the catcalls behind them were any indication.

Once he released his grip on her waist— she didn't recall when his hands had gripped her— he rumbled, "Don't leave here unless you call me first." She nodded her agreement. Satisfied, he left Triskelion without another word to walk the short distance to the O Building, the O'Faolain four-story home next door.

Still feeling hot vibrations zinging her lips, she turned around to face her friends, all of whom were leaning against their desks, knowing smirks firmly in place.

She tried for a small smile, but she could feel the wide, toothy grin break out instead. "I know. I know. He does it for me. What can I say?"

"Damn," River said, fist-pumping, "your Scotsman's got game."

"I would say, 'You have no idea,' but you all are married to O'Faolain men, so... you do know."

"Truth."

"Truth."

"Truth."

Sometimes, it was easy to forget the Byrne sisters weren't triplets. Laughing at their banter, she followed them to the office's comfy couches, where the four of them collapsed in heaps of smiles and chatter.

"I missed you guys. Video calls aren't near as good as the real thing."

"Tell that to River and Patrick. I think they forget they're married and together and don't need to have video sex." Rowan poked her sister's side.

"Did River ever tell you that I was there for her first dabble into virtual sex?" Jo asked, attempting to keep a straight face.

"Don't you dare, bitch," River threatened.

"Oh my God," Raven gasped. "Tell us."

Rowan was laughing and clasping her belly. "Details!" she demanded.

Winking at River, Jo said, "I'm not a listen to someone having sex type of tell-all woman. Sorry, ladies."

"Fine," Rowan conceded, "tell us everything new about you and Thomas then."

Over the next hour and a half, they all traded stories. The camaraderie had always been the best part of being friends with the Byrnes. They also called Aileen. Mirren shouted her two cents from another room, of course, and within twenty minutes, Jo would have sworn Aileen's sad meter was back to zero.

"Thanks for calling me, you guys," Aileen said. "I can't wait to show you all my favorite places around Scotland when you come next month."

Aileen's chemo treatments were doing their thing. She was responding so well that in another few weeks, she would be moving back to Inverness.

From the background, yet again, Mirren yelled, "Did you tell them what Mary did today?"

All of the women flinched, knowing how 'over-the-top' the older set of women in their families could be. The Byrnes' grandmother, Nan, Matilda O'Faolain, and Diana Gaines enjoyed nothing more than butting into the younger generation's lives. Jo's mother was the youngest of the nosey set, but Mary O'Connor held her own in the pushy department. The key was to remember that they meant well.

"Oh, geez, what did Mom do now?"

Aileen's cheeks pinkened as she explained that a stylist showed up at their condo that morning with clothes and wigs for both she and Mirren to have fun trying on.

"And it was fun," Aileen admitted, "but she already paid the woman some money so that Mir and I had to pick a few things. Your mother is a loving, amazing woman, Jo, but I would like to strangle her."

"Singing to the choir, Aileen, singing to the choir," Jo repeated. "She had to come back to Rome for a work thing. She believes my brother and his wife are keeping a pregnancy from her. She's acting out by shopping through you. If I thought I could stop her, I would." She chuckled when Aileen threw her hands up in the air.

"You want to sing in the ultimate choir, Aileen? Feel free to join ours," River chuckled. "We have Matilda O'Faolain, Hugh's mom, our Nan, and Diana Gaines. Against Diana, Mary looks like an innocent lamb."

Aileen snorted in amusement. "Well, Diana is the one who led me to call Jo, so she kind of holds a special place in my heart."

"We'll tell her you said hello. We're eating dinner with Matilda and Diana tonight," Raven offered.

"The guys were happy that Jo and Thomas were in town to join," River grinned. "They think Diana won't pay them any mind with new meat to torture."

"Hugh still grumbles about the time she called him dramatic. Personally, I think it was one of her best setdowns," Rowan admitted.

"Don't expect sympathy from this crowd, Aileen," Jo warned.

"Show us what you and Mirren got," River urged.

Jo could see that Aileen was flagging. Her eyes had soft bruises, and she'd covered her mouth to yawn a few times. Too polite to say no, Jo helped her out.

"Hey, you know, I still have to shower and get dressed for dinner. Why don't you guys give us a fashion show tomorrow? I'm dying to see what sexy wig you chose too."

Aileen looked relieved. Everyone said their goodbyes until it was the four of them again. Dom, Triskelion's manager was out running errands and had insisted they close the shop for the rest of the day. Jo would have felt bad that she was taking them away from their work, but she was selfishly pleased.

"I'm glad you did that, Jo," Raven began. "I could tell she was exhausted, but I hated to say anything."

"Chemotherapy really takes it out of people," River sympathized.

"It's working, though, so that's the only thing that matters. This shitty chapter of her life will soon be written and shelved," Rowan said with resolution while rubbing her belly deep in thought.

They all were quiet for a few moments, each thinking their own thoughts until River asked Jo for an update on Veleno.

She explained the latest developments and that Interpol didn't want her to deviate from her normal routine until they raided the place Saturday night. "If there are any issues with the new POS system, and I have to go in, I'll have trackers on my person. There will also be undercover officers in the dance club and the ground-floor bar.

"Thomas also put an icon on my phone screen that if I press it, he'll have a live audio link."

Rowan sat forward on the couch, curling her legs beside her

before she said, "I hate that you even have to walk back through those doors. I know it sounds safe enough, but these people are sick."

"And there's no way they or any of their associates will ever know you turned them in?" Raven asked.

"No. Thomas' people, especially Coll, Aileen's brother, are monitoring all their communications. So far, it looks like they are none the wiser. Members for Viper go up every day. I hope most of them truly believe it's just a secretive, consensual kink club."

"Yeah, let's hope some of them just want to get off in public, live out their fantasies, or whatever and are not all rapists and pedophiles," River added grimly, her lip curling in disgust.

"How are you really doing, Jo?" Raven asked, placing her hand on Jo's knee.

River and Rowan scooched over on the sectional and grasped Jo's hands.

"We know you haven't told us things," Rowan started. "We understand. You have Thomas, and that's enough for us."

"We are always here." Raven squeezed her knee once more before letting go.

"Always here," River echoed.

Jo could only nod. Her emotions threatened to spill over. In a matter of weeks, her life had felt like she was being slowly asphyxiated. Shallow pants, black dots in her vision, fear... shame. Now... strength filled her veins. She'd forgiven her teenage self and was determined to take back her life. It was like Rowan had said about Aileen's cancer. Jo's shitty chapter had been written eight years ago. It was about time she shelved it.

## 26

"I'm pleased to see that you are more brain than brawn, after all. You had me worried for a while," Diana Gaines said before he and Jo had taken their seats at a fancy restaurant where he was being forced to wear a suit just to enter the hallowed dining establishment. Jo's appreciation of his appearance went a long way to soothing any feathers that Mrs. Gaines was attempting to ruffle.

Ignoring the meddling, old-money snob, he pulled out Jo's seat and pointedly didn't look at the older woman. Jo looked stunning in a simple, dark-red, silky dress that flowed around her delicious body. It was modest and high-necked in the front, but the back was bare, the silken edges moving and gliding against her flawless skin. When he'd placed his hand against her naked back as they walked into the restaurant, he had to bite back a groan.

He leaned close to her ear and whispered, "I would rather eat you than whatever they serve here."

She gave him a commiserating pat on his forearm. "Raincheck," she whispered back, "but no way are we leaving."

"You wanted to eat here the last time we were in town," he

mentioned as she took her seat. When he felt her stiffen, he could have kicked his ass.

The last time they were in Dublin as a couple was when she'd found out he was married. It was not a brilliant move on his part to bring it up. *Jesus.*

"Perhaps I was too hasty in my assessment," Diana grumbled. Her sniff perfectly reflected her derision.

Before the older woman could say anything else to set his teeth to grinding, Jo attempted to brush over the moment. "Chapter House is supposed to have the best canapés, and I'm dying to try the Foie Gras Royale."

Thomas took his seat and leaned in so no one else at the table could hear. Not that he was concerned. The O'Faolains with their wives and babies in tow made enough ruckus to drown out a heavy metal concert.

"It was thoughtless to bring up our last trip here together. Please say I haven't ruined your evening," he pleaded.

She covered the hand that he had lying on her thigh. "You haven't. I promise," she added at his skeptical look. "I just hate remembering the day I left you. How I felt."

He continued to watch her face to make sure she was telling the truth. "I've been in a lot of difficult, even devastating circumstances between my military career and the security firm. None of that came close to when I lost you." He bent to press his lips to hers. No passion, only promise. "I will never give you reason to leave again," he vowed.

She lightly touched his cheek before sitting back in her chair. "I know."

*I know.* He could breathe again. The talk around the table was lively. Jo, he was relieved to see, joined in. Unfortunately, he couldn't put off his dreaded task of… thanking Diana Gaines for butting into his life. He cursed under his breath, already feeling heat fire his cheeks.

Turning to the diminutive woman on his right, dressed in haute couture— he only knew that because Raven had gushed over the old woman's garish outfit— he girded his loins.

"You're looking well, Mrs. Gaines," he began, hoping his compliment would soften her up.

"Call me Diana. Your wife does," she quickly rejoined.

The woman might be old, but she was quick-witted... and obnoxious.

"I would thank you for reaching out to Aileen. Had she not spoken to Jo, she wouldn't now be in one of the best cancer treatment facilities in France."

Thomas was shocked to see her face soften, not so far as to be considered kind but several rungs below ferocious.

"Mary O'Connor told me. I wish she didn't have to go through that. Your daughter is well?"

Thomas couldn't stop a small smile from forming. "She stayed with her mother during the treatment. We both wanted her back in Scotland and in school, but she managed to work around our wishes."

"That child is smart as a whip."

"She is at that," Thomas agreed.

"I had you investigated."

"I'm aware."

"Matilda O'Faolain is my best friend. She loves the Byrne girls, and they love Josephine. When Josephine was upset, it upset the girls, which upset Tilly, and that didn't work for me. Do you understand?"

For all of Diana Gaines' grating ways, he appreciated her zero-bullshit policy. "I do."

"You'll invite me to the wedding." It wasn't a question.

"Of course. Are you still living with Evan Dunn in New Orleans?" Evan was Devlen Dunn's twin brother. Devlen was the second husband of Bébhinn Byrne, the Byrne sisters' grandmother. He was satisfied at the comically horrified look on her face. He almost laughed, but she would have made him suffer tenfold.

"I am most assuredly not living with that annoying blowhard. I have my own home in New Orleans. That I live quite alone in, young man. Tilly has the address." With that, Diana sniffed dramatically and shifted her angry attention to Hugh sitting across the table from her. The O'Faolain patriarch's flinch was satisfying.

The meal was very good, though Thomas preferred simpler fare, and he was still hungry. At his size, it took a lot to fill his belly, and courses that consisted of two to three bites weren't his idea of a grand meal. Jo loved it though, and that was all that mattered.

Matilda O'Faolain was taking Raven and River's sons home with her. A nanny was waiting at her apartment to help with the "heavy lifting" so "I can enjoy all the fun parts of my great-grandsons sleeping over without worrying over the not-so-fun parts."

The large, and only slightly less noisy than on arrival, group left Chapter House and climbed into waiting cars to take the four couples to Murphy's pub... where he planned on ordering a second dinner.

It was only him and Jo in one of the smaller cars. He chose to sit in the backseat with her, not willing to sit in the front with the driver where he couldn't touch her in some way.

Watching her climb in the low-slung sedan was the best part of the night so far. Her thigh-length dress rode high on her legs as she bent forward, revealing sheer, nude panties that made his dick twitch in response.

"Christ, lass," he growled as he settled beside her, placed a hand over her leg, and gripped.

When she gave him a small smile and winked, he realized

she'd given him the show on purpose. As he gave the driver the address, she nonchalantly slid her fingers over his thigh to secure her fingers in the crease of his groin. Jo was a flint strike to his tinder.

"There are about to be consequences," he warned.

"I hope so," Jo laughed. There were always lovely consequences when she teased Thomas. She loved the way his muscles flexed under her hand and wished for the hundredth time after seeing Thomas walk out looking so sharp in his suit that she could crawl onto his lap and feel him harden between her thighs.

She moved her fingers slightly in the crease of his groin and received a growled "Josephine" for her troubles.

"Any more, and we won't be going to Murphy's," he warned.

Sighing, she removed her hand. "Fine, but you can't blame me. You always look mouthwatering, but something about you in that suit... yummm," she hummed the last in his ear. She meant it. The dark-brown blazer and slacks with a barely off-white button-up— bottom line, calling him handsome was too plebian.

In the back of the darkened car, she watched the flashes of streetlights ripple over his face, highlighting that his dark eyes were fixed on her. It was her turn to press her legs together and try not to squirm.

"Have you ever had sex in a public place?" he asked in a shockingly even tone.

Jo felt her cheeks heat and glanced quickly at the driver. Thankfully, the man had music playing and hopefully couldn't hear anything. "Never," she answered, swallowing around her suddenly dry tongue. *Was he suggesting...*

"When I was guarding you, I thoroughly scouted the interior of Murphy's before you went one night with the Byrnes," he continued conversationally. "There is a small supply room in the back, separate from the kitchen. It has a lock on the door," he added in the same steady voice. "I have the key in my pocket."

She was utterly trapped in his predatory gaze. Did she want to be his prey?

*She wanted.*

"Have *you* ever had sex in a public place?"

"No. Tonight will be my first time."

"Someone is confident," she purred softly, sliding closer to his side.

"Should I not be?"

The driver turned the radio down and announced they had reached their destination. She saw their friends already standing outside the bright lights of the Murphy's Pub neon sign. The light was enough to see Thomas discreetly adjust himself through his pants before reaching for the door handle.

"You should be. Confident, that is," Jo told him in a normal voice as he helped her from the car.

THOMAS HAD to replay his conversation with Diana Gaines earlier in the evening to help slow the blood flow rushing through his nether bits, hoping he wouldn't have to join their group with a massive tent in his pants. Josephine may have started the teasing, but he admittedly escalated it. He also planned on finishing it.

As they joined the group and walked into the busy pub, live music and laughter surrounded them. Thomas was fond of small Scottish pubs himself where old timers sipped whisky and gossiped about their neighbors or complained about the country's current political woes, but he could admit that Murphy's was always a good time.

As they maneuvered the crowd and headed to a reserved table close to the stage, Thomas tapped Bran's shoulder to get his attention. "Jo needs the ladies' room. We'll find you." Bran nodded and said he'd get their drinks started.

Jo hadn't heard what he said as she was walking slightly back and to the side of him, not to mention the band was in the middle of a ruckus drum set. She looked at him in question when he turned to face her, taking her hand and leading her back the way they'd come.

She raised her voice to be heard and asked, "Where are we going?"

He only looked at her and raised his brows. The perfect O her lips formed when she realized his intentions and their destination was comical. He didn't laugh at her stunned expression and red cheeks because his whole focus needed to stay on not getting hard as they made their way back to the storage room.

It was quieter and darker in the back hall. He dug the pub's master key from his pocket, the one Cormac Murphy had given him when his men needed to clear all the rooms before Jo, the Byrne sisters, and the O'Faolains were allowed to enjoy an evening out while their stalker was still at large.

"Mr. MacGregor," Jo singsonged, "how long have you been planning this?"

"Since you were packing your bags in Rome," he admitted. Unlocked, the door swung open easily. The light switch was to the left of the doorframe, and he flicked it on. A soft glow from the swinging lights above illuminated the tidy rows of supplies. He could hear his ragged breathing in the quiet room once he shut and locked the door. Jo was panting beside him, whether from nerves or desire. He couldn't guess.

For himself, it was all desire. He'd spent the plane ride today dreaming of taking her here. The clandestine nature of having sex while hundreds of strangers wandered outside the room was surprisingly exhilarating.

"We haven't much time, lassie," he rasped, backing her against the door. Her long legs and high heels put her mouth closer to his own, and he groaned as he licked across her lower lip. "Take your panties off. The see-through ones you were teasing me with in the cab," he clarified.

"Could you really see through them?" she asked before taking his mouth in a desperate kiss.

"You know I could." Stroking his hand up her leg and past the hem of her dress, he wondered, "How ready are you for me, Jo? Are your panties wet?" He hissed between his teeth as his fingers brushed the damp silk covering her center.

"Christ," he muttered as she moaned, "God."

"Take them off. Now." She obeyed. Her eyes trained on him as he shucked off his jacket and shirt, tossing them over one of the shelving units holding paper supplies.

She was just stepping her last heel from her panties when he unbuckled his belt, sliding the leather through the loops and tossing it near his jacket. His zipper was next, not an easy pull with his erection pressing against the teeth.

Jo's breathing was coming in faster and faster pants as one last snick of the zipper sounded. He let the waist sag at his hips, pulling his soft boxer briefs down so his aching flesh was freed.

"I love your body," she admitted, her tongue darting out to dampen her lips as she watched him slowly stroke his length.

"I know you do, baby. Now come here and let me show you how much I love yours. Slip your dress off first. I want to be able to see everything when I slide inside you."

It was his turn to be riveted as she easily grabbed the hem of the loose dress and pulled it over her head, revealing her naked breasts and puckered nipples. She tossed her dress behind him as she walked into his arms.

He wrapped both arms around her back and lifted her body until her legs wrapped around his middle. Her heels dug into his back, the prick of pain ratcheting up his desire.

He took one of her breasts in his mouth, tonguing the nipple until she was moaning and writhing in his arms. By the time his mouth covered hers, she was in a frenzy. He let her body slide down until he was fully seated in her heat.

And then it was like a bomb had gone off. He let go of her mouth so her body could lean back enough for him to have an unobstructed view of his flesh pounding in and out. She was whimpering and moaning, crying and demanding he go harder, which he obeyed. He fisted her ass and used it as leverage to pump harder and faster.

"Oh, God, yes, baby, yes! Don't stop! Close, close, close," she repeated.

He was so turned on at that moment that when her orgasm hit, and her body began convulsing around his, he shouted hoarsely and filled her full of his seed.

Jo slowly fell forward to rest against his chest, her blonde waves mussed and flowing down her back and flushed body. He knew he needed to let her down. He didn't want to, but if their absence was any longer, it would be noticed if it hadn't been already.

"No naps yet, love." He spoke against the crown of her head where it rested against his shoulder.

"I know." She chuckled. "I can't believe we just did that. What would my parents think?" she teased.

"We'll never know because they'll never know," he answered, lightly slapping her ass as he set her on her feet. He couldn't help groaning as his sensitive member pulled free.

He straightened his pants and put on his shirt. Recognizing

the need to hurry now that the frenzy of orgasming was past, Jo donned her dress and was fluffing her hair while presumably scanning the floor for her panties. Grinning, he pulled the pale silk from his pants pocket.

"Looking for these?"

"Yes, you ass." She held her hand out to retrieve them. He had other ideas.

He maneuvered her back to the door once more and kneeled on the floor as she leaned back against the heavy wood. "Hold your dress up. I'll put these on for you." It pleased him when she complied without a word. He helped her place first one foot and then the other in the garment, sliding the nude silk up her legs.

He couldn't stop himself from leaning forward and licking slowly up her wet seam. "I wish I had time to taste us both on your skin— better than any dessert," he said wickedly. She moaned his name and touched the top of his head, where his mouth was still sending hot breaths over her flesh. She definitely liked the idea.

"We better get you to the ladies' room. Your panties won't hold back what's about to start leaking from between your legs."

Before he let himself get lost in her body again, he slid the material home and stood.

She helped him adjust his jacket and, hand in hand, they left the storage room, locking up as they went. A quick restroom stop and then they were, after sixteen minutes and thirty-eight seconds, weaving their way back through the rowdy crowd to find their table.

Six sets of inquisitive eyes met their approach, knowing smirks and outright grins openly displayed.

"Sorry that took so long," Jo tried for nonchalance. She didn't pull it off. "We saw Saoirse and Tim as we were leaving the restrooms."

"Really? Because Cormac said to tell you he'd like his key back when you guys finished touring his storeroom." Rowan laughed at Jo's chagrined grimace at being caught outright in a lie. "You can give it to me," she offered with a grin.

River held up her hand. "Don't give it to her, Thomas. She'll only give it to Hugh, and then we won't see them for the rest of the evening."

Hugh stoically watched the band, not reacting to River's teasing, but his sharp cheekbones were tinted pink under the beard he was beginning to grow back.

"Give Jo a break, guys." Raven smiled sweetly. "Roger Rabbit wanted to show Jo some of his favorite hangouts."

*Ignore. Ignore. Ignore.*

Thomas never thought he'd long to return to Rome.

Where have you been?

Jo's pulse instantly stuttered as she read the text. Percy Donovan. *Damn him.*

> Visiting friends in Ireland. Did Aldo need something while I was gone?

He ignored her question.

George mentioned your boyfriend was in town.

Knowing her phone was monitored was some comfort. At least it made her feel like she wasn't having a private conversation with the sick bastard.

> He was.

She'd been instructed to say Thomas was no longer here. It gave the appearance that she was unconcerned with them knowing she was alone. Her parents had already sent an email to Russo thanking him yet again for his business and dropping that they would be leaving Rome immediately for a vacation.

I didn't think you dated.

Percy had never questioned her personal life like this before. It was odd.

Of course, I date.

You haven't dated in years.

That sent chills up her spine. Being told he had been keeping tabs on her and hearing the evidence were two different animals.

I'm unclear why my personal life is any of your concern.

Jo choked on her sip of tea as his next text came through.

"Oh God, oh God, oh God," she whimpered. He sent a still picture taken from what must have been the... video.

She was reclined against several pillows, her arms loose at her sides, hands resting on their tops, fingers lightly curled up. In peace?

In supplication?

In horror at being immobile?

Her eyes were open, staring vacantly at the ceiling.

She was naked.

Her legs were wrapped loosely around Percy's waist.

He was naked. And aroused.

A keening wail escaped her lips as her knees gave out, and she fell to the floor of her bedroom where she'd been unpacking her bags from Dublin.

Thomas burst through the door, causing it to hit the wall

hard enough to leave a jagged wound in the plaster from the handle.

She was scooped off the floor and crushed against his chest before she registered his intent. The moment she felt his strength surround her, great heaving sobs burst free— water tearing through a dam's moorings.

"No, Josephine. No, my love," Thomas attempted to soothe her. "You are safe. You are safe," he repeated.

"Coll, damn it!" he growled ferociously into his phone that she just now realized he was holding. "Take me out of the call now, and I want that image blurred immediately. For everyone."

"Fogging now. Done. You're dropped."

Coll's unemotional response helped calm Jo's ragged edges. With one hand, Thomas yanked the comforter off the bed, dragging all her clothes with it. He gently laid her against the mattress. He must have picked up her phone because he was holding it to her face.

"Look, Jo. Look," he insisted. "The picture is gone, baby. Gone."

It was. Gone. She wished her memory could be fogged like the picture. Before he could pull the phone away another text from Percy came through. With shaking hands, she took the phone from Thomas' outstretched hand.

> This is why your personal life concerns me, Josie.

And then another came through.

> I was your first.

Another.

> You were always meant to be mine.

"Jesus Christ," Thomas choked. "Stop reading them. Give me the phone back," he pleaded, reaching out to take it from her.

Instead, she placed it on the mattress next to her and sat up, scooching away from the headboard. "Sit behind me, Thomas. Hold me while we figure out what to do. I'm stronger when you hold me." She was pleased that her tears had stopped, and her voice barely vibrated with emotion.

He didn't say a word as he climbed in, his bulk making the request a little rough and tumble, but soon enough, she reclined against his chest, his knees bent to cage her body between them.

"It took me by surprise," she admitted, patting his forearm where it lay over her waist. He needed comfort, too, she knew.

He didn't say anything, but she heard several ragged intakes of breath, his body shaking ever so slightly.

"Don't cry, Thomas. I'll be okay."

"I can goddamned cry over your hurt if I want, lass," he answered thickly, tightening his arms around her.

"I love you."

He bent to lay his forehead against the top of her shoulder, sighing deeply before speaking. "I would die a hundred times over before I would ever hear you cry like that again."

"I know."

"I love you, Josephine."

"I know that too." Each of them took a moment to just breathe and feel each other's beating hearts.

"I hate to say this, but I need to respond, or he'll get suspici—"

"No."

"Yes. He's clearly psychotic as well as a... a rapist. He's unhinged," she insisted. "Call Coll. Tell him that I'm going to respond." Before he could try to shut her down again, she added, "I told you I didn't want him to have any more power over me. I will not allow anything to screw up tomorrow night's raid.

"Even if I go in, I won't be alone. Coll brought in several of your European team members, and they'll be there as guests too.

"Call him," she said again.

Coll answered mid-first ring. "Tommy."

Jo had never heard the stoic man sound anything but staid, but his voice was gruff with emotion, and he called Thomas by his childhood nickname.

Thomas explained that she would be texting back to alleviate any suspicion.

"No."

"Christ, save me from overbearing Scotsmen," Jo groused, trying to relieve the boiling tension.

"I want Viper Club, and all the deviants associated with the place caught, but if something goes wrong, I want to do everything I can to make sure I get enough on Percy Donovan to send him to prison for what he did to me," she stopped to swallow down the tears that threatened to escape again, "and for what he's probably done to many others."

Silence. And then, "I'll let the team know."

We had sex. Once. That doesn't mean we were meant for anything. I'm not breaking up with my boyfriend.

Jo HAD to play it coolly and calmly. Just like she was conducting a business meeting or speaking with clients. Collected.

You will, or I'll ruin him.

Jo shuddered. Just the thought of this crazy person doing

anything to Thomas... Speaking of Thomas, he kissed her shoulder in reassurance.

> At least he didn't have to drug me to get me to sleep with him.

She had to swallow bile at so casually mentioning the assault.

> I'm not sure it would have been as much fun if I hadn't.

He practically admitted to drugging her.

> You'll never know now.

> I took your body in every way a man can take a woman. Without my helpful dosing, your little eighteen-year-old virgin body wouldn't have handled it so well.

"Jo," Thomas warned. The conversation had gone on long enough, and he wanted her to finish it.

> Again. You'll never know. As soon as the opening is over, I'm moving in with my boyfriend, and you'll continue to be a vague memory.

# 28

Veleno's opening was in full swing. Jo was keeping in contact with the floor managers and the bartender from the ground-floor bar, Adder. It was closing in on eleven-thirty, and no emergencies so far.

Medusa had shut their fine dining doors to customers an hour ago, many of which moved to the cigar lounge or to the dance club. Surveillance intelligence tracked numerous patrons making their way to the basement. Viper.

According to reports, every floor was full to capacity, the staff was keeping cool heads, and the point-of-sale system was working as advertised. If no snags called for Jo's attention within the next hour or so, there was a good possibility she wouldn't have to go in.

It was hard not to feel proud of what she and the O'Connor team had accomplished at Veleno. She knew that she only had a few hours to appreciate the accomplishment because, soon enough, the snake-infested establishment would be crushed. Cold-blooded reptiles like Aldo, Percy, and Angelica would shortly be made examples of.

Hopefully, the worst prisons had to offer would be their reward.

For now, Jo was logged in and closely watching the POS sale entries stacking up. Each floor was killing it. Jo smiled when she estimated Veleno's future projected income that Russo would never see.

"What put that smile on your face, lass?"

Thomas walked back to the living room, having gotten up to grab a couple bottles of water. There would be no whisky for either of them tonight. Work now, and hopefully, drinks on the flight to Scotland tomorrow.

She grinned at his handsome face. "Calculating how much money Aldo Russo and his partners will never get to enjoy." She scooted over and patted the cushion beside her. "Sit, and I'll show you the latest sales spreadsheet."

His eyebrows winged up in surprise. "Damn. That's impressive."

"Right? I had a thought," she began when he interrupted.

"You want another orgasm? I just gave you three an hour ago, but I'm not tired," he said straight-faced, beginning to lift her laptop from where it rested on her thighs.

Laughing, she swatted his hands. "Does your momma know what a naughty boy she raised?"

He huffed in answer. "I blamed any misdeeds on Coll. I was her angel," he preened, trying to lift the laptop once again.

Jo elbowed him that time. "Stop!" He kissed her before backing off. It lasted five minutes... but when she felt her laptop start to slip from her legs, she groaned and pushed his chest. "Angel, my ass."

"Back to my thought," she frowned at his unrepentant grin. "Dad is good friends with Grainger Leftstoff. Have you heard of him?" At his negative headshake, she continued, "I would have been surprised if you had. He is very lowkey.

"Grainger is old money from Britain. He has continued to invest and grow his family's fortune, but he rarely spends any of it on himself. He is one hundred percent invested in his philanthropic pursuits, specifically rehabilitation for those rescued from trafficking.

"I considered that he might be interested in acquiring Veleno, rebranding from the snake theme, of course, and using the proceeds to help more people. He could even hire formerly trafficked individuals to work there. I think the fact that Russo tried to use Veleno to hide the very thing Grainger has spent his life to uncover will pique his interest."

"It would be worth asking for sure. Have you considered offering your services to this Leftstoff?"

"In what capacity?"

He shrugged, clearly round tabling. "It seems you enjoyed training the staff in the new sales system. Maybe you could offer to teach classes for the rescued men and women— not just those who were trafficked. People are hurt in lots of ways." He reached over to gently touch her cheek before relaxing against the cushions.

"You could create a class that teaches them the ins and outs of the hospitality industry. Not everyone can go to college. Not everyone needs college to be successful. What if your class gave them the tools they would need to be hirable— but more importantly, gave them the courage and confidence to take back their lives. What if you helped set up these classes worldwide with Leftstoff's backing?"

Jo felt tingles in her gut the more Thomas spoke— seedlings of possibility beginning to grow and take root in her psyche. She grinned at him. "Thomas MacGregor, you are a brilliant man."

"However will you repay me?" His wink ruined his current solemn stare.

"You have to be the horniest man in security." She poked him in the chest.

"Call me a caveman, but I've been picturing you swollen with my baby since the day I met you and your sassy mouth," he shared. "You know how babies are made, right?"

It would be a lie to say she'd never thought of having children someday. She definitely wanted them, or one specifically. Her womb flexed, picturing a mini version of Thomas running around or a long-legged little girl with her gray eyes. Boy or girl, they would most certainly be led into all sorts of trouble by their big sister, Mirren.

She didn't admit any of that, but she did set her laptop aside so she could crawl onto his lap. "I wouldn't say no to the practicing part." As soon as she settled over his legs, he began unbuttoning her blouse.

"I can't stop thinking about the storeroom at Murphy's."

His admission made in that rumbling voice had her hips making an involuntary slow roll against him. "I try not to think about it." His hands froze at her admission. "I had to change my panties twice today because thinking about it makes me so—"

Her ringing phone cut off her admission. "It's George," she flashed the screen to Thomas before answering the general manager's call on speaker.

"George, hello."

Relief was clear in his thickly accented voice. "Josephine, thank goodness. Mr. Russo hoped you might be able to handle a situation that's come up at G&E."

Jo heard a thumping beat in the background and assumed George was in one of the offices on the dance club's floor. She started to shift off Thomas' lap, but he held her firmly in place. She looked at him, but his blank expression gave nothing away. If she had to guess, he knew she'd be going to Veleno, and he didn't want to let her go.

"Of course, but can you explain the situation?" It was almost midnight. The raid was set for one. She was surprised G&E would have any issues, especially this early. The club didn't close until four in the morning. Food service issues would be minor since they only served light apps and drinks, which were easily put out.

The door bouncers were trained to check IDs, weed out people who already appeared drunk or on illicit drugs, and to make sure everyone went through the metal detectors. It wasn't a written rule but most understood that in high-end clubs like G&E, only the best dressed would be allowed in.

"The bouncers were seen on camera, but it was too late to stop them, taking monetary bribes from people wanting to get in. As a consequence, the club is over capacity. Way over. The staff can't keep up, and many of the patrons are starting to act up. The bathroom has already been trashed twice and the bartenders are having glasses thrown at them.

"I've pulled cleaning crew off the other floors and offered staff from Medusa overtime to help, but it isn't enough."

Jo tipped her head back in contemplation of the problem. "Hmm. Well, lucky for you, I'm not leaving for Scotland until morning," she said cheerily, exuding calm to counteract the manager's clear panic. "Okay, George. Call Mia. She's in charge of Donovan's PR promotions. See if she has any of the G&E apple and snake glow bands she made up for one of the promotion parties last month. If she does, have her bring them to you.

"I'll head to the club now, and we can hopefully 'gift' some of the patrons with the special bracelets to attend an exclusive, invitation-only party next month. They have to leave the premises immediately if they accept. If this fails to work, we may have to shut G&E down to avoid injuries and damages."

"Yes. Yes, yes. This is a good plan. Thank you! I'll call Mia now."

Before he hung up, he gave her the location of which second-floor office he would be in. She squeaked in surprise as her phone tumbled from her hand when Thomas stood from the couch abruptly. His body was unyielding stone under her hands.

"I can't let you leave. I can't let you go near the man who hurt you. Please, Josephine. Don't make me let you go."

"Honey," she whispered against his cheek, "I want to be at least a small reason he's caught. I won't go if you can't let me, but... I'm asking you. Let me."

His whole body shuddered, but gradually, he let her body slide slowly down until her feet touched the warm, hardwood floor.

"Never again, Jo. Never again can I let you walk into danger. Promise this is it. Promise me."

His fierce entreaty washed over and through Jo's chest. It was an easy promise to make. "Never again, Thomas."

Once Jo was able to pry Thomas' bear paws from her waist, she grabbed her crossbody, phone, and hair clip, all of which had microchips and tracking apps, before she rushed out the door.

Interpol and Coll barked orders while she trotted down the sidewalk toward Veleno. She was to get in and get out as quickly as possible. *Obviously...* Thomas and Coll were clearly on the same page.

She was not only bugged, tagged, and practically tattooed with trackers, but she would have eyes on her as well. Officers were already in place for the raid and knew she was coming in. It was imperative that no suspicion was raised by her reacting oddly— and oddly would have been to ignore a problem.

Jo excused herself a gazillion times as she dodged partygoers up the two flights of outdoor stairs leading to G&E's "front door." Jo gave the bouncers the evil eye as she flashed her employee badge before walking into... chaos.

George hadn't exaggerated. If anything, he'd been a master of understatement. The dance club was a hot, smokey, over-peopled shitshow. She didn't bother rubber-necking the train-wreck but made a beeline for the back offices.

She didn't waste time knocking but burst through the office door to find George standing behind his desk, wringing his hands, and Percy Donovan grinning like a serial killer, holding a bag of at least two hundred promotional bracelets.

Not ideal.

# 29

Thomas was tracking Jo's every step from the moment she walked out of the apartment. Coll and the team were as well. After the sickening texts Donovan sent to Jo, MacGregor's people were doubly invested in her well-being.

Sweat beaded his brow, thinking of her being anywhere near those sick bastards. Not following her was hell. She'd had to remind him twice more before she left that he could track her and listen to everything, and that the moment she got close to the four-story building that housed Veleno's clubs, she'd have eyes on her too.

Agents surrounded the place, and several more were disguised as guests. He had also hacked into the surveillance cameras around the building and was intently staring at the camera's feed, which should be picking up Jo any minute. His phone began ringing, irritating as they were supposed to remain radio silent. No one wanted to miss who Jo spoke to and who spoke to her.

It was Coll. He answered with a curt, "Talk." The moment Coll's strained voice began speaking, Thomas' stomach dropped.

"I've been considering why Donovan, who's clearly been interested in stalking Josephine from afar for years, suddenly decided to play his hand. What triggered him to ask Russo to hire the O'Connors for this job?"

Fresh sweat bloomed across his back. Coll wouldn't have called with speculation alone. Not tonight. "And?"

"I left the team and Interpol to study Russo, the partners, and Viper's members while I focused on Donovan and Josephine over the past several years. Percy Donovan corresponded with Samuel Delton for several months before his death."

Thomas felt his body sway at the news. Never would he have put those two together, though he should have considered it. Both were sick fucks. Samuel Delton had been a serial stalker and rapist. Delton had made the O'Faolains' and Byrnes' lives a nightmare and had targeted Jo and her brother because of their close friendship with the O'Faolains.

Delton was dead. He could no longer target Jo, but Percy Donovan was very much alive and very much still a threat.

"Christ. How did you find the messages?"

"One of the FBI on Delton's case gave me access to his dark web account where people subscribed to watch his date rape videos, @SammySoGood — King of Twisted Love Stories. Donovan was a subscriber.

"Delton had pictures of Rowan Byrne and Josephine on the site. He detailed his plans to rape them both together. He had preorders, and again, Donovan was one of them. The day after Delton posted their pictures on his website, a series of DMs between Delton and Donovan began.

"Donovan sent the video to Delton, bragging that he'd gotten to her first. I want nothing more than to see this man pay."

Thomas had known about Delton's dark web account and

his threats against Jo. The FBI took the account down. "How did they miss Donovan's messages? Why wasn't he flagged?"

"He was flagged. There just wasn't enough evidence to go after him yet. They always thought the Donovan family was into some shady shit and have been working to see how deep it went. Now, with his ties to Russo, the money laundering was uncovered, and the rest of their crimes are beginning to domino. Donovan and his family are well and truly caught. They just don't know it yet."

The music playing through Jo's mic just went up several decibels. "She's inside G&E." While Coll had been talking, he'd watched Jo approach Veleno and walk to the side of the building where the dance club's stairway entrance was.

"I've got her location pinged. She's closing in on the offices now," Coll calmly relayed.

Thomas heard a short knock before Jo, presumably, entered the office. *"Good evening, Percy."*

He and Coll swore at the same time. "Don't lose your head, Tommy," Coll cautioned. "Everyone is aware of the situation. The agent just messaged that Donovan had been at Viper up until twenty minutes ago. There is one agent at the bar and another on the dancefloor. She's covered."

Thomas took several deep breaths, but remaining immobile was taking a toll. Even with Coll's reassurances, he felt minutes away from an honest panic attack. He'd never had one, but surely the excruciating heart palpitations beating bruises against his chest wall were sufficient indication.

Since he and Coll were the only ones privy to this conversation, he admitted, "I appreciate your reassurances, Coll, but the woman I love is standing face-to-face with her attacker. Her rapist. She isn't covered. Not by a long fucking shot."

"You're right. What do you need me to do?"

Thomas sighed, knowing their choices were limited. "Damn

it," he growled in frustration. "Keep listening. Jo is smart and will tip us off if she needs any type of saving." Just speaking that made Thomas feel less panicked. Jo was smart. Really smart. She would never take chances with her safety.

"*I'm glad you called, George. It's a definite crush out there.*"

"*I admit, Josephine, that I'm in over my head. Mr. Russo said you would know how to handle it, and he was right.*"

"*I hope the bracelets work. Thank you, Percy, for bringing them yourself. Was Mia tied up?*"

"*Something like that.*"

Thomas could hear the smarmy quality of Donovan's answer. Mia might very well be tied up in the basement. Gritting his teeth, he continued to listen.

"*It was kind of you to make sure the opening ran smoothly. George, let's take these bracelets that Mr. Donovan kindly brought us and go try to get at least a quarter of the G&E patrons to take a hike.*"

It was clear that Jo was keeping her cool and staying cordial but professional with Donovan. Smart.

"*George can hand them out. I'd like a few minutes of your time, Josie.*"

"She has this, Tom," Coll reminded.

"*Hahaha. George can certainly handle it, but with me, it will be twice as fast. I don't know about you, but it's closing in on twelve-thirty, and I want my bed. Let's go, George.*"

"*Fine, my love. Help pass the bracelets out, but you won't be returning to your apartment so soon. Viper is having its soft opening... well, hard opening is probably a better descriptor, and I want you to be my date.*"

"Coll," Thomas growled. His tenuous grasp on his anger was frayed past saving. *My love...*

"She's handling him. Twenty minutes."

"*I was clear with you, Percy. I am not breaking up with my boyfriend. He's waiting for me to call him when I get back. I'm leaving tomorrow for Oklahoma. As intriguing as Viper sounds, I would never go without him by my side. I do appreciate the invitation, Percy, but once again, no."*

*"George, wait outside. Ms. O'Connor will be along shortly."*

"Get out of there, Jo," Thomas spoke to the empty living room.

*"I had no idea you were so persistent."*

Jo was the perfect mix of exasperated and slightly interested.

*"How about this. I get this G&E situation taken care of because we both know Aldo will not accept excuses. Personally, I would have just let the crowd have their way for the night, but I understand he wants to make sure the authorities have no reason to come down on Veleno.*

*"I'll help George. Then... I will call my boyfriend and see if he minds if I join you at Viper. He knows... I have certain tastes. He also knows I'm working. If he doesn't mind, I'll text you, though, I'm sorely underdressed for Viper."*

Thomas swore again and again, praying the sick fuck believed Jo's line of BS.

*"Go help pass out the bracelets. Call your boyfriend or not. It matters little to me. Meet me in thirty minutes, or I'll make sure your video is queued next for Viper's VIPs."*

Thomas heard the sound of a door opening and then, *"Did you know Samuel Delton and I were great friends? Hurry, and I'll tell you all about how we met."*

Thomas heard Jo's gasp. She must be alone because he heard her barely whispered, "Thomas." He hung up with Coll, who was still on the line, and immediately called her.

"Thomas," she whispered again when she answered.

"I'm here, baby. You've never been alone. Listen to me, Josephine." he said in a commanding tone. "Walk out of the office and go find the two bouncers. Take one with you to hand out the bracelets and have him escort the guest out the door. Tell the other bouncer to clear the stairs of any remaining hopefuls trying to get in.

"Help George, walk out those doors, and come straight to me. I will meet you. The raid happens in less than half an hour. You're done, baby."

"Okay."

## 30

Jo and Thomas were packing for Scotland the following morning while listening to Coll give them the details of last night's raid. Armed Interpol agents broke through the back-alley entrance and swarmed Viper.

He said there were a few men who tried to escape but local Roman authorities had all the exits covered and caught them up quickly.

"Once it was confirmed it wasn't simply a kink club and that people were being held against their will, the place was locked down tight, and arrests were made. They're still processing them now. Unfortunately, most of the men and women at Viper are extremely wealthy and immediately called their solicitors.

"It's a shit show, but Interpol expected it and was prepared. Russo was arrested first as the owner of the establishment. Even then," he sighed, sounding tired, "there's no telling if he'll ever see the inside of a prison. People like the Russos have fail-safes in place. People set up to take the fall, whether knowingly or unknowingly.

"The good news, Russo's been on the outs with several of his family members. They're all rotten like Aldo, but Interpol has learned that the family believes Aldo takes too many risks. It's hoped that they will hang him out to dry for this latest debacle."

"What of the people who were rescued?" She immediately pictured the stack of cages in the back room, nausea curled in her belly.

"Masks are required to enter. Hiding the patrons' identities, yet not really. It's all a game to them, I guess. When the agents got there, a teenage boy was chained to the stage and in the middle of being auctioned off. The sick fucks bidding on him will have a tough time weaseling out of the charges.

"There were open orgies on several of the raised couches surrounding the stage. My contact said the orgy goers admitted to enjoying performing for an audience but were unaware of the auction. The bidders could get off on the writhing couples while they bid on the poor naked boy in the center of it all." Coll slammed his fist into something in anger. "I hope he was drugged enough that the whole evening is a haze for him, but Thomas, you and I both know those people would want him sober and frightened."

"It's what we've found before," he agreed, pinching the bridge of his nose, probably trying to stave off a headache.

"A few women and one man were already being used in the rooms as well. They were taken care of immediately and sent to a hospital.

"The main attraction..." and here, Coll stopped speaking for a moment. "The main attraction was twin girls between four and five years old. They were being led around by collars to work the crowd up in a frenzy to bid on them.

"They appeared to be unharmed. Christ," he swore. "I hate this type of shit."

"We all do, brother," Thomas spoke softly. "You are one of the reasons so many of them were saved tonight. I'm very impressed with you and your team."

Thomas had admitted to Jo early this morning that he was hopeful this case had helped Coll recognize that he was still able to do his job. He lost a leg, not his ability to take down criminals. Thomas admitted he didn't have the stomach for that kind of work. He'd always preferred the research and hacking side of things. And guarding clients. She'd smiled at that. Thomas had been a very dedicated guard. Grumpy but dedicated.

Coll went on as if Thomas hadn't spoken. "There were five women and two more men still in the cages and a handful of children from toddler age to ten or eleven. All of them had been drugged to keep them compliant."

"Will even a quarter of those sick fucks see the inside of a prison?" Thomas asked in disgusted defeat.

"One is better than none," Jo reminded him gently.

"Our team will hand over all our research that we've compiled in case Interpol hasn't found everything that we did. Several club members won't be able to buy their way out of this.

"There are just as many members that probably believed they were truly signing up for a high-end kink experience, but once they walked through Viper's doors, there was no denying that it wasn't a simple sex club. They chose to stay, making them complicit."

She waited for Coll to mention Percy. He didn't, and she didn't want to ask but needed to know— needed the closure. "Percy Donovan?" She felt more than heard Thomas' rumble of anger at hearing the name.

"I haven't heard. I'm sure he's one of many waiting to be processed. His father was arrested, and the family businesses have all been seized. That family has no hope of staying out of prison. They were in way too deep and had their fingers in too many shady dealings. Our people are invested in your safety. You know this. They are monitoring the situation closely. The minute Donovan is booked, they'll know, and I'll call."

Jo felt warmth bloom in her cheeks. Coll's team had read Percy's filthy texts, saw the picture, and heard their conversations. She inhaled deeply before exhaling her embarrassment. She had nothing to be ashamed of. Coll's team had taken her under their wings, showing nothing but quiet understanding and support during video meetings.

"Thank you, Coll. I'd appreciate that." Jo let him know, though she wouldn't feel completely safe until she knew.

Finding out that Percy and Samuel Delton had messaged each other about her before Delton's death had sent tendrils of unease sliding under her skin. Like seeks out like, so she shouldn't have been so surprised that two men who thrived on assaulting women would find one another. It was the unanswered questions that plagued her the most. Samuel Delton's motives had been clear— hurt the O'Faolains by hurting their loved ones. Percy's motivation for eight years of stalking was far less straightforward.

At least one of them was no longer a threat, but Percy... she'd tried to be brave in the face of his disgusting words, but they had gotten to her.

It might be her Oklahoma soul, but she didn't think men like them were capable of redemption or deserving. When something was rotten to the core, it should be thrown into the garbage. The diseased men and women at Viper getting off on other people's suffering and degradation deserved to be dumped in with the rest of the sewage.

"I appreciate the update," Thomas told Coll.

"Of course," he replied in a growly tone similar to Thomas'.

"Aileen and Mirren will be moving home next month if all continues to go well with your sister's treatments. Jo, Cat, and Mirren want to plan a party for her soon after. Will you be able to come home for it?"

Thomas' invitation would have appeared casual to someone

who wasn't aware of how much he wanted his best friend to say yes.

"I don—"

Thomas cut off Coll's brushoff before it could fully be formed. "I... could use your support. Mirren asked me to reach out to her birth father, Charles."

"The hell she did! Did you tell her no? Jesus, Tommy. What could you be thinking, man? She's been your daughter for these past sixteen years."

Clearly, Coll wasn't a fan of the man who'd impregnated his sister in college.

"She will always be mine," Thomas shot back. "You know Mir once she's made up her mind. She thinks your sister has been pining for the piece of—" Thomas cut off the slur in favor of, "... for the man she loved all those years ago and wants them to meet. I think... well, I think she's also curious to see where the other half of her genes come from. I won't stand in the way, but I think we should talk to your sister together."

Ninety seconds later, after silence punctuated by cursing and heavy breathing, Coll finally agreed. "I'll come." He hung up without another word.

Jo laid her head against Thomas' bicep. "He's coming home, babe. That's something, at least. Mirren will be ecstatic. I think Aileen will appreciate it the most. She told me once that since Coll's accident, he's pulled away from her. You are definitely not the only one who misses the surly SOB," she lightly teased.

He chuckled like she hoped he would. "I know one person that hasn't been mourning his absence. My wee sister, Cat. She'd sooner scratch his eyes out than give him the time of day."

"Really?" In the few times Jo had spoken to Thomas' younger sister, she'd never mentioned that they didn't get along.

"She's never forgiven him for ruining her senior prom. I never thought it was as big of a deal as Cat made it."

"What did he do?" She was thinking to herself... *Fear a teenager wronged.* Thomas' cheeks pinkening was a dead give-away that Coll deserved all of Catriona's ire.

"He followed her. In Coll's defense, her date was shifty-eyed."

Thomas started packing again, ignoring her open-jawed horror. "He followed an eighteen-year-old, on her date... for prom?"

"Like I said... shifty-eyed. Coll had the right of it. He never spoke to them, just... you know, ate dinner at the same place and... well, okay," he hesitated with the last part, which meant it was even worse, "... he chaperoned the dance."

"Thomas MacGregor! If he tries to pull that bullshit at Mirren's prom, I'll cut his nuts off! Good Lord, no wonder she isn't a fan."

"She's twenty-two, a college graduate, and a successful horticulturist, surely she can get over a bit of overprotectiveness," he defended.

"Mmmhmm... don't hold your breath, Honey Bunny."

THOMAS WOKE to his cell ringing. Instantly wide awake, he was sitting on the side of the bed and looking at the screen within a second. It was one in the morning. *Coll.* Jo moved behind him.

He answered. "Talk."

"Put me on speaker."

Thomas tensed. This was about Donovan, then. "You're on." Jo sat next to him and placed her delicate hand on his thigh. Its slight tremor betrayed her nerves.

"Donovan didn't go back to Viper after he left Josephine. Carly tracked his movements using Veleno's cameras. He left G&E and made his way to the front ground-floor entrance elevator. We can clearly see the doors open and him hesitating. He didn't take the lift. Instead, he retraced his steps to G&E's side entrance.

"It's possible Donovan decided to wait on Josephine. Video footage shows him looking at his phone right before he was about to climb the stairs. Whatever he read had him running. Carly hacked into the city's street cameras. He ran one block past Veleno to a parking garage where he had a car. She lost him once he drove into an area without camera feeds."

"Christ," Thomas bit out. He switched the phone to his other hand and wrapped his free arm around Josephine. "He was tipped off?"

"He had to have been because when I say he was full-out running, it's not an exaggeration. It could have been a server with misplaced loyalty to the prick. We may never know. Go home as planned, Tommy." Coll's voice held regret. "The bastard doesn't know you're Jo's boyfriend or that she planned on flying to Scotland. The team's priority is tracking him down. It will stay our priority until he's behind bars."

"Fine then." Thomas ended the call and tipped Jo's face up to meet his. "They'll find him. You are strong. So am I."

Jo nodded stiffly, but she did soften enough to return his firm but chaste kiss. "I'm moving forward, Thomas. With you. With our life. That man doesn't get any more of my time."

# 31

"**D**one." Jo was satisfied with the email she'd composed during the flight to Inverness and just sent to Grainger Leftstoff. When she'd spoken to her dad on the way to the airport this morning, he agreed that his buddy would probably be interested, certainly intrigued.

"Even if he isn't interested in Veleno, I believe he will want to speak to you about your hospitality training program proposal."

She smiled at the man on her left. Thomas' unsmiling countenance couldn't hide the fact that what he said was meant to be a compliment. She poked his side, teasing, "You're proud of me."

She expected him to say something grumpy back. Thomas MacGregor could only say so many heartfelt, sweet nothings in a row, but he surprised her.

Gently taking her hand and placing it on his leg, he said, "Very proud."

Somehow, she didn't believe he was only referring to her possibly stepping into a new career. She cleared her throat to corral the tears trying to slip free and changed the subject. "Mom said that you spoke to Dad yesterday."

"He asked me to take the house alarm off and for the door code."

This was said with zero inflection. "Why in the hell would he ask for that? You didn't give it to him, did you?" Gasping, she begged, "Tell me you aren't letting them stay at your house."

"Our house."

Jo sighed. He wouldn't tell her anything else until she agreed. "Our house."

He narrowed his eyes at her huff of exasperation. "You did promise," he stubbornly added.

"I did, and I am, but my parents better not be moving in too." The plane was taxiing toward the terminal, but she didn't bother looking out the window. Her sights were glued to his face. "Thomas, spill your guts."

His mouth quirked in... amusement... resignation? "They are not. Your father rented something in Inverness proper, outlandishly expensive, I'm sure."

It was true. Her parents did nothing on a small scale. "So why did he need your... our," she corrected, "house code?" The slight smirk her question engendered made her nervous.

"Your mother's made a new friend that she wanted to show the house to."

Her mother had never met a stranger. Shaking her head in dread, she asked, "Who?"

"Dougal Donaldson. Remember that woodworker we met in Nairn last year? The one with the lovely personality?"

"No way." Dougal Donaldson was a short, belligerent Scotsman with a penchant for foul language and intoxication. She and River Byrne had visited his workshop, hoping he'd sell them some of his pieces for their clients. The only reason she and River had been invited to view his carved masterpieces was because Thomas had been with them and had been rude right back. Dougal was thenceforth charmed.

"Apparently, Dougal agreed to look at the primary to get inspired to create us the perfect bedroom suite."

"Christ." Taking the Lord's name in vain was all she had left in her vocabulary. Mary O'Connor lived to do whatever she wanted and ask for forgiveness later.

"That isn't the best part," he taunted.

Now she realized his sober manner was only a cover to hide his amusement. *How long had the asshole been holding in his giggles?*

"Your dad found a house to purchase in Inverness with plenty of rooms for friends and family to stay. Oh, and they're putting their home in Tulsa up for sale."

Her head was spinning. No, that wasn't right. Her brain was melting. Dougal Donaldson traipsing around her new bedroom. Her parents buying— not leasing, not renting, but buying— a home in Scotland. Selling their family home in Oklahoma.

"But... why?" she whined. "Is this some sort of... are you joking with me?"

The plane had come to a stop while Jo's life as she knew it was currently in a blender just... blending.

Thomas stood and pulled her up with him. He looked at her then with a serious face, no hidden joviality. "I asked Dean. Your dad said that he and your mother would never take your happiness for granted again. He told me, 'When Josephine tells her mom and me that she's happy, I'm going to be looking at her face and know if it's the truth.' You won't be changing their minds, lass."

"Well... well, okay. That's that, then," Jo finished, flustered because she could hear her father clearly saying that.

"Jo." Thomas gripped her chin and made her look at him. "What happened to you wasn't your fault. It wasn't your parents' fault either. It's the 'after' that haunts all of you. You still have healing to do, but so do your parents. Let them."

She didn't want to cry, but damn it! She'd been a minute away from calling her mother and haranguing the hell out of her and Dad for trying to stick to her like cockleburs, but... *Let them...*

She nodded her resignation. "Okay."

"That's my brave girl," he praised.

She chuckled. "Not so much brave as resigned. I mean... Dougal Donaldson! Mom is a certified nutter."

"We better get going. Did I mention your parents are at our house now with an architect?"

"MacGregor Castle, here we come," she mumbled under her breath.

BUNCHREW WAS a lovely village only three miles west of Inverness, so Jo's parents were only minutes away from being able to stop by and visit their daughter. *Yay me.*

The MacGregor property ran close to Beauly Firth, and the views were spectacular. She'd always be an Oklahoman, born and raised, but she had no doubts about moving to Scotland.

There were several very good reasons to make the move. The first, the whole country was stunning.

The second, Raven, River, and Rowan Byrne, as well as her college bestie, Saoirse Kennedy, were only a hop, skip, and a jump away in Dublin, Ireland.

The third and most vital, Thomas, lived there.

She couldn't wait to explore the area. She really couldn't wait to spend time with Catriona. From their few phone conversations, Jo could tell they would easily become close. Thomas' grandmother had been asking him every time they spoke to bring her for a visit. There were so many experiences to look forward to.

Unfortunately, her wish list took a back burner to her parents... overparenting. This was her first time to see Thomas' home, anything of Thomas' private life really, but after stepping two feet into the lovely two-story cottage, she was greeted by her parents, a kitchen center island full of— Christ— a catered buffet, and a man in a navy suit and tie presenting, what she assumed, were sketches of the cottage 2.0.

Thomas only grunted at the chaos, choosing to tuck into the buffet. Mom announced, "Thomas, dear, save some for your sister and grandma. They're excited to see the plans. Speaking of, Harvey, this is our daughter Josephine and her... significant other, Thomas MacGregor."

"Mom," Jo said in warning. Helicopter parenting paired with meddling was one thing. Hinting at an engagement was just far past enough for Jo.

"Whoops, sorry. I'm just so excited about... everything really." Her mom cringed, grabbing her husband's hand for support.

Dad just smiled at his wife and shrugged his shoulders at his daughter. Thomas paid none of them any mind. He wanted her to let her parents do this. Sighing, she resigned herself to seeing her new home and meeting Thomas' family for the first time while gushing over architectural renderings and a buffet.

"I'm excited, too, Mom. This was all such a surprise but very thoughtful." Her mom teared up. *Oh God.* Turning to the table of sketches, she held her hand out to the architect to shake. "I can't wait to see your ideas."

"These are only modest sketches done mostly as I walked through the place a couple of days ago. The house is well made. A classic Scottish cottage."

Thomas grunted at the compliment. "I built it during my

time off when I was in the military. It's simple, but I was always more interested in the view."

He glanced at Jo. Most people would think he was disinterested, but she wasn't most people. He wanted her to like the house. "Mom, Dad, Harvey," she addressed the room, "I want Thomas to give me a tour of the place before I look at the sketches. If we decide to make any changes, it'll be easier if I have the whole picture." Looking at Thomas, she asked, "Willing to play tour guide before your family gets here?" She couldn't help the slight smirk that crossed her face, thinking about her mother inviting his family without asking his permission.

"I am."

Thirty minutes later, they were walking back toward the kitchen, having toured the house and the immediate property.

"I love it, babe. I can't believe you built this all by yourself."

"Friends helped as they could. It wasn't just me," he downplayed.

She held tight to his hand and stopped so he would be forced to stop with her. She wanted to finish telling him her thoughts before joining the peanut gallery waiting for them. He looked at her curiously but remained silent.

"Nothing about this house needs to change. I only care that you and I will be together." She wrapped her arms around his waist and kissed his chin. "You know my mom is extra. I have no qualms about shutting her down," she assured.

He studied her upturned face, gently tucking a blonde strand of hair behind her ear. Swallowing, he admitted, "I know this house isn't grand. I only want you to be happy with... some of it. I'm trying not to be prideful," he admitted with a wince and shrug.

"Oh, Honey Bunny, you're precious," she teased. She slid

her hands around his ribs and over his chest. "If I were you, I'd be prideful. You big stud."

"Josephine," he rolled his eyes and swatted her ass for teasing him. "I know it needs a lot, and I won't be happy if you don't choose one of those sketches and make this a house you see yourself in for the rest of your life." He exhaled a long breath. "I have... well, I know we've never spoken of finances, but I have more than enough to change this house into anything you want or tear the whole thing down and start over.

"You are the one making all the sacrifices, Jo. You aren't just moving one town over to be with me. You're changing countries... continents. Nothing, certainly not this house, is more important than your happiness."

It was her turn to study his sincerity. "Anything I want?" she clarified.

"Anything."

Pulling out of his embrace, she grabbed his hand and tugged him the rest of the way into the kitchen. "Come on, then. I've got this." She grinned.

Thankfully, Grandma Macgregor and Catriona had yet to arrive. Having toured the house and surrounding property, she had a clear vision of what she'd be changing. This wouldn't take long.

"Are you ready to look at the sketches?" her mom asked as they rejoined the 'party.'

"Actually, no. Harvey, I appreciate you brought a few offerings for me to look at, but they won't be necessary." At his bewildered look, Jo moved on without a hitch. "I want you to design a huge, gorgeous, wraparound porch around the whole house. I've always loved them.

"I want those fancy mechanical blinds that can be raised and lowered depending on the season and weather. Think forever luxe, Harvey. Make the porch design a place where families want to gather. A design that begs for brass fixtures and commercial grade ceiling fans. The design needs to seamlessly match the lines of the existing house.

"I want an attached outdoor kitchen facing the Firth and the best baby swing money can buy hung from that gorgeous oak tree for the mini-MacGregor I plan on having one of these years. Thomas will need to design the outdoor kitchen, but Harvey, you'll need to design the covered breezeway that will attach the house to the outdoor area." She glanced in her mother's direction, her face a picture of rapture. Good thing, as she wouldn't like the rest.

"As for the main house, there's only one thing. The kitchen needs a floor-to-ceiling makeover. Harvey, you might consider pushing that west wall out a smidge while you're designing the porch. I'm sure I'll eventually learn how to cook, and if not, I still want it to look pretty." She winked at Thomas, whose mouth twitched.

"Oh, and we're also on a time crunch. So, as soon as you can get the plans to us, the better."

"But... that's it?" her mom stuttered.

"That's it. The house is perfect. It's cozy. The primary has a stunning view, there's a room for Mirren when she stays over, a lovely, paneled den for Thomas and me to make into our home office, which Dad can help me design, and an extra bedroom for... baby M. Oh!" Jo remembered excitedly. "I hope Thomas' sister will design the flower beds around the porch, but yes, that's it." She hip-bumped Thomas, who had yet to speak. *Shocker.* "I've dreamed of a home that was warm and made for a family. That's what this house is."

Her mom was glassy eyed at the mention of a grandchild. Dad pulled his wife against his side and softly kissed her cheek, whispering something in her ear that made her smile as she returned a kiss to his cheek.

Mom quickly switched gears. "I have so many ideas for the kitchen. Viking floor-to-ceiling. The Tuscany line is a must. Oh, Jo, I can't wait. Do you remember the color you fell in love with when the Byrne girls were decorating their apartments?"

"Antique bronze," Jo said dreamily.

"Antique bronze," Mom repeated with a squeal. Her mom was so excited. It kind of made her excited too.

Turning to Thomas, she asked, "Well?"

A slow smile tipped his normally stern lips. "Perfect."

That settled, Jo was about to dig into the buffet when her mother decided to open her mouth and over-parent again.

"By the way, I spoke with Aileen and Mirren this morning. They'll be moving in with me and Dean." Patting her father's arm, she gushed, "Your dad bought me the most precious house in Inverness with tons of rooms. Anyway, I'll only have four weeks to get everything ready, so I'm feeling a bit overwhelmed. I'm sure I'll manage." Jo barely contained a snort. Her mother had never been overwhelmed in her life. "Aileen will need to be closer to the city for all her after cancer care, so it's perfect."

"After cancer care?" Thomas was blinking at her mom in wonder.

"You know, a personal trainer to help regain her strength, a dietician, and, of course, spa days for skin, nail, and hair growth stimulation. Things like that." She waved a hand in front of her as if her calling Thomas' ex-wife and inserting herself was completely natural.

"Mirren will be finishing online school early, in two months, actually, so really, there's no reason for her to rush back home. Prom isn't until June, and they'll be back in their home by then."

Thomas leaned his hip against the refrigerator, the only indication that her mother had knocked him for a loop. Talking clients into believing that her ideas were the best ideas was her mother's superpower. She was clearly attempting the same technique on Thomas.

"Plus, you and Jo will be living at Aileen's during the remodel. Really, there was no other choice but for them to live with me."

Grandma MacGregor and Catriona had arrived during her mom's word vomiting sesh. Jo noted their shoulders were jiggling in quiet mirth. They probably loved watching her mother take charge of Thomas' life.

Wisely, he only nodded, murmured a thank you for thinking of them, and went to kiss his sister on the head and give his grandmother a hug. Introductions were made, and Jo got her own hugs. Harvey, or Harv as her mother now called him, like he was family, left with handshakes and smiles, promising to call in a few days, and then finally, it was time to begin enjoying her new home. With family.

An hour later, Jo was sitting on Thomas' lap, listening to hilarious stories of him and Coll as children from his sister and grandma. It warmed her to see her parents enjoying themselves. She could tell Thomas was thrilled, though you'd never know it by looking at him.

"I love you, HB," she whispered in his ear.

"I love you too," he whispered back. "I'm blown away by your ideas for the house. They're brilliant."

"Wait until you hear my brilliant ideas on how you can thank me tonight. When we're in bed. Naked."

# 32

THREE WEEKS AFTER THE VIPER RAID...

P ercy Donovan had seen better days. He didn't believe he'd been this tired and rumpled since his sophomore year in college when his fraternity had hosted a three-day kegger.

*At least he didn't have a near-death hangover this time.*

*He'd been slouching around Inverness for a couple of weeks now— since that damn raid at Viper. He hadn't seen that coming. He knew Aldo hadn't, or the man wouldn't currently be counting jail cell bars. Gossip underground was that Aldo's family had turned their backs on him in the hopes of distancing themselves from the scandal.*

*The Russo family was entrenched in arms dealing, trafficking, and drugs. They would consider the Viper raid negligence on Aldo's part and do everything to protect the family. Aldo was a weak link they would no longer shield. The perfect fall guy. He was sure Aldo's assets were frozen, meaning he couldn't afford the type of defense attorney the Russos typically used to get them out of trouble. Aldo wasn't leaving his current shithole accommodations anytime soon. If ever.*

*Percy's father wouldn't have thrown him away like that, not on purpose. Percy had spoken to one of his New York sources after the FBI raided Donovan's many laundering fronts. He said it was well-planned and thorough. The loss of income was a blow.*

*His father had begun laundering for various crime families years ago, and it had been lucrative. Their profits had skyrocketed once his father had brought him into the family business.*

*He wondered if his link to Aldo Russo had sparked the investigation into his family or if this had been destined before he'd ever stepped foot in Rome.*

*According to one of their employees who had fled before the FBI raid, Dad was in jail, their assets were frozen, and family and friends were being interrogated. Donovan Public Relations was done.*

*Thank God Dad had made arrangements years ago for emergency contingencies, which was why he had a burner phone, cash, fake IDs, passports, and a plane and pilot waiting to take him to a sandy beach somewhere.*

*When he'd left Josie at G&E, he'd fully intended to return to Viper, but before he could take the elevator down to the club, he'd stopped. Just stopped. He couldn't bring himself to let her out of his sight. He'd had a woman waiting on him below, chained against a wall, naked and spread wide for his pleasure, but to his frustration, he'd taken little pleasure in the woman's tears.*

*Without Josie watching him work, he'd lost his hard-on partway through cutting her inner thighs. It was one of his favorite first cuts to make. An obsession born from seeing blood smeared between Josie's thighs all those years ago. There was nothing more beautiful than that. Nothing more beautiful than her.*

*While they'd been waiting for Josie to come in that night, George mentioned her plans to fly to Inverness the following morning, which was why he found himself there. Her dedication in coming in that late in the evening to fix an issue for Veleno* made him positive that she'd had nothing to do with the raid. He'd taken pride in her work ethic over the years.

Sure, she'd played hard to get, throwing her so-called boyfriend repeatedly in his face, but he knew they'd end up together.

Percy tried to move past his want of her over the years, only making a lowkey effort to follow her personal life and career, but something had clicked for him that night. She was beautiful and pure and had eyes only for him. She'd been impossible to forget.

When she'd left the wedding festivities early, he'd been crushed. He had spent hours daydreaming about meeting her for the first time after their night. Would she be shy? Would she want him again? He desperately wanted to see how his marks looked on her pale skin. No matter where he traveled in the world or what woman he fucked, it was always her face... her gray eyes watching him.

It had been enough for a while to know that she was simply out there. Eventually, he needed more than that. Private detectives filled in the blanks. Through them, he knew she rarely dated and never seriously. Percy knew he was the reason. No one could ever make her feel the way he had.

He liked watching her life, wondering how often she dreamed of him. He'd been willing to keep his distance, enjoying the cat-and-mouse relationship. That ended when one of the dark web channels he subscribed to posted Josie's picture.

He'd been a frequent visitor to @SammySoGood's website for several years. Sammy loved his 'dates' extremely willing as well. Drugs were amazing— they created a mood. Imagine Percy's surprise when Josie's picture had shown up on Sammy's site. Sammy planned on kidnapping her and filming their date together. What were the odds? Clearly, a higher power wanted to bring him and Josie back together. He decided that day that he'd *let her go her own way long enough. It was past time their two paths converged.*

*She'd been so beautiful that night so many years ago. So young. So willing. He had a picture album of all the things they'd done to each other. He never went anywhere without it. His father had been on him to marry for the past couple of years. Josie was the only woman he would tie himself to.*

*She would never want her family to see their video, which meant it made the perfect blackmail. Threatening to leak the video would ensure he had a wife who would stay in line. He had special tastes when it came to sex, and he wanted desperately to teach her to like it too. When Aldo told him her fetish was voyeurism, Percy became almost manic to lock down their relationship.*

*The thought of her watching him do his work on women, that she'd get off on it, almost had him coming in his pants.*

*The raid had changed the trajectory of his life, but not who he'd be spending it with. After walking the streets of Inverness, he finally spotted her. Josie. She was shopping with her mother. She was wearing an oversized sweater, jeans, and stylish tennis shoes. She looked effortlessly chic and beautiful. She always did.*

*Josie was smiling and laughing at something her mother must have said. He was entranced at how lovely and carefree she seemed, wishing he was standing next to her, his arm around her waist, having her smile at him that way instead of watching from across the narrow street.*

*He pocketed his phone and set out to follow his future wife. He needed to find out where she was staying. He needed to find a way to convince her to go away with him.*

*Of course, if there was one constant in Percy's character, it was that he didn't need consent to get what he wanted.*

# 33

Jo missed Thomas terribly even though he'd only been gone for two days and would be home that night. He'd gone to France to help Aileen and Mirren pack and move home. More specifically, to move in with Jo's mother. She snorted to herself at the absurdity of it all.

The fact that she'd spent months wrecked over Thomas being a secretly married man to loving his wife like a sister was a testament to how crazy her life was.

Jo, her mom, and Thomas' sister, Cat, were planning a welcome home party for Aileen. She was meeting her mom in town to pick up more supplies. Catriona picked up the alcohol yesterday. The doctor had given Aileen the green light on partaking in a moderate amount of spirits, and she loved champagne, so champagne it was!

It was supposed to have been a smallish affair, but Raven, River, and Rowan wanted to come. When they were on their weekly video chat with Jo, the girls said they would make it a quick day trip without the guys. She snorted in amusement at how that went over.

"You aren't going without me, Rowan," Hugh O'Faolain, the most overprotective husband in the universe, decreed.

Jo heard Rowan's exasperation when she snapped back. "I'm not due for another ten weeks. Not next weekend!"

Raven and River were laughing. Hugh didn't say anything else, but he must have been giving his wife the "I'm not changing my mind" thousand-yard glare.

"You are impossible," Rowan relented.

"If Dad gets to go, then I'm coming too," Patrick wheedled.

"See what you've started, Hugh?" River laughed.

"I want to meet Aileen, of course, but Thomas promised he'd take us to Castle Stuart for a round of golf, so I want to come too," Bran reasoned. "We can all take our clubs and get in a game."

"I think Jo was trying to keep things lowkey for this particular get-together, Bran." Raven gently tried to veer her husband away from his current course.

"No way, babe. She doesn't mind. Do you, Jo?"

"She doesn't," Patrick answered for her. "Plus, Grandma will want to come. Diana went home, but her brother, Owen, is visiting, and Gran will want to bring him to meet Aileen and Mirren."

"Christ," Hugh growled. "Why does Owen have to visit Mom? She's going back to Tulsa in a few weeks."

"Stop being an ass, Hugh," Rowan chided. "Your mom likes Owen, and he likes her. He is a wonderful man."

"How wonderful can he really be if he created a son like William?"

Rowan simply said in a breezy voice, "I see you're in one of your impossible moods. You and William are friends."

"A generous classification."

Jo had to put a hand over her mouth to keep in her laughter. No one else bothered, of course. William Stanton and Rowan briefly dated last year, and it was obvious Hugh was still salty over it.

After another twenty minutes of plan making and teasing, Jo signed off with her friends and their husbands. The Dublin crew added ten more people. Two were the babies, Raven and Bran's Daniel, and River and Patrick's Jonathan. She and her mom adjusted the food quantities with the caterer and rolled on. Hospitality was their bread and butter, after all. No sweat.

Her mom was thrilled. She would have loved to have all of them stay at her new house, but she felt Aileen would need a lot less hullabaloo— her mother's word— during her first few days home.

Mom and Matilda O'Faolain had known each other for years because Jo's brother, James, and Matilda's grandsons, Bran and Patrick, were best friends. Mom called Matilda as soon as she found out they were coming and offered to get rooms reserved at a local hotel. She declined the offer with many thanks. Apparently, Owen made them for everyone as soon they heard about the trip.

Jo smiled. Hugh would have to say thank you to his mother's boyfriend.

Coll would stay with them at his sister's house since her and Thomas' house was in full makeover mode, and he didn't get along the best with his parents. Mom offered him a room, but he declined. Thomas said he preferred smaller crowds since the accident.

In darker news, Percy wasn't the only member of Viper that fled the country. For many of the rich, the famous, and politicians, being members of a sex kink club would have been career-ending. A sex kink club that supported trafficking and child abuse... social suicide. There was no coming back from that.

A man matching Percy's description booked a flight to the states and was apprehended at the New York JFK airport upon landing. Turned out, a man had paid him two-thousand dollars plus the tickets to take the flight. Interpol believed Percy used the man as a distraction while he wore a disguise and flew somewhere else. The car Percy had driven the night of the raid was discovered in covered, long-term parking at Rome's Leonardo da Vinci airport.

It could take months to track him down. Donovan assets were frozen, but that didn't mean a contingency plan wasn't in play.

Coll's team was still relentlessly pursuing the Viper members, especially Percy. They traced a few, but never him. Everyone believed she was relatively safe in Inverness, but Thomas insisted that certain safety precautions be implemented. She could never drive a vehicle that didn't have a tracker. She had trackers in her purses, and she even wore a bracelet that was a tracker with an emergency button she could press. She was required to wear it every day. Jo didn't mind. She felt safer, and it gave Thomas some peace.

Jo also got a new number because she hated the thought of her abuser knowing how to get a hold of her.

The day after she and Thomas had landed in Inverness, he set up a Zoom call with an attorney based in New York. A member of MacGregor Security recommended her. She specialized in sexual assault cases. Coll sent the attorney all the files from Samuel Delton including the messages between Percy and Samuel, his website, a photo of the letter Percy had left Jo all those years ago, his current text messages, and... the video taken from his phone.

She hated all of it, but she hated him more.

Jo's knee-jerk reaction had been to let it go. Percy Donovan was destined for prison. Why put herself through the trauma of it all? But that was selfish, and she knew it. There was no way she was the only person he'd hurt in his life. She owed it to them to share her story.

She still didn't want to. Thomas said she was strong enough, and she was, damn it, but that didn't mean she wasn't losing sleep over it.

Her parents knew she was pursuing a lawsuit against him. She didn't want them caught unaware when the news hit, and it would. They both cried, but they supported her decision a hundred percent. Assault didn't just hurt the victim. The family was impacted too.

So, here she was, trying to shake off all the negative bullshit and enjoy party planning with her mother. Except a dark cloud seemed to be following her lately. Whenever she left the house, it felt like she was an ant under a microscope. She never said anything. Clearly, she was oversensitive.

Thomas was loving and supportive, but she wasn't sleeping well. She had a sense of being watched. Every day. Everywhere. Since Thomas had been in Paris, the feeling had increased tenfold.

Her therapist in Inverness, one that Rowan's Dublin therapist had recommended, told Jo not to worry so much about all her feelings, good, bad, or paranoid. She said that in her case, finding out eight years later that she'd been assaulted made Jo's brain react like it had just happened.

Her body didn't care that the video and the still pictures that Percy had sent her, were old news. To her, it happened the moment Thomas told her she'd been assaulted.

It wasn't 'drunk girl gone wild who made a mistake' anymore. The veil had been taken from her eyes, replaced with a flashing, neon light announcing... rape.

Her therapist told her that dealing with old trauma was no different than dealing with new trauma. Jo needed to give herself a break. Allow the mood swings and the random tears, know that she was handling things the way *she* needed to.

If there had been even a minuscule doubt as to Thomas' character, the past few weeks had proven his worth a million times over. Thomas MacGregor was a demon slayer. He was an easy man to lean on when her emotions got the best of her, but she was committed to standing on her own. If she vanquished her own demons, then she would feel more like a partner and less like a woman in need of saving.

With all the positivity in her life, which included antique bronze Viking appliances, Jo was pissed that she felt a shadow stalker trying to ruin her day. She needed to tell Thomas when he got home tonight. Maybe speaking about her fears out loud would take its power over her away.

Once the decision was made, she felt ten times more relaxed. If the tingle between her shoulder blades twitched off and on the rest of the afternoon, she'd resigned herself to ignore it.

## 34

G etting Josie's address had been embarrassingly easy. It was
   obvious she was planning a party after following her and
her mother, Mary, for a few hours. Linen store, tableware, décor,
caterer, and finally a florist.

If he was going to get the information he needed, he would
have to stop following them and risk losing Josie in the crowd.
Sure, if he stayed with the women, he would learn where she was
living, but he needed more than that.

Ten minutes of loitering on the sidewalk after Josie's exit, he
entered the flower shop, walking straight to the front counter.

"Good morning," he told the woman behind the counter, a
bright smile on his face. "My friends must be running late, Mary
and Josephine O'Connor. I'm supposed to escort them to lunch,"
he said with a self-deprecating smile.

"Oh no, you just missed them. If you ring them, I'm sure they
can't have gone too far," the woman said unhelpfully.

The woman was older than him, perhaps in her forties, with
an apron tied tightly around a trim waist. With a critical eye,
Percy noted, with a modicum of interest, that her tits were full to
bursting, and her hips flared nicely.

*She would look lovely tied to a table. Women with a little more meat on their bones made his cuts more satisfying. The jiggling flesh seemed to encourage blood to run faster between their legs.* Shaking his head to disperse the fantasy, Percy got his head back in the game. Getting Josie away from her family was the priority, and he needed information to do that.

"You've got to be kidding me," he hammed it up. "Mary is best friends with my mother. We're from Oklahoma," he explained. "Mom couldn't bear to miss one of Mary's parties, so I accompanied her. If she finds out I was too late to escort them to lunch, she'll tan my hide." The woman was chuckling now. An attorney and an actor had a lot in common.

"You better make me a small bouquet to give Mary at lunch. Maybe flowers will sway her not to tattle on me." He grimaced as if he was concerned about any such thing.

"Oh yes!" She clasped her hands to her chest. "Thoughtful gifts are never wasted. Do you have something in mind?"

"No, no. You choose. Pretty, but small enough to carry until she gets home. I'm sure you have an idea of Mary's tastes. The party sounds like it's shaping up to be a beautiful one," he said offhandedly as he began browsing around the shelves of vases and knickknacks.

"Yes, and Saturday looks like it's going to be the warmest we've seen in months," she provided helpfully, busy putting some white and yellow flowers together with green wire.

"I suppose I better offer to pick the flowers up. I'm sure they'll be swamped with last-minute hostess duties."

"It's only a small dinner party, so Mary just ordered one large table centerpiece. Her daughter offered to pick it up Friday morning before their guests begin to arrive. I'm sure she would appreciate you taking over the errand." And with that last bit of information he needed, the florist handed him a fistful of flowers, beamed and said, "There. Simple and lovely. Mary mentioned loving the Seaside Pansies I had on display."

"Very pretty. Thank you." As he paid, he asked, "What time is Josephine picking up the arrangement? I'll tell her at lunch that I spoke with you and will do it."

"Ten o'clock."

"Would you mind if I picked it up at nine-thirty? I promised Mom I'd take her to her hair appointment, which is at ten, so I can make one trip and get both things done."

"Of course, Mr..."

"Sorry! My manners really have deserted me today. Ralph Johnson." He used his uncle's name. He was dead, so he wouldn't mind. His father had him killed several years ago when he didn't agree with how the Donovan's made money. "Thanks again for your help. See you Friday morning," he threw over his shoulder as he left the shop.

He took his first deep breath since escaping Rome. He walked slowly down the sidewalk, quickly turning into an alley where there would be no chance of running into Josie. He tossed the bouquet of flowers in a dumpster as he walked confidently between buildings.

He allowed a grin to split his face. "See you Friday, Josie."

## 35

Thomas was not enjoying sleeping in his ex-wife's house, in his ex-wife's bed, while trying to get Josephine naked. His relationship with Aileen might have been platonic these past sixteen years, but it went against all his Catholic upbringing to have sex with his girlfriend in her house.

But Christ Jesus, men went to war for things less coveted than Josephine's body. Coll had gotten in last night, keeping his taciturn self holed up in Mirren's room or visiting with his reptilian-like parents. The Barrs were a cold-blooded lot. Coll could be standoffish, especially since his injury, but he was loyal and loving despite his recent reserve, and Aileen, of course, was always warm and tangibly kind.

Coll was visiting his sister in Inverness at the O'Connor's new place, which meant he had the house to himself. Aileen's house... His brain might stutter over the fine details, but his body was apparently a pro at amnesia and didn't care whose house it was in.

He didn't blame his body's reaction. Josephine was wearing soft, baby-blue pajamas, making tea in the kitchen. The bottoms were short enough to see the gentle swell of her ass peeking below the hem.

She finally noticed his focused stare where he stood in the kitchen's doorframe... and his bare chest. He'd purposely left off a shirt after his shower, choosing instead to slip on an old pair of gray sweatpants. He wasn't too old that he hadn't heard about the gray sweatpants TikTok craze.

After pouring hot water into a mug, she dropped a teabag in, but her eyes were more on him than her task. He saw a flush begin to creep up her neck.

"Are you trying to seduce me with that stare... and those pants, Mr. MacGregor?"

"Yes. Is it working?" he asked as he prowled into the kitchen, stopping short of touching her.

"You had me at shirtless," she admitted while picking up the tabbed string connected to her tea, swirling it through the steaming water.

Thomas used his bulk to back her against the edge of the kitchen counter, dipping his head until they were cheek to cheek. "I want you. Badly," he growled in her ear.

She angled her head until their mouths met, exhaling as he moved her hands to his back and pressed her against him while dipping his tongue leisurely inside her mouth. Their tongues slid together in a rhythm that imitated sex— it was his turn to exhale.

He could come from kissing her alone. Her mouth tasted that damn good. His balls were tight, his erection stiff and wanting, tenting his pants. His throbbing flesh searching.

Jo spread her knees wide to accommodate his frame as he stepped between them. Her hands were propped behind her as she wrapped her long legs around his waist, squeezing tight so she could rub her core against him over and over.

He clasped her thighs to hold her still. She'd thrown her

head back, her long hair making blonde waves around her shoulders and over the counter. When he stopped her gyrating hips, her head raised, and her eyes opened.

"Wha... wha... why did you stop?" she finally got out. He felt smug at her stuttered words. "I'm close. Let me move," she squirmed in his hands.

"No, baby," he gently admonished as he took her silky sleep top off, revealing creamy skin, round, full breasts, and puckered nipples. He couldn't stop himself from pinching the hardened peaks, reveling in her moans.

"If you want to come, Josephine, it'll be with my dick buried deep inside you," he explained while pulling her bottoms down her legs.

"But... Co... Coll might walk in," she halfheartedly protested, and that was generous because her slim fingers were already inside his waistband, fisting his heat and stroking.

"He's not due back." He yanked his pants below his ass. "Nothing and no one will stop me from going balls deep in your body. Right here. Right now." He punctuated his words by running his thumb up her slick seam, mesmerized by how her juices coated his skin.

He grabbed her hips, bringing her as close to the edge of the counter as he could. "Take what you want from me," he taunted.

She took it without hesitation, hooking her ankles around his ass and pulling him to her. Her moan was drowned out by his shout of satisfaction as he slid slowly in. Both he and Jo were transfixed as he disappeared inside her body.

Soon enough, she was panting his name, close from edging the line already. "Not slow, Thomas. I need fast and hard," she demanded.

No more teasing. Watching her body take him so well and hearing her cries had pushed him faster and faster. When he felt her body begin to convulse around his shaft, he followed her climax with his own, a shout escaped as his body released.

Jo went boneless, gradually laying back on the counter, a groan of contentment deep in her throat. With some regret, he slid from her body and righted his pants. "You look like a golden goddess laid bare on all that creamy granite, lass."

She smiled sleepily. "The perfect woman for my golden bunny," she snickered.

"God, you used to make me so mad when you teased me in front of your friends. It took every ounce of willpower I'd learned in the Marines to ignore the razzing."

"And now?" she asked, sitting up and scooting off the counter to get dressed.

"My mother loved reading Robert Burns to me when I was a child at bedtime. Her favorite was *A Red, Red Rose*. She read that one so often I memorized it. This was my favorite bit.

*So fair art thou, my bonnie lass,*
*So deep in luve am I;*
*And I will luve thee still, my dear,*
*Till a' the seas gang dry.*

"I consider myself the luckiest of men that you call me anything at all." He could feel the tips of his ears burning and his cheeks heat, but he didn't care. She made him willing to spout poetry.

"You might want to tidy yourself, lassie. Coll is due."

"Good Lord! I completely forgot!"

Thomas laughed as she frantically began to straighten her pajamas and fluff her hair. She stopped mid-pants twisting and hugged him around the waist. "Just so you know, I want you to teach me that poem. That was the single most romantic moment of my life." She leaned back so they could see each other's faces. "It's going to be really, really, really hard not to tell the Byrnes."

Without so much as a blink, he tossed down a threat. "You

tell the Byrnes that I spouted poetry. I'll tell Aileen your naked ass was on her kitchen countertop."

"You win," she conceded quickly.

Jo COULDN'T HELP the smile that spread across her face that morning. Her friends— and their husbands— were coming into town tomorrow afternoon, babies and nannies included. The O'Faolains and Byrnes together made for a loud, boisterous, good time.

Today, she and Mirren were going shopping and to lunch. She might be most excited about that. She'd spoken numerous times to Thomas' daughter, but this would be the first one-on-one they'd enjoy, and Jo could not wait. She was running to Bunchrew's local gym and hopefully burning a gazillion calories.

She'd put on a few pounds the last couple of months, not much, but she'd weighed the same since she was a teenager, and five pounds seemed like fifty. Thomas still liked her figure. She grinned, thinking about last night.

Aileen had been invited to go shopping, too, of course, but she still tired easily and wanted to save all her energy for the dinner party Saturday night. So that Aileen wouldn't feel obligated to entertain guests two days in a row, she and Thomas were going out to eat with their friends Friday night.

All the guys were going to play golf Saturday morning while the women were to be treated to lunch and spa treatments that Matilda O'Faolain put together. For Saturday afternoon, Mom hired a few glam hair and makeup artists to get all the women gorgeous.

Aileen had a new wig she planned on debuting. This

weekend was about celebration. Family, friends, love, and especially health. Aileen was a cancer ass-kicker.

Jo heard Thomas and Coll in the kitchen before she saw them. They sounded like two growly tigers enjoying a morning coffee. She braced herself to see Coll. He was kind and professional and loved Thomas, but he also knew her darkest secret and had seen the video, at least a flash of it... and that picture.

She had to force herself to make eye contact and hated her inability to get over the awkward hump. For his part, Coll did his best to make her comfortable, which meant he grunted and huffed out one-word responses like he did to everyone else.

"Good morning." She smiled, adding a silly half-wave where her hand rested at her hip. Avoiding eye contact, she went to the fridge and grabbed a bottle of water. "I'm headed to the gym now, so I'll have time to shower before I meet Mirren," she added cheerily. Cringe cheery.

"Josephine."

That's all Thomas said but there was no way to avoid that tone. She walked to his side, avoiding Coll's stare on the DL. She bent to give Thomas' cheek a quick peck. "What are you doing today?"

"Coll is visiting his parents." The other man snorted at this. "And I'm helping Catriona move several pallets of fertilizer into her greenhouses."

"Maybe we could have dinner at your grandma's tonight?" she asked, wanting to get to know his family like he knew hers. Thomas' parents were coming back for a week soon, and she was looking forward to meeting them in person.

"I'll tell her. She'd love that, lass. Thank you for thinking of it. Coll, you'll come."

"I have—" Coll began.

"It would hurt her feelings. You haven't seen Grandma in months."

"Fine."

These men were intense. "I'm heading out. Aileen's letting me borrow her car while we're living here."

"Call me when you leave for Inverness." Thomas wasn't asking. Mr. Overprotective.

She was about to agree when Coll spoke. "Josephine." When she finally made eye contact, he said, "You're embarrassed to be around me because I know something private about you."

"Coll," Thomas warned.

"Thomas is my family. You are his, which means you are my family too. You'll stop being nervous around me. Now."

*Well... well...* Coll's stern gaze met hers straight on.

"I can do that."

He only nodded before returning his attention to the television's local news.

"Plus," Coll began in a bland tone, "I had to see Tommy's bare ass in the kitchen last night. You owe me."

He never even looked away from the TV's screen. Her horrified gaze whipped to Thomas, whose whole body was shaking with silent laughter. "You are dead to me, Thomas MacGregor," she snarled before storming out of the kitchen, which only made him laugh harder. She hid her grin. Barely.

# 36

Jo and Mirren sat down for a late lunch after they finished shopping. The little café had the best beef stew served in sourdough bowls. The bread was made fresh every morning— exactly what her waistline didn't need. Jo's appetite had been nonexistent, though. More than likely, she'd waste the majority of her meal anyway.

Before Jo could climb down a dieting rabbit hole, Mirren quietly announced, "I talked to my... birth father. Charles Morrow, that is."

Talk about an appetite suppressant. Jo put the menu aside and stared wide-eyed at the blank expression gracing the normally effusive face of the sixteen-year-old teenager.

"Wha—" Jo started before Mirren jumped in.

"I messaged him first with a detailed accounting of the past, my parentage, Dad, Mom's cancer, and that I thought he was a shithead."

"I... well, you're nothing if not brutally honest." Jo grasped Mirren's hand lying on the table. "Does your mom know you reached out? How did he respond?"

"She doesn't. I couldn't risk him being a waste of space. As for how he responded. Shock and awe, of course. I told him I would take a DNA test at his convenience."

"I see." And Jo did see. Mirren was being matter of fact about it all, but clearly, this was huge. "But... how did he take it?"

"He..." and here was the first break in Mirren's brave face, "he said if Aileen said he was my father, he didn't need a test. He ruined all that, of course, by trying to be angry about not being told he had a daughter."

Jo gently tried to explain that that was an understandable reaction, but she wasn't having it.

"Humph," she snorted in irritation. "I told him that my mother had tried to contact him, and he told her he'd moved on with another woman and didn't have the flipping time of day to spare her."

Mirren's lips were pinched, and a mulish expression blanketed her sweet face. The rapid blinking and glassy eyes gave her away, though. "Mir," she started gently, "he was in shock. Surely, you can give him a bit of grace."

"Not likely." Stubborn MacGregor.

"I thought you were going to let your father handle contacting Charles."

She gave a typical teenage shrug. "I don't know everything about the case Dad and Uncle Coll were working in Rome, but I read the news and filled in some of the blanks. Dad was being purposely vague. I understand. Trafficking is a sickening business and I'm proud of Dad and Colly. I guess I figured he had enough on his plate, and he never brought up Charles again either," she added quietly.

Jo swallowed bile. She didn't want such vile news to soil a single hair on this child's head, but Mirren also needed to understand that nothing was more important to Thomas than his daughter.

Meeting Mirren's sullen eyes, she explained, "Before I say anything else, you need to be reminded that your father keeps his promises. He did plan on contacting Charles, but he's also had to work on bringing your uncle around to the idea." Mirren looked shamefaced at doubting her dad. "Also, there was more to the case in Rome than reported in the news. One of the men involved in that horrible club Interpol raided hurt me when I was a teenager. Veleno hiring my family's hospitality company was a setup to get me there by... that man.

"I would... well, I would like not to tell you anything else about that. Is it enough to know that your father was busy saving me?"

"More than enough, Jo. You are... okay?" she asked tentatively.

"My physical hurts were eight years ago. Mentally... I've started therapy."

Mirren expelled a full breath. "Good."

"I didn't tell you about this to make it about me. You are smart and knew your dad was keeping things from you. I understand the frustration. Your father can be irritatingly close-mouthed. I told you so you'd know the severity of the situation, but even then, there will never be anything more important than your happiness to your father. Tell me you believe that. He planned on reaching out to Charles. He didn't forget," she assured.

"I know he would have," she grumbled. "I was impatient."

Jo chuckled. "I get that. Promise me that you'll tap the brakes on your anger toward Charles. Allow him to explore his feelings about suddenly finding out he has a sixteen-year-old daughter."

Blank stare. "You've always known your birth father was out there," Jo tried again. "Give him a hot second. After all, your mom loved him once, and it sounds like she still does. Surely, her instincts weren't completely broken back then. She chose your dad to be your father. Aileen has good instincts where men are concerned."

"Whatever. Fine."

"Great." Jo's enthusiasm was lost on the teen. "Are you ready to order?"

"Yes, but first, ugh, do I have to tell Mom what I did?"

"I won't tell you that you have to, but I imagine she would appreciate being kept in the loop."

"Fine. And Dad?"

Real worry crept into her expressive face with the question. "Yes. For one, when he reaches out to Charles, it would certainly help the conversation's tenor if he was aware that you'd already reached out. More importantly, your father is sensitive about Charles. He knows if you have a relationship with your birth father, things are bound to change."

"They would never change," Mirren said hotly.

"Everything changes, Mir. Most of the time, they change for the better. Four months ago, I didn't even know you or your mom existed, and now I can't imagine my life without you in it. Loving you guys didn't make me love my old friends less.

"Your Dad needs reassurance. You two need to trust in your relationship. You'll always have it. Why don't you come back to Bunchrew with me when we finish shopping. Do it face to face."

"Today?" Her eyes went wide.

"Today. Consider fessing up to your dad penance for your impatience." Jo laughed at Mirren's sigh-eye-roll combination.

She and Mirren enjoyed the rest of lunch, as much as Jo could anyway. Her taste buds were wonky, and she felt bloated. She pictured herself lying by Thomas in bed that night swollen, flatulent, and grumpy. Super attractive.

Other than her gastro issues, shopping had been a success.

After three hours of retail therapy, she'd finally had to admit to Mirren that her stomach was off. Now that the teen had confessed her worries, she was all about unprofessionally diagnosing Jo's stomach ailment, making Jo describe each symptom in detail.

"Constipation. I guarantee it. Did you know constipation can cause headaches and nausea?" Mirren said with such a superior air that Jo was hard-pressed not to believe her.

"I hesitate to ask, but why are you such an intestinal encyclopedia?"

"Mom's treatments." She shrugged. "Treatments can give you diarrhea, constipation, or both. Unfortunately for Mom, we had to learn a lot about both."

"Okay, Dr. MacGregor. Give me the treatment." Jo sighed.

"Easy. We'll stop by a Boots on the way home. Laxative suppositories for if you're crazy bad and want to blow up the loo in ten minutes or a high fiber drink that 'works gently overnight,'" she air quoted. "Gentle is debatable."

*Oh, joy...*

Jo was nervously watching Thomas and Mirren talk outside through the living room's picture window. Thomas was still as a statue while his daughter was pacing and wildly gesturing with her hands. It would have been comical if she wasn't worried Thomas might get his feelings hurt.

Jo was about to turn from the private tableau when she felt Coll move to stand at her shoulder. He was surprisingly silent for a large man wielding a prosthetic leg. He didn't say anything for a minute, but it wasn't an uncomfortable silence. Clearly, demanding that she get over being embarrassed around him worked.

"There were years when I berated myself for not stopping Tommy from marrying my sister. He did it for me as much as for her."

"He was meant to be Mirren's father."

He glanced at her then, a serious expression marring his mouth and downturned brows. "He was. I don't know what to think of this Charles Morrow."

She was surprised he would admit that. Coll was private with his thoughts. He made Hugh O'Faolain's taciturn, borderline belligerent behavior seem warm and fuzzy. There was only one thing that would probably make this soldier stand down.

"Your sister is lonely."

Coll braced his big, callused palm against the window frame. Exhaling, he only said, "I know."

Jo turned back to the scene outside. Mirren was still gesticulating like a mime enacting a circus act when Thomas placed his hands on each of his daughter's shoulders, effectively stilling her body before pulling her gently against his chest.

He tenderly smoothed down her soft, brown hair before cupping her head. Mirren finally reached her arms around her father's waist and hugged him back. Tears clogged Jo's throat, and she tried to surreptitiously use her t-shirt to dab her eyes.

"That other man will never be the father he is," Coll quietly spoke.

"If he's even half the man, Mirren will be fortunate indeed."

## 37

Percy felt adrift even though he had the means to live comfortably and future employment opportunities. In fact, he'd been in contact with one of Aldo's uncles, who had heard Percy was quite proficient at falsifying documents and funneling money until it appeared as clean as the day it was printed.

Tommaso Russo handled the majority of the family's trafficking business. Percy had been wanting to expand in the skin trade. With his money laundering skills, the possibilities were limitless. To be sure, his family had done quite well for themselves, but the real money was in the crime, not in the cleaning crew.

His father had let him enjoy his first prostitute at twelve. She hadn't been much older than him, but she'd taught him how to enjoy a woman's body. As he grew older, he discovered just how many ways there were.

Which brought him back to tonight's mood. Frustration. He ached for Josie. He wanted her now, but the timing had to be perfect. Following her had lost its thrill. Each day, time slipped away from him— he could feel the police restraints tightening around his body if he didn't make a move soon. There was no doubt they were still looking for him. His life before Rome was over, but the new life he would be creating might even be better. With his Josie, anything was possible.

He swirled his vodka and lime absently, moodily staring at the flames in the hotel room's wall gas fireplace. He never recalled having such deep, contemplative thoughts. Josie was already impacting him for the better. Life did have its funny twists and turns.

Perhaps he should consider this time in his life as a rebirth— a chance to reinvent himself. After all, by tomorrow, Josie would be on a plane with him headed to their new home.

A new life. She would learn to relish his deepest, darkest desires as if they were her own. She was diligent in her work, intelligent, and detailed. He had no doubt she would take to his training with the same passion. It would take a few weeks to get the drug dosage just right, but once her inhibitions were lifted, Percy knew she'd be the partner he'd longed for.

Percy smiled, thinking about the children he would plant in her belly. He pictured her in a sunny villa with sandy beaches, sparkling waves, and cloudless skies. She would run naked through the surf, calling his name to join her.

Tomorrow, she would be in his arms one way or another.

No. He had no reason to feel adrift or anxious.

He slipped his memory book from the bag at his feet, the pictures calming and thrilling.

Josie. Josie. Josie.

# 38

Meals at Thomas' grandmother's home were always an experience. Grandma usually spent eighty percent of the meal berating him over some supposed misdeed.

He, Coll, Jo, and Catriona had barely sat down at the table when she announced, "You'll need to meet with Father Kevin about the divorce. The shame of it all." She tsked, shaking her head in despair.

Jo was attempting to cover her mouth, clearly amused. "Gram," he admonished. "You've always known that my marriage was in name only."

"Yes, yes, young man. I'm not senile," the older woman snapped back. "I didn't want you to marry wee Aileen back then because I knew it would have to end this way, but you did what you thought was best, as you've always done. You are Mirren's father, and I am happy about that. However, none of that matters, boy." Grandma shook her finger in his direction. "You'll still need to make a proper confession, and that's that." Her small fist lightly pounded the table in finality.

"Of course," he agreed, glancing at Jo and her poor attempt at hiding her grin. Coll was looking all smug as he shoveled beef stew in his smirking pie hole until Grandma turned her attention his way not five minutes later.

"And you, Coll Alexander Barr..." she paused to silently stare at his best friend, making him squirm like a little boy, "never come home."

It was all fun and games until the old woman sniffled. "I worry." And that did it. Coll broke like glass dropped on asphalt.

He lowered his eyes briefly before meeting the woman who had a hand in raising him when his own family couldn't take the time. "I'll do better, Gram."

He watched Jo look at Catriona, eyebrows raised. His sister smiled and shrugged. Clearly, it was rare for all of them to witness Coll apologetic. Thomas was happy to see he would humble himself for the older woman.

"Fine then." Once the group was stuffed full— though he noticed Jo only took a few bites and spent most of the meal pushing bits of beef around her bowl— Grandma stood and began gathering the empty bowls near her. Jo instantly stood to help clear the dishes.

"I made caramel tablets for you, Tommy. I want to know what your favorite treats are, Josephine, so I can make them next time you come around." Grandma tapped Jo's shoulder as she walked to the kitchen sink. Jo's small grin made a matching one appear on his face. "Wee Cat made your favorite, Colly, tea cookies with apple butter."

Coll's clenched jaw and blush were sweet payback for all the times his friend had teased him about his grandma spoiling him. "Thanks, Gram, and Jo likes anything with even a hint of chocolate."

"Oh, Josephine." She clapped her hands. "You'll love my chocolate scones. I top them with a dark chocolate clotted cream."

Jo grinned his way before replying, "I can't wait, Mrs. MacGregor."

"Grace," Grandma corrected. "Here's the tablets for Tom. I think you'll like them. Cat, grab Colly's biscuits."

He watched his sister grind her teeth. She really wasn't a fan of Coll.

"He can get them himself if he wants one," she replied tartly. When Grandma whipped around to stare at her granddaughter, Cat huffed before pushing her chair back and standing. She went over to the wooden shelf below the kitchen window and grabbed a covered plate, walking the few steps back to the table before tossing the plate in front of Coll. He didn't so much as flinch as the plate clattered between his resting forearms.

Choosing to ignore Thomas' sister's antics, Coll peeled back the waxed paper and grabbed a biscuit, stuffing the whole thing in his mouth. As he chewed, he managed to smirk at Cat, making her fair skin turn crimson in anger.

After swallowing and licking his fingers, Coll announced, "I haven't had tea cookies this fine since the night of your prom, Kitty Cat."

Thomas had never witnessed Coll poke the Cat Bear that hard since she was an easily enraged, fire-headed toddler. Thomas admitted that watching his wee sister ignite like a stick of dynamite had been amusing when she was child, but she wasn't a child anymore. Jo must have noticed the preliminary opening to World War III and quickly grabbed a biscuit for herself.

"Mmm, Cat. These are amazing. You and Grace will have to teach me how to make them."

Jo placed her body between Coll and Catriona like a human shield. He could have done without Jo's sweet ass being so close to his best friend's face, but if it was that or Cat going Tasmanian Devil, he wouldn't move her.

"Of course," Catriona said with a tight smile before turning and walking toward the door. Over her shoulder, she said, "I have an early day tomorrow. Thanks for the help today, Tom, and thanks for dinner, Gram. See you tomorrow, Jo."

Her body was stiff as if his sister was barely keeping herself together. Thomas frowned at Coll. "I don't understand what just happened, but you hurt her feelings." For Coll's part, he looked just as bewildered. The look turned into a grimace after Grandma smacked him on the head with the serving spoon she was washing, leaving soap suds clinging to Coll's dark hair.

"You will cease teasing that poor girl about that night. You have no idea how much those kids hurt her feelings because you followed her."

ONE SECOND, Coll was rubbing his head where Grace had whacked him, and the next, both men were standing and facing the older woman.

"What are you talking about?" Thomas demanded, which got him a raised brow of warning from his grandma.

"Who the fuck hurt her? I was there. I didn't see anything."

"You will not use that language in my house, young man, unless you want a second lump on that thick head of yours."

Jo enjoyed his mumbled apology immensely. There was something satisfying about a tiny silver-haired woman putting two grown men in their places. It was a shame that Catriona wasn't there to witness the set down, but something about Coll's taunting had hurt or embarrassed her enough to leave.

"Will you explain, Gram?" Thomas tried to modulate the growl from his voice. Jo might need to learn that spoon trick.

Grace sniffed in indignation a few times before turning back to the dishes. Jo grabbed a drying cloth to help. After another full minute, probably to torture the guys, she said, "I won't tell you any specifics. Cat told me in confidence that night. She ran over here sobbing and told me the whole of it."

"Because I was there?" Coll asked quietly.

Grace sighed but continued to scrub her stew pot. "Yes, and before you feel too terribly about that, Cat did understand that you and Tom are very protective of her. Truth be told, she wasn't even that surprised to see you there that night, Coll."

"So, what then?" he asked.

"I can't tell you, boy. She made me swear. I believe... I fear she still believes some of the hurtful things they said, but that's enough of that," she said suddenly. "Catriona wouldn't thank us for speaking of her behind her back. I won't say another word except to tell you to drop it."

Coll didn't say anything else. He gave Grace a short nod, which could have meant he understood, or it could have been a thank you for dinner. Either way, he silently left the kitchen and then the house. Thomas watched the slight limp in his best friend's stride with frustration.

Thomas sat heavily in his chair, looking at Jo in misery. "He's been better the last few days. Almost like it used to be. I'm afraid that this," he swiped his hand in front of himself, indicating the scene they just witnessed, "will make him... quiet again."

Grace shocked her and Thomas when she turned from the sink and smiled. "I wouldn't worry too much about that. Coll won't be able to let it go— not knowing what those kids said to her. It'll eat him alive until he gets the story from wee Cat."

"And that's a good thing, why?" Jo asked, unsure where Grace was going.

"Simple. Coll needs to think of something besides his

missing leg. Cat is Thomas' sister and therefore family to him as well. He'll want to fix it. He won't have nearly as much time to brood about himself. Then there is Catriona. She needs to tell someone besides me what hurt her feelings and have someone besides me tell her that those kids were full of manure.

"They'll help each other. Win-win." Grace brushed her hands over her apron, clearly proud of her scheming.

Jo looked at Thomas, he looked at her, he shrugged, she smiled. Grace might be on to something.

## 39

Jo was the last to enter the kitchen Friday morning. Thomas and Coll were already silently contemplating their days. Unless she was by herself, coffee with friends was normally a time to chit-chat. Not so with those two.

Thomas touched her hand in passing and gave her a warm look as she got her cup down from the cabinet. "I'm running into town in a few hours to pick up the flowers for Mom's table," she told them over her shoulder. "What do you guys have going on today?"

The pained look he gave her when she sat down almost had her snorting in her coffee. "I have the pleasure of meeting that pain in the ass, Dougal Donaldson, at our house. He wasn't 'inspired' enough the first time," Thomas drawled.

She laughed at Thomas' hangdog look. "So, is he looking at the bedroom again to spark more inspiration? Or is it drinks at the local pub?"

"Mmpf." The grunt indicated his disbelief as well. "He's not fooling me either. The man probably wanted to day drink with someone besides his housekeeper. Jesus, that man could try a saint's patience," he muttered.

She barely refrained from mentioning that most of the Scotsmen she was acquainted with could do the same. It was close, but she choked back the guffaw that wanted to break loose. She caught Coll grinning in his coffee mug, clearly guessing the direction of her thoughts.

"What about you, Coll?"

"Cleaning Aileen's garage. Repainting," he muttered, his amusement of a moment ago gone and his normal melancholy mood engaged.

Thomas glanced her way before saying, "Damn, I didn't know you were doing that today."

"Why? Did you need me to do something?" Coll asked.

"No, that's fine. Cat's website had some glitch she needed looked at. I might have time this afternoon if Dougal doesn't talk me into too many shots. She acted like it was a big deal, but surely, she's overreacting."

If Coll couldn't pick up on Thomas' poor acting skills, she and George Strait had some ocean front property in Arizona for sale he might be interested in.

"I can take a look at it."

Coll's careful eye avoidance meant he was oblivious to his friend's manipulation. *Calendar note: Sunscreen for Coll's Christmas stocking. He's going to the beach!*

"Great," Thomas said, practically preening. If Catriona ever found out about her family's scheming, there would be hell to pay.

Standing, she said, "Tell Dougal I said hello... or not. I'm off to the gym."

"You've tripled your gym time lately, babe. Be careful not to overdo it," Thomas warned.

"My stomach's been off, and my weight's been climbing. Gym time is life right now."

Thomas gave her a stormy look. "You didn't tell me you

weren't feeling well," he accused. "Is that why you haven't been eating?"

Kicking herself for mentioning her stomach ailment to Captain Overreact, she only said, "I'm fine. I probably just need to stop skipping my placebo week and let my body have a per—" She was abruptly cut off by Coll's chair scraping back and the man suddenly looming over the breakfast table.

"Do not discuss woman shit in front of me this early in the morning, Josephine. Christ." Coll shook his head and stomped off toward the garage.

Thomas didn't spare Coll's retreating back a glance. "I don't like that you didn't tell me you weren't feeling good."

"I'm fine, truly. I just feel full all the time, so I'm not super hungry. Mirren tried to doctor me, but I promise, if I don't feel better soon, I'll make a doctor's appointment."

"Let me guess," his shoulders were already shaking in amusement, "constipation?"

*Kill me now.* "How... how did you know that?"

"Mir told me my mood would be greatly improved with more regular... movements," he grimaced. "I got a next day Amazon Prime box filled with suppositories, finger condom things, and... lotion."

Jo bent at the waist, she was laughing so hard. "Oh, God," she said between giggling, "I'm so glad it wasn't just me she 'diagnosed.'"

He stood and followed her to the sink, circling her waist with his hands and leaned down so that his face was close to hers. "Don't keep things from me. You've been suffering, and I didn't know," he growled.

She huffed impatiently. "Hardly suffering. Minor discomfort, if that," she argued. It was likely due to the stressful past few months, and her body just needed a bit longer to work itself out. Nothing to further worry the worrywart with. "I almost took your daughter's advice, but it felt dicey at best," she teased. "If it were something serious, I would tell you. I promise," she conceded, knowing her overprotective man wouldn't relent without assurances.

His acceptance of her vow was to kiss her until she was limply leaning against a row of kitchen drawers. "Have a good workout, lass. I'll be gone before you're back. I'll meet you back here this afternoon. That'll give us plenty of time to get around before we pick up the O'Faolains for dinner."

His grip on her hips tightened when he spoke. "Is 'plenty of time' code for sex?"

"Yes."

# 40

Percy had been following Josie along High Street the moment she parked in the Eastgate garage, a few blocks from the flower shop. Her glorious head of golden hair was a beacon. He was starving for her eyes to be on his, even if they were angry.

The first time he'd met her, Josie's gray eyes mesmerized him. While he took her innocence, her unblinking gunmetal stare seared into his brain. That night, she'd looked like a mannequin, silent and perfectly crafted. His real-life doll.

Today, she was wearing a stunning green wrap dress, the perfect foil for her lovely blonde hair. He couldn't wait to see her in sundresses and bikinis. Their new life together was going to be beaches and soft breezes.

And cuffs, chains, whips, and knives.

# 41

Jo was walking down Inverness' congested High Street, window shopping as she made her way to the florist's. She was feeling particularly prickly after her workout and shower. When she'd stepped on her scale that morning, she was only three pounds over her normal weight, which wasn't a big deal at all. She was down two pounds.

She should be happy. It was her bloated lower stomach that was making her tetchy as hell. There was really no difference in her appearance, she just felt... full.

Too nervous to try Mirren's over-the-counter answer to her problems— the possibility of an embarrassing public accident was a gamble she couldn't make herself take— Jo made an appointment with a doctor that had a small practice only a few miles from Bunchrew Village. If the doctor confirmed it was constipation, she would take the diagnosis to her grave. Otherwise, Mirren would crow about it for months.

Her mother always told her buying a new pair of shoes could solve life's most difficult problems. She was early yet to pick up the arrangement, so she decided to take her advice and slip into a lovely shoe store. It smelled of leather and lavender. Perfect therapy.

The saleswoman sent her a cheery hello. She was to let her know if she wanted to try anything on. A hands-off retailer. Jo's favorite.

She moved to one of the front displays that showcased woven belts and leather-stamped purses and caught her reflection in the front window. She wore a soft wool wrap dress in a dark, leaf green. The dress was one of her favorites. Too bad Thomas had missed seeing her in it. Or maybe it was a good thing because she would have definitely been late this morning instead of early.

She was about to turn around when a man walked by the window outside. Tallish, slim build, sharp suit. It was the charcoal felt bucket hat that caught her attention. It really was an odd accessory pairing with the suit.

She was about to turn back to the purses when the gentleman turned his head, barely a tilt to the side, but that one glimpse had Jo's heart stuttering in her chest.

She was letting her imagination run away. There was no way Percy Donovan was in Inverness, Scotland, of all places. He couldn't have followed her. He would have had no way of knowing where she was going when she left Rome.

She took several deep breaths in an attempt to bring her heart rate down from needing an ambulance level. The man had continued to walk down the sidewalk, not a care in the world. When she leaned further into the display window, she saw him stop and ask a woman something. She smiled and pointed further down the street. He bobbed his head in thanks and continued on his way.

He'd been just a normal guy. A normal guy with bad taste in hats, she chuckled to herself. *Did constipation make people hallucinate?*

Except... she could have sworn the man had a cleft chin, which was not exactly uncommon, but the small mole below his lower lip just like Percy had... At the angle his head had turned, she hadn't seen anything of his upper face, but the sun had lit the lower half. Shaking her head, she determined to forget it. Running her fingers around her emergency bracelet further calmed her nerves. She was safe.

Jo finally settled on a buttery, yellow leather clutch, and matching ballet slippers. The leather was exceptionally soft, and she couldn't wait for the weather to finally warm up so she could wear them.

Thanking the sales lady, she decided she had time for one more quick stop. There was a jewelry store between the shoe store she'd just left and the florists. Mirren had oohed and aahed over a pair of small gold earrings in the shape of a bird in flight. They were delicate and lovely. Mirren had refused to let her buy them for her yesterday.

She wasn't here to say no now, though. Picturing the teenager's surprise made her smile in anticipation. She was about to cross the street, so she glanced behind her to make sure she didn't cut off a pedestrian as she moved toward the crosswalk... and glimpsed the man with the bucket hat not too far behind.

Her fingers went icy cold with dread. Surely, another coincidence. She glanced a second time over her shoulder, the man had stopped and was either window shopping at a woman's boutique or pretending to window shop.

Thomas would kick her butt if she didn't take this possible threat seriously. Neither Interpol nor the FBI had found Percy, after all. Making up her mind, she dug her phone from her tote and dialed Coll. Thomas was with Dougal, and it wasn't that she minded interrupting the meeting. It was that Thomas would panic, and this might be nothing at all but nerves.

Instead of crossing the street, Jo retraced her steps until she was at a tweed retailer right next to the clothing store where the man still stood. If he was following her, she wanted him to hear her conversation so his suspicions wouldn't be aroused.

Coll answered on the first ring. "Jo."

"Hey, Mom," she said brightly.

"I'm pulling your location up now. Talk to me." Coll caught on immediately.

"I'm about to pick up the arrangement from the florists and drop it off to you, but you know me, I couldn't resist a new pair of shoes from a shop on High Street. So, here's my question, I'm standing outside Harris Tweed. Do you remember it from the other day?"

"Keep talking. Only a few minutes away. Donovan?"

"Maybe. I just can't decide. Would Dad wear a tweed vest if I got him one for his birthday?" Pretending like her mom answered, Jo laughed and said, "That's true, dang it. He'd rather pick it out for himself. Just like his suits."

"Is he wearing a suit?"

"Yes. I'll think about a gift card. Maybe just buy a hat to wrap with it."

"Hat? Color?" Coll asked.

"Dark gray would be a nice color. Did James ever finalize his fishing expedition?" She waited a beat for her mom to 'answer.' "I guess I'll have to give him back that bucket hat I wore to the pond last summer."

"Like a fishing hat?" Coll asked.

"Yeah, kind of, the material's a little warm for summer, I think."

"Parking now. I texted Thomas to notify the police. He's giving them the man's description."

Jo sighed. "Great. He'll be lots of fun to deal with. Oh, I almost forgot," she slowly turned from the window and started to make her way across the street to the jewelers.

"I'm walking across the street to the jewelry store, High Seas, where Mir saw those earrings she fell in love with that I told you about." She paused before saying, "Yes, the little gold birds. She's going to die when I show her. I hope they have a matching necklace or bracelet."

"I can see you. He's following you across the street. Two cops who work High Street have been briefed, and they are closing in. Tommy is parked and coming fast. You'll be in trouble for not calling him." There was a hint of laughter in his voice, which relaxed her considerably.

She chuckled. "I have no doubt." Since the man following her could no longer hear her conversation, she admitted, "I knew you would keep your cool where my safety might be compromised. Thomas loves me enough to come in like a Miley Cyrus wrecking ball." She winced at the thought.

"He has every right. If this is Donovan, which we both know it has to be, or you wouldn't have called me, he hurt you badly once, Josephine. Tommy wants to protect you. Walk into the store. We will take him while he waits for you to leave. There are a few alleys between the jewelry shop and the florists. He probably didn't plan on taking you until you reached one of them."

She shivered, wondering how long he'd been following her. How many days? She held out a small hope that this was all a mistake, but she had a bigger hope that it was him and he'd finally be arrested.

Determined to let the debacle on the sidewalk play itself out, she asked the salesclerk about the gold bird earrings.

WHEN THOMAS WAS close enough to the jewelry store, he could see Coll leaning against the building's façade, one foot propped behind him. With a hand casually resting on his upraised thigh, he signed where the uniformed police were stationed, Josephine's location, and where their mark was hiding.

Percy fucking Donovan. Thomas had to viciously shove down the rage threatening to burst from his skin. That he'd been following Josephine... He couldn't bear the thought that her rapist had been stalking her. It had been bad enough when she had to face him at Veleno. The difference was that she'd walked into that place knowing there was always a possibility of contact.

As Thomas walked by Coll, his friend fell in line at his shoulder. Thomas nodded to the police. It was time. Donovan was standing partially concealed in a recessed alcove right past the jewelry shop's door. The arrogant shit was flipping through pages on his phone, not a care in the world.

Before the police could cross the street, he and Coll walked directly up to Donovan. Coll snatched his phone, which his team would use to track down even more of Donovan's contacts and hidden offshore accounts, and Thomas grabbed the man, pulling him out and into the sunlight by his suit vest.

"What in the hell do you think you're doing?" Donovan barked while twisting and turning his body to break Thomas' hold.

"Making sure you never have the chance to lay eyes or hands on Josephine O'Connor again." That stunned the struggle out of him. His hat had come off in the scuffle, revealing a monster's face.

Chuckling in a condescending manner, he said, "You must be the boyfriend Josie thinks she's not leaving for me." His chuckle was unhinged. He hadn't seen the police yet and thought this was just a simple domestic dispute. "How about I do this for you, buddy? I'll send you pictures of me taking her body in all our favorite positions. Have you gotten to experience how clever she is with her mout—"

Thomas punched his filthy mouth then and kept punching until Donovan's body was flattened against the wall he'd recently been leaning against. A big hand landed on Thomas' shoulder, stopping him from lunging at the filth currently sliding bonelessly down the brick.

Coll's voice rumbled near his ear. "Enough, Tommy."

"It will never be enough while that piece of shit is breathing," he shot back.

"No. It will never be enough," he agreed. "Not after what he did to Jo, but the police are ready to arrest him, and you'll need to let them by." To the police, Coll said as he stepped back, taking Thomas with him, "Sorry about the trouble, officers, but the criminal attempted to flee, and my partner used his common law power to restrain him."

To the officer's credit, they didn't bat an eye over the falsehood. Having been briefed on Donovan's crimes, they certainly would have no sympathy.

As one officer stepped forward to read Donovan his rights, the other pulled him from the ground to place him in handcuffs. Donovan glared at Thomas through his swollen and bloodied face.

"Enjoy prison. I hear inmates love meeting rapists and pedophiles." Thomas relished Donovan blanch in fear. Other officers, several in plainclothes, had begun to arrive. Thomas gave a brief statement before turning to Coll and asking him to finish up. "I'm for Jo, then."

"Go." He nodded his head, acknowledging that Thomas needed to lay eyes on the woman who meant everything to him.

∼

"Oh, yes, aren't they lovely?" she said. "They are actually from a local artist, Finn Campbell. He's highly sought after and quite the mystery," the clerk tittered. "He's been asked to do interviews, both in person and online, and he's refused them all. The fact that my father was able to get a complete collection for our store is unheard of.

"I put the earrings out yesterday, but I put the rest of the pieces out today. He named the collection An Unkindness of Ravens. It's a good thing you came in just as we opened. I've had several calls before I even unlocked the door this morning. He makes duplicates of several of his pieces, but this particular collection is one of a kind."

Jo was trying her best to ignore anything happening beyond the store's interior. She trusted Thomas and Coll to take care of any danger, and she didn't need to watch Percy, if it was really him, get arrested. Her closure had been walking out of Veleno. She hadn't looked over her shoulder then, and she sure as hell wasn't going to look back now. Outside her therapy, Jo was determined to not let that man touch any bit of her new life. Her anxiety melted away. It was time to buy some jewelry.

"Oh my," Jo said softly, her eyes rounded at the display. She had a ton of jewelry; gold, silver, platinum, precious, and semi-precious— it wouldn't matter what materials this artist used. He was brilliant. Truly brilliant. There were two sets of earrings, a necklace with different pendants, three different rings, and four bracelets. Some were all gold, like the earrings Mirren had spied yesterday. Some had black onyx with embedded diamonds. Each piece was extraordinary.

"Have any pieces been bought?"

"No. Besides the earrings you saw yesterday, the rest of the pieces came in after store hours last night."

"I want every piece." Mirren had been working her butt off since she'd been doing online school. Jo wasn't sure of the exact date, but she would graduate high school early. She'd been accepted into an early studies university program just last week because of her dedication and exceptional grades. This jewelry would be the perfect gift to celebrate the achievement.

The store owner's daughter, Matilda, was still frozen over the case as if she hadn't quite understood. Shaking out of her stupor, she finally managed, "I'll get the artist's logbook, then. The artist insists on the name and country of the person who purchases his pieces." At Jo's raised eyebrows, she admitted, "It's a quirk, I realize, but he is adamant."

As Jo signed M. MacGregor, Scotland, at the top of the collection list and drew a line down through all of the pieces' descriptions, she noticed the number of uniformed men and women outside had quadrupled since her last glance. It had been Percy.

"Oh, my goodness. What in the world is going on outside, I wonder," Matilda fanned her face dramatically, probably noting the hulking forms of Thomas and Coll blocking the store's entrance.

Jo slid her credit card from the billfold and handed it over. There were fourteen pieces that could be worn separately or together. It was truly a keepsake gift that Mirren would cherish for the rest of her life.

"The total is—"

Matilda froze as Thomas stormed in, practically tearing the front door off its hinges. He stalked his way toward her, a single-minded berserker. Jo was happy to note that Percy Donovan, his arrest, or his future did not hold any interest.

"Josephine O'Connor," his deep voice rumbled, echoing in the suddenly quiet shop.

"Thomas MacGregor," she answered. His knuckles were swollen, and flecks of blood dotted his hands. *He wants to protect you.*

He ignored Matilda's wide eyes and moved until his body caged hers against the front glass counter. He grasped her chin and forced her to meet his eyes.

"You didn't call me."

"I had reasons."

"Tell me."

"I believed you loved me too much to be rational. I didn't want to just be saved. I wanted him caught. You would always put me above anything else."

His stare said a million things and only one. She felt her breath hitch at its intensity. After all the months she'd known this man, he could still slay her with a look.

"You didn't call me."

She sighed. "I didn't."

"Why. Tell me the truth this time."

She realized this interrogation wouldn't end until she told him. "I didn't want you to have to clean up a mess that I started eight years ago." She cursed the tear that slipped down her cheek at the omission.

"I am honored to be the one who gets to clean up your messes, Jo, even though you did nothing... nothing... to deserve what happened all those years ago. You hurt me today."

Oh God. That was it. She gulped in air like it might stave off her emotions. She wrapped her arms around his middle and laid her head on his chest. "I'll never do it again."

"Don't cry, Jo," he soothed, brushing his hand down her hair over and over. "He's in custody and gone. That man has so many charges brought against him that there's not a court of law in the world that will let him go free."

She squeezed her eyes shut tight, taking his words in. She felt at peace, but she'd felt that for a while now, thanks to the man before her. "Thank you, Thomas." She poured every ounce of her soul into those three words.

"I called Dean."

She sighed. She seemed to sigh a lot these days. "Might as well have one more overbearing man rushing to my side, I suppose." She felt Thomas' mirth beneath the soft sweatshirt stretched across the broad expanse of chest she was currently nestled against.

"I'll tell you everything we found out about Donovan, but later, lass. Would you mind putting that..." his voice hitched over, calling Percy Donovan a man. She understood. He was more monster than human. "... piece of shit out of your mind for now. I'm of a mind to take the love of my life out on the town with a group of our best friends."

She had to blink back tears, but for once, when Percy's name was in the mix, they were tears of joy. Relief. "Convince your sister and Coll to attend, and I'm in."

"Done. Now tell me, lass," he began while shifting her body to face Matilda's stunned countenance once more, "why is there an invoice with your name on it for 48,000 quid?"

## 42

The last two weeks had been a whirlwind. Percy had been taken back to Rome to stand trial as it was proven that he and his father were partners in Viper. McGregor security, Interpol, and the FBI found evidence of his guilt. It was clear that he was involved in trafficking.

He was also identified by one of the women who had been found chained to a wall the night of the raid as her abuser. She was only sixteen. Mirren's age.

It would probably be months before he was extradited to the United States to stand trial for his family's involvement in money laundering and probably a whole slew of other criminal activities— including the charges she planned on bringing against him.

She'd already been in touch with an attorney from New York. Coll took care of sending all the intel that had been gathered on Percy, including the original video and the note he'd left that night.

There was also a book the police found on Percy when he was arrested. It was a small, leatherbound scrapbook of Jo. Pictures from the video as well as pictures taken from social media and her work. That was sent to the attorney as well to be turned in as evidence. The attorney believed more women were bound to come forward.

He'd been carrying an engagement ring at the time of his arrest.

He told the police she was his fiancée.

He wasn't only a predator but clearly insane. He'd asked repeatedly to speak to her. She always refused. There was no need to see him or hear his voice again. Closure had already come. Thomas had firmly told Percy's attorney never to contact her again.

Percy *would* have been tied up in court battles for years— if he hadn't been found murdered in his jail cell.

Rome authorities believe that Aldo found out that Percy planned on turning over evidence against his partners to reduce his prison sentence. One of Aldo's people, still loyal to him, must have hired a fellow inmate to murder him.

The New York attorney would now be filing a lawsuit against the Donovan estate. If any monetary restitution was granted, it was to be donated to shelters and clinics for assault victims.

Jo would be lying if she said she wasn't glad that women got to live in a world where Percy Donovan no longer existed, but... damn him. He got away with his crimes in life and would suffer no consequences in death— except, hopefully, he was literally burning in Hell.

Her therapist believed that she'd unconsciously hung her recovery or healing on Percy being convicted of sexual assault, and his death had subconsciously yanked that feeling of power out from under her. She might be right, but regardless, it made no difference at this point. She would continue therapy until her brain was as healed as her heart.

Besides, par for the course of her life, she had more important things to worry over. She'd finally been able to keep a doctor's appointment to find out what in the hell was going on with her stomach.

She was four months pregnant. Turned out, their Paris runway plane sex did a whole hell of a lot more than feel good. The bright side— she couldn't wait to tell Mirren she wasn't constipated.

The less bright side— she believed she and Thomas were in a forever relationship, but no woman wants forever to start with being a baby mama. Jo cringed at the moniker. Josephine O'Connor; educated, successful businesswoman, world traveler, and birth control dummy.

She and the doctor went over the timeline of events and believe they figured out where she might have dropped the ball — her words, not the doctor's. She'd taken her NuvaRing out the week before she was with Thomas so she could have a period. Her period stopped after three days of light spotting, but she decided to give her body another few days of rest before putting a new ring in. The 'plane' happened on day six. She put a new ring in the next day, but she was already pregnant.

She would never have taken that chance had she been thinking clearly. The shock of seeing him at the hospital and then having him stop her plane to talk— thoughts of safe sex hadn't even made her top twenty biggest things to worry about that day. It was no excuse. It was her fault she was pregnant.

Call her an old-fashioned Oklahoman, but she'd wanted to be a wife first. Sighing for the hundredth time, she rubbed her temples to relieve the building tension. There was no help for it now. She'd have to tell him. Soon. She would swear that her stomach moved out an inch after the news.

The doctor said she was healthy, and the baby was measuring exactly the size it should be, and not to be worried that she wasn't showing more. A lot of mothers who didn't know they're pregnant or are in denial were slow to show.

When she'd gotten into Aileen's car outside the clinic, she sat there for a good fifteen minutes before she picked up her phone.

"Hey, Jo," Aileen's sweet voice sounded over the car's speakers. "How are things going for your pre-housewarming barbeque?"

Most of the wrap-around porch was complete, the kitchen was coming along and should be done in another two weeks, the bed was on DT, Dougal Time, but the outdoor kitchen was finished, so she and Thomas decided a cookout would be fun. Not necessarily a celebration of Percy's death, but more to celebrate... life. The irony. Little did Thomas know how on point the theme was.

"You know, I'm kind of pissed you haven't asked me to do anything. You do realize I am feeling *perfectly* fine. Who wouldn't with Mary having me go to every type of healer in all of Scotland massaging my damn... everything." She huffed in exasperation.

"Happy ending everything... or just tradish massages?"

"You're terrible. Jesus."

Jo couldn't help but tease Aileen. She was just so damn sweet. "Hey," she hesitated for a second, "is Mir around?"

"No. She's gardening with Cat. Why?" Aileen's mirth of a moment ago was replaced with concern.

In for a penny... "Because I wanted to tell you something without her hearing."

"Get it out then! Your hesitation is too much for my poor, tired body."

Jo smiled at Aileen's dramatics. The woman knew she was beating about the bush and was trying to pull her out of the hedge. "I just found out I'm pregnant." Crickets. "Say something, damn it! You're the first person to know, so make your words memorable."

"I know I'm not really related, but can I be an honorary auntie?"

And that fast, Jo was crying, big gulping tears. She didn't dare look in the rearview mirror to witness the jag of ugly crying. Choking on a hiccup, she finally got out, "I'm four months. It happened... damn it, I'm sorry, but it happened that one time in Paris when he held up my plane. I swore I wouldn't be with him while he was still married to you... but I was," she wailed. "Tell me you aren't disappointed in me and that you'll still be Auntie LeLe."

"You big dummy. I told you then, and I'll remind you now. You and Tommy are better together. You were meant to be. I'm thrilled for you. He'll be... stunned, elated... overprotective, but babe, Auntie LeLe. Try Auntie Ai. In Scots, it'll always sound like Baby is saying yes to his favorite aunt."

"Thank you for being such a great friend to me. Seriously."

"I'm honored to be the first to know. That'll really piss Miss Know-It-All off." She giggled. Mirren would have a few choice words for Jo, no doubt. "When are you telling him?"

"It's hard to just blurt it out. Like... Hey, guess what. You're going to be a dad again in five months."

"Good God, I hadn't done the math yet. Christ, Jo. How are you not showing? And before you answer, let me be the first woman to call you a bitch. I looked like a two-ton Tina at sixteen weeks."

"I'm surrounded by short women. I have more room."

"Surprise him at the cookout. You only have to keep the secret for a couple more days."

"That's actually not a bad idea. I already feel like my belly is pooching out by the minute, but I can embrace baggy chic clothes and candlelit evenings. Thanks, Auntie Ai."

That night, she managed to evade anything more than snuggling, which was no hardship as having Thomas' body wrapped around her own was one of the snuggliest things ever.

It didn't appear like her body would be satisfied with platonic comfort tonight, though. When she walked into Aileen's bedroom and saw a naked Thomas stepping out of the shower, she got the touchy-feelys. *Lord have mercy, that man's body...*

As nonchalantly as possible, Jo dimmed the bedroom lights. Glancing at her reflection in Aileen's huge floor-to-ceiling mirror propped against one wall, she smoothed a few strands of her hair back into her loose bun before sliding her hands down the black silk mid-thigh robe she'd put on after her shower, tightening the bow at her waist. The wide loops of the sash nicely hid the slight rounding of her lower abdomen.

Cupping her barely there bump brought a smile to her lips. She'd caught herself smiling often since she found out she had a baby MacGregor on board. She was beyond excited for tomorrow. She was pretty damned excited for tonight. Directing her feet to the open bathroom— Thomas wasn't a fan of closed doors— she found herself leaning against the doorframe, taking in the show.

She missed him drying off, but watching him shave was the next best thing. Each scrape of the blade revealed more smooth skin and the strong angles of his jaw. Her gaze flicked to the bathroom mirror, using the reflection to see the rest of his body.

His broad shoulders and the great slabs of his chest were flexing with each stroke of the razor, making his muscles bunch and release. She let her gaze travel over the dips and furrows of his abs... her breathing quickly turning into pants, her tongue tingling at the thought of tasting all that glorious skin.

Her eyes easily followed his deep v-line, slipping over his thick, muscular thighs to the heavy sac hanging between his slightly parted legs. His sex was impressive in length and width, even in its flaccid state. As her eyes were locked on his groin, she didn't miss his penis twitching, getting fuller. Thomas had been aware of her watching him from the moment she'd stepped into the room.

She didn't say a word as she shut off the bright overhead light, leaving a soft glow in the bathroom. Jo walked to him until she stood at his back. As he rinsed his razor again, she placed her palms flush over his shoulder blades, gently running her hands over his back. When she pressed her silk-covered body against his naked flesh, he groaned.

She let her hands begin a light massage over his neck and back, arms and ass. By then, he'd already tossed his razor aside and wiped the remainder of the white, foamy cream from his face. His hands were braced on the marble countertop, his back curved to give her better access.

Leaning back enough to give her hands room to enjoy the firm, round globes of his ass, she massaged those too. His breathing was becoming more and more ragged, especially as her slender fingers made a foray between his spread thighs. Her knuckles grazed his sensitive perineum before cupping his balls.

"Christ, Jo. Don't stop." His voice was rough and begging, his legs spreading just that much more apart.

He was trying not to move, but his hips were beginning to thrust. She peeked around his body and saw his erection full and bobbing. Keeping one hand between his legs, she slid around to his front, her body now between him and the counter. When he started to grab her hips, she stopped the motion.

"No, Thomas. Tonight, I want to pleasure you," she instructed, nipping and then licking his nipples until he grasped both sides of her cheeks to keep her mouth on his skin.

"I want to pleasure you too."

"If you knew how wet my panties are right now, babe, you

would know how pleasured I am already." Bringing both hands into play, she used her knuckles on his seam to drive him insane while her other hand stroked his length. "Kiss me." A demand.

He took her mouth while she worked his body, the grind and grunting spiking her body's heat to madness. Releasing him, she pushed his damp chest away just enough to maneuver out of his grasp.

Taking his hand, she led him to the bedroom in front of the huge mirror, turning them both where the glass was in their peripheral. "I want you to see everything I do to your body." She felt his body shudder under her fingertips.

Leaning up, she slowly kissed each side of his mouth before dragging her tongue across his closed lips. He parted his mouth to let her in, but she'd already moved on. She kissed his neck and chest, licking and biting as she went. When she flicked her eyes up, she saw that he was looking down.

Making a tsking sound, she gently moved his clenched jaw to the side. "Eyes on the mirror." She smiled at his compliance and got back to work. He shivered when her hands glided up and down his sides and over his abs. She never went quite as low as he wanted.

Grabbing a pillow off the couch behind her, she tossed it at his feet. He started to look away from the mirror, but she made a discouraging noise. He huffed but turned back. As slow as she could, she sank to her knees, licking his abs while avoiding his engorged sex. Once on her knees, she began kissing and massaging his thighs, reaching around to knead his ass.

"Spread your legs more for me, Thomas." She met his gaze in the mirror as she cupped his balls, swollen from his arousal.

"Untie your robe, baby. I want to see your body."

Her thighs clenched at his demanding tone. She acquiesced but only loosened the tie enough to make sure her nipples could be seen from the side. "Tonight isn't about what you want. It's about what I want."

"Fuck me, Jo," he growled.

"Not this time," she sassed, intentionally misunderstanding. "Tell me exactly what you want. I want every detail of what you are imagining right now." Goading him might not be the smartest idea because when Thomas MacGregor lost control...

In two blinks, he had her neck in his grasp, and his thumbs shoved into her mouth, opening her to his body— and then he told her exactly what he wanted from her mouth and hands. He had a vivid imagination, but then, so did she.

If he looked away from their reflection, she couldn't have said.

## 43

"Thank you, but no," Coll declined the invitation politely. It was the morning of the cookout, and Jo was trying to convince him to stay another day so he could go. "I realize I only live a few hours away, but I've been gone several weeks now, and I need to get home and take care of my place after I get Aileen and Mirren moved back in here."

"I want you there, Coll." Her stance was purposefully aggressive, arms crossed over her chest, feet wide, and a scowl—his classic pose. "I realize taking down a trafficking racket was just another day in the life of you being a... a... superhero or something, but Percy Donovan was one of the men you helped put behind bars. We aren't celebrating that he's dead, but maybe that he'll never hurt anyone else."

"I'm celebrating that he's dead," he growled back. "I'm still going home."

Wanting him to understand why his presence was important, she tried again. "He stole my innocence, but he also took years of my peace of mind. You and your team are a big reason why I'm finally able to heal. Let's celebrate that. It isn't just me that wants you there tonight. Thomas and Catriona do, as well."

She hated to pull the Cat Card, but she wasn't going to let her man's best friend slip back into the shadows just because another MacGregor Security job was completed, and his sister's health was on the mend.

"You are one of the strongest women I know, Josephine. Donovan never broke you. He was never strong enough, and Thomas doesn't need me, lass. I can assure you of that. He isn't some toddler wailing for his friend to come play, and Catriona refuses to let me within a mile of her person. I'm for home."

She clapped her hands together for dramatic effect. "How about this then? Charles Morrow was invited."

Coll stood so quickly his chair tipped over with a loud thwack. The noise brought an underwear-clad Thomas storming the kitchen like it was the beaches of Normandy.

"The fuck are you on about?" Coll shouted, ignoring his bestie shouting, "What the hell, Colly?" and his much sweeter, "Baby, are you okay?"

"Forgot to tell me that fucking Charles," he dragged the name out with a mocking tone, "was invited to your fucking house. To be around my sister," he added with a fist to the kitchen table, its squeaking annoyance ignored. "I thought we talking to Aileen about this first."

Thomas crossed his arms over his barrel chest, unconcerned about having a conversation in his undies. "My daughter invited him," Emphasis on 'my.' "Mir thinks it will make her mother happy. I don't like it either... for more than one reason... but I do want your sister to have a chance for happiness. I trust Mirren. You need to give this a chance, Coll."

"Christ Almighty." He stood statue still, staring at... nothing. Clearly deep in thought. "Fine."

THE COOKOUT WAS SUPPOSED to be "chill," Jo's word, since her parents couldn't make it. Translation— her mother wouldn't be there to turn the cookout into a fine dining experience. Her folks were picking up Jo's brother and wife, James and Jane, at the airport. The couple were stopping by Inverness for the day to visit Mary and Dean before heading on to Passau, Germany, for a short vacation after finishing a big job in Oklahoma.

Aileen surprised Jo by inviting the Byrne sisters, which meant she invited all of the O'Faolains too. Thomas wasn't sure Jo or Aileen understood that Raven, River, and Rowan were the opposite of chill.

Everyone was enjoying the fine day, chatting, drinking, and wolfing down snacks— most of which Jo and Aileen had made together that morning. It still had his head shaking in wonder that they'd become such good friends, and of course, Mirren and Jo loved one another as well.

He was pleased that their friends seemed quite impressed with the outdoor kitchen. The space would undoubtedly be one of the most used spaces on the property. Thomas should never have been nervous about the changes Jo might make to the home he'd built. She had brilliant vision and had taken his humble cottage and, with minor changes and additions, created a home.

However, only two things were currently clamoring for attention in his brain, and it wasn't crisps and beer. First, he was proposing to Jo today, the engagement ring was in his pocket, and second, his daughter's birth father was expected to show. When he'd been a second away from asking Jo to join him on the new covered porch for a semi-private moment away from the crowd, Charles Morrow walked around the corner. Selfishly, Thomas had held out hope the man wouldn't show.

Mirren had finally fessed up to her mom about them contacting him. Thomas could grudgingly admit that Charles had been nice and polite on the phone. Aileen had been running around like a chicken with its head chopped off since the news broke. Her nervous energy spiked his own. The evening he'd been preparing for, dreaming about, was suddenly a parody of a clusterfuck.

River Byrne's red dirt country playlist played on as he watched the man tentatively join the party. Several things happened at once. Aileen gasped, covering her mouth with one hand and touching her wig with the other. If that man made her feel like she wasn't beautiful just because she'd lost her hair, he'd throw him in the ocean.

Next, he saw Coll lurch out of the corner where he'd been lounging in the shadows— which had become his natural habitat since his accident— making a beeline toward Morrow. Catriona slapped one of her tiny hands in the middle of his chest and said, "No." To Thomas' utter shock, he complied.

The third, and by far the worst bit of chaos to punch his stomach, was watching his daughter walk toward the man who was... her other father. He felt Jo slide her arm around his waist and give him a side hug.

"She will never love you less, Thomas, and she certainly could never love you more. In her eyes, you hung the damn sun, moon, and stars. Don't you dare leave her to that awkward reunion alone."

That single moment would have solidified his great love for Josephine if he didn't already love her beyond understanding. He nodded once before leaving her side. "See to Aileen, love," before following his daughter.

To give Morrow his due, a man would have to be brave or foolish to meet his ex and his daughter in such a public manner. Thomas had done his own research on the man and believed it was the former.

While Mirren stared in wide-eyed fear, rooted in a spot some four feet from the man that she'd invited to visit, Thomas walked past his daughter, touching one of the clenched fists that lay at her side, and approached a man he'd never met but was excruciatingly jealous of.

Morrow's DNA ran through Mirren, and that killed Thomas.

He put his right hand out to the dark-headed stranger and threw him a lifeline for Mirren's sake. "You must be Charles Morrow. I'm Thomas MacGregor. You'll have heard of me?"

Relief and perhaps even gratitude rippled over the man's face. "Aye. Mirren sent me... a file." That almost made Thomas smile. Of course, she did.

The party goers moved a respectful distance from them and continued the cookout as if there was nothing out of the ordinary going on. "I would ask," Thomas began somewhat gruffly, but only because emotions were riding him, "why you've come."

To his credit, he glanced at Mirren and then further on through the crowd, presumably looking for Aileen, and answered, "I want to know my... daughter." He swallowed hard, his own emotions riding him. "I want to speak with Aileen face to face. I didn't know I... I didn't know we had... had created a child."

"Mom called you, but you didn't have the bloody time of day for her. You said you were seeing someone else. Should she have begged you for a moment of your time? Her parents would have disowned her had she not married Dad. You left, and you never looked back," Mirren said vehemently.

"Mir," Thomas warned. He saw Coll edging his way toward the spectacle and wanted to head off further outbursts, because God knew, Coll would escalate the situation.

"No, MacGregor." Charles waved his hand as if to stop Thomas from reprimanding Mirren, which he wouldn't have done. She had every right to her feelings, right, wrong, or misplaced. He only wished she would speak when her emotions weren't so high. "Mirren is correct. I fuc—" Charles stopped before saying, "I messed up in every way I could.

"I was hurt that Aileen didn't move with me to the States. I was young and immature and handled the whole damn thing wrong. I wasn't even seeing anyone. I just wanted to hurt her like she'd hurt me. I've had time to consider the past since Mirren reached out to me, and I can assure you both that I am not proud of my behavior. It cost me everything." The sad look he gave Mirren was heartbreaking.

Thomas appreciated his honesty. "I don't believe any of us have always conducted ourselves as gentlemen. I almost lost the only woman I loved because I was an idiot."

Charles dipped his head at Thomas, acknowledging the support. Turning to Mirren, he said, "I would ask your forgiveness. I was shocked to find out I had a daughter all these years. I was angry that I hadn't been given the chance to be your father. I reacted badly. I desperately want to know you now," he finished softly. Looking at Thomas, he added, "I would like to speak to Aileen if I may."

"She's free to make her own mind up about that." He hesitated a moment, not wanting to say too much but also not wanting to say too little. "Mir will have told you about Aileen's health scare?" At his affirming nod, he went ahead. "She's recovering well, but I don't want to see you upsetting her. You can begin a relationship with Mirren if she wishes," he thought to add, "but I don't want Aileen to think you want to... get to know her again if you aren't serious."

"If she'll only speak to me, I desperately would like a chance to be the man she used to believe I was."

Thomas placed a gentle hand on his daughter's shoulder. "Mirren. What do you want? I know you invited Charles to visit, but still, now that he's here, I want to know that you're still okay with it."

She turned her glassy eyes up to his before looking over at Charles. "I want to know him." She looked toward him once more and added, "But only if it doesn't hurt you in the doing of it."

"If anyone could handle two fathers loving her, then I imagine it's you." At her relieved sigh, he knew he'd made the right decision. "Should we go introduce Charles to the group and find your mom?" To Charles, he said, "We've a bit of a crazy group. Best to get you familiarized right off."

"I can come back another day," he offered, looking like a man about to face a firing squad.

"You might as well jump into the deep end, Morrow. If you plan on spending much time with my girls, then you'll need to be acquainted with this lot sooner or later."

Charles' face pinkened, but he gamely tagged along. Unsurprisingly, everyone was kind and welcoming. It might have been blind luck that Aileen invited the extra guests. With all the joking banter, the first meet and greet went well.

They were finally standing in front of Aileen and Jo, Coll looming behind them. Aileen was red-faced and holding Jo's hand in a white-fisted grip.

He decided to start with Jo first. "Charles Morrow, my girlfriend, Josephine O'Connor." *Fiancée soon, he hoped.*

"I've heard so much about you, Charles. So nice to meet you."

Thomas decided not to acknowledge Coll for now. "And you'll know Aileen, of course." Jo pulled her hand from Aileen's so that she could make room for Charles to step forward.

Jo was fighting tooth and nail not to cry, but this reunion might have been the sweetest moment she'd ever witnessed. Her lips quivered as she watched the long-lost couple reunite. *Damn hormones.* As inconspicuously as she could, she moved behind Mirren and stepped to Thomas' side.

"Aileen."

"Charles."

"You've not changed a day in almost seventeen years." His voice held wonder, sadness too.

"I'm wearing a wig," Aileen blurted out before slapping her hands over her face in embarrassment and mumbling, "Oh God."

He hesitated for a brief moment before moving closer. He gently took her hands from her face so that she was forced to look at him. "And I don't care. I wouldn't care if you looked nothing like the girl I once knew. I only care that you're still you and that you still... that you might someday look at me like you used to."

At Aileen's soft look, Jo knew they needed to walk away and give the reunited couple some privacy. She glanced at Catriona and nodded her head to Coll. She'd drag him off his sister's back if anyone could. "Mir, I need to speak to your dad about something. Hold the fort down?"

"Sure thing," she agreed. She looked so happy seeing Aileen and Charles murmuring to one another. "Mom looks happy," she told Jo, grinning.

"She does," Jo agreed. She briefly squeezed the girl's hand and, grinning, said, "You did a good thing, Mirren Mòr MacGregor."

"You need to talk to me?" Thomas asked as they entered the breezeway that would take them to the new wraparound porch and, hopefully, a modicum of privacy.

"I do." She barely resisted the urge to place her hand over her small bump. Now that Charles was sorted, her nerves had kicked in. Thomas would be happy. She knew he would.

"I need to speak to you too."

His serious tone increased her nerves tenfold. Mirren chose the moment right before she and Thomas turned the corner, putting them out of sight, to be... Mirren.

Thomas winced when he heard his sweet, little daughter announce to all and sundry that "Dad and Jo will probably be awhile. The way they were looking at each other when they left should require prophylactics."

"Christ, that girl," Thomas growled.

"Thomas—" she began, once they were away from prying eyes, only to be interrupted. She finally noted that his cheeks were flushed, and he was sweating profusely. He kept exhaling giant breaths of air, and his hands were all over the place. On her shoulders, her waist, holding one hand and then two. He finally stopped moving and fidgeting and just looked at her.

"Would you mind if I go first?"

She said, "Okay," but at this point, she wasn't sure she wanted to know what was making him this nervous.

"I'm just going to come out with it. Damn it," he winced. "That wasn't what I meant to say."

*Red alert. Red alert. Red alert.* "You're making me nervous. Just tell me already." He began fumbling around again, digging in first one front pocket of his jeans and then the other before he pulled out a... Oh my God.

He shoved the ring in her face and asked, "Will you marry me, Josephine? Please."

Her first thought was that he found out she was pregnant and felt obligated. But then he said, "It's a gray diamond. The color intensity is Fancy. Dark is the best. Fancy is second best. Not," he swore under his breath, "that you are second best. The jeweler spent two damn months trying to find a Dark. I almost switched jewelers, but once I saw this one, I thought it matched your eyes. So... umm... I had them solder a simple gold and white-gold band together because you always wear different stuff." He cringed again. His precious, nervous rambling finally petered off.

Her second thought— he had no idea about the baby. Her third thought— she was about to be engaged to the most romantic man in the world.

"Yes, Thomas," she said decisively. She couldn't help but grin when this tough ex-Marine whispered, "Thank God," before grasping her left hand and slipping the stunning ring onto her finger.

"I'm so glad you went first." She placed her hands on his chest, enjoying the sun sparkling off the gray stone.

He looked bemused. "I'm sorry I cut you off. I was too nervous to wait another second. What did you need to tell me?"

"Are you ready to be a dad again in five months?" His rounded eyes and slack jaw were satisfying. It was more satisfying when he grabbed her up in his arms and twirled her around.

Voice choked, he asked, "You're happy? I'm happy."

"So happy."

"Honey Bunny came through and is already making kittens," River faux whispered somewhere behind them. Clearly, they had an audience.

"Josephine's getting married. Who do we call first?" Raven clapped her hands in excitement.

"Are you telling me that secret-keeping bitch is four months gone and not showing? The unfairness is a horror to humanity," Rowan whined. "How did we not know this?"

"I knew," Aileen said smugly.

"I can't believe it wasn't constipation. I was so sure." Mirren sounded put out that her diagnosis wasn't accurate after all. "Clearly, neither one of my fathers is a big believer in birth control," she lamented.

Jo snorted in amusement against Thomas' chest. She pulled his head down to whisper in his ear. "I love you."

"You make me better. You've made me better since the first day I heard your sassy mouth. I love you."

"Forever."

"Always."

## ALSO BY ANNE GREGOR

### The Scottish Lions

Josephine

### The Irish Wolves Trilogy

Raven

River

Rowan

# ABOUT THE AUTHOR

Anne Gregor has a Master of Arts in History with an emphasis on the Civil War. For her thesis, she focused on Irish immigrants working the transcontinental railroad across America, specifically those who settled in Oklahoma amongst Native Americans. A love for research turned into a love for fictional writing, and soon, every old document Anne ever studied became the premise for a novel. Anne Gregor has been writing book reviews for several years and is a freelance proofreader. Oklahoma is near and dear to her heart as she lives on Grand Lake O' the Cherokees. **Anne is the author of two contemporary romance series, The Irish Wolves Trilogy and The Scottish Lions Duology.**

Milton Keynes UK
Ingram Content Group UK Ltd.
UKHW040722300924
449047UK00005B/361